PRAISE FOR SOPHIE WHITE

'Unputdownable ... a darkly funny, raw story about friendship, vulnerability and honesty'
Irish Times

'A sharp, funny story of female friendship at its best, with characters you'll fall in love with'
Beth O'Leary

'One of the best flawed heroines in Irish commercial fiction since Rachel Walsh in Marian Keyes' ground-breaking *Rachel's Holiday*'
Sunday Times

'A modern, witty, razor-sharp page-turner'
Emer McLysaght

'White's pages fizz with earthy wit and [Marian] Keyes fans will definitely find plenty to enjoy here'
Sunday Independent

'Fresh, current and thoroughly enjoyable'
Eithne Shortall

'Witty and wonderful – I devoured this in a single sitting'
Image

'Whip smart and very, very funny'
Sarah Breen

'White's sharp-eyed take on modern life couldn't be more on target'
Irish Independent

Sophie White is an award-winning writer and essayist and her work has been translated into numerous languages. She lives in Dublin with her husband and three sons. She writes regularly for many Irish publications, including her weekly 'Nobody Tells You' column for the *Sunday Independent LIFE* magazine, and also co-hosts two podcasts, *Mother of Pod* and *The Creep Dive*.

ALSO BY SOPHIE WHITE

Fiction
Filter This
Unfiltered
The Snag List
My Hot Friend
Where I End

Non-fiction
Corpsing
Recipes for a Nervous Breakdown

Such a Good Couple

Sophie White

HACHETTE
BOOKS
IRELAND

Copyright © 2025 Sophie White

The right of Sophie White to be identified as the author of the work has been asserted by her in accordance with the Copyright, Designs and Patents Act 1988.

First published in Ireland in 2025 by HACHETTE BOOKS IRELAND

1

All rights reserved. No part of this publication may be reproduced, stored in a retrieval system, or transmitted, in any form or by any means without the prior written permission of the publisher, nor be otherwise circulated in any form of binding or cover other than that in which it is published and without a similar condition being imposed on the subsequent purchaser.

This is a work of fiction. All characters in this publication are fictitious and any resemblance to real persons, living or dead, is purely coincidental.

The lyrics to 'True Friends' by Jerry Fish and the Mudbug Club, written by Gerard Joseph Whelan and John Moloney, appear with permission.

Cataloguing in Publication Data is available from the British Library.

ISBN 9781399746540

Typeset in ArnoPro by Bookends Publishing Services, Dublin
Printed and bound in Great Britain by Clays Ltd, Elcograf S.p.A.

Hachette Books Ireland policy is to use papers that are natural, renewable and recyclable products and made from wood grown in sustainable forests. The logging and manufacturing processes are expected to conform to the environmental regulations of the country of origin.

MIX
Paper | Supporting
responsible forestry
FSC® C104740

Hachette Books Ireland
8 Castlecourt Centre
Castleknock
Dublin 15, Ireland

info@hbgi.ie
Authorised representative in EEA

A division of Hachette UK Ltd
Carmelite House, 50 Victoria Embankment, London EC4Y 0DZ

www.hachettebooksireland.ie

For Emer

A NOTE FROM THE AUTHOR

Dear Reader,

Firstly, thank you so much for being here. Your support means everything to me.

Secondly … some prior warning. Please take care while reading *Such A Good Couple*. This book deals with some difficult subjects, namely fertility struggles and eating disorders. Especially regarding the eating disorder depicted in the book, I have endeavoured to take as much care as possible to avoid gratuitous descriptions or stray into territory that could be inadvertently instructive in these matters. Eating disorders are the deadliest of all mental illnesses and I would never, ever want to glamorise these tragic disorders.

I am indebted to the courageous women who spoke to me about their experiences. I also drew on my own life, as well as the words of many excellent writers, in particular the vital work of Aubrey Gordon, Virginia Sole-Smith and Cole Kazdin.

For a full list of resources, please refer to the page at the back of the book.

If you are struggling or have struggled with fertility or disordered eating, I am sending love and hope you know that, even though society wants you to be quiet about your pain, your grief is real and deserves to be acknowledged. When you are ready, your friends and loved ones are ready to listen and hold you.

All my love,
Sophie xxx

'I can't believe _____ and _____ broke up. After twenty years? They were always such a good couple.'

'You just never know what's going on in other people's relationships.'

— Old WhatsApp Proverb

CHAPTER 1

'Are you *still bloody in there*, Ollie?'

Clara stood jiggling on the small landing of her house and hammered on the toilet door while her children continued to play around her legs, oblivious to her plight.

'Are you alive? Has something prolapsed? This wee is *seconds* away from simply falling out of me.'

'I'm coming,' came Ollie's completely unruffled reply. 'I just want to be thorough.'

'Shut *up*! No additional information, *please*.'

Clara bent over and squeezed her thighs together. When they weren't feuding over the one and only toilet in the house, she and Ollie called this stance 'assuming the position'. Now two of the boys, the older two she reckoned from squinting at them – she needed to put in her contacts – were using her legs as an obstacle around which to chase each other.

'Get away,' she hissed, inching a leg out to bat them off while continuing to clench every muscle in her body. Unfortunately the tiny movement of her leg was enough to compromise her, sending a tiny, depressing trickle of piss into the gusset of her knickers.

'Have you packed my goggles?' Ollie asked from the other side of the door. It was Wednesday the 2nd of July, and instead of them both being in work, they were getting ready to escape on holidays.

Ignoring him and still bent over with legs fused, Clara shuffled towards the top of the stairs. She needed a receptacle fast. Initially the three kids – the youngest had now joined – tried to come with her but she managed to shunt them in the other direction towards the two bedrooms.

'Play. Up. There. You. Madzers,' she muttered. 'Mummy has to go and stoop to the lowest of the low.'

Her boys, ten-year-old Josh, six-year-old Tom and three-year-old Reggie, duly moved, though still scrapping and thumping each other.

'I'll just be a couple more minutes,' Ollie announced airily from the loo.

Clara couldn't even roll her eyes at this – she needed all her focus on not pissing herself. She quickly eased herself down the stairs and into the pokey little galley kitchen that was filled to bursting with dirty breakfast plates, lunch plates and snack plates. It was 3 p.m. She had less than forty minutes before they needed to leave for the airport.

Think about that in a minute, she thought, tearing through a cupboard looking for the big plastic bowl they used for popcorn and (weirdly) the occasional vomit – did every family have the vom-popcorn bowl? Was it just an Irish thing? Or a *them* thing?

She pulled it out, then paused.

'You know what?' she announced to Reggie, who had just ambled in. 'This bowl has been through enough.'

Instead of the bowl, she grabbed the large pot they used for soup and Bolognese. And now urinating, apparently. She reefed her pants down to her knees and wedged the pot between her thighs. Unfortunately she hadn't accounted for the power of her piss stream when calculating the proximity of the pot, and the backsplash of the piss immediately started to go everywhere.

'What are you doing?' Ollie arrived in time to witness the latest of Clara's humiliations.

Life just seemed to be back-to-back indignities once you had kids (though perhaps only if you were a person who had cavalierly ignored all advice to do the pelvic floor exercises).

'Obviously, I'm pissing,' Clara replied.

'Badly, I see.' Ollie leaned languidly against the doorframe to observe her. Immediately the toddler commenced scaling his body.

Clara laughed. 'Shite off!' She briskly dried her inner thighs with a tea towel and pulled up her knickers and leggings. 'Now.' She held up the pot. 'Will we make soup?'

'I'm just glad you didn't use the vomit-popcorn bowl.'

'Right.' Clara put the kettle on, opened the back door and poured the pee directly down the drain outside. Next she grabbed the anti-bacterial spray and went back out to give the pot a liberal dousing.

'Holy water would be better,' Ollie called from inside, where the other two boys had found him and were dragging him to the ground for one of their customary wrestling sessions. He was so used to being under siege at all times that he could easily scroll his apps and send texts while they clambered all over him.

Clara was similarly unfazed by the violent affection of their kids. Each one had come out of her vadge madder than the last and Clara had pretty much been speaking at screaming pitch for nearly ten years now. They still never listened unless she said she was running them a bath. They were allergic to being cleaned so all she had to do was whisper 'I'm running the bath' and they would flee. Running a bath could buy her up to ten minutes of sitting in the loo basking in some lovely scrolling-on-my-phone alone time. If Ollie hadn't beaten her in there first, of course.

'Fuck me, we need another bathroom,' she said aloud to no one in particular.

'We need another house, one that actually fits us,' Ollie piped up from the floor, just as a child's foot got him in the jaw.

Clara flung the pot into the dishwasher and began chucking in other random items after it.

'Not realistic,' Clara singsonged, trying not to let his words sink her mood. There was not a hope that they could afford a bigger place. 'And not the time to talk about it. We still have a shit tonne to do. The taxi gets here in thirty minutes. I've only packed for the lunatics. And I imagine, even though we live our lives in servitude to them, we'll still need a few things ourselves in case we're allowed to have a bit of a holiday.'

'Oh, babe! The only people in servitude on this holiday will be Fionn and Maggie's staff.' Ollie stood up, shedding children as he rose. 'Did you check out the itinerary that that Brody guy sent?' He held up his phone displaying the PDF Fionn's executive assistant had made. There was a loose timetable for the two weeks they would all be together in Cape Cod comprising sunrise yoga, boat trips, walking tours and barbecues on the beach; plus an exhaustive list of additional activities they could pick and choose from.

'I know!' Clara replied. 'There's cooks and nannies and the whole shebang. Did you see there's literally kid-free time built into the schedule? The poor help will be taking them off for ice cream and magic memories so we can chill.'

Clara shook her head in amazement. She could not imagine her friends' lives. In the WhatsApp group she, Maggie and Annie shared (called Slags For Life) there were four different phone numbers for Maggie. She changed numbers like other people changed handbags, switching from phone to phone throughout the year as the Strongs jetted from house to house in LA, London, Saint-Tropez and, of course, Dublin.

'I'm definitely doing the jet-skiing again,' Ollie declared. 'That was amazing in Hawaii last year.'

'We're not doing anything on the timetable if we don't get our shit together now.' Clara shoved the dishwasher closed and stooped to listen to make sure it started. You couldn't always assume that it would. Like everything else in their chaotic, full-to-bursting, terraced red-brick cottage, it was a vintage model. Ollie, still buried in his phone, skipped out the door into the hall while Clara did her best to tidy the kitchen, then pushed through the many-headed beast that was her children, still gleefully pounding the shite out of each other on the floor.

In the hallway was a large suitcase blocking the front door. Ollie was nowhere to be seen. He had an incredible knack for disappearing when annoying bullshit like packing had to be done.

'Ollie?' she scream-shouted up the stairs.

'I'm up here getting some stuff together like you said!' he shouted back.

'Amazing,' Clara roared.

So much of marriage with kids is just yelling to each other from different locations, she mused, crouching down by the big open suitcase to do one last check of the kids' things before closing it up. Even when she and Ollie were in the same room they often had to shout at each other to be heard over the constant monologuing of their children.

Clara took stock of the boys' things.

Clothes? Check.

Swim stuff? Check.

Random items they'll need/freak out if they didn't have? Check.

The sounds of grunting and furniture being disturbed in the dining room were hitting a fever pitch. 'Boys! Stop fighting and get out here.' She zipped the suitcase closed and pulled it out the front door.

Back inside, Ollie was dragging the other suitcase down the stairs.

'All set?' she shouted.

'All set,' he shouted back, muscling past her with the bag.

'Really?'

Clara stared after him as he brought both bags down the garden path. She was slightly amazed at his efficiency, though it was hardly such a feat – she'd left all their clothes folded in neat piles on the bed so it'd been straightforward enough. *The credit we give men for doing the most basic things*, she thought. At dinnertime, Ollie often reported to her all the housework and life admin tasks he'd completed that day as if waiting for some kind of certificate of commendation. Women, meanwhile, just got on with doing this shit. She plucked her phone from her pocket to say as much to Annie and Maggie in Slags For Life but then caught sight of the time. The taxi'd be there any minute. She hurried back into the dining room.

'Okay, boys, stop *now*. The taxi's coming.' Clara used a level four shout – nothing crazy, the kind you'd use for a cat trying to get at the Christmas turkey.

Not one of them looked up. The younger two had pinned Josh, who was writhing and laughing hysterically.

'Jesus. Christ. Get. Up. Now.' She'd gone full level ten (the type of shout that actually caused you to hurt your own throat).

Josh who, at ten, had the most experience of Clara's shouting, shot up at that moment. 'Yeah! Jesus. Christ,' he shouted down to his little brothers, before beaming up at her angelically.

'Taxi's here,' came Ollie's voice from behind her. He shunted her to the side – the hall could really not accommodate more than one person at a time – and strode in to where the younger boys were still giggling on the ground. He hiked them up and tucked one under each arm.

Clara backed out the front door, trying not to stumble over the potted plants on the step as Ollie strolled towards her with the squealing boys, Josh stomping along behind him. Clara grinned and experienced one of those glimmers of gratitude that so often arose even amidst the complete chaos of parenthood. This trip was going to be good, even if it was a bit awkward – Maggie and Fionn were paying for everything, right down to the taxi being loaded up at that very moment.

Clara eased herself into the back seat, dodging the excited flailing limbs of her children. *Someone needs to write some kind of handbook for what to do when your lifelong best friends become millionaires,* Clara thought.

Fionn and Maggie's millionaire status had come pretty much out of nowhere. By their mid-thirties, Clara and Ollie had managed to scrounge a mortgage from the bank, and Annie and Conor had settled into a long-term lease, but Maggie and Fionn were still living a nomadic existence, moving from one live-in dog-sitting gig to another, soon with Maggie's pregnant bump in tow.

Back then Annie and Conor were the most had-their-shit-together on paper: she had landed her dream job in art restoration in the National Gallery and Conor was an accountant.

Ironically, Fionn and Maggie were the ones the others had worried about. Maggie lived from arts grant to arts grant, staging beautiful but extremely uncommercial site-specific theatre productions, and Fionn acted when he was cast and did restaurant work in between. They had moved to London to pursue the theatre life but they were still fairly broke.

At home in Ireland, Clara and Annie had pored over the 'Maggie problem'. When was she going to get practical? When were they going to 'get real' and 'settle down'? Surely once the twins ('Twins! God luv them,' Clara'd wailed on hearing) were born, they'd have to get proper jobs.

'Right,' the driver called to them from the front seat. 'Which terminal are ye going to?'

'Terminal 2, please,' Clara replied, checking that all the boys were wearing their seatbelts.

At that time, the 'proper job' Clara had was in customer service for Google. Meanwhile, Ollie was a gardener, which was perfect. He loved the freedom and creativity and had always had steady work because anyone who could afford to have a garden in Dublin never had time to garden because they worked all day and all night to be able to afford the gardens they were never home to be in.

All was reasonably fine, until a *fucking* pandemic meant everyone was at home for literal years. Gardening their little arses off all of a sudden.

Then Clara had been made redundant. To save face she'd told her friends that she'd made the decision to leave. Now she was eight months into her job at ComYOUnicate. It was a garden-variety call centre with a particularly cringe name. She was struggling with it – she felt like a snob but she hadn't pictured herself at forty-two working in a call centre. Sure, in Google, for all those years, she had essentially been making calls. But there'd been a cachet in working for Google. In ComYOUnicate there were no splashy murals on the walls shouting moronic slogans. It was windowless, grey and functional. Aesthetically, compared with the fancy tech places, it was like working in the basement where a serial killer keeps his victims.

Clara gazed out the window as the taxi merged with the sluggish mid-afternoon traffic. In two weeks' time, she'd be back in the office, a place so clogged with the fug of warm tuna sandwiches and instant coffee it was practically a microclimate all of its own.

Look, she reminded herself, *only a handful of, let's face it, insufferable people like their jobs; everyone else just gets on with it.*

Now that the cost-of-living crisis had them by their necks, she and Ollie spent all their time tagging in and out of home life. Clara usually worked from 7 a.m. to 3 p.m. and when she got home, Ollie went out to put in as many hours as he could with the clients he had left before it got dark. They passed kids and laundry and school notes and homework back and forth between them all week. On the weekends, Ollie did full days at a garden centre an hour's drive from Crumlin, where they lived, and Clara spent her days 'off' attempting to clean the ever-rising tide of shite in their house. And screaming lovingly at the kids – never not screaming at the kids.

The really hard part about the days and overtime hours she spent tethered to the headset was that they didn't buy her any ease in her home life. Working at full tilt still only meant that they were just about keeping up. Clara tried to relax her jaw as the taxi swung off the motorway and passed under a sign for the airport. The cause of the hovering sadness she had felt but not quite articulated in the previous weeks suddenly pulled into focus: without Maggie and Fionn, her boys would not be going on a plane right now. There'd be no holiday. It was a very hard thing to not be able to give your children the things they deserved.

Back in March, when they were all nailing down the dates for the Provincetown holiday, she and Ollie had joked about selling their spot on the trip on DoneDeal.

Clara hadn't been able to bring herself to tell Annie and Maggie about how much they were struggling. It was hard not being able to vent about it to the two people she was closest to in the whole world but, for very different reasons, Annie and Maggie were not the best audience for the Wrung-Out Parent Lament.

From the floor of the taxi, Clara pulled up her shoulder bag (Mulberry from Maggie; Annie had one too) and did another check that she had all five passports. She glanced over at Ollie, who was playing (and winning) rock-paper-scissors against Tom while also furiously thumbing his phone.

'You haven't even asked *once* about the passports,' she said pointedly, pursing her lips. 'What if I'd assumed *you* were sorting them?'

'Hmmmm?' Ollie was a good multitasker but adding a pass-agg married-couple thought experiment to his current roster of activities was too much even for him.

'The passports, babe,' she said loudly. 'I only have mine and the boys', did you bring yours?'

That got his attention. He blanched, then grinned. 'Hahaha, shut up. You're evil.' He resumed texting.

'I always vowed not to be one of those straight couples where the man is some honorary child the wife looks after and steers through life.'

'Honorary child? I wish,' he muttered. He looked up from his phone. 'Do you even know when the car's up for its next NCT? Or who our health insurance provider is? You're not exactly a paragon of maturity!'

Did she detect a slightly sneering edge to his words? They'd been best friends for two decades but ten years of child-related broken sleep had definitely seen some snippiness creeping in here and there. Was it more lately? It was hard to tell.

'Also,' Ollie continued, 'spending the child benefit allowance in the pub after you've gone "for one" with your twenty-five-year-old workmates makes *me* feel like I've got an unruly teenager.'

Clara debated throwing something back at him: *At least you get to do a job you actually like?* came to mind.

But playing the Married Couple Hardship Olympics right before a holiday wasn't worth it. They needed this break very badly so she settled on: 'That was one time, Ollie!' She kept her tone playful. 'And it wasn't the *whole* payment. A few euro on blowing off steam! My job is hard – it's very draining working with young people who're happy and full of optimism about life. The sheer effort it takes to not punch them in the face.'

'Why did you go out with them, then? Do they need to be burped after their pints?'

Clara grinned. This felt better, this was more them. 'Listen,' she said, 'parenting is very stressful. If the government doesn't want us to spend the child benefit on self-medicating, they should provide better state-funded childcare.'

This raised a bit of a laugh from him at least, though a second later he'd already slid back onto his phone.

She frowned. The phone obsession was just a fact of twenty-first-century married life, wasn't it? Maybe it was even prolonging millennial marriages? Less pressure to continue being entertaining for each other for years on end. You could just keep a steady stream of memes and TikToks going back and forth and, voila, you had a reasonably good approximation of a fun relationship.

Clara wished that she could see his screen, though. She also wished that she didn't wish this but she couldn't help it. He was on it so much. Everyone was on their phones a lot, of course, but recently Ollie couldn't seem to leave it down for a second. Was it something nefarious? Unlikely.

Though the truth was Ollie *had* been acting strangely in the last few months. She'd been on a committed jag of explaining it away but the unease was growing like a tumour. Along with being glued to the phone, he was regularly coming home from work much later than usual, often after dark, with shrugging explanations about tweaking irrigation systems and whatnot. She knew there were some jobs gardeners could do at night but she couldn't imagine his wealthy clients wanting him skulking around their properties at that hour. Then he'd always hop straight into the shower when he came home even though it was late and could wake the kids. Sometimes, in her sleep-addled state, she even sensed him gone from the bed during the night but he'd always be back snoring beside her in the morning. Most unnerving of all, she was noticing that the money coming in from his Saturday hours in the garden centre seemed less than usual.

The taxi passed under a sign for the airport and she pulled away from the growing abyss of unease. She resolved to talk to him, but not until after the holiday. Under no circumstance was the holiday to be ruined with reality. Especially as it was all probably in her head anyway.

He literally doesn't have the hours in the day for an affair, she thought wryly.

CHAPTER 2

As crowds milled around her, Annie snapped a selfie holding her passport and sent it to Slags For Life.

Annie: It's happening! Cannot wait to see you guys!

Beside her, her partner Conor was grim-faced as he hauled the big case up onto the conveyor belt at the bag drop. 'We need to get to security before Clara and Ollie. I am *not* getting involved with their chaos.'

He snatched the receipt from the machine and immediately turned and started marching through the crowds, a good head taller than pretty much everyone. Annie hurried after him, smiling apologetically at every disgruntled person left in his wake.

'I need to go to the toilet, Conor,' Annie tried to whisper-shout over the din of the departures hall. It'd been a frantic day and Annie had still not had time to test her urine from that morning. Between packing and fielding Conor's customary travel panic that was escalating with every passing minute, she'd left it in the jar she always used and forgotten all about it, only remembering right as they were leaving.

With no time to get the ovulation strips out then and there, she'd decanted the wee into a small plastic water bottle, planning to duck away to test it at the airport.

Before leaving the house, she'd sent a pic of the bottle of wee in her handbag to her friend Rachel:

Carting my wee around with me feels like a new low.

Rachel had replied:

From what I hear there's a whole host of new lows after people become parents!

As Annie had read this reply, it'd struck her that this was definitely the type of thing she would've had a laugh with Conor about before.

Before when? She wasn't quite sure anymore. Eighteen months of Babygate was really affecting the atmosphere between them but lately Annie had started to wonder if things had been more strained than she wanted to admit even prior to that.

Annie knew that sprinting (completely unnecessarily) through the airport was not the place for the grim soul-searching that accosted her with more and more frequency now but she couldn't really pick and choose when these thoughts assailed her. She had stopped trying to vocalise them to Conor. It was strange that after twenty years together, after effectively *growing up* together, there was suddenly a topic of conversation off the menu. And such an important bloody topic. But any mention of it Conor seemed to see as a dig. He had been the one urging them to put off trying for a baby – he was obsessed with them having all their 'ducks in a row' before becoming parents. And now that having a family was starting to seem like an increasingly remote possibility, it was hard for her not to give in to the creeping resentment.

No one is ever ready for kids, for God's sake. Usually, she was quick to pack away these thoughts because feeling angry and resentful was not going to make their efforts to have a baby any easier. Plus, she had also probably been a bit laidback about it until she'd turned thirty-nine and insisted they get real about their age.

Still, she thought, as she watched him muscling through the relaxed holidaymakers, his backpack jostling them, she should be able to bring it up without him getting defensive and then distant, which had become something of a pattern.

The distance was especially hard to take and Rachel had come into Annie's life at a particularly lonely time. She'd joined the gallery as artist-in-residence at the beginning of the year and they'd bonded fast. Rachel was very open and Annie found that encouraged her to be more open also. Also, Rachel understood much better than Maggie and Clara what Annie was going through. Rachel was on a similar trajectory; she wanted a baby too and was keen to adopt, but it was proving painful and extremely frustrating.

'The system's not loving that I'm single and self-employed.' She had rolled her eyes ruefully. 'Apparently painter is not exactly a bankable, stable career for a would-be adoptive parent. I've made some excellent life choices, haven't I?'

These days Annie's own life choices didn't feel much better. She'd be forty-one in October.

She tried to get Conor's attention again. 'Conor! Babe! I gotta wee!'

'Again?' Conor tossed over his shoulder, still ploughing through the ambling holidaymakers. 'You went before we left.'

We should be ambling. Annie felt resentment rising as her shoulder bag banged rhythmically against her hip. *This is a fun trip. We've loads of time. Why am I sweating and tense already?*

Conor was never a chill guy but put him in an air-travel situation and he could quickly become rabid.

'Conor! Please can we stop for a minute, I need—'

'Annie.' Conor turned. His handsome, sharply hewn features were taut, but she sensed he was making the effort to sound placating rather than irritated. 'Can't you go on the other side of security? I'd just feel way better if we got through in good time.'

Annie hesitated. Things between them had been flat, with occasional spikes of anger and frustration, for as long as her period had been showing up, unwelcome, for a year and a half now. She didn't want to start the holiday on a bad note, and bringing up the domineering little strips that had been dictating their sex life for so long would darken the already murky mood.

'Fine,' she said. She could do the test on the other side once Conor was distracted with the bookshop and the duty free.

Maybe it wouldn't be so tense if we hadn't held off on trying for so long ... ? Though a lot of the time, it really felt like she was the only one trying.

As she'd said to Rachel, it should feel like they were in this together, but in the last six months their relationship had felt unnervingly unpredictable, as though the emotional space between them was shrinking and contracting at different times. They had moments of closeness and moments when there was something hard to name in Conor's eyes when he looked at her. This invariably sparked panic in Annie. What was he thinking and why couldn't she face asking him this straight out?

Annie'd read the whole internet on the matter: Trying to conceive, or TTC as the forums called it, was hard on a couple: *Your DH* [meaning 'darling husband', vom] *was experiencing his own set of anxieties. There was a lot of pressure on the men to perform. Despite being partners on the road, a distance could open up between you both on your quest for a LO* ['little one', gag].

They'd reached the security queue now, and seeing that things were moving at an efficient clip, Conor reached back and took her hand, pulling her to him. 'Sorry, sorry. I know I'm a dick in airports.' He kissed the top of her head, immediately causing her blonde hair to cling to the velcro of his stubble.

'You are a complete lunatic in airports.' Annie smoothed her shoulder-length bob back behind her ears. 'You're like a velociraptor on cocaine.'

He grinned, shaking his head. 'I dunno why, but I get this uncontrollable impulse to get ahead of everyone, beat them to the bag drop, beat them to the queue … Also, like I said,' he widened his eyes meaningfully, 'we need to outrun Clara and Ollie. We don't need their bullshit.' He winced.

'You better get used to it.' Annie giggled. 'We've got two weeks of it.'

Conor looked around furtively. 'Look, I love them but I don't want it to start a second sooner than it has to.'

'Stop! They're our best friends, practically family.' She mussed his dark brown hair that he kept short and no-nonsense and felt the welcome release of relief that they seemed to be acting normal with one another again. She tried not to think about the fact that you shouldn't be *acting* normal with your other half, you should just *be* normal with your other half.

'You know what they're like.' Conor nudged forward in the line, practically breathing on the neck of the teenager in front of him. 'If they'd got to us before security we'd have been given a child each to field. Their shite would be everywhere, they'd be holding up the whole queue. They're *those* people.'

'They are,' Annie agreed. 'It's part of their charm.'

'Is it?' Conor was checking their boarding cards on his phone and opening their passports as they shuffled on.

In university, Annie, Clara, Ollie and Maggie had all been in the same year, though Annie was slightly younger, having skipped transition year in school. They had all studied different subjects. Annie'd done art history, Clara had a very random degree in zoology and Ollie scraped a degree in business while Maggie was in the drama department. Fionn and Conor had been two years ahead of them, and when Maggie and Fionn got together through their drama department productions, the twenty-year-old Annie had fallen hard for Fionn's friend, Conor. He was serious but had a dry sense of humour. At twenty-three, he'd seemed impossibly grown up and together – an opinion Annie had formed based purely on the fact that he had a George Foreman grill in his flat and owned a spare set of sheets. What boy – no! – what *man* thought of such things? Even though they'd been together ever since, he wasn't, as the forums said, her 'darling husband'. While the others had gotten married in their mid-twenties, in the same summer, no less, she and Conor had felt no great need.

From drunken red wine nights with them, Annie knew that Maggie and Clara were convinced that Annie was upset about this.

She genuinely wasn't. Her own parents, Liam and Shiv, had also not been married and that worked out grand, insofar as when they split up they didn't have any major bureaucratic headaches. He just moved to the shed down the bottom of the garden and came up most nights for dinner with Annie, her mum and her three sisters. It would probably have seemed like a more unusual setup if they hadn't lived in west Cork, where everyone had some kind of story and there was a distinctly bohemian vibe. Annie didn't feel much different from her friends in school; a few of them were the kids of divorced homes and several never even *saw* their dads. At least Liam was just at the bottom of the garden doing his whittling (yes, really – he sold hand-whittled fairy doors to tourists at the local markets. *Very* west Cork). With their daughters now mostly gone, Liam and Shiv no longer shared a meal all that often but every Sunday night they watched a movie together. Annie thought it was nice, though she didn't quite understand it. But she knew other people's relationships were a foreign country – you could never fully know them.

Just then, Annie felt a not entirely friendly poke from the woman behind her and the airport around her swam back into focus. She shuffled forward, following Conor as he approached a man in a high-vis vest checking boarding cards and passports.

No doubt the focus of the Red Wine Chats in Provincetown would at some point turn to her lack of wedding, they always did. That's something that she both did and didn't love about being with the friends she'd had for more of her life than not. They had a tendency to circle around the same subjects over and over. Sometimes the subjects were fun, like the time in their twenties when all six of them had been excruciatingly hungover during a surf lesson in County Clare and Ollie had fully fallen asleep on his board, which had then washed ashore, violently taking out a group of small children in the process. Of course, sometimes the subjects were tiresome, such as the weddingless Conor and Annie. Thank God they had just about enough tact to not mention the other thing Conor and Annie didn't have.

Now through the boarding pass check, Conor absentmindedly took Annie's hand again and they joined the nearest queue for the metal detectors. Annie rubbed her thumb over the familiar little vein on the back of Conor's hand and thought about how relationships were so much more than a wedding. It was about the life you built together.

Annie and Conor had a large apartment outside the city in a complex close to the foothills of the Dublin mountains. The view was gorgeous – all of Dublin Bay unspooled before them. On summer evenings Annie and Conor ate on the balcony and watched the small boats in the distance gliding over the water. How calm it all looked at such a remove but, Annie knew, down on the boats there would be shouted directions and ropes whipping in the wind. Sea spray and salt in the air. The squall of life.

All life was like that, Annie thought. Like a painting, observed from afar it made sense and appeared ordered. It was up close that you could see the frenzy of creation in the brush strokes and impatient smudges and sometimes, embedded in the pigment, a rogue bristle from the artist's brush. Up close the painting throbbed with life.

Since the baby game had begun, Annie had felt like her own life was a painting observed at a distance. There was order: she went to work and made small but satisfying inroads in restoring the artwork in her care. There was colour: she kissed Conor between his shoulder blades as he made coffee in the mornings. There was a life being lived: she bought a new dress. She bought another new dress. She put new flowers in the vase. They ate dinner on the dining table, their image reflected in the sliding glass doors to the balcony.

However, if you observed the scene closer, unlike a painting, there was no thrum of life, no exuberance. Annie had come to realise that being locked into a state of terminal waiting was not compatible with living. You simply *couldn't* live. You couldn't rush at life with an open heart when your every day, every hour and every minute were given over to waiting.

And along with the waiting came the calculating. The leaden days were units of time to get through. Her mood, at any given moment, depended on where she was on her cycle. Her best days were in the lead-up to ovulation when possibility shimmered. *This could be the month, this could be it.* She actually tried to beat back the hope because she was convinced that allowing the hope to swell would only make it harder when, yet again, she felt the familiar clenching in her womb and found blood.

Each month, she had to brace herself against the terrible silent howl of disappointment that wracked her. When the disappointment abated, the fear rose up: *It's never going to happen.* And then, at night, the blaming would begin. Cold and unpitying recriminations, mostly of herself but yes, sometimes Conor too. *You waited too long, what did you think would happen? Sometimes you can't wait for every single duck to be in a row. There's no perfect time when you magically become ready to have children.*

At last they reached the top of the queue and Annie was happy to turn away from these roiling thoughts. *FFS, it's holiday time, Annie!*

Conor leaned down to take her cabin bag and hike it up on the rollers leading into the large X-ray machine. Balancing on the side of the conveyor belt, Annie pulled off her thick-soled lace-up boots and turfed them into a tray along with the washed-out vintage denim jacket she was wearing over her dark floral tea dress. That morning Conor had joked about her commitment to the bit: 'Summer must be so hard for goths! You can't relax the rules even for a six-hour flight!' His flying attire was an extremely practical grey tracksuit and trainers.

'I'd lose my goth credentials,' she'd explained matter-of-factly and had carried on piling her suitcase with mostly black garments in linen and lightweight cotton.

Standing in her socks now, she took in Conor's broad back and small waist. He was committed to his own bit: working out incessantly. When he wasn't taking meetings with team leads – he worked for Cobalt, a small start-up that specialised in HR – he was working out. Annie felt a pull of tension in her jaw at the sudden montage of Conor leaving for the gym that began to roll in her head. He wasn't storming out as such but his swift exits nearly always coincided with talk of the Baby Project.

The first months he'd been excited, just like her, but as the first-year-mark passed, he'd become quieter on the subject. They both had. They edged around the topic. They didn't talk about the family they were one day going to be the way they had at the beginning. Now Annie took the recommended vitamins and supplements, tracked her basal body temperature, noted all the information and basically just told him when they'd be having sex. While he didn't play a proactive role, he had bought her flowers and other gifts every single time she got her period in the last year.

Ahead of her, Conor was now passing through the machine. She needed to stop being hard on him. She knew he worried about her, though he said little, just occasional concerned references to the level of focus she was giving the whole enterprise. *But it requires focus, that's the thing he doesn't get*, she thought as she watched a security man giving Conor a thorough frisk. She inched forward, waiting to be called.

With trying to conceive, details mattered. Take the ovulation tests, for example, you had to make sure you used the first pee of the day as it was most concentrated.

WAIT. Shit, shit, SHIT. Annie pulled back from the mouth of the large body scanner. The fucking pee was in her bag. Her bag that was rolling through the machine this very minute.

'You can step forward, madam,' the security guard was now calling, as Annie continued to back away.

She stumbled into several people, including the unfriendly back-poker from the queue. 'I'm sorry, so sorry. I have to—' She wedged herself back into the crowd at the luggage conveyor belt and implored an irritated-looking man. 'Excuse me? I just remembered something in my bag.'

'Annie?' Conor was calling from the other side of the glass divide. She ignored him. She did not want him to see her grappling with her piss at security. This would definitely fall under the umbrella of her 'being too intense about trying to conceive'.

'Which one's your bag?'

Annie leaned forward to see whether it had already gone through. There was no sign of it. On tippy-toes, she could see on the other side of security a woman carrying her shoulder bag and asking the milling passengers if it was theirs.

'She has it,' Annie pointed.

The man shrugged. 'Well then, it's already gone through, hasn't it?'

'But I need to take something out,' she whispered urgently. She could see Conor making his way towards the bag, which was now sequestered on the other side of the conveyor belt where all the bags that needed searching were. 'It's a liquid.'

The guy looked openly tired of her. 'Calm down, luv, they'll just take it off you on that side. Now go through, you're holding the whole place up.'

She couldn't believe she'd cocked up. She didn't love that Conor was about to learn that she'd been schlepping her piss around in her bag, but mainly she was worried that if this started a row, they'd waste a potentially fertile day – she'd been planning to somehow squeeze sex in when they reached their accommodation that night. She edged back into the queue for the metal detector, her eyes fastened on the exchange between Conor and the woman with the bag. He was gesturing towards Annie, obviously explaining that it was his partner's.

At last, Annie slipped through the security sensor, only to be waylaid by a woman with some kind of wand who wanted to investigate her more closely. *For God's sake.* Annie waved over at Conor. 'I'm *coming*. Don't start searching. It's *my* bag,' she yelled. Apparently too loudly, going by the reactions of at least thirty people in the vicinity.

'Do you mind not screaming?' Another security person was now approaching. 'There's no need for hysteria, please de-escalate. You will get your bag back.'

'I'm sorry. I just …' Annie lowered her voice. 'I don't want my boyfriend looking in my bag.' Beyond the crowd and the glass, the woman and Conor were chatting amiably as she began to unfasten the satchel.

'Is there something you are deliberately trying to conceal?' The uniformed woman with the wand straightened up sharply.

'No.' Annie felt utterly defeated; her grip on the situation had evaporated. 'There's a container of wee in there. I'd forgotten about it. We're trying to conceive. I just don't want him—'

'Say no more, hun.' The woman quickly stepped aside and waved her through with the wand. Unfortunately, it was too late. Annie arrived at Conor's side as both he and the security woman were examining the small bottle of piss.

'You've got some … what … cider here?' The woman held it up to the light, looking perplexed.

Annie nodded. 'Sorry, I meant to take it out and then completely forgot it was in there.' She could feel Conor looking at her but she kept her eyes on the woman.

'Well,' the lady smiled, dumping the bottle in the bin to her right, 'there's plenty of cider in the Runway bar! I just need to pop this through again and you're good to go.'

She trotted off with the bag and Conor turned to Annie. 'Did you just try to bring urine through airport security?' To Annie's relief Conor didn't look annoyed, just slightly perplexed.

'What do you mean?' Annie was ready to style it out. 'You know I need tiny portions of Handbag Cider to get through the day.'

Conor smiled, but Annie saw a wariness creep into his expression.

'Okay, you got me!' She kept her tone breezy. 'I'd forgotten to do the ovulation strips this morning. So I just popped it in my bag—'

'Annie ...' he began, 'I think this trip we should maybe—'

'Here you go!' The woman had returned with Annie's now urine-free bag.

'Thanks a million.' Annie gathered her things and pulled on her boots. As they moved away from security, she continued to explain. 'I thought I'd do the testing in the loo here. Look,' she beamed, trying to banish the odd formality that had suddenly wedged stubbornly between them, 'the test strips thing doesn't matter anyway. There's nothing to stop us just having sex!'

'Hmmm.' He nodded, sounding about as excited as if she'd said, *There's nothing to stop us just performing the procedure without anaesthetic.*

He looked like he was psyching himself up to say something, and unease stirred in the pit of her stomach.

'Conor! Annie! Thank fuck! I need *help*!' The mildly psychotic shout that rang out behind them could only belong to Clara.

'Shit.' Conor tried to duck but it was futile. Across security, with possessions and bags and children scattered all around her, Clara was waving to them, oblivious to the muttering of passengers and security personnel everywhere.

'Can you guys take this one?' Clara shouted over to them, giving the toddling Reggie a push towards the metal detector. 'He needs a change,' she called, quickly stuffing a nappy and wipes into his tiny hands.

CHAPTER 3

The buzzing of her family WhatsApp group chat caused Maggie Strong to stir a full fifteen minutes before her alarm.

She pulled her phone out from under the pillow to see an unsettling missive from her mother.

Mam: Dirty fecker. I always knew he was a slimy little prick.

She could see that it was indeed stupid o'clock. Aka 6.15 a.m. The injustice! The alarm was set for half anyway, they would be leaving for LAX soon, but a mother of two in her forties needed every scrap of sleep she could get.

She rolled over and landed directly into one of the strips of white-hot sunlight that was slicing through her blinds and across her huge bed – it was no doubt already in the thirties outside.

Los Angeles mornings were somehow the most *morningest* mornings of anywhere. The sun was barely up but she could tell from the distant sounds of traffic and general vibe of activity audible in the house beyond her bedroom door that the outside world's day had already started in earnest. People in LA took meetings at 6 a.m. Lots of people, like Fionn, her husband, went to the gym at 4 a.m., when it was still dark. It was a deranged, though unavoidable, part of his job.

It was after lunchtime in Ireland so her group chats were already bopping. The family chat, unnervingly named It's A Finger – a reference so old, neither her parents nor her two younger siblings, Emer and Donal, could remember the origin story – was brimming with indignation about a just-leaked story of an Irish politician doing the usual Irish Politician Stuff.

This is what had elicited her mother's message, a message which the others were now violently protesting.

Emer: Gah, Mam, too early for the image of a slimy prick. Now that's burned indelibly on my retina. 🍆💦

Donal: Look at Emer pretending she isn't balls deep in slimy pricks round the clock.

Dad: Can we go one bloody day without the aubergine and splashy drops emoji in this group? It's bloody obscene. On a less lewd and more cultured note, I was reading about Fionn's new indie movie! He's becoming so well regarded, delighted for him, and working with Adam Abramson is incredible. Can't wait to ask him all about it when ye're back at the end of the month.

Maggie thumbsed-up his message and flicked over to her other most active thread, Slags For Life, where Clara and Annie were comparing notes on what they'd packed and generally squealing about how excited they were to be all together in just eight more hours.

Maggie typed: *Cannot WAIT to see you two gorgeous hags*, then she x'd out and brought up the internet to check the weather for Provincetown but was instead met with the headline she'd read last thing before falling into an agitated sleep the night before.

SEE: These Pics Of A-List Actor Finn Strong's Wife Are Giving Us All Hope.

Queasy shame made her stomach curdle. She hadn't clicked in when the article had shown up in her newsfeed last night. But it had taken everything in her to resist. Now her finger hovered over the underlined link. *Don't, Maggie! This is stupid. It's not productive. Nothing good ever comes of this*, her rational side was desperately trying to remind her.

Her Fuck-It Side clicked the link. Sometimes knowing something was out there but not quite knowing what it was was worse, she reasoned.

She scrolled past the sycophantic opening paragraph …

He's Hollywood's hottest leading man …

… down past the list of accolades and achievements:

There's Oscar buzz around his role in Adam Abramson's Fires in Vermont premiering at NYC Celluloid Fest this autumn …

… and then on to the sick-making fawning over the fact that 'despite it all, he's still with the girl he met in college'. Underneath this paragraph was a carousel of images of a woman shopping. Maggie clicked through them, observing herself looking hassled as she crossed a Santa Monica car park with her twins, Dodi and Essie, trailing behind her. She was juggling the holy trinity – phone, coffee, handbag – and wearing high-waisted blue jeans, sunglasses and a white shirt. In one picture, her phone was wedged between her ear and shoulder as she unlocked her colossal white Grand Cherokee Jeep with blacked-out windows. It wasn't a great angle: the position had caused her jawline to disappear into a series of cascading folds. In another picture, she was placing her coffee on the roof of the car, her raised arm causing her shirt to lift. Her exposed belly was in the process of devouring the waistband of her jeans.

'We love that Mrs Finn Strong (aka Maggie!) is just your totally average girlie, embracing her imperfections,' the final words of the piece trilled.

Maggie clicked out of the article just as her phone's alarm began to beep. She hit 'dismiss' and stuffed the phone back under her pillow. Just a few seconds on the internet had thrown her nervous system into high gear and she now needed to climb down off the ledge of anxiety that any encounter with the press or social media inevitably inspired these days.

Maggie had married 'Finn' back when he was Fionn and they were just two of the many struggling theatre people in rainy, downtrodden Dublin in the 2000s. Now Fionn Strong was Finn Strong and he went to the gym at *4 bloody a.m.* with the rest of the lunatics.

His side of the bed was empty currently, not because he was out honing his body (voted top ten torsos in *GQ* magazine three years running) but because he'd spent the past month in Quebec shooting the third instalment in the *Endurance* movie franchise. He had agreed a short hiatus though and would be flying in on Friday to meet her and their friends in Provincetown for the 4th of July weekend and a long-overdue vacation.

Vacation! Maggie caught herself. *Holiday, for feck sake, Maggie. Don't become one of them.*

Maggie pulled herself from the tangle of the bed and hit the keypad on the wall above her side table to raise the blinds that covered the entirely glass wall that cleverly folded open onto the private patio of their renovated-to-within-an-inch-of-its-life 1920s bungalow on Lime Orchard Road, Beverly Hills. Neighbours included Penélope Cruz and Jennifer Lawrence.

Fionn and Maggie had been living in the bizarre land of fame for five years now and it had never become normal. The movie-star wives fell into two categories: Civilians and Stars In Their Own Right. Maggie had noticed after her first twenty or so Hollywood parties that the two groups didn't mix. She stuck to her allotted group but the other Civilian Wives seemed to assimilate more easily than she had. They told her to just get on the train and enjoy the ride.

'Don't read the press,' Eva Dreyfus (yes, wife of *that* director and the only real friend Maggie had made since she and Fionn moved to LA) had advised sagely.

Impossible.

'Don't compare yourself to the actresses.'

Impossible.

'Ignore the rumours or, better yet, don't even *hear* the rumours.'

Luckily for Maggie, Fionn hadn't hit the stage of a star's ascent when the rumours tended to begin. He probably had a couple more years until his 'golden boy' status would sour and mutterings about affairs and substances would kick off.

Maggie crossed the palatial bedroom, shedding her white button-down pyjamas (sourced for her by Sylvia, the stylist-slash-personal-shopper the whole family used).

Her room overlooked its own sectioned-off area of the property, complete with outdoor bath and trailing begonias. Despite the slightly terrarium effect of her bedroom's design, this patio space was totally private. What was *not* private was the bloody en suite shower, which was basically *in* the bedroom with them. The slatted floor-to-ceiling screen of imported European white ash that vaguely partitioned it off did nothing.

It was such an LA thing to do – have a wide-open shower so you could have a fecking audience in the bed watching you lather up. LA people worked so hard on their bodies, it kind of tracked that they'd want to have them on view at every available moment. Maggie showered in the guest room when Fionn was in town. She was forty-two – she wanted to soap her various puckered lumps and crevices in peace. She turned on the shower and stepped under the water, grateful to drown out thoughts of what it said about her marriage that she had taken to hiding her body from her husband.

Over the last five years, Maggie had made something of an anthropological study of celebrity marriages. Not an altogether healthy activity according to Maggie's long-suffering personal trainer, Britney, who, quite against Maggie's will, had also taken on the role of therapist since Maggie didn't have one (considered the height of eccentricity in LA).

The average lifespan of a celebrity marriage according to one study (carried out by a divorce firm, natch) was seven and a half years. She and Fionn had long outlasted that already. Next month, on the 17th of August, they'd be celebrating eighteen years of marriage.

Eighteen years. Though, come to think of it, they might not even be on the same landmass for it; she'd need to check the schedule.

Their elderly marriage more than doubled this gloomy statistic, but Maggie still fretted: did the clock start at the beginning of the relationship or at the beginning of the fame? Because in that case ... she only had a couple of years left. Fionn's big break had been slow in coming. He'd been thirty-nine when he was, at last, able to give up his side gig as a waiter.

At least *his* big break had shown up. Maggie tried to focus on lathering her shoulder-length dark hair and swallowed the regret that could crowd in on her at the slightest thought or mention of her own dormant (extinct?) ambitions. Her mind strayed to the half dozen or so abandoned documents on her laptop. Scraps of scripts. Notes on the ideas that prodded at her even after a year away from theatre turned into two and then eventually into what felt like a defeated sort of retirement.

'You should go back to writing, Maggie! You have so much talent,' Fionn often tried to encourage her. This latest bit of coaxing happened only a few months before as they'd watched the live announcement of the Tony Awards nominations together. The Tony Awards were the biggest theatre awards in the world and both of them had always tuned in. It was their version of being sports fans; Maggie loved rooting for the shows she'd seen and loved.

'I'm too long out of it,' she'd tossed back curtly, hoping to shut down the conversation. He meant well, of course, but more and more his well-meaning words just served to underscore how far from her old self she'd drifted. 'Anyway, I've forgotten all about the hero's journey! Something something quest, something something descent.' She tried to sound jokey, while biting back the urge to point out that if she started back down the theatre road, things would change a lot in their family.

Was there room for two big careers in a marriage? She often looked at the paired-off A-listers at premieres and industry parties and wondered how they did it. After a few years in the orbit of these people, Maggie had realised that for every John Krasinski and Emily Blunt there were hundreds of Hollywood couples where one lagged behind in the dust trail of the comet that was the other's career. And let's face it, it was usually the wife, especially if they had kids.

In Maggie's mid-thirties she had definitely gained some ground in the London theatre scene. She hadn't made much money but her shows were favourably reviewed. However her achievements seemed so insignificant compared to Fionn's. It made more sense to prioritise his dreams.

Theatre directing and playwriting was such a different animal to acting. Was there such a thing as a big break in theatre? Kind of, but nothing compared to making it in Hollywood. When Fionn was cast as the lead in a relatively small Irish TV show, she had just been commissioned by the Abbey Theatre to write a new play but had pressed pause to look after the twins and travel with him while he shot scenes in Ireland and Italy. It was a solid opportunity for Fionn but she hadn't thought it'd be particularly life-changing. When it aired during the first lockdown of the pandemic, no one could ever have anticipated the global impact.

People everywhere were mesmerised by this quiet, understated drama about a doomed love affair, and quite literally overnight (sometimes clichés are bloody clichés for a reason) Fionn had been catapulted into the stratosphere.

You could be successful in theatre, even famous, but Hollywood didn't even occupy the same solar system: it was a different galaxy. Maggie had never pressed unpause on that commission; the beginnings of the idea languished on her laptop along with the other false starts of the last five years.

Maggie rinsed her hair as her mind spun into different, equally dreary, territory.

Fionn didn't refer to the fact that he'd never seen her use the tits-out, bits-out washing area. *He probably knows why*, she thought darkly. He couldn't have not noticed the huge disparity in attractiveness that had developed between them ever since 80 per cent of his job had become staying rock hard and jacked up to feck. There was a gym in all the homes they owned (LA, London and Dublin) and all the homes they rented (New York, Paris, Saint-Tropez). Fionn used his gym-time to run lines with his assistant Brody and watch movies.

Maggie cleansed her face with the $400 gel Eva swore by and made a concerted effort to think about the days ahead.

In their twenties, their gang had always gone on holidays together, but they had been camping trips or music festivals mostly. They did the odd package holiday, money permitting. They were broke but it was a normal level of broke for their age.

In their early thirties, with slightly better jobs, they'd graduated to Airbnbs down the country at home in Ireland.

But for the last few years, Maggie and Fionn insisted on paying for everything on these twice-yearly trips with their friends because it had just gotten to the point where it was insane not to.

It was mad for them all to go to Sherkin Island and be piling into an Airbnb just a fraction of the size of one of Fionn and Maggie's actual homes when Fionn and Maggie had the means to rent out the entire island, never mind the Airbnb.

After a lot of awkward cajoling, their friends had finally agreed to accept this. But just because they'd come to an agreement didn't mean it felt entirely normal. Maggie knew that when they all converged on Boston later that night, there'd be some initial awkwardness as the first wave of extravagance hit her friends. The first millionaire moment would no doubt be the yacht that had been chartered to bring them all across to Provincetown. Maggie had implored Brody to find something reasonably restrained.

Just thinking of the lavishness made Maggie cringe as she adjusted the temperature of the shower. Still, she'd come to a place where fighting it seemed pointless. Why pretend that they were who they used to be? Sure, she'd *try* and be her normal self with Clara and Annie and Conor and Ollie; they needn't know that in the lead-up to the holiday, her self-care consultant Antonia had created a timetable of treatments – Botox, filler, peels, laser, transfusions, enemas. Maggie, on a sort of autopilot, just made her way to the various salons as dictated by the appointments in her calendar.

Maggie's friends also wouldn't know that Maggie wasn't even packing a bag. She'd bring her Kindle and phone and charger in her handbag but Sylvia had already purchased and arranged the family's holiday clothes, to be sent ahead. While her friends unpacked that night, Maggie would just open the garment bags hung in her room and check out the outfits Sylvia had put together based on the various fashion spreads and Insta outfit posts she'd sent Maggie.

Sure, Maggie could *act* as normal as she wanted, but it didn't change the fact that nothing about her life felt normal anymore. But pretending it was in front of her friends felt like the only option. She couldn't say her life was hard and lonely and weird and maybe not even what she had ever wanted for herself – *she'd* want to punch herself, never mind how Annie and Clara might feel about their rich friend moaning.

Her thoughts turned to the coming Friday. In three days, she'd see Fionn. At least Fionn would be one person on the trip that she wouldn't have to pretend with. He knew their life was bizarre as hell. She just hoped he wouldn't be too *Hollywood* around their friends. When they were skiing in January, she was sure she'd caught a few glances passing between them when fans approached him asking for selfies and he'd dialled up the *Finn Strong* persona.

She was excited to spend time with him. Just over a month had passed with Fionn away on set. But along with the anticipation, Maggie felt a strange tilt of dread when she thought of seeing him in the flesh. Or was it more the thought of him seeing *her* in the flesh? She ran her hands over her stomach. Eight years since giving birth and it still flapped down over her C-section scar.

'Mam! Mam!'

Maggie could hear her daughter Dodi out in the hall and welcomed the distraction.

It was hilarious to hear 'Mam' in an American accent. The twins were eight, they'd been in America since they were three, the accent was going nowhere – but Maggie and Fionn were pretty firm on them not saying '*Mom*'. Using 'Mam' was fast becoming their only connection to Ireland.

Dodi was only distinguishable from her sister by a faint freckle just under her left eye. A very fucking handy freckle, Maggie and Fionn agreed, because otherwise it'd be a real struggle to tell them apart. They'd assigned the twins colours as babies to minimise confusion. Dodi was yellow and Essie was pink – they'd even put ribbons on their ankles. She remembered the day Fionn had come up with the idea and they'd gone to the fancy gift shop in Hackney to buy the ribbon. Along the way, she and Fionn had played a game they'd devised. Dodi and Essie were about six weeks old at this point and Maggie had noticed that passersby invariably had *something* to say upon spotting the twin buggy and so Twin Commentary Bingo was born. Whenever a stranger got that slightly crazed eager gleam in their eyes and descended on them, Maggie and Fionn would mutter guesses as to what cliché was coming.

Frequent flyers were:
You've got your hands full!
No fucking shit, hun.
Two for the price of one.
Tell that to the crèche we're gonna be paying for.
Did you have them naturally or …?
No, luv. We went the *super*natural route: We sacrificed a virgin to Satan for them.

Maggie smiled at the recollection but also felt a twinge of sadness. She and Fionn couldn't really just stroll down the street anymore. There were fans and photographers and, while Fionn enjoyed it, Maggie found it suffocating and found the idea of being tracked so assiduously more than a little bit unnerving. It also made her feel even more left out of his life, as she was quite literally swept to the side by the people so eager to metaphorically devour her husband.

Just then Dodi swooped into view and leapt on the bed, gatecrashing Maggie's ruminations. Maggie reflexively sucked in her stomach before Dodi spotted her. She didn't want to be weird about her body around her daughters. She definitely didn't want to pass down her propensity for self-loathing. But Jesus, it was very hard to go against a lifetime of social conditioning.

Noticing the sound of running water, Dodi jumped down off the bed and peered around the screen. 'Mam, Essie says she doesn't have the second Xbox controller but then she keeps laughing. She is being totally suss.'

'I will be out in ten, okay?' Maggie made a futile effort to cover her body. Pointless – her arms hid exactly nothing. It was a needless effort too – Dodi was at the age where she barely paid attention to her mother's body. To her it was like an old piece of furniture she'd grown up around.

'Fine.' Dodi shot back out of the room as fast as she'd come in, screaming, 'Essie, Mam's coming so you should just cough it up already.'

Maggie pulled at her stomach as the suds streamed down over her belly. *Bodies are just bodies*, she reminded herself. But the headline from earlier muscled in anyway.

SEE: These Pics Of A-List Actor Finn Strong's Wife Are Giving Us All Hope.

On the face of it, it was an innocuous headline, but the implication was there – she wasn't good enough for Fionn. Wasn't he great for having such an astoundingly ordinary wife?

Ugh, could the shitty internal monologue ever just take a day off?

Maybe she should stop ignoring the check-in emails from her old therapist. Though how much good had the therapy ever done her if she was still locked in these spirals?

She turned off the shower and squeezed the water from her hair. *Fuck that article. Fuck my stomach.*

The two weeks in Cape Cod were coming at a good time. It would also be the longest they'd spent together as a family in 2025 so far. She'd been thrilled when Fionn had insisted the break be written into his *Endurance 3* contract.

The flight to Boston from the LAX VIP terminal – housed in a different building to the general departure gates – would leave in a few hours. She'd be with Clara and Annie so soon, and she actually felt tears rise just thinking about seeing them. She was fond of Eva but LA friends were never going to be the same.

'Are we nearly there?' Maggie asked the driver who'd collected them from Boston airport. Tucked in on either side of her, Dodi and Essie were dozing as they wound their way to the port. Outside the streets were busy as the day shift of work and obligation switched over to the night shift of languid drinks with friends and fizzing possibilities. It was nearly 7 p.m. and Maggie felt herself fizzing too as her reunion with her friends drew nearer and nearer.

'We're just here.' The driver pulled over. 'Woah!' he exclaimed, looking out his window.

Maggie leaned over to see what he was looking at. Crap, it was the *insane* yacht, gleaming in the dock. It looked like a medium-sized hotel on water. Fecking Brody.

'Is that for you guys?'

'Mmmmm.' Maggie nodded, distracted by notifications on her phone.

Brody: I'll call you in 20 to explain, okay? No need to get worked up.

In spite of her irritation, she grinned at his timing – how had he guessed that she'd just arrived at this boat-monstrosity?

'Holy crap, you some kind of high roller?' The driver was intrigued.

'Mmmmm.' Maggie smiled again. She had learned by now that when you are a celebrity plus-one, the best option was to be as low-key as possible about absolutely everything. To paraphrase *Law & Order*: anything you said could be used against you in the court of social media. Drivers, wait staff, shop assistants, people in the street, people on planes, the parents at the girls' school were all potential 'sources' for the media, Reddit forums and blind items. She winced thinking of a recent one on Deuxmoi that could've been her for all anyone knew:

What wife of an Irish A-lister has been doctor shopping all over Manhattan for prescriptions she does not need?

Given the small crop of Irish A-listers, both Clara and Annie had been straight on to her to discreetly ask if everything was okay. Sheesh. Though in their defence, it wasn't the most insane conclusion given Maggie's past.

Maggie could now see a huddle of boat personnel standing at the bottom of the bridge. She roused her daughters as the driver came around to open their door.

'So, no luggage?' He was squinting with curiosity at Maggie. Perhaps trying to place her as someone notable.

'Nope!' Maggie shook her head and typed a quick message back to Brody:

K. Just boarding boat now. It's ridiculous.

'We don't need luggage!' Dodi chirruped breezily. 'Sylvia has pulled looks for our vacay already!' She and Essie trooped down the gangplank and were ushered aboard by a young man in a crisp white and navy uniform.

The girls didn't so much as glance at the boat. Their blasé attitude to the luxurious circumstances of their lives was unnerving to Maggie. Another buzz from her phone pulled her attention back to the thread with Brody.

Yes! Of course it's ridiculous!

She dropped her phone back into her bag and paid the taxi driver.

On board *Poseidon's Palace*, Dodi and Essie were soon ensconced in the cinema eating popcorn and being served elaborate mocktails from the extensive menu. Maggie meanwhile was on edge in the vast lounge that was upholstered to within an inch of its life in beige leather. Anything that was not leather was dark mahogany and the whole thing was topped off with an elaborate gold chandelier. Deranged.

Maggie checked her reflection for the tenth time in the glass windows of the boat. It was dark outside now so she could get a good look at herself – she was suddenly hyper-conscious that none of the gang had seen each other in person since skiing. Had she put on weight? It felt like it but she knew she couldn't trust herself when it came to this. Historically, she hadn't been a reliable witness when it came to her own body. At least she'd had time to ditch her travel clothes and don a floaty navy kimono dress covered in tiny stars that Sylvia had arranged to be hanging in her cabin. It looked chic but relaxed and was doing a good job of pretty much covering her.

'Maggie! Maggie! Is there a slag aboard?' Clara's unmistakable husky voice was ringing through the still night air.

Maggie hurried out to the deck just as Josh, Tom and Reggie barrelled down the gangplank and into her arms, all talking at once.

'Aunty Maggie!' Reggie squealed.

'Our plane had free drinks and your own TV and bed-chairs,' Tom yelped breathlessly.

'That's cuz it was first class, babes.' Josh rolled his eyes, apparently already entirely adjusted to luxe living after just one transatlantic flight. 'The whole plane didn't have it.'

Coming down behind the boys were Clara and Annie and Conor. Ollie was on the dock still checking and double-checking that the porter didn't need a hand with the bags.

'C'mon, Ollie,' Clara called back to him while Annie and Maggie embraced. Maggie was enveloped by the comforting smell of Annie's rosewater perfume, a fragrance she'd been devoted to since college.

Clara was still shouting at her husband. 'They're grand, Ollie. You're being a hindrance and they're too polite to tell you to piss off. You're holding us up.'

Clara turned back and beamed at Maggie. Clara was dressed in full Clara regalia – a lurid lime green sweatshirt, joggers in a paler green and gold Converse with a chunky heel. Her long brown hair was scraped back into a bouncy ponytail and after hours in the air most of her mascara had relocated to under her eyes. She looked as effortlessly cool as ever but also mildly shattered. Maggie felt guilty for thinking it but she also couldn't help but feel sorry for her friend. Clara had boundless energy but her life looked unbearably hectic.

Clara pulled Maggie in for a hug. 'You okay, babes?' she asked. Over her shoulder, Maggie spotted Annie looking concerned.

'Me?' Maggie drew back from her. 'Of course!' She looked at the two of them, trying to gauge the slightly off vibe between them. Were they worried about her? They had a tendency to, even though she had been steady for years now (or at least as steady as anyone could be).

Maggie blazed past Clara's question and smiled big. 'You both look gorgeous! And ...' Maggie turned to Conor, kissing him on the cheek and hugging Ollie, who'd just jogged up, '*you two* look gorgeous!'

'So, where can I store my children?' Clara asked, just as the uniformed waiter materialised with champagne and narrowly avoided being knocked over by Reggie, who was rolled up into a ball and being pushed along the wooden deck by his brothers.

'Dodi and Essie are watching movies and eating their weight in treats. Do you lads want to see the cinema?' Maggie asked.

'Hell, yes!' Josh sounded more and more like a teenage YouTuber from the Midwest every time she saw him.

Another member of the boat staff appeared on cue and gently herded the boys off down a red-carpeted corridor that led deeper into the boat.

Annie, Maggie noticed, was declining the champagne, and Maggie felt a tug of pity. It was unlikely she was pregnant – she'd shared last month's negative test in the group chat. It was probably more to do with the strict lifestyle choices being pushed by the internet forums. Maggie wished she could be a better support for Annie but the truth was she didn't have any experience of what Annie was going through. She and Fionn had gotten pregnant with minimal effort and, while twins had felt like a lot, there were advantages – they had an instant, ready-made family and Maggie never had to get pregnant again.

Maggie mentally shuddered, remembering the full-body takeover of pregnancy that had left her unrecognisable to herself. It had been so hard not to slide back into old habits during that first year of motherhood when life felt so completely out of control. The babies cried. She cried. She couldn't get them to feed, sleep or shit. She was tormented by the all-pervasive feeling that she was fucking it up in every direction. Still, she'd managed not to give in to the old urges. It had helped that her mum had moved in temporarily to their tiny flat in Peckham for the first months. Maggie's little crutch was not very compatible with living in close quarters with other people.

Recently, Maggie and Fionn had discussed paying for IVF for Annie and Conor but Maggie was very wary of suggesting it. It felt so personal. How did you even bring something like that up? The few times Annie had referenced IVF, she'd said that they 'weren't quite there yet'. Though with Annie being nearly forty-two, Maggie couldn't help but think there was some denial going on.

'So!' Annie smiled at the waiter, who'd produced a glass of pink, non-alcoholic fizz for her. 'According to the itinerary, we're on this boat for ninety minutes! Do we get a tour?'

'Yes! Tour, please!' Clara chimed in, swigging from her glass.

Maggie laughed. 'I'd say it'll take hours to get around this boat.

I swear, I told Brody to just get us a nice, normal yacht. Let's have some snacks in the leather lounge? Ye must be wrecked from the flight.'

Maggie led them through the double doors.

Conor looked around. 'The leather lounge sounds like a place for seventies couples to do some swinging. Oh, look! Everything's wipe clean.'

Giggling, Clara plonked herself down and immediately tucked into the charcuterie plates that were dotted on small tables among the seating. 'I guess it figures that there'd be loads of meat in the leather lounge.' She laughed. 'So, Maggie,' Clara spoke through a mouth full of prosciutto, 'I'm gonna need a full rundown of what you're doing to your face, at some point. You've gone full *Death Becomes Her* – and I mean that as a huge compliment.'

'Oh God, in LA this is considered, like, fully unkempt.' Maggie gestured at herself. 'Wait till the party on Monday night. There'll be loads of movie people there and you'll see what I mean.'

'Oooooh!' Annie murmured. 'I saw the celeb bash in the schedule. Exciting!'

'Yeah.' Maggie tried to look enthusiastic. 'I think Brody kind of talked Fionn into it. Good networking, yada yada yada …'

She took a seat beside Conor, who was enthusiastically spooning caviar onto a piece of crusty bread. Ollie was on the other side of him buried in his phone and muttering about roaming charges.

'I'm out of Botox until we've finished paying off the new sofa.' Clara drew the skin of her forehead up to her hairline to demonstrate how smooth and expressionless she'd prefer to be. 'I wish they'd hurry up and start selling home injectable kits. Imagine *that* in the Aldi miscellaneous aisle.'

'The dream,' Annie echoed wistfully. 'There'd be riots, though. You should see the queues when they have the inflatable hot tubs on special. A few weeks ago, an elderly woman broke some ribs in a Ballyfermot supermarket when they had a forty-five-euro pizza oven. It was carnage.'

'Botox is probably not even a thing in California anymore, is it?' Clara mused. 'What do ye have now? Are ye harvesting the skin from babies' arses and grafting it to your faces?'

'Yes! Exactly.' Maggie giggled. 'It's a procedure called Baby Arse Face and it's all the rage.'

Clara laughed, but a second later Maggie noticed her shooting a slightly irked look at Ollie's frantic tapping. Nothing more annoying than your other half on their phone, Maggie reasoned.

When Fionn was around, his phone was like a third person in the marriage. If it wasn't Brody ringing him, it was Steven, his agent, invariably delivering news that, depending on whether it was good or bad, would see the atmosphere of the house instantly altered. If Steven opened with 'They're going with someone else', Fionn was liable to disappear into the gym for upwards of two hours to blow off steam. If Steven said, 'You nailed it!' Fionn would probably still head to the gym, just in a bubble of excitement rather than frustration. Either way, Maggie was on the outside.

'Ollie, can you stop pawing at that phone like it's your willy.' Clara was withering. 'What are you at? Pretty much everyone you know is in this room with you.'

Ollie grinned up at her. 'Now, now, no need for a snit. I'm just sorting out roaming. There's this digital SIM you can get that saves a fortune—'

'Grand! Fine!' Clara interjected. 'No need for boring details. Can you just play with yourself elsewhere?'

'Surely the leather room is the designated play with yourself area?' Conor mugged.

Ollie stood shakily. The boat, at last, was on the move. 'I'm gonna head out and see if I can get signal. We've got like an hour, right?'

'Yup, bit longer even,' Maggie replied.

'Eh,' Annie piped up, looking over at Conor meaningfully. 'Actually, is there somewhere we can maybe have a bit of privacy just for—?'

'I'll join you, man.' Conor shot to his feet and was out the doors after Ollie before Annie could quite finish her question.

'Just for … what?' Clara asked her.

'Ah nothing, never mind.' Annie kicked off her boots and tucked her legs up under her, looking, Maggie noticed, a bit deflated. 'What's the story with Provincetown? What's it like?'

'Well, I haven't been before,' Maggie admitted. 'Fionn was really pushing to go. It's got this really rich history in terms of writing and theatre. And my friend Eva says it's like gay Vegas, so extremely fun clubs, great food and amazing general vibe.'

'Gay endorsement is *big*, this is very reassuring.' Annie nodded sagely. 'As a card-carrying queer, I approve.'

'Would that be Eva *Dreyfus*? Wife of *the* Leon Dreyfus?' Clara's eyes were shining; Clara loved a celeb.

Maggie grinned. 'Yup. Eva says the place is a celeb stronghold. The Coen brothers have places there. And John Waters, Julianne Moore, Annette Bening and Warren Beatty.'

'So proper old-school celebs!' Clara beamed. 'Not newbies! Excellent. We only want the very best to stalk!'

'Discreetly, of course!' Annie added.

'Now, I have a concern.' Clara was now fully reclining on her little leather sofa, dangling Parma ham slices into her mouth. 'Brody doesn't seem to have factored in much lying-down-dying-of-a-hangover time.'

'Jesus, you're right,' Maggie laughed. 'He's only twenty-five – he doesn't realise that after forty every glass of wine equals an hour of crying and hating yourself the next day. I'll have a word. He's actually due to ring me any minute.' Maggie consulted her phone to make sure her volume was turned up. 'It's so weird, he never calls me.'

Maggie caught her friends exchanging uneasy glances.

'Okay. What? I saw that, you know, you two are shite at being subtle.'

'It's nothing, Maggie,' Annie said, just as Clara sat up and blurted, 'It's just doses on the internet.'

Dread immediately flooded Maggie. That bloody article she'd read earlier. She was mortified thinking of them seeing it.

'Listen, it's okay, gals, I don't go near the internet anymore,' she lied, wanting to reassure them so they could go back to talking shite and laughing at injured OAPs. 'I've read one too many fawning articles commending Finn Strong for being with such a totally average forty-something with a fupa.'

'Don't be mad. There's not a fupa in sight,' Clara said.

'Good for you, Maggie,' Annie chimed in, though Maggie spotted her glancing at Clara, who was now busying herself with chorizo.

Maggie tried not to let her growing unease puncture the happy buzz of their reunion, but the girls were acting so odd. What if it was a different post? Now she *had* to check the bloody internet.

'I'm just gonna go to the loo.' She stood, pocketing her phone. It was probably more of the same *Finn Strong's wife is a total minger, isn't he great altogether for continuing to look at her*. Annie and Clara were just being over-protective; they didn't realise she was used to it. Or sort of used to it, at least.

She headed out the doors feeling her friends' eyes on her back. In the corridor she kept one hand on the wall to stay as steady as she could – the boat was moving through the darkness at a clip. As anxiety dragged at her, Maggie felt an unnerving unreality descend. Everything about the hallway started to look surreal – the vivid red of the carpet was dialled up, the black of the portholes looked like an abyss. It was like a scene from a movie. She took a couple of deep breaths. The feeling of being at a remove from everything had visited her many times over the years. It was her special flavour of anxiety, one she'd started experiencing in her twenties that was very knit into some of the other problems she'd had back then. The buzz of her phone in her hand severed the pull of the panic and she was actually grateful to answer Brody's call.

'Brody.'

'Maggie, hey! Thanks for taking the call. I know you already said you think it's ridiculous but I just want to make doubly sure you're okay with everything.'

'Brody, what are you talking about? I meant the boat you hired is ridiculous. Now my friends are acting weird. What is going on?'

'Oh crap. Right.' Brody sounded momentarily wrong-footed. 'Sorry, I thought from your message you knew. Look, it's nothing big. Just a few blind-item social accounts posting stuff that people might mistake for Finn.'

'Like … ?'

Drugs? Rehab? Inappropriate behaviour? Maggie's mind shuffled through the possibilities.

Brody hesitated and Maggie balled her left hand, feeling her nails digging into her palm.

'Irish A-lister, on-set affair with co-star.' Brody exhaled as if the awkward moment was too much for even him.

A sickly adrenaline began to invade her body. She took a couple of shallow breaths but felt her lungs hit resistance each time she tried to fill them.

Maggie'd spent so many hours worrying about this very thing, weirdly she almost felt a sense of release that it was finally happening. No more pre-emptive worry which felt like a waste of energy. Now she could just *worry* worry. *Yay!* she thought bleakly, glad that this wasn't a video call so he couldn't see her face as she blinked back tears.

She didn't have to ask who – there was only one main female character in the *Endurance* franchise, only one co-star it could be: Emilene Jones. Twenty-six. Blonde. A nightmare. *Why don't they ever cast women the same age as the male stars? Surely this would prevent this from happening.*

If this is even definitely happening, a small part of her suggested hopefully.

'Why are *you* telling me this instead of Fionn?' She tried to sound dignified.

'Well, Maggie, he's on set; you know how strict he is about contact with the outside world …'

Maggie felt a surge of irritation. Fionn's insistence on being totally immersed in shooting was something they'd argued about. 'You're a father of two and a husband,' she'd said. 'You can't go dark on us for weeks on end.' What she *didn't* say was that she probably wouldn't be quite so annoyed about it if she didn't constantly come across pics of him out to dinner with the cast and crew on the other actors' social media.

She'd visited a set once during one of the early *Endurance* shoots. But from minute one, she'd realised it was a huge mistake. Fionn and the rest of the cast and crew were polite and cordial but she'd felt like a parent gatecrashing their party.

'Movie sets are funny,' Eva had counselled her kindly when Maggie'd rung in a panic on the first night. 'These people are together all day every day for weeks and months on end. A little society just evolves. Even the in-jokes have in-jokes. And anyone who tries to break into that is going to find it very hard.'

Maggie swallowed now, listening to Brody's awkward breathing. 'Are you saying Fionn doesn't know something's leaked?' she asked, trying to sound matter-of-fact.

'Not leaked, Maggie. Been cooked up out of thin air! The item could also be about any of the other Irish actors. There is absolutely no truth in it, I promise you.'

'Do you swear on my daughters' lives, Brody?'

'Well, I don't feel comfortable with that question, Maggie.'

'How about just one of them, Brody? Dodi. Do you swear on Dodi's life?'

'Haha.' He gave a fakey LA laugh. 'I'm glad you're seeing the funny side. Look, no need for us to acknowledge anything. It's blind item nonsense and completely untrue to boot! I'll be seeing you Friday. In the meantime, enjoy all the fab things in the schedule.'

Maggie ended the call and debated her options. Full-scale breakdown? Spend hours sobbing and trawling the internet googling *Finn Strong affair*? Or go back to her friends and pretend it's all grand?

Or ...? She looked down the hall to where a discreet door led to the cabin where she'd changed earlier. She drifted towards it almost without conscious thought.

I'm just going to check my face, she told herself. She pushed the door open. Her travelling clothes, a pair of Yves Saint Laurent jeans and a top from The Row, were still strewn across the bed. In the bathroom, she fixed her make-up and then leaned on the sink, resting her forehead on the mirror. It would be so easy ... It would feel good. It had always made her feel calmer in the past. And it's not like it was a real problem anymore, she hadn't done it in ages.

A bang of the bedroom door jolted her back upright.

'Maggie?' It was Annie. 'Are you in here?'

'Annie?' Clara knocked.

Shit. Maggie gathered herself, feeling a sharp tug of regret at being interrupted. She headed out to them.

'Hey, sorry, I was just going to the loo, remember?'

'Yep.' Clara smiled, but Annie wasn't as quick to hide her anxiety.

'Are you okay?' she asked.

Maggie knew there was no point pretending with them. 'Sorry, I was talking to Brody. I know about the blind item which, from all your exchanging of loaded glances, I presume you've both seen.' She gave a weak smile.

'Look, who hasn't had a crush at work?' Clara joked, clearly attempting to reassure her in the most *unreassuring*, Clara-esque fashion ever.

'Which may not,' Annie hastily added, glaring at Clara, 'in fact has *definitely* not happened here with Fionn.'

'Well, most workplaces don't require the employees to pretend to be in love and fake-ride each other for cameras.' Maggie pressed her fingers into her temples.

'Everyone at my job is basically a foetus,' Clara continued, evidently trying to lighten the mood. 'But even my eye can be drawn in a moment of madness. There's a very cute boy-man who works Mondays and Tuesdays … I could be persuaded.'

'Fionn isn't being persuaded of *anything*.' Annie was talking loudly, to drown Clara out.

'I know, I know.' Maggie threw her arm around Annie. Even though a cacophony of worries clanged in her head – *could Fionn cheat with a co-star? Is he really that predictable?* – she didn't want the holiday to totally crumble into drama before it even began. 'Look, the story is of course bullshit,' she said, with a confidence she wished she truly felt. 'I think what gets to me more than the gossip is that Fionn doesn't know because of his whole "need to stay in the moment when on location" rule. He brings an old flip phone, for God's sake. *And* mostly keeps it off. So I'm, like, out here trying to deal with people saying this stuff and saying my marriage is a piece of shit and he's just oblivious.'

'That is a fucking outrageous rule,' Clara announced. 'What a fucking *man* thing to insist on. Like, you have kids, mate, what if one of them needed an organ?'

'Or one of *us*, his lifelong friends?' Annie chimed in. 'Fionn and I are both B-negative. I've had my eye on his right kidney for a while now.'

Maggie giggled, feeling a powerful rush of affection for them. 'It is shit, right? Like, you become a parent, your life *does* have to change a bit.'

'Not for men,' Clara seethed. 'This is going to sound totally unreasonable but I'm really not happy with Ollie doing anything for himself, which, God love him, he barely does – a few pints here and there. I know, I'm a bitch, but it's how I feel. I'm in the shit 24/7, I want him to be in the shit 24/7. I feel like there is an invisible leaderboard tracking who gets to have time to themselves and if either of us gets ahead of the other, it can get *veerrrry* tense. And to be clear here, a trip to the supermarket *sans* kids counts as time to ourselves. I went for drinks with the gang from work ages ago and Ollie was at me about it in the taxi *today*. Like, how long had he been storing up *that* little grievance? They're all a bag of dicks.'

Maggie grinned, already feeling a bit calmer. She was happy that at least this shit had arisen while she was with them instead of by herself rattling around the LA house with too much time to ruminate, but she didn't want them raging at Fionn when he finally joined them. She wanted this trip to be perfect. 'Look, it's only a couple more days. Fionn will be here on Friday and we can talk about this whole no communication thing then. I know he's super excited to see you all. He moved mountains to get this break written into his contract.'

'C'mon.' Annie headed back out to the corridor. 'We only have half an hour left in our beloved Meat Room. The waiter said we'd arrive in Provincetown very soon.'

CHAPTER 4

The bedroom was dark when Clara woke up groggy from a champagne and cured meat hangover. She was so parched, her tongue literally felt like a thick slice of Serrano ham flopping around in her mouth. For a couple of disorientating moments she wondered if she was still on the boat, until she realised the slight feeling of listing was just the after-effects of the journey over the previous night. This was no boat cabin but an enormous bedroom furnished entirely in white – a daring decor choice for a rental. The Venetian blinds on two big picture windows were just about holding the searing morning sun at bay. Clara turned to rouse Ollie, only to find him already gone from the bed.

Her throat tightened slightly. Was it weird that he hadn't woken her? On the very first morning of the holiday? Hadn't he wanted to lounge in bed with her? She'd considered telling Maggie and Annie about her building disquiet about Ollie the night before but had instead papered over her real feelings with jokes about the parental leaderboard.

She rolled over and tried to bury the thoughts. An affair just seemed so not Ollie's style. He was a good husband.

Also, he had always been extremely outspoken about his feelings on what he called 'the shittiest thing you could do to another person'. When Ollie was a teenager, his dad had cheated on his mum and the family came apart. Ollie, to this day, kept his interactions with Don to the absolute bare minimum.

Plus, she and Ollie had always been such a *team*. Not like bloody Fionn, who she was not impressed with at all at that moment. She'd be scheduling in a word with him at some point for sure, if he ever even appeared.

She took a breath and forced herself to return to this moment of pure luxury; she wanted to savour it. As much as it felt uncomfortable to be indebted to their friends for this reprieve from the grind of life, she needed to soak it up. She breathed deeply and made a conscious effort to release the tension in her jaw. Mortgage thoughts and bills thoughts were not going to smother her. She needed this.

She stretched out and pondered how strange it was to not be woken up by every one of her children bounding around her bed and lovingly breathing morning fug into her face. On this trip, all the kids were staying in two rooms on the lower floor of the house along with a small team of childcare professionals. This was Maggie and Fionn's world: parental obligation and discomfort simply did not exist.

Clara rooted through the bedclothes to find her phone. 10.30 a.m. Jesus, when was the last time she'd slept past seven? With the time difference, 10.30 a.m. was really 3.30 p.m. but so far no weirdy jetlag feelings were circling, though as the day wore on they might set in. Nothing a nap and more booze wouldn't solve. The thought of all the delicious empty hours stretching ahead was intoxicating. Clara could practically *feel* her chest loosening. She knew her workload and the mountain of housework and family admin was still waiting for her at home, but for now she could forget about it all. Though as she untethered herself from the sheets, another glance at Ollie's empty side caused a further unwelcome niggle of worry. Maybe he'd felt uncomfortable with the nannies doing all the work with getting the boys up and went to help?

That must be it. She shook off the thoughts and got up.

Pulling down the long George Michael T-shirt she wore to bed, she padded to the windows and began a trying battle to open the huge blinds. She had a vague memory of a button or some kind of clapping sequence closing them the night before. She searched the walls around the frames. She was dying to see the view – it had been total darkness when they'd arrived on Provincetown's wooden pier the night before.

Even in the darkness, the sheer *American*-ness of it all had been delightful. By the light of the tall white lamps dotted along the walkway – each adorned with a proud American flag – they could see the little shuttered clapboard huts that during the day sold seashell ornaments and tickets for cruises and paintings by local artists.

Two huge vans with blacked-out windows had met them where the pier ran out and the main street of Provincetown began. While the port was deserted and draped in shadows, the main street had been hopping. Music had blared from every bar and club – Gaga, Chappell, Harry and Beyoncé were all jostling for dominance. On Commercial Street, the ubiquitous American flags were joined by pride flags, and gangs of gorgeous young gays, theys and gals were strutting, arms linked, into town. Clara had tried then and there to abandon bedtime and persuade everyone to go for a dance but sense had prevailed in the form of Annie shooting agitated looks at Conor (no doubt they had mandatory sex planned) and Maggie looking drawn. Instead they'd all been whisked in the opposite direction, soon leaving the buzz of a July night in P-town behind them. The vans had headed along Shore Road which hugged the coast and curved south before turning down what appeared to be effectively a single-lane back road that ran for miles with houses dotted between dunes and occasional glimpses of the dark and glittering ocean to the right. The rest of the north side of the island lay to the left.

The house they'd arrived at was beautiful. Its white clapboard exterior had glowed in the moonlight. It was straight out of an American movie about rich people 'summering'. Verandas and balconies wreathed the many stories and a large wooden deck extended on stilts out over the beach to the rear. Waves could be heard crashing from the fathomless black of the ocean somewhere out in the night beyond the pearlescent sands.

Now, the sound of the door opening behind her drew Clara back to the present. 'Good morning,' Ollie called.

'Hey.' She turned. 'How do you open these?'

He seemed to be hanging back by the door – keeping away for some reason? *Or maybe he's just standing there, Clara! Paranoid much?* she silently admonished herself.

'There's a remote on the bedside table there.' He pointed.

Clara located the slim silver device and pressed the arrow pointing up. The room gradually filled with light. As Clara's eyes adjusted to the sudden brightness, the vast blue sea materialised like a mirage in front of them.

'Fuck,' she breathed. Beaming, she turned to make her way to Ollie but he was already ducking towards the bathroom.

'Quick shower,' he said, disappearing behind the door.

'Cool,' Clara replied, as the door shut abruptly. 'It'd be terrible to share a bloody moment here.' Her words dissolved in the glare of the room.

Her phone buzzed with a message from Maggie in the P-town group chat they'd created for the trip:

Breakfast on the deck, gang. There's a chef here doing mad shit – he just made me a blueberry, lemon and ricotta soufflé. Unreal scenes.

Clara heaved the suitcase onto the bed and pulled out a pair of high-waisted short shorts and an orange crochet bralet. She'd made a vow to dress well on this holiday, trawling Depop for good deals on a few nice bits. She wanted Ollie to see her as more than just his co-wrangler of children. It was a very dispiriting part of marriage – God, she *hoped* it wasn't just *their* marriage – that you could literally go weeks without really looking at the other person, without really *seeing* them. With three kids ten and under, sex was once a week on a *good* month. Various podcasts she listened to seemed to promise light (aka sex) at the end of this tunnel when the kids were older and more self-sufficient.

Clara and Ollie's sex had become extremely efficient when it did happen. *Bluey* was their sex babysitter and they could basically both finish in less time than an episode. The standard *Bluey* episode was seven minutes long.

Plus, if you had kids, the reality was you were likely having sex with someone who, best-case scenario, had seen you effectively shite out a baby while grunting obscenities. Surely no amount of fake tan and nice underwear could help them unsee that?

Once she was dressed and had lashed on a bit of the expensive CC cream Maggie'd sent in one of her many care packages of spendy treats she claimed she was given for free and didn't want, Clara headed to the deck where Maggie, Dodi and Essie sat at a long table with a pretty gingham tablecloth. They were being tended to by various staff in uniforms of crisp navy shorts and sleeveless white shirts.

Maggie was wearing a loose white dress with flowers embroidered across the shoulders and sipping from a delicate flute. Her daughters wore sun hats and swimsuits and looked impossibly cute eating their berries and chocolate pancakes.

'Good morning!' Maggie called.

'Hi!' Clara took a seat and was handed a menu.

'Coffee, ma'am? Mimosa?'

Clara laughed. 'Both! Thanks a million!' Then mouthed 'ma'am' at Maggie.

Maggie giggled. 'Did you see Annie or Conor?'

'Not yet, I got the feeling that they were under pressure to ...' Clara lowered her voice, throwing a glance at the twins, 'to ... eh ... get to bed last night. I'd say they're on the old sex diet this week. Boning on a timetable must be such a fun-suck.'

Maggie nodded. 'I sensed the edginess alright. Has she said much about how it's going lately?'

'She doesn't really talk about it anymore.' Clara accepted the proffered glass of fizz from the waiter's tray.

'Yeah,' Maggie agreed quietly. 'Apart from the odd snap of the negative tests, she's not doing the monthly bulletin in the WhatsApp.'

'I think the whole slog has just beaten the quippiness out of her.'

Maggie leaned closer. 'Surely it's time for them to, ya know, take some action. Fertility treatment, like.'

'I'm not sure they can afford it, Maggie. The rent on their apartment is probably crazy.' Clara stopped, worried she'd said too much. She scanned the menu, avoiding Maggie's gaze. Maggie and Fionn were always trying to give them all money. They'd fully wanted to buy her and Ollie a bigger house outright a couple of years into Fionn's ascent. Annie and Conor had said they'd received the same offer. Clara felt a squirm of guilt remembering the boozy dinner the four of them had had bitching about Fionn and Maggie's house proposals. Clara knew they meant well but there was something just a bit fucking off about the whole thing. It was so *obvious* that Maggie and Fionn must talk pityingly about them all. And it was kind of insulting and presumptuous assuming that everyone must aspire to have fame and money. Okay, of *course* Clara would like to have more money but not charity from friends. Besides, money and friendship rarely mixed well.

'I've been thinking.' Maggie was clearly not ready to drop the fertility matter. 'I really want to help them.'

Clara welcomed the arrival of another waiter with a pad and pen. 'Hiya.' Clara smiled. 'Can I please have the eggs royale and three chocolate pancakes for my kids? I better go get them up.' Clara started to rise, grateful to be ducking out of the conversation.

'Don't.' Maggie raised a palm. 'Ed, the day nanny, already got the boys! They've been playing down there for ages!'

'Well,' Clara paused awkwardly, not quite sitting, not quite standing, 'shouldn't I get them dressed and stuff?' Just then a caterwauling started up from inside the house. The noise was increasing in volume and drawing nearer. 'Ah.' She dropped back into her seat. 'My children, no doubt,' she said just as the three boys exploded out of the house trailed by a grinning guy of about twenty.

'Ed! This is Clara.' Maggie waved him over. 'Clara, this is Ed. He's on the day shifts this week.'

'You're amazing.' Clara shook his hand. 'If you feel the need to sedate my kids or trap them under something heavy, feel absolutely free. Sit *down*, Reggie!' The toddler was already up on the table and immediately plonked himself down amid the glassware and cutlery. 'I meant on a chair,' she added, starting to reach for him, only for Ed to swoop in.

'I've got it.' He smiled. 'Come on, big guy.' He plucked Reggie up and settled him on a chair. Already the pancakes had arrived and all the boys began tucking in, grunting away at the usual volume.

'I can only apologise. I would say that they're never like this at home but that would be a lie.' Clara picked up her drink, watching Ed patiently tending to Dodi and Essie, wiping their chocolatey hands and reapplying their sun block.

'I *do* parent my kids at home, I swear,' Maggie said wryly, evidently following Clara's gaze. 'This is special "holiday levels" of nannying. The girls don't even have a nanny in LA.'

'Hey,' Clara raised her glass, 'you don't have to explain yourself to me. If you *can* do it, you *should* do it.' She regretted her words more or less straightaway.

Maggie looked pained. 'Clara, you know we'd love to help—'

'Maggie! If you start offering me money for childcare while I'm on a holiday you are paying for, I might fully pass away from mortification.'

'I know, I know.' Maggie's words rushed out. 'I'm sorry. It's just, like, you all work so hard and ... well, you know I think what Fionn earns is stupid money. And—'

'Please stop, I'll start getting irritated!' Clara made sure this sounded jokey, but frankly, she *was* feeling an edge of annoyance, probably goaded by the surely imminent jetlag and the blaze of the sun. Plus, Ollie had still not appeared. *He's a big guy, but seriously, how long can one man need for a shower?*

Her eggs arrived, perfectly poached with elaborately arranged smoked salmon and slathered in buttery hollandaise. Finally, Ollie, Annie and Conor appeared.

'Morning!' Maggie called over the sounds of Josh, Tom and Reggie scarfing down pancakes. Ed had returned and was hovering nearby, ready to clean the boys' faces.

'Maggie, this ...' Ollie swept an arm wide over the pastry- and fruit-laden table, the deck and the beach beyond, 'is, frankly, a let-down.'

Conor laughed, though Annie, Clara noticed, didn't join in. She was looking at the view but her eyes were faraway. It was a face Clara'd grown accustomed to seeing. Annie was most likely doing the calculations that Clara knew took up enormous real estate in her head. When should they have sex? How many times could they manage? Or maybe she was wondering if she was standing up too soon after the most recent sex. She'd mentioned that concern once during the first year of it all.

As they took their seats, Clara spotted Ollie once more staring intently at his phone. She stuck her knife into one of her eggs and watched the yolk spill out.

'Looks like we're on the boat for the afternoon.' Ollie was holding up his phone, the itinerary visible on the screen, and Clara was reassured immediately. *I'm over-analysing. And it's going to ruin the bloody holiday if I don't stop.*

On the yacht, the afternoon drifted by languidly in a rosy haze of easy chat and hot, hot sun.

While Ollie and Conor cannonballed with the kids into the ocean, Clara, Maggie and Annie discussed the social media presence of one of their old college friends who was doing a committed line in 'life begins at forty' after an acrimonious divorce and tense custody battle.

'Ollie and I just wouldn't have the time to get a divorce – the sheer paperwork,' Clara mused from under her arm, thrown over her face to shield her from the dazzling rays as she lay on a lounger.

'That's one thing me and Conor would have an easy time of.' Clara squinted over at Annie, who was reapplying her sun block, despite the fact that she was sitting in the shade of the enormous taut sail overheard and wearing a diaphanous black beach cover-up. 'We've all the time in the world for paperwork. Not that there'd even really be any. Renting, separate bank accounts, no dependants …'

Clara could see Maggie shuffling herself upright on her lounger and starting to tilt her head in the international sign for commiseration.

'How is it all going—?' Maggie began, before being cut off by Annie, who spoke loudly and deliberately:

'With everything else being done for us on this trip, I'm kind of amazed there's no one putting our factor 50 on!'

Clara winced. Annie was clearly not willing to allow an opening for any 'u ok hun' chat.

'Yeah, my bad.' Maggie grinned, settling back down, evidently resigned to the fact that Annie was not in the mood for any Big Chat. 'We've got hair and make-up before dinner this evening, though!'

'Shut up!' Clara couldn't even say for sure that this was a joke. The staff had done everything short of digesting their meals for them since that morning.

'I am actually serious,' Maggie continued. 'I decided to do it cuz I don't think I can take one more grim pap shot of me on social media. This is bad enough.' She waved a hand vaguely over her body. 'At least my face is one thing I can control, so I'm fucking doing it.'

'Maggie!' Clara glanced at Annie, who'd straightened up at this. 'You look absolutely beautiful. You're Rich Lady Hot!'

Rich Lady Hot was a term they'd coined back when they spent a summer in New York after college. The phrase was inspired by all the moneyed women with impossibly sleek hair and yoga bodies they'd served in the Hamptons' Riviera Country Club.

'Yeah, well.' Maggie shrugged. 'Turns out there's a much hotter type of hot than Rich Lady Hot – LA Girl Hot. So yeah, the old confidence isn't amazing. Drinks?' She stood abruptly and headed into the cabin, where a bar was stocked with gleaming bottles.

With a twang of nerves, Clara thought back to Maggie in the bathroom on the ship the night before. Hearing Maggie be so down on her body was unnerving, especially as she looked objectively lovely.

'That fucking blind item,' Annie hissed over.

'I know,' Clara whispered back. 'I kinda thought she was okay but … it's obviously upset her, like, of course it would.'

'I didn't love having to get her out of the loo.' Annie checked that Maggie was still inside. 'Bit déjà-vu-ish, wasn't it?'

'Uh-huh. Like old times,' Clara said quietly. 'But I genuinely think she was just taking a minute. God, it must be so hard having shit like that splashed around the internet … No wonder she's feeling a bit low in confidence.'

'You don't think there's truth in it?'

'Nah.' Clara kept her voice low. 'There's no way he would. Not after everything … He's been with her through it all. Remember Ollie drove Fionn to the facility? Ollie told me Fionn broke down in the car afterwards, really lost it. Seeing her like that scared the shit out of him. I just can't see him doing something so hurtful. He's a good guy, even if the fame thing has him being a bit self-absorbed.'

'Hmmmm.' Annie pursed her lips, then quickly flipped to smiling as Maggie returned with a large pitcher full of booze and fresh mint.

'It's time for rum,' she said. A white-aproned barman followed behind her with glasses.

'Amazing.' Clara made a concerted effort to sound brighter. 'I'm just going to get my hat.'

In the gloom of the yacht's below-deck living space, Clara's eyes took a moment to adjust before she spotted her wide-brimmed straw visor. Another Depop purchase. She pulled her long ponytail through it, then fixed it in front of the mirror. That was when she spotted Ollie's pile of clothes heaped on the banquette. She grabbed his T-shirt, thinking she might throw it over her shoulders. Even though it was past 4 p.m., it was hot as ever, with the sun burning in the cloudless sky overhead. Disturbing the clothes caused Ollie's phone to drop out of his shorts and onto the floor. Clara stooped to grab it, then hesitated. Had she really wanted the T-shirt? Or had she wanted the phone to fall into her path? She didn't even want to fully interrogate this idea. Anytime she articulated her suspicions to herself, it made the knot in her stomach draw tighter.

Just take a look. There won't be anything to see anyway, she told herself. *I can look, see that there's nothing and then I can relax and enjoy the holiday.*

She glanced back out towards the cabin door, though all she could see of the day beyond was a rectangle of harsh white that left an impression on her retina when she turned and blinked. She quickly bent down, scooped up the phone and hunched over it, facing the cabin wall, ready to drop it back into the cluster of garments should anyone walk in. She tapped the home button and the lockscreen appeared. Her and the three boys were sitting on the roof of their car on the back road out by the airport where they often went to watch the planes land and take off. Some months, that was what passed for a family outing. Just leaving the house with kids could be so expensive – they wanted stuff from the shop, the toll bridge each way cost four euro. At least the boys looked happy: the older two were clearly in the middle of shouting at something while Reggie held his arms aloft with a soother stuck in his mouth.

For their sake, I should check. Then at least I'd be rid of this crazy overthinking, she told herself. She knew that suspicion in a marriage could all too easily metastasise and grow malignant even if there was nothing to have misgivings about.

Clara tapped in Ollie's code and it was rejected. She tapped it in again, more slowly this time. The digits shook again and the lockscreen remained unchanged. Rejected.

Clara felt a twinge of unease. *When did he change his code? And more importantly: why?*

'Clara?' Ollie's rangy frame was suddenly blocking most of the light from the door as he lowered himself down the small, awkward steps.

She dropped the phone and nudged it under his shorts, then quickly moved into the centre of the cabin.

'Hey.' She knew her voice sounded odd, a little strangled, and she subtly tried to steady her breathing.

'The kids are dying for you to come play with us.' He was grinning, and his usually springy, curly hair was wet and flat to his head.

She nodded slowly in answer but she was distracted. He was looking so toned. He'd always been slim but was there more definition? When had *that* happened? How had she not noticed? Though when did they last have sex? Had they even put the lights on?

'So will you come jump in?' He moved a little closer and put his hand on her waist. 'This is nice, isn't it?' He lowered his lips to hers and Clara had a sudden, deeply unpleasant feeling that she was kissing a complete stranger. A stranger who had changed his passcode for some reason.

Clara felt the cabin close in around them and she pulled away.

'Better get out to the boys.' She hurried past him up into the light.

An hour later, the boat returned to the shore just across from the house and a small speedboat ferried them back to their own private dock. They all got off and Ed and two more nannies began an impressive military-style operation to transport the five kids and untold amounts of paraphernalia across the sand and up to the house. Clara, Maggie and Annie trailed behind while Ollie and Conor headed out into the waves for the last swim of the day.

'The glam squad are arriving at 6.30.' Maggie had one eye closed to squint at her phone – a sure sign that she was well on her way to being blitzed.

'Uh-oh, she's doing the one eye open move!' Annie giggled.

'Shut up!' Maggie laughed. 'We've been pretty restrained today. Some fizz at breakfast. Two cocktails on the boat!'

'Well, we're not twenty anymore. You'd better actually make it to dinner.' Clara winked.

Maggie was not a talented drinker and Clara hadn't seen her finish a single meal since arriving.

'So,' Maggie carried on, drifting slightly off-course, 'we have time to shower and get the kids settled, then dinner's at 8 p.m. Let's all reconvene in my room in an hour? Cool?'

'Uh-huh.' Clara tried to refocus on Maggie's words but it felt like there was a sea of booze and growing worry pitching around inside her. Ollie's new code felt so ominous.

'An hour, that's cool,' Annie echoed, squinting over her shoulder at Conor disappearing into a wave.

'So, you and Conor are on a pretty tight schedule?' Clara asked delicately.

'Hmmm.' Annie gave a slight nod.

'Does *he* know this?' Clara waved a hand back to the guys, now nearly at a pontoon that was floating about fifty metres from the shoreline.

'He's *supposed* to.' Annie's smile was tight but then she shrugged and seemed to reset herself. 'He'll be up in a minute. He knows we've got two sessions in the calendar for tonight. This first one will be just under the wire but we'll manage it.'

'Fun,' Clara said sympathetically. You didn't get to forty-two without learning what a slog the road to children can be. Either you or someone you knew went through it. She and Ollie had gotten lucky but so many didn't.

'I'm gonna just give him a nudge.' Annie turned back to make her way down to the water's edge. 'See you guys in an hour.'

Up at the house, the kids, who had wilted on the walk back from the boat, were soon freshly showered and assembled in the dedicated screening room down in the basement in front of the new *Sonic* movie.

'It's not even in cinemas yet,' Josh told Clara breathlessly. 'Essie and Dodi's dad gets all the movies before they're out! And he's the voice of one of the squirrels.'

With the boys settled, Clara jumped into the shower herself and took her time conditioning her hair and cleansing her face. It was a luxury showering without her kids trying to get in with her but Clara's thoughts were swirling. *Why change the code? Why change the code?* Day-drinking and unsettling revelations did not mix.

Ollie was still not back from the beach when she got out and started getting dressed. She chose a short mint-green dress and Doc Marten sandals and hurried up the stairs to Maggie's room on the second floor. She wanted to get there before the stylists arrived. She had to tell the girls about the phone passcode. She needed the reaction of an outsider to decide how serious or not serious it was.

She pushed open the door, which led into an airy seating area. Maggie and Fionn's room was a suite, with a bedroom and bathroom off a living room. The sound of running water suggested Maggie was still showering, so Clara ambled over to the windows. Just like Clara's own room, the view was spectacular, only this room had a wrap-around wooden balcony – a sort of widow's walk. She stepped out onto it and looked down to the beach below. She could see Ollie and Conor ambling back and she felt irritation flare. Conor had clearly stood Annie up and Ollie hadn't even been up to the house to check if the kids were sorted. Obviously she hadn't had to do a thing with Ed on hand but Ollie didn't know that.

Clara realised that the shower had stopped and she slipped back inside, moving into the bedroom area.

'Maggie?' Clara called. She heard the toilet flush and some elaborate throat-clearing noises, then the doors swung open and Maggie, catching sight of Clara, leapt backwards.

'Fucking hell!'

'Sorry! Sorry!' Clara laughed. 'I thought you'd heard me call you!'

'No, sorry.' Maggie, recovered from her fright, strode across the room wrapped in her towel and began pulling a dress in a deep red from a garment bag that hung on a rail in the corner along with more than a dozen others. 'I'm just going to get dressed.' She slipped back into the bathroom.

'You really don't have to hide from me, the amount of times you've mooned me!'

'That was in college,' Maggie called through the door.

'That was last year in Saint-Tropez!' Clara reminded her.

Clara slid over to the clothes rail. There were laminated sheets affixed to the outside of each bag showing what looked to be pictures of the dresses inside, along with notes on what shoes and jewellery go with each one. Fascinating. Clara filed this away to tell Annie about. Just then, as though summoned by Clara's thoughts, Annie appeared in the living space behind her.

'Oh my God!' Annie said, taking in the chic wicker sofas with plump white cushions and enormous, almost sculptural wicker lighting feature overhead.

'Shhhhh.' Clara pulled her into the bedroom and indicated the rail. 'Check it out,' she whispered. 'Rich People Shit is getting crazier.'

Annie's eyes were wide. 'This one's Marni!' Annie tugged on a bag. 'She didn't have this dress buffet on the last holiday, did she?'

Clara shook her head. 'Maybe because it was skiing, she didn't care as much?'

'She is caring a lot now, I'm noticing.' Annie kept her voice low. 'Where is she?'

'In the bathroom, changing.'

'You don't think …' Annie paused. She seemed to be searching for the right words. 'You don't think she's doing anything … bad?'

'No!' Clara shook her head. 'She would never. She's just a little self-conscious. Those shits in the press. Plus there was another one of those pieces about her being Fionn's, like, super "ordinary" wife …'

Just then Maggie breezed out, looking beautiful. Her dress was to the knee with a scoop neck and the rust-red colour was a stunning contrast to her dark hair.

'So, Annie? Did you get the ride?' Maggie asked.

'I did not.' Annie shook her head, looking mutinous. 'I'm getting so sick of it. I do all the work of making the plans, figuring out the fertile windows, and then half the time I've to cajole him into it. Do you know how hard it is to bang someone when you've had to remind them, like, a hundred times to fuck you?'

Clara nodded sympathetically. 'I can imagine.'

Maggie put her arms around Annie. 'If it makes you feel any better, I don't think you're alone. I'm starting to suspect that fucking your husband starts to feel like a chore no matter where you're at.'

Maggie drew back from Annie and started fussing in a large velvet box on the dressing table that was full of neatly arranged jewellery. Annie, Clara noticed, didn't look remotely cheered up by that bleak statement.

'I don't remember the last time Ollie and I had sex,' Clara piped up. 'It's easily been a month. And no doubt it was brief. He's ...' She hesitated for a minute; she wanted their opinion but, also, saying it made it real.

'He's what?' Maggie was now layering on several delicate gold necklaces.

'He's ... I dunno. It feels like he's barely around. He's late from work and then he's tired and I'm tired.' Clara sat down on the edge of the bed. 'This is going to maybe sound silly but he's started taking showers at weird times, late at night and stuff.'

'Maybe he's just sweaty after work?' said Annie.

'No, I mean *really* late at night. He showers after work but then a couple of times I've woken up at, like, one in the morning and he's back in the shower again.' Clara messed with the hem of her dress. 'He's changed the passcode to his phone,' she announced flatly. 'That's strange, right?'

She spotted the girls exchanging looks.

'Maybe it's not?' Maggie leaned back against the table. 'Maybe he had to. Maybe he got locked out?'

'I never thought I'd have to worry about this with Ollie after everything with his dad. And, like, I've always thought that if Ollie tried to have an affair, I'd have to organise it for him.' Clara tried not to sound like she was about to cry. 'And then have to remind him to actually go to the secret hook-ups.'

Annie snorted. 'He is *not* having an affair. This is Ollie. Devoted-to-you-since-forever Ollie.'

'Yeah,' Maggie chimed in. 'If anyone's having an affair, apparently it's Fionn. If Deuxmoi says so.' She shrugged unhappily.

'*He's* not having an affair either,' Annie interjected. 'Of course he's not. Neither of them are!'

A brisk knock startled them all.

'Ladies!' A beautiful man with shiny American teeth peeked around the door. 'Ready to be transformed?'

Clara made her way back to her room. Her face felt about two pounds heavier with the make-up and she was pretty sure she looked borderline ridiculous. Still, it had been fun being pampered, and a glass of champagne had relaxed her somewhat. The code was a stupid thing to read into and neither Annie nor Maggie had been particularly fazed, which had helped to assuage her worries.

In the bedroom, Ollie was in the shower. Where else?

Clara rooted in her suitcase for her evening bag and dropped in the new Pat McGrath lipstick and powder her make-up artist had given her, along with the phone she'd grabbed up from the end of the bed. As she bent to retrieve her shoes, she saw another identical phone on the carpet half under the bed. She and Ollie had the same make so she pressed the home button on the one from her bag to check whose was whose. The picture of her and the boys flared into view. It was Ollie's. Across the lock screen was the preview of a text. Her stomach dropped.

I had such a good time, Ollie. The best yet.

CHAPTER 5

Conor arrived back in the room looking sweaty, just as Annie, fed up waiting, had finally gotten dressed.

'Where have you been?' She stood to face him.

'I was just squeezing in a workout before dinner, the gym is in the basement, it's amazing. There's a guy down there. Like, stationed at all times. Completely batshit. He's there alone 90 per cent of the time, wiping down the equipment. Anyway, he gave me some tips on my deadlift.'

'I'm sorry, but what the actual fuck, Conor. I've been waiting here. We were supposed to have sex.'

Conor ducked his head but Annie still caught the grimace his features had twisted to form. He moved towards the bathroom and reached in to swipe a towel off the rail. Now armed with the towel, he could completely avoid meeting her eyes as he made a big production of wiping sweat from his face and neck.

'Conor?' Annie stared at him and felt a kick of sadness. Sadness she'd been on the run from for so long now, certain that if she could just get pregnant then it'd all go back to normal. 'Conor,' she repeated, 'you don't even have the balls to just tell me, do you?'

He stilled and then straightened up. 'Tell you what?'

Annie rolled her eyes and went to the full-length mirror to check her reflection. She was wearing a black wrap skirt with tiny white flowers all over it and a black sleeveless top. She eyed up the chunky black boots, wondering if the evening would be cooler than the scalding day they'd had. She looked up to find Conor's eyes in the mirror.

'I don't feel like explaining it to you.' She was exhausted. It felt like not just the weight of the day but the weight of many months was bearing down on her.

'Annie.' He at least looked upset, as he came up behind her and put his arms around her.

'Conor, if you don't want this anymore …' She could barely bring herself to say the words.

'Don't say that.' His face was buried in her hair and Annie wished she could see his eyes.

'Don't say it because it's not true?'

'Don't say it because …' He took a deep breath. 'Because—'

A loud knock on the door interrupted whatever he'd been about to say, and Annie wanted to scream in frustration.

'The fleet of Mercedes-Benz Sprinters with blacked-out windows is here, guys.' Ollie's voice came through the door.

'Shit. I've gotta rinse off. I'll be ready in two.' Conor grabbed his towel and headed into the toilet. Annie had the strong impression that he was delighted to cut the conversation short.

Dinner was not going well.

Everything about the setup was perfect. They had the entire back patio of one of the most famous restaurants in Provincetown, The

Canteen, to themselves. The water lapped just metres from where they sat under strings of glowing bulbs. Diners inside had looked them over with curiosity as they'd passed through to the reserved area, before losing interest when it was clear none of them were famous. The food was insane. They'd shared an enormous seafood plate to start, and now Annie was nibbling at a quintessentially P-town take on the humble grilled cheese that boasted additions of fresh crab and gruyere.

The surroundings were so perfect that it was dialling up how *not* perfect the atmosphere around the table was. The food was delicious but barely touched by her two friends. Maggie was noticeably distracted and kept getting up under the guise of taking calls when there'd been no sign of her phone ringing. Clara meanwhile had only spoken when ordering from the waiter, which was not like her. Ollie and Conor were the only ones having anything remotely resembling a good time.

Across the table from her, Ollie was on an absolute roll, lamenting the lunacy of his sons.

'Each one came out crazier than the last.' He shook his head dolefully. 'I honestly have no idea where they got it; we're pretty chill.' He looked to Clara beside him but she just shrugged.

She's really taking the passcode change very seriously, Annie thought, with a vague flash of irritation. It was very *Clara* to have the least serious bloody problem and still make the biggest deal about it. Annie was also sick of the moaning-about-the-kids schtick that they were carrying on with. *Have a bit of self-awareness.*

'Ollie, man.' Conor was laughing. 'I love you both but you two are not chill, have never been chill. Ye were chaos from the moment I met you.'

'I'm sorry, but when you met us we were pilled off our faces. It's not fair to make assessments about someone when they are extravagantly high,' Ollie pointed out.

Conor grinned. 'As I recall, you were "pilled off your faces" at a chamber music recital on a Sunday afternoon. Context matters, Ollie!'

'I hope the boys never take pills,' Ollie mused. 'They'd be completely unstoppable then.' He winked at a very distracted Clara. Annie could see she seemed to have completely lost interest in the conversation and was now staring at Ollie's phone on the table just inches from her hand.

Ollie and Conor, either unaware of or ignoring the atmosphere among the women, swung into a new conversation about their jet-ski plans and Maggie stood suddenly for the third time since they'd been seated. 'I better take this.' She waved her phone, screen turned away and hurried down the side passage of the restaurant.

Annie tried to catch Clara's eye but she seemed to be lost in her own head, oblivious to how odd Maggie was acting. Maggie had been well for years now but Annie knew that recovery from these kinds of things could be extremely complicated. The media attention on Fionn had spread to her and, even without her history, being photographed in your private life had to be incredibly destabilising.

Annie wiped her mouth and stood. If Clara didn't care, she'd go find Maggie herself. 'I just need to send a message,' she also lied, and stood. She walked over to the passageway, the same one Maggie had disappeared down seconds before. It was deserted; just bins and empty crates lined the space on one side and a couple of weather-beaten wooden doors on the other. This place was rough and ready but still a local institution. One of the doors said 'Staff only' and one was a toilet. Annie tried the handle but it was locked. She stood still, listening for a minute, but could hear nothing. Maybe it wasn't in use; it looked pretty dilapidated. Maybe Maggie had gone out front. Annie carried on out to the street, where the evening revellers were spilling out of bars and eateries on all sides.

She glanced around for Maggie in her distinctive red dress but there was no sign of her, and Annie felt her mood sink lower. She unlocked her phone and checked WhatsApp.

Rachel had messaged a few hours before but Annie hadn't got around to replying.

How's it all going? Is it luxury out the arse? Rachel was asking.

Looking at the text, Annie smiled, in spite of the mounting drama of the day. Rachel *looked* like the sweet, rosy-cheeked innocent in a period drama but she was blunt as they came.

Annie started to type:

It's luxurious but definitely not as fun as usual. I feel like maybe we all have brought extra baggage on this holiday, there's a weird amount of emotional fuckery going on – know what I mean?

Annie hit 'send' and watched the grey double tick appear. Rachel wouldn't see the message for hours. It was around 3 a.m. at home. It didn't matter. Annie felt comforted just by sending it to her. Sometimes confiding in Rachel felt somehow easier than confiding in her oldest friends. Less history there. And Rachel wasn't all tied up in the tangled dynamics of the group. She hadn't actually seen

Rachel for more than a week as she'd been over hanging a show in London and Annie was dying for a catch-up when they got back, especially given how things had been with Conor with this month's trying effort.

Annie pocketed the phone and then headed back towards the back patio of the restaurant once more. As she neared the banjaxed old toilet door, Maggie emerged in front of her, running a hand through her hair. Annie was about to tap her on the back when an unmistakable smell hit her. Annie stopped. She looked ahead to check that Maggie hadn't noticed her, and it seemed she hadn't, as she disappeared around the corner into the patio area. Annie peered into the bathroom. Air freshener had been sprayed but it was mingling with the sour stench of vomit. Annie took in the dingy bathroom, the grotty sink and the damp floor. She couldn't imagine Maggie kneeling in here to be sick but she knew from experience that, unfortunately, it wasn't that far-fetched. With the smell of the loo and the image of Maggie bowed before it, a churn of nausea gripped Annie.

She quickly shut the door and made her way towards the others, taking in big gulps of fresh air. An undeniable sense of doom started to envelop her. *Please let me be wrong*, she made a silent plea.

She was going to have to get Fionn on his own. If he ever bloody showed up.

After dinner, they arrived back to the house to a scene of mild chaos. Reggie was hot to the touch and crying for Clara, who seemed to at last stir to life after barely speaking the whole night.

She took her son from the night nanny. 'Great.' She smiled ruefully. 'I love when parenting collides with the arrival of my day-drinking hangover,' she said, though Annie immediately heard her cooing 'You're alright, sweet boy' as she headed away down the stairs.

Annie debated going after her; she had been hoping to talk to her about the Maggie thing but the alarm on Annie's phone was vibrating insistently from her skirt pocket. Sex was on the to-do list before the night was out. Was it bad to pick sex over figuring out what to do about your friend possibly relapsing?

Yes, it was, but with Clara gone and Maggie already drifting towards the stairs it seemed the decision was made for her. It'd have to be tomorrow. Nothing bad could happen in ten hours.

'Night,' Maggie called. 'Sleep well, everyone.'

'Anyone up for a nightcap out on the deck?' Ollie looked from Conor to Annie.

'No, thanks,' Annie said firmly.

'Eh …' Conor paused, then shook his head and Annie resolved to ignore his slight hesitation. Starting something would derail the sex they were supposed to be having. If she'd ditched sex every time Conor pissed her off in the last year … well, it probably wouldn't have made a difference, she thought grimly. They'd still be in the same baby-less boat they were in now.

Upstairs in the bedroom, she and Conor didn't bother turning on the lamps. They undressed in the path of moonlight that stretched from the windows towards the foot of the bed.

For them, Annie realised sadly, sex wasn't really about the other person anymore. Where once Conor had kissed every curve of her, now it had become so far removed from pleasure that they barely looked at each other. Sex had also become extremely quick. They could get it done in under ten minutes. Though they'd never vocalised it, it was clear that neither of them were remotely interested in prolonging it.

Annie lay back on the bed and Conor positioned himself between her legs and began the routine that had replaced their old passion. He propped himself up with one arm and with his other hand gripped his dick and began to jerk it to help him get hard. Annie looked over to the side table where her cornucopia of prenatal vitamins were assembled forlornly. A tear slipped from the corner of her eye and into the fine hair at her temple. Usually she could give some kind of perfunctory performance. She felt under particular pressure to, seeing as how it felt more and more like she was the one putting them through this. With a concerted effort she pulled herself back from the edge of crying. *Crying is a boner killer*, she thought as she reached up and drew Conor's face down to her and kissed him, trying very hard to ignore how long it seemed to be taking him to get going tonight.

'You ready?' he whispered at last, and she nodded. She was about as turned on as if she'd been filling out a bank form, and it rubbed uncomfortably as he entered her and began the desultory thrusting that to date had gotten them exactly nowhere. He buried his face in the hair at her neck and she squeezed her eyes shut. This position was part of their dreary routine. That no one had to look at anyone was their unspoken agreement. She made some murmurs of pleasure and so did he. This was also part of their routine so that no one had to face the reality that this situation had gotten bad. Really, really bad.

A few minutes passed and Conor's movement became a bit more urgent.

'You go ahead and come,' Annie said quietly. 'I don't think I'll be able to. The wine …' She said this as if her not coming was some kind of anomaly and not, in fact, the same thing that happened – or didn't, as the case may be – virtually every time these past few months.

'Are you sure?' Conor asked as per their script, and Annie nodded.

He continued to press into her, but then Annie detected his rhythm falter slightly. She reached down and pulled him by the hips to draw him deeper inside her but found, to her dismay, some resistance on his part.

'What?' she said as he propped himself back up to look down at her. In the dark of the bedroom she couldn't quite see his eyes, but the grim line of his mouth didn't look promising.

'Annie …' He pulled away from her and knelt on the bed between her knees, cupping his genitals. Feeling impossibly exposed, she pulled herself up to sitting and drew her legs together. God, it was all so undignified.

'Why are you stopping?' She asked the question even though she suspected she knew the answer.

His eyes remained down as he fiddled with a fold in the bedsheet.

'Okay, I get it.' Annie leaned toward him. 'I know it's really shitty doing it like this. It's so much pressure. I hate it too, you know. Maybe it's time to start thinking about the IVF. We could find a way to make the money work.'

He looked up at her and seemed on the verge of saying something but then just nodded and climbed off the bed. He shut the door of the bathroom behind him and Annie heard the shower start; no doubt he wanted to wash away their latest failure.

She turned over and squeezed her eyes shut. A wasted window of fertility. The sense of defeat and disappointment landed like a stone in her chest and her eyes began to sting with tears.

CHAPTER 6

Finn is so excited to see everyone today! 👍👍👍

Every time Maggie read Brody's message she could feel the dial on her rage twisting upwards. He'd sent it at 6 a.m. and she'd read it first in bed amid the feverish sheets – she had not slept well. Her stomach had been acting up. Too much food and booze the night before. And all the wrong sort, she admonished herself. Cream and butter – everything fucking good in life. In LA not eating nice food was easier, as none of the nice food was within reach. The twins ate normal kids' stuff but, for Fionn and Maggie, their chef cooked according to whatever strict regimen Fionn was on for a role. It was pretty much always steamed something with a side of steamed something else. When he was prepping to shoot the first *Endurance* movie, they'd gone plant-based and sugar-free. His diet had even limited fruit. Maggie never thought she'd be craving an apple so much. But holidays were for binning the diet so no wonder her tummy had been in bits at dinner. She'd been so uncomfortably full that she'd actually been unwell in the restaurant toilets. Mortifying. Luckily Clara and Annie hadn't noticed; they would no doubt have read into it.

When she went to pee, Maggie read the message again.

Finn is so excited to see everyone today! 👍 👍 👍

She switched over to her thread with Fionn, noting that her last text had been several weeks ago. It was a picture of the girls on their roller-skates at the boardwalk. He'd simply hearted the picture.

I hear you're 'so excited to see everyone', she typed.

She flushed the loo and trudged back to the bed – it wasn't even 7 a.m. yet, though getting back to sleep seemed to be an unlikely prospect; her thoughts were too stirred up.

Later today Fionn would be landing. Tonight he'd be in this bed with her. Not so long ago, this thought would have comforted her. She used to miss him when he was gone. On the nights of their reunions, they couldn't get the girls to bed fast enough. The minute they were free they'd make their way to the bedroom, where she used to get on top of him and delight in his big hands gripping her waist.

In the last couple of years, however, Maggie had found a sudden yearning to take back the territory of her body, the territory that had been so occupied since her teens. Colonised by boys in school and then men in college, and then Fionn and, lastly, in new ways, by her daughters. At forty, Maggie'd unearthed an unexpected desire to retreat from them all. Especially Fionn. She turned the lights off when he sought her out in the night, she didn't want to be looked at while they fucked, and she didn't want to be held by him afterwards. His arms came down like shutters around her, stifling and claustrophobic. They hadn't slept together in months and she sensed she should probably care a bit more about this but she couldn't help it, she wanted her own room and her own body back.

She could not intuit whether this was rooted in the miserable but deeply held conviction that her body was ugly. Or did it all stem from something more existential? Was her body going into a sort of retirement, a middle-aged retreat, having served its purpose? She'd been looked at and fucked and had reproduced, and now what? She could be invisible? There would be a sort of relief in it after a lifetime of being a woman and being judged on her appearance.

Fuck sleep. She sighed and untangled herself from the knotted sheets. After the night before, her stomach felt cleaved and empty – but even despite not feeling amazing, the anger Brody's text had kicked off made her want to eat. If she made it down to breakfast early, before anyone else got there, she could maybe have something a little extra.

'Good morning, ma'am.'

The toothy waitress was new, Maggie noted.

'Morning.' Maggie smiled, squinting up at her.

'You're up early!'

'I am.' Maggie smiled again. 'Can you bring me some coffee and melon?'

'Sure.' The girl nodded, turning to leave. Maggie flipped over her phone to check the time: 6.50 a.m. Still good and early, no one would be up anytime soon.

'And, sorry ...?' Maggie blurted, then lowered her voice. 'A plate of pancakes for my girls, they'll be here any minute and they get *so* impatient.'

'Of course, Mrs Strong.'

While she waited, Maggie googled her husband. This activity was pure self-harm, as both Eva and Britney frequently lectured. But today was different. She needed to know what the internet was saying, if she was going to be frank with him about how these stories and his disconnect from their day-to-day life impacted her. Though was she actually going to confront him?

She paused in her googling to consider this, her thoughts drifting this way and that. If they started fighting on the holiday it would wreck the buzz and waste what little time they had with their friends. If she didn't say anything, nothing would change. Then again, what did she want to change? Did she even *want* Fionn home more at this point? And, Jesus Christ, what did *that* mean if she didn't? Mercifully, the coffee, melon and a stack of fluffy American-style pancakes arrived before she could become even more mired in the knotty questions of her marriage.

She checked the group chat to make sure Annie and Clara hadn't messaged in yet. No sign of life there. They had to be still asleep, surely; yesterday had been a heavy one, soaked in booze and sun. Maggie glanced up at the windows of the upper stories of the house above her. They were mirrors in the sun, giving no hint to whether there were stirrings in the rooms within.

Someone *could* be standing on the other side of the shining glass admiring the shimmering view.

The volume on the more insistent thought in her head was starting to amp up. *Fuck it, just get it done. Eat them fast before someone comes along.* She wanted the numbing calm that came with consuming with abandon.

She shifted her chair so that her back was to the house, and hunched slightly over to try and shield the pancakes from the view of any staff possibly drifting around inside.

At least it'll keep me from googling Fionn.

She propped her head up on her left hand, allowing a sheet of hair to fall and provide a fraction more cover. With her right hand, she rolled the top pancake into a scroll-like shape and ate it in two bites. In another minute, she'd dispatched two more in the exact same efficient manner. Her hands were tacky with syrup. She didn't even like syrup. Or this kind of thick pancake. She liked lemon and sugar on her pancakes – the thin kind that they'd had at home when she was a kid. Still, the satisfying weight of carbs and sugar hitting her stomach was good. She rolled up the remaining two pancakes and sucked them down as well. She quickly ran a finger around the edge of the plate where the last of the syrup glistened and discreetly brought her fingertips to her mouth. This speedy hit of food pacified her and she could practically *feel* her body slacken. Thoughts of Fionn felt more distant, if only momentarily. She snuck a glance back at the house; it looked the exact same as it had just minutes before. She considered the empty pancake plate. She could slip it underneath the plate of melon in front of her and just say nothing or she could—

'Maggie! Morning!'

Maggie started at her name coming from below on the beach. It was Ollie, just a few feet from the bottom of the steps up to the deck.

Shite. She'd been so preoccupied with being seen from the house that she hadn't even checked the beach side.

'Hey,' she called back, and then used the time it took him to jog up the stairs to wipe her face. Her right hand was a sticky mess but there was no water on the table to clean it off. She could see the top of Ollie's wavy hair and made the split-second decision to plunge her hand into her coffee – her still quite fucking hot coffee! She grabbed a napkin to dry her hand as Ollie bounded up to the other side of the table.

'You're up early.' He squinted down at her.

'You too!' Maggie speared a chunk of watermelon. 'Where've you been?'

'Just a little jog.' He squinted back towards the beach. 'It is unbelievably gorgeous out there. Beats the treadmill, those things are mind-numbingly boring.'

'Yeah.' Maggie nodded, a little amused. 'I can't say I'd ever pictured you on a treadmill. Or up before seven to jog! Except maybe to get to the next session on a roll-over.'

'Ha.' Ollie grinned. 'Look, we all have to have our midlife crisis. It could be so much worse. Half the lads at home are becoming extremely tedious about coffee – it's the new artisanal IPAs. At least I'm not boring anyone about my running. Or trying not to.' He started a few sweaty lunges by the railing. 'Are you planning a little midlife crisis yourself at all? I feel like it'd suit you.'

'Just the usual *I look older than Nosferatu, my ass is heading due south and my husband scores twenty-somethings for a living.*'

'Ah yes, the "usual".' Ollie chewed his lower lip, looking concerned. 'It's a fucking tough gig, Mags. I can't imagine. I know it's just acting and all but if Clara kissed someone else …' He shook his head. 'It'd wreck me.'

'Yeah …' Maggie sighed. 'I guess I'm just used to it with Fionn. He's always been an actor. So I've had to get used to the intimacy required. But the speculation online. That's been hitting another level of hard.'

Maggie'd forgotten how easy it was talking to Ollie. Rather than rush in with desperate reassurances, he gave a lot of space for people to share.

'You know he adores you, right? You don't feel like there's something actually going on?' He pulled his hands through his hair, looking worried.

'No.' Maggie stabbed at another chunk of melon just to have something to do. 'But … it's still hard.'

'I know.' Ollie pressed his lips together. 'You should know, though … you don't look as old as Nosferatu. You look like his cute little sister.'

Maggie laughed, but he fixed her with a serious look and she was reminded that, being one of Fionn's closest friends, he'd had a ringside seat to some of the worst fallout from her eating disorder. He'd even come to the hospital, which she'd never allowed Annie or Clara to do. She would've barred Ollie too only he'd just showed up. But sometimes you needed those people – the people who didn't ask and just showed up – during the hard times in life.

He leaned down to her. 'Are you doing okay?'

'Yeah, of course!'

'Maggie …' he said gently.

'I am! Genuinely.'

'Because the last time …'

'Ollie. Stop. I am fine.' She smiled. 'You're being way overprotective! This is Fionn's gig and I am cool with it 99.99999 per cent of the time; I was just joking around.'

He held her gaze for a moment more, then straightened up. 'Okay, okay! I'm gonna have a quick shower. See how Clara's getting on with Reggie. She never even came back to our room last night.'

Ollie was only gone a few seconds when Clara appeared, followed by Annie.

'Just saw Ollie, he looked fresh off some vigorous masturbating.' Clara collapsed into a chair.

'He's been for a jog!' Maggie laughed, despite the fact that her previous calm was now being replaced by an uncomfortable fullness, and with it the inevitable recriminations. *Why did I do that? Why am I so gross and weak?* She remembered her old doctor in college trying to gently coach her through feeling full after she'd gotten back on the path to recovery and was learning to eat normally again. Whatever *that* was. Did any woman of their generation really eat normally? she often wondered. Even if you weren't explicitly on a diet, was there a woman alive who didn't overthink every little thing she put in her mouth?

'Feeling full is just a physical sensation,' her doctor had advised. 'Lots of people eat to the point of feeling full and it is not a character weakness, Maggie.' But to Maggie this bursting, impacted state felt like powerful evidence of her own greed. It seemed like irrefutable proof that she was what her illness told her she was: a fundamentally disgusting person. The purge was the remedy to this, and with the lightness and emptiness of the purge came a sense of control and safety and power. If only that feeling could stay, but invariably the hunger returned and the cycle repeated. And repeated. Until it felt out of her hands. That was, she'd reluctantly come to accept, the problem with the system. All the initial sense of control soon morphed into something much darker and more relentless. At the height of it, she could lose hours to eating and purging, eating and purging until her throat felt shredded and her stomach could handle no more.

Annie leaned over to pour a cup of coffee. 'If Ollie's up with the larks and out masturbating in public at forty-two, then I can only commend him,' she said with a tight smile She paused mid-pour and looked up at the house, before continuing in a quiet voice, 'Conor didn't even finish last night.'

'Oh.' Clara looked disconcerted at this uncharacteristic frankness from Annie. 'God, I'm sorry, Annie. What's going on? Is it a … medical thing?'

'No, I think it's a, I dunno, pressure thing. There's just so much riding on every … ride, you know?' Annie pressed her lips into a grim smile, shaking her head.

Clara stood and went over to Annie to put her arms around her, while Maggie debated how to phrase her next words. 'You guys have been on this road a while,' she started. 'It's understandable the stress is affecting you both. Do you think it's time to try another way?'

Annie was still focused on the coffee, but over the top of Annie's head Maggie could see Clara's eyes flick towards her. But she couldn't quite read her expression. Was there a warning there? Or something like irritation? Maggie shifted nervously, readjusting her waistband, trying to relieve some of her discomfort from the food.

'Stuff like that is expensive in Ireland, Maggie.' Clara sounded vaguely accusatory and a sudden rash of anxiety spread through Maggie's chest.

'I know, I'm sorry.' Maggie immediately regretted saying this in front of Clara. Clara, Maggie suspected, was the most resentful of Fionn and Maggie's money.

Maggie reached for Annie's hand and gave it what she hoped was a supportive squeeze. She wanted to add, *Please let us pay*. But the way the atmosphere had suddenly become leaden convinced her this was not the way to go.

The buzz of her phone abruptly seized all their attention. The screen filled with Fionn's chiselled face, signalling an incoming video call.

'What the fuck,' Maggie yelped. 'He didn't say he was going to video call me.'

'Ugh.' Clara returned to her seat. 'A *phonecall* without prior text is a violence, never *mind* a *video* call. At least it's just Fionn.'

Her snippiness had seemingly dissipated. Thank God, it was only day two. Maggie couldn't hack an extended Clara mood.

'I can't answer this.' Maggie held the phone away from her. 'I look like shit.'

'What?' Annie looked incredulous. 'For starters, you don't. And secondly, he is your literal husband. Who cares what you look like? It's just Fionn.'

Maggie ran a hand through her hair; unfortunately, it was the one that was still vaguely sticky from the maple syrup. She stood and scooted away from them over to the far corner of the deck and hit 'accept' on the call.

Her husband, tanned in a pair of yellow-tinted aviator Ray-Bans, appeared on the screen.

'Heya, gorgeous.' Fionn grinned broadly and Maggie, per usual, felt the little jolt of uncanny valley she often got when seeing him for the first time in a while. Back when he was an unknown, Fionn had always been the most handsome man in any room in Ireland, and the same in London when they'd lived there. But once they'd arrived in LA, where every room was filled to bursting with the hottest people in the universe, the tweaks had begun. His agents had a laundry list of things he 'needed' to improve on if he was realistically going to become a fully fledged star. Jaw implants and bits of filler, plus the requisite bulking up. Fionn had been broad but lean in his youth. This was fine for supporting actors, he'd been told, but for leading men not so much. Fionn had eschewed most of the more invasive procedures but had acquired the requisite muscles and relented on the matter of the Hollywood Teeth, and Maggie often found herself missing his old endearingly jumbled set.

'Hey.' She smiled back, turning slightly to find a more forgiving light.

'So. Couldn't help but notice some sarcastic inverted commas in your last text?' He smiled but looked completely sincere. 'I'm sorry Brody was messaging. I was caught up, tryna tie up the last few bits before this break and it was just a random moment when it was easier to just ask him to text. I am really sorry. I know it's not exactly the stuff long-awaited reunions are made of. I cannot *wait* to see you.'

Maggie thawed a little. 'I can't wait to see you too.' She tried to smile, though an unexpected sadness was rising in her. This clearly must have shown on her face, as Fionn's expression swiftly shifted to concern.

'Are you okay?'

'Yeah.' Maggie pressed the back of her hand to her forehead, trying to keep herself in check. 'Sorry, I think, it's just … it can be so hard having, like, zero contact and then to see you, even if it's just on a call. And I'm hungover. Plus there's all that stuff online.'

He looked upset. 'Ahh, Maggie—'

'I know I shouldn't be looking.' She spoke over him, afraid that if she heard him deny it, it wouldn't sound convincing enough. 'And I'm not! Not really …' She didn't want to ruin their reunion before it'd even happened.

'I'm not making excuses here but Brody hadn't told me …' He pulled off his shades. 'I hate that you were all on your own thinking about that bullshit—'

'I wasn't all on my own,' she interjected. 'I have the gang here. And I've barely thought about it that much, don't worry.' Patently untrue, but she did *not* want to be some figure of pity in her husband's eyes. 'We've been having a really good time here.'

Have we? She glanced back to Clara and Annie, both bent towards each other over the table examining something on Clara's phone.

'That's great,' he said firmly. 'Ollie and Conor have been sending pics to the lads' chat round the clock – it looks awesome. So, right, we're scheduled to land around 6 p.m. aaaaand,' a big (impossibly shiny, white) smile spread across his face, 'I've got something really cool planned for everyone. It's not in Brody's itinerary as I wanted it to be a surprise but it's going to be really special, a once-in-a-lifetime thing.'

'Okay, that sounds deadly.' Maggie was feeling better. She remembered that sometimes the anticipation of these reunions was the worst thing. The lead-in time could make her anxiety spiral, and then the second they were together again, it'd level off when she remembered that, for all the things that had changed so irrevocably, they were still just Maggie and Fionn.

'Are the girls up yet?' Fionn asked hopefully.

Maggie shook her head. 'Sorry, all the kids are still in bed. They're on holiday mode so off their tits on sugar and up torturing the nannies half the night.'

'No probs, can't wait to give them big squishes. See you really soon.' He blew her a kiss and they ended the call.

'Are you done, Maggie?' Annie called with a strange urgency.

Maggie made her way back towards them. Their eggs and bacon and mimosas had arrived in her absence. 'What is it?'

'It's irrefutable goddamn proof.' Clara seethed.

'Of?'

'Proof of Ollie fucking around,' Clara hissed.

'It may not be proof, Clara.' Annie sounded calm but she did look a bit rattled. 'Clara saw a weird text on Ollie's phone before dinner last night.'

Clara leaned across the table and lowered her voice. 'It said, and these are the exact words, "I had such a good time, Ollie. The best yet."'

'Oh God, Clara.' Maggie bit her lip. This explained Clara's strange quiet of the night before. Maggie scrambled for the right thing to say and came up short. 'It really mightn't mean that. What did he say when you asked him about it?'

'I haven't had a chance to talk to him. There was dinner – I was so blindsided I just said nothing – and then when I got back I was with Reggie all night. He's fine, by the way, just a bit of a temperature. To be honest, I was glad to have the excuse to stay away ... I'm still trying to compute this. This is Ollie, like! You know what he's like after his love-rat dad and all that. Mr You-so-much-as-kiss-someone-else-it's-over.'

'This genuinely could mean something else. What was the name of the contact?'

'Stevie. Like Stevie Nicks your husband.'

'It could just as easily be a lad?'

Clara ignored her. 'Maggie, look at our debit card transactions.' She shoved the phone over to Maggie. 'There is some really strange-sounding shit on here.'

Maggie took the phone and tried not to look visibly shocked at the total on the account that was displayed up top. *Maybe they have a savings account separate to this one?*

She scrolled down but couldn't see much of anything. 'What am I looking for here?'

'He spent 140 euro on a website called HardBodies.com. I looked it up. It's like a sex shop with toys and outfits and everything.'

'Maybe he's got you a present?'

'It was back in March. As you know, my birthday's in April and I got an off-brand Dyson hoover-wannabe.' Clara took the phone back to scroll further. 'He doesn't even like lingerie and dress-up stuff,' she muttered, irritated. 'Anytime I ever got a nice bra or knickers he'd just get them straight off like they were a nuisance. Now here he is spending money we *so* don't have, being spicy at last and it's not even with me.'

'Ollie is one of the good ones. I can't believe he'd be sneaking around.' Maggie felt certain there had to be an explanation for it all. 'You have to have it out with him. What are you going to do?'

'I honestly don't know.' Clara picked up her glass. 'Fume? Confront him? Cry? Day-drink? All of the above?'

Clara was not a crier. Maggie hadn't seen her shed a tear in two decades of friendship. She was more of a railer. She railed against injustices small and large with the exact same level of venom.

Maggie looked helplessly over at Annie, who gave an impotent little shrug.

Clara spied the exchange. 'I'm sorry, gals, I realise discovering an affair while on a group holiday with friends isn't exactly ideal for everyone else.'

'Okay, but you haven't actually discovered anything definite,' Maggie reminded her. 'Ollie's a softie, Clara. He was literally just saying to me earlier how he doesn't know how I can cope with Fionn kissing actresses at work, that he'd lose his mind if it was you.'

Clara swigged at her cocktail, ignoring this. 'I think more than anything, I'm just furious that he's had the time for this when I haven't had the time to so much as go to the toilet on my own in what feels like ten years.'

'Babe,' Annie reached across and rubbed Clara's upper arm, 'you need to talk to him.'

'I know, I know.' Clara's look of rage was rapidly giving way to one of pain. 'This is going to sound bonkers but I also just reeeeally don't want to ruin the holiday. I was looking forward to this.' She looked to Maggie. 'I don't suppose Brody could fly in Esther Perel at a day's notice?' She barked a rueful laugh.

'Ugh, no thanks.' Maggie crossed her legs, trying to ignore the wodge of knee fat that she'd lately become fixated on after hearing Eva had had hers lipo'd out. Maggie checked the time – it was coming up to 8 a.m.; soon Ollie, Conor and all the kids would be upon them. 'Maybe we need to declare a girls' day?' she suggested. 'Give us all a bit of breathing space to think. We can figure out a plan with Ollie, and we can give you,' she nodded gently at Annie, 'and Conor a break from the whole baby stress. Fionn says he has some surprise planned for tonight. Let's get through today and then figure it all out. This really could be nothing, Clara. Ollie is not a guy who would do this.'

'They never are,' Clara replied darkly. 'Look at Fionn.'

'Clara!' Annie cried.

'What do you mean "look at Fionn"?' Maggie's jaw clenched. 'Only yesterday you both were full of "oh it's just losers on the internet talking shit". So which fucking is it? I talked to him there and he was the same as ever.'

'They *are* just bullshit rumours based on nothing—' Annie's insistent words came out in a rush.

'I'm sorry, I didn't mean it that way about Fionn.' Clara met Maggie's eyes looking matter-of-fact. 'I'm not tryna be a bitch here, like, I love the guy, he's one of my oldest pals, but the reality is Fionn is being a bit of a shit, all this disappearing out of your and the girls' lives for weeks and months on end.'

'It's my life, Clara. Not yours to have an opinion about. Fionn is not a shit.' Maggie was edging ever closer to saying something unsayable. *He's paying for the food you're eating. He's paying for the booze that you are clearly hitting way too hard.* She pulled herself back; Clara didn't mean it, she was upset about Ollie.

'Guys, stop.' Annie spoke quietly. 'It's obvious we're all a bit stressed. Can we agree that we're all coming from a place of love here? No one wants to hurt anyone. We've all got a lot going on. I think Maggie's idea is the best. I don't wanna spend the day with Conor, trying to act like I feel super amazing after last night. Clara needs to take a breath and figure some stuff out. Maggie, you've been anxious since we got here.'

Despite this being accurate, Maggie wanted to argue. 'I haven't. I'm good.'

'Okay, you're great. Whatever.' Annie shrugged. 'Let's just get out of here. It's the fourth of July, let's get some independence from these fucking men. At least until later.'

'What'll we do?' Maggie asked.

'What all straight women do when they're worn down from the hetero bullshit,' Annie replied.

'Find some gays?' Clara suggested. 'We're in the right place for it.'

Maggie smiled, grateful that the sudden spike in tension was dissipating. She was feeling discombobulated enough with Fionn's imminent arrival and all the whispers online, never mind the food she'd been wolfing down; she didn't want to waste the precious time they had together snipping and fighting.

CHAPTER 7

'When I said we should hang out with some gays, I didn't mean in an edifying, educational way.' Clara was griping as Annie, following the blue dot on her phone, led them down P-town's main drag, Commercial Street, to the town hall where they were to meet their tour guide, Geraldo.

'Will you relax,' Annie muttered, steering them around the hordes of tourists. 'The TripAdvisor reviews promised camp anecdotes about Provincetown's history and a walking tour of all the hottest bars and clubs.'

They'd managed to dodge Conor, Ollie and the kids for the whole morning, spending three hours being pampered by the onsite holistic therapy team. The facials, massages and pedicures had been somewhat relaxing, though Clara had asked every single one of the therapists what *they* thought 'I had such a good time, Ollie. The best yet' could mean.

Annie consulted the maps app. 'I think we're here.' They'd come to the red-brick square in the centre of town, presided over by the town hall. The girls scanned the crowd.

'How will we recognise him?' Maggie asked, just as a striking man in his late forties, dressed in breeches, knee-high socks and an elaborate shirt appeared on the other side of the concourse ringing a large brass bell.

'Eh, without much difficulty!' Annie giggled, heading towards him. 'Geraldo?' she called.

'Annie Sweeney? Party of three?' He grinned and gave a neat little bow by way of greeting. 'You all look ravishing.'

'Back atcha,' Clara said. 'But are you not fecking roasting?'

'Irish! Three cailíns!' He pronounced 'cailíns' like 'cawlins'. 'I love it! Saoirse Ronan was just here on vacation a few weeks ago.'

'No way!' Clara replied.

'Okay, ladies, let's stand over here in the shade and I can give you a rundown of P-town.'

They headed over to a bench underneath a beautiful elm tree and Geraldo stood before them. 'Right, firstly I'm going to give you a little potted history about the pilgrims and how the town got its very grand motto of the "Birthplace of American Liberty". Then,' an impish twinkle appeared in his eyes, 'I'm going to give you all the best gossip. How P-town became a mecca for artists and writers and celebrities from the 1920s right up to today. Aaaaand lastly, we'll conclude our tour with a little P-town tradition: the tea dance.'

'The tea dance? Sounds sedate.' Clara was shooting Annie a vaguely accusatory look. In her current agitated state, Clara was obviously gunning for something a bit wilder.

Annie just glared back. *She can organise the fucking day if she's going to be bolshy about it.*

Then Annie felt bad. It was a fairly huge deal to find out that your husband was maybe cheating on you. Annie turned to Geraldo. 'A tea dance sounds a bit more formal than we were thinking?'

'Ha, just wait.' He laughed. 'The tea dance is legendary. It's three hours of dancing and *mayhem*. Strictly adults only.'

'Ohhhh, okay.' Clara was perking up. 'I can tolerate the history bit so.'

It was nearly 2.30 p.m. when Geraldo announced, 'Some lunch is in order before tea dance time!'

He led them to a restaurant called Bayside Betsy's just a few doors down from The Canteen where they'd eaten the night before.

'We cannot have anyone going in to the tea dance on an empty stomach; it would be certain death by debauchery.'

'Can we sit inside, please?' Annie was wilting in the relentless heat of the afternoon.

'Annie identifies as an ageing goth,' Maggie informed Geraldo.

Inside, Annie ordered shrimp linguine and sparkling water, though she was starting to wonder if it was time to quit being so careful; it didn't seem like this was going to be any different to all the other months she hadn't gotten pregnant. Especially if Conor had yet to even ejaculate inside her.

As Geraldo filled the others in on the annual P-town Bear Week celebrations coming up soon, Annie examined the gallery of black-and-white photographs arranged on the wall across from their table.

The largest of them showed what looked to be a house of sorts out on its own, barely standing on spindly supports above sandy scrubland. There wasn't a straight line in the little hut and the overall impression was that, rather than any formal construction having taken place, instead weathered old slats of wood had somehow drifted together on the wind to create this rudimentary dwelling.

'What's that?' Annie interrupted, pointing at the photograph.

'Ahhh well, you're way ahead of me on the history tour! I was just about to get on to the dune shacks. Have you ever heard of them?'

They all shook their heads.

'Wait, is that,' Maggie squinted at another picture on the wall, 'Eugene O'Neill?'

'Absolutely! America's best playwright, if you're into being deeply depressed after a show. Good eye, Maggie.' Geraldo looked impressed.

'Maggie's a theatre person!' Clara piped up.

'Oh, I'm not,' Maggie protested, looking awkward. 'I did a few nothing bits back in the day. That's all done, it was—'

'Maggie!' Annie hated hearing her friend demoting her work to a footnote. It also made her realise with deep sadness that she hadn't heard Maggie talk about theatre in years. She turned to Geraldo. 'Maggie was called "a powerful and beguiling new voice" by *The Guardian*.'

'Yeah in 2013 when I was thirty!' Maggie scoffed. 'Anyway, tell us about the dune shacks. I feel like I'm remembering something now … about a commune or something?'

'So,' Geraldo settled himself back in his chair, 'the dune shacks are about two miles out of town, nestled in, you've guessed it, the dunes. There're nineteen or so of them left at this stage though there were more when they were built by the Coast Guard to house rescue teams back in the late 1800s. It's a wild place over there, there's no electricity or running water. Some of the shacks have literally fallen into the sea since then, others have been bulldozed – a crime.' He shook his head. 'It should be a historic site. Jack Kerouac wrote part of *On the Road* there. Norman Mailer and Jackson Pollock and E.E. Cummings holed up there to do their work. To think they've boarded up some of them. The one positive is that artists can enter a lottery to spend weeks out there on kind-of residency things.'

'Wow, that's amazing. Though also nightmarish.' Clara laughed. 'I'd probably die without my phone. Too much time with my thoughts.' She speared an asparagus. 'So the dead celebrities loved it here. But who are the current celeb residents? We heard the Coen brothers had places …'

'They do!' Geraldo nodded. 'They're soooo nice, I've been over to Joel's place for cookouts. Who else comes here? Let's see …' He casually reeled off a veritable galaxy of stars. 'You know what, though … it's not the P-town vibe to totally lose it over these A-listers, yanno? We don't fawn.'

'Hmmm.' Maggie was doing a committed impression of being engrossed in her crab salad but Annie sensed she wasn't comfortable in this territory.

'Like,' Geraldo lowered his voice conspiratorially, 'the more interesting ones are very low-key. Edwin Ensel – you know that director who's supposed to be very eccentric – he's apparently out in one of the dune shacks right now, working on some new film. Though without electricity, God knows how. He's probably writing the thing with a quill! In his own blood! I hear he has some very odd little peccadilloes. A voyeur.' Geraldo arched a brow. 'Apparently when he's auditioning actors he likes to observe them without their knowing. Then,' Geraldo grinned, 'you have the celebs who think they're big shots. It's very funny, they get annoyed when no one cares about them! Like I've heard that Finn Strong is coming this way *today* no less! My money's on him doing a bit of this. These ones are like the nouveau riche only they're the nouveau famous. He'll come in all dick swinging then be furious when no one wants an autograph.'

Maggie'd completely frozen. Clara was holding her breath and Annie pressed her lips together to suppress a laugh. Then Maggie snorted and set them all off.

'*What?*' Geraldo was looking from one to the other as they howled.

'Nothing, nothing.' Maggie wiped her eyes. Then immediately started laughing again.

'It's just the mental image: swinging dicks,' Clara said helpfully, to redirect the conversation.

'Well,' Geraldo raised his glass, 'our next stop is nothing *but* swinging dicks! Eat up, girls, the tea dance starts in thirty minutes.'

There were about seven women and about seven hundred impossibly gorgeous, impossibly fit men at the Boat Slip, which was the club and hotel that hosted the enormous outdoor tea dance. There was a pool and bars and Geraldo had even booked them a private cabana from which to savour all the action. He left them there, disappearing off to find his friends. Music blared and muscles gleamed under the afternoon rays. Annie had finally succumbed to some booze and was feeling at a pleasant remove from her real life. Well, a tiny remove at least.

'I have to send this to the family chat!' Maggie was filming the melee. 'They will die over this.'

'The sheer beauty of this crowd.' Clara was in her chair, in a neon orange bikini, legs crossed, scanning the heaving ocean of masculinity. 'It's so hard to look at them knowing that they're all fundamentally repelled by me and my vagina.'

'They may not *all* be. Some could be pan or bi.' Maggie was hunched over her phone captioning her video. Annie could see the strap of Maggie's bikini tied in a knot at the back of her neck. When Annie and Clara stripped down to their togs, Maggie had said she'd forgotten to wear hers.

Annie felt the familiar pull of anxiety. Maggie being so preoccupied with how she looked was old territory. Bad territory. And there'd been the unmistakable smell from the restaurant toilet the night before. Though as the hours had passed since, Annie'd started to question her suspicion. It was a public toilet, after all. Maybe it wasn't fair to assume it was Maggie's doing. Maggie had been in recovery for nearly twenty years; if she seemed on edge, it was far more likely to be because she hadn't seen Fionn since reading the stupid blind item.

'I should shift one of these beautiful men.' Clara had now pulled her sunglasses down to better assess the offerings at the tea dance. 'The perfect fuck-you to Ollie "I had such a good time. The best yet" Delaney.'

'Will they get a say?' Maggie put the phone aside and sat back on her lounger, drawing her knees up. Without the strap of the halter bikini in sight, it was easier for Annie to gloss over her friend's lie. Anyway, Maggie was a grown woman – if she didn't want to be half naked in the afternoon with a pack of strangers, that was her prerogative.

'I just want something to throw back in Ollie's face when I *do* confront him, and this is what's available currently.' Clara stood, presumably to get a better view.

'Would having an adult discussion not be the better option?' Annie couldn't think of anything worse than flirting with a gay man. Their standards were so high for beauty it was intimidating, but Clara did not lack confidence.

'I would be throwing it in his face in the *course* of an adult conversation.'

'Ah yes, the Revenge Shift, a cornerstone of every adult conversation,' Maggie said wryly, her eyes closed.

'You wouldn't get it. I feel so humiliated ...' Clara trailed off, apparently belatedly realising what she'd just said and to whom. 'Gah, fuck, I'm sorry, Maggie.' She threw Annie a pleading 'help me' look.

Annie swooped in. 'Clara means that ... like ... em ...' She trailed off as Maggie sat up and eyed them both, looking half-amused, half-exasperated.

'It's okay,' she said. 'Your husband's very possibly having an affair. Everyone *thinks* mine is. We're probably even in the humiliation stakes. You *should* go catch a gay.'

'You're dead fucking right.' Clara threw her shoulders back and stormed in the direction of the bar. 'I'll get drinks on my way back,' she shouted over her shoulder.

'You shouldn't have encouraged that!' Annie swung her legs off the lounger and faced Maggie.

'Oh my God, I was joking!' Maggie turned towards her. 'She's not gonna kiss someone!'

Annie frowned. 'I wouldn't be so sure,' she said darkly. 'We *know* how kamikaze she can be. And they've got kids!'

'Well, Ollie's clearly not thinking about that if he's texting someone. Fionn's not giving it a thought when he's doing his "radio silence on set" schtick. Men just ... like ... spit kids out their dicks and then get to carry on with their lives.' Maggie stopped abruptly. 'Shit, sorry, that came out badly. I'm so sorry, Annie. I'm so sorry you are going through all this.'

'We're all in the shit on this holiday all of a sudden, aren't we?' Annie sighed. 'Though I think Clara's probably winning. Or losing?'

Just then a chant started up in the direction Clara had gone in.

'Straights! Straights! Straights! Straights! Straights!'

Maggie got to her feet to check it out just as a small crowd of giddy men passed, flocking to the source of the commotion.

Annie stood and intercepted one of them. 'What's going on?'

He paused, beaming. 'Well, word's gone round that there's a guy and a girl kissing and grinding on each other up by the bar. Straights! At the tea dance! It's got to be a first! A blue moon event!' he finished breathlessly, then hurried on, pulling his phone out from the band of his gold lamé Speedos.

'Well, that Revenge Shift took all of five seconds,' Annie said as she and Maggie made their way after the guy, his little gold-clad ass cheeks providing a guiding beacon through the crowd.

At the centre, where the chanting was at a fever pitch, Clara was indeed kissing a young guy in miniscule shorts and a green plastic visor, though the grinding had been something of an exaggeration. A few people had phones out and were photographing the 'historic' event. Clara and the boy pulled apart, laughing, and even posed for a few of the pictures.

'She took my virginity,' the guy yelled, while Clara ruffled his hair and sauntered off to the bar.

'She is Mother.' Geraldo had reappeared beside them and was gazing adoringly at Clara's back. 'That was straight excellence. Not even Gaga could get a guy in here to kiss her when *she* came!'

'How did Clara manage it?' Maggie wondered.

Annie just shook her head. 'I don't know but it's going to be *impossible* to get her out of here now that she's queen of the place.'

Forty minutes later, as predicted, trying to extract Clara from the club was proving incredibly difficult.

'Clara, it's nearly 6 p.m. The car has come for us,' Annie pleaded, while Maggie gathered their things from the cabana. 'Fionn's arrived and we're supposed to be doing his surprise thing.'

'Okay, okay.' Clara finished taking a selfie with three young guys in feather boas. 'But am I or am I not a legend? People are asking for my autograph! I just signed a literal penis.'

'You're a legend,' Maggie said obediently.

In the car on the way back to the house, Annie discreetly updated Rachel on the latest drama as, beside her, Clara's giddiness was palpably draining. It figured. As the house came closer, so too did the ever-evolving shitshow that this holiday was morphing into. Conor hadn't texted all day. Ollie meanwhile had been obliviously dropping snaps into the group chat of them and the kids snorkelling and eating ice creams the size of their heads.

Across from Annie, Maggie was the only one in any way perky, no doubt eager to finally get some time with her husband.

'Okay.' Maggie was leaning over to Clara. 'Come on, spill. What did you tell that poor boy to make him score you?'

'Honestly, I just told him about the text and my sad-as-fuck life,' Clara said plainly, 'and he agreed to kiss me.'

Annie and Maggie said nothing.

'God. A gay man kissed me, that's how sorry for me he felt. That's really saying something about the whole situation, isn't it?'

'Well, the gays are the best among us,' Annie consoled her. A buzz on her lap drew her eye to the phone and she unlocked it. Rachel's reply made her smile despite the mood:

I hope Clara appreciates what a good friend you are. I'm not sure hanging out at a gay bar is making the most of the fertility window. Though I'm happy Clara got her Revenge Shift ... I think?!

Annie grinned, then, while she had her phone in hand, tossed off a quick message to Conor:

Quick conjugal before dinner? No presh but also ... presh! Tick tock.

When they pulled up outside the house Fionn was waiting for them, holding a daughter in each arm.

Seeing Fionn in person these days was destabilising, like looking at a familiar stranger. It felt a bit like seeing double. The friend she'd basically grown up with was overlaid with the 'airbrushed into oblivion' person who stared out from posters on the sides of buses and cruised languidly down red carpets among the other celebrities in videos online.

As soon as the driver turned off the engine, Maggie hopped out and hurried over to him. He gently lowered his girls and swept Maggie into a big hug. Annie and Clara hung back as their friends stayed in the embrace for a few minutes, and Annie felt reassured. She had resolved to get Fionn on his own to share her concerns about Maggie, but seeing them so close, could there really be anything going on that he wouldn't know about?

Of course, the thought of Maggie, alone, wandering the house in LA during Fionn's on-set radio silences was unnerving Annie. A lot of hours to fill. A lot of dumb internet posts to read about herself. What a weird world it was they lived in.

Talking about anyone's appearance was fucked up, but talking about the appearance of someone in recovery was downright dangerous. Of course, the people online couldn't know that Maggie had survived a killer disease. During Maggie's stint in hospital back in '06, Annie, Clara, Conor, Ollie and, of course, Fionn had tried to find out as much as they could so that Maggie's mind would never slide to such a terrifying place again. But there was so much less online back then. Eventually they'd visited the campus health centre and a doctor there had filled in the blanks somewhat. Maggie had collapsed on stage in the middle of directing a scene for their Beckett module. Dehydration and a severe loss of electrolytes coupled with low blood pressure had been the disastrous cocktail of woes her body had been contending with as her secret purging had ramped up.

Even though it seemed impossibly bleak, the doctor had warned them it could've been even worse. Maggie's illness could cause heart problems, oesophageal damage and even life-threatening internal bleeding. It had been sobering. But they'd all been in their early twenties. Death as a possibility was remote and couldn't possibly apply to any of them. Plus, Maggie was in hospital and hospital equalled getting better, right? And when Maggie was released she did seem much, much better. They'd all finished college, pissed about together all summer in America and then Maggie and Fionn had set off on their theatre dreams in London.

'Check those out.' Clara nudged her, interrupting Annie's agitated stream of thoughts. She pointed to a trio of bizarre-looking vehicles with no roofs and huge wheels parked in the shadow of the house.

'They look like something out of *Mad Max*. Part of the surprise, no doubt,' Annie whispered. Foreboding niggled. She would've liked to collapse into bed at this point. She felt like she'd lived several days already today. She and Conor probably needed to have their own adult conversation, and being locked into a 'surprise' event of Fionn's creation would be unlikely to allow that.

'Annie! Clara!' Fionn had released Maggie from his arms, arms that Annie swore doubled in size every time she saw him. 'Get over here!'

That accent. Annie didn't chance looking at Clara in case they laughed. It was becoming harder and harder to tell where Fionn Strong ended and Finn Strong began.

She and Clara were accepting his hugs and air kisses just as Conor and Ollie emerged from the house.

'Hey, lads,' Ollie called. 'Hope ye're not completely hammered or you are *not* going to like the evening plans!'

Annie tried to catch Conor's eyes but he remained focused on Ollie in a slightly forced-looking fashion and didn't so much as glance her way.

Fionn flashed his creepily perfect celebrity teeth at Annie, Clara and Maggie. 'We're going for a ride in the dunes! In these dune buggies.'

'Cool!' Maggie said warily, looking the buggies over. Each one had two seats inside something vaguely cage-like that sat atop four huge wheels. 'Only … Fionn? There's not much of a roof, is there? And no doors? And where will the kids go?'

Fionn laughed. 'Oh, the kids are staying here – we'll be out in the dunes most of the night. Brody arranged a surprise for the kids too though, don't worry; he booked Blippi!'

'Blippi,' Clara repeated. Annie could see she looked stunned.

'What's Blippi?' Annie asked.

'Which Blippi? There's two now,' Clara questioned him.

'Original Blippi,' said Fionn, clearly thrilled with himself over this coup, whatever the hell the coup was.

Maggie had shooed Dodi and Essie back into the house and was tugging on Fionn's arm. She spoke quietly but they could all hear her, the house blocking what little breeze was left in the day.

'Don't you think on your first night back you should be with the girls?'

Ollie, looking awkward, herded Conor, Clara and Annie away from the other two. 'We should check these things out,' he said. 'See what we're gonna die in!'

Annie glanced back. There was now palpable tension in Maggie and Fionn's body language, though there was palpable tension among the rest of them as well. Only Ollie seemed happy and oblivious.

He was explaining that Blippi was a YouTuber.

'I was actually pretty starstruck meeting Blippi.' Ollie grinned. 'And,' he called to Conor, 'we've gotta keep Maggie and Clara away from him. He's got this cult following of pervy mums who have a Reddit forum called Blippi After Dark.'

Clara slumped into the passenger seat of the buggy furthest away while Conor was pulling at the seatbelt of the nearest buggy. 'These things do not seem safe.'

'Yeah,' Annie echoed him. 'Also, what did Fionn mean "we'll be out there most of the night"? Out in the dunes? Where, like?'

'Oh, well.' Ollie shifted awkwardly. 'I'd say Maggie won't be happy.' He glanced back across to Fionn and Maggie, who did indeed appear to be involved in some kind of quiet altercation. 'There's this director and he says he wants to work with Fionn but only if Fionn will come out to where he's staying. Don't tell Maggie but Fionn kinda let slip that he basically planned this entire holiday to coincide with this meeting.'

'The director guy is based somewhere off the beaten track, supposedly,' Conor explained.

'No way.' Clara spoke up from her seat. 'That's yer man, Edwin Ensel! Our tour guide today told us he's staying out in these mad shacks.'

'I don't know *what* Fionn's thinking,' Ollie remarked. 'It's hardly the stuff of heartfelt reunions ... How long's it been since he and Maggie saw each other?'

'Well,' Clara threw him a withering look, 'you'd know better than anyone that just cuz you're with each other all the time doesn't mean the relationship is good.'

'What does *that* mean?' Ollie looked baffled.

Before Clara could say more, Maggie's voice travelled over to them. She sounded upset. 'Wow. Just wow, Fionn. That is so typical.'

'Please, lads.' Conor looked from Clara to Ollie. 'Only one couple fighting at a time – that's the rule of this holiday.'

Annie noted that he didn't look her way at all.

When they'd left the proper road, the route to Edwin Ensel's dune shack was two miles of scrappy sand trails that bounded over the hills and down through the gullies of the almost lunar landscape. Fionn had told Conor and Ollie not to drink that day and so the guys were driving. Via a series of meaningful looks, Annie, Clara and Maggie had communicated that none of them wanted to ride with their other half and so that was how Annie came to be bouncing around beside Ollie as he whooped and giggled. There was still a bit of light left at the horizon but Annie couldn't help worrying about the drive back.

'How do you know how to drive this thing?' she shouted over the roar of the engine.

'The lad who dropped them off gave us a tutorial.'

'That sounds … thorough? Hopefully?' She winced as they bumped over a small outcrop of rocks.

'Did you guys have fun today?'

The image of Clara's tongue in that random guy's mouth flashed into Annie's mind.

'Yeah,' she said, cautiously.

What the fuck. How did I get stuck with my friend's potentially cheating husband just hours after she cheated on him back?

Annie twisted to look back at the rest of the gang careering around the track behind them. Fionn was clearly having a blast with his buggy. He had just one hand on the wheel and was steering it expertly around obstacles and up banks of sand. With his shades, tan and white teeth, Annie felt like she could literally be watching a scene from one of his movies. Beside him, Clara was whooping tipsily. Trailing far behind, Annie could see Conor inching his way cautiously forward with a very tense Maggie beside him. They'd probably arrive an hour after everyone else.

'I'm glad today was good.' Ollie jerked them to the right to get around a withered-looking bush. 'Clara really needs this holiday.'

'She does,' Annie agreed.

'She works so much. The last time she got a night to herself, she went out drinking with her work crowd, but drinking can't be her only outlet. Plus, they're in their twenties – getting shitfaced is still a novelty for them. What's Clara's excuse?'

'Blowing off steam, I guess?' Annie had a surge of remorse (along with a surge of nausea as they swung a violent left); the last couple of times Clara had suggested they get together, Annie'd been meeting Rachel. *I should've suggested she come, especially as it's hard for Clara to make time with the kids and work. The next time I will*, she resolved.

Beside her, Ollie continued, 'I feel kinda guilty because …' The buggy bounced, cutting him off, and Annie clenched, both from the jolt and hearing Ollie announce that he felt guilty. She did not want to receive some kind of confession.

'Maybe less talking, Ollie.' She gripped her seat, though she knew it was a completely futile gesture – wherever this buggy was going, the seat was going too.

'Don't worry, I can drive this, no probs! I drive the truck for work, sure. But yeah ... I feel bad for her. Can I ask you, though ... has Clara said anything?'

'Of course she's said things, we've been on holiday together for two days now.'

'C'mon, Annie.' He glanced her way. 'Has she said anything about me? About us? I feel like ... Look, I haven't been totally honest with her lately and I'm worried that if—'

'Ollie, you can't put me in this position.' The buggy swooped down a steep depression in the terrain and Annie's stomach did a flip.

'What position?' Ollie pulled the buggy sharply to the left to keep from veering right off the trail altogether. 'I just want to be upfront with her and I want to get the lie of the land before we talk.'

'Why are you proposing to have some big heart-to-heart that might upset her while on holiday?' Annie glared at him. 'Why would you think that's appropriate?'

'Jesus, relax! I know it's not great that I haven't been honest but I think now's actually a good time. At home, we don't get a second to talk, Annie. The kids are up our holes round the clock.'

'I cannot believe I'm having to explain to you why here, on a group holiday, isn't a good time to come clean about your behaviour.'

'Okay, calm down! You're acting like I'm confessing to an affair or something. I only want to tell her that I've been training for the marathon.'

'*What?*' Annie froze.

'I know. I'm completely shitting it about telling her. We're both so busy and it just feels really selfish of me to be doing something like this for myself, not to mention something so time-consuming. She's working so hard and the kids are so full-on. I've been trying to train when I can squeeze it in, at times when it doesn't affect her, late at night and stuff.'

'I ... see ...' Annie's thoughts whirred. *This is not an affair. Oh God, it's so wholesome as well ...*

'You think she's gonna be upset?' He pushed his shaggy curls back from his face, looking nervous.

'Ehhhm.' Annie cast around for something to say. So he wasn't having an affair at all? What about the text Clara'd seen? *I had such a good time, Ollie. The best yet.*

'I'm training with my buddy, Stevie. He's done one before and we're tryna give each other encouragement. It's been good for my mental health.' Ollie still looked worried. 'She'll understand that, right?'

Annie thought again of the text. 'Do you keep track of your timings? On your runs?'

'What?' Ollie glanced over, seeming surprised at her apparent interest. 'Yeah, of course. Stevie just had his best time yet yesterday! Lucky fucker. My knee's been a bit dodgy so having to mind it a bit.'

'Right.' Annie sat back. *Fuck.*

CHAPTER 8

Night was starting to fall and, ahead of her, Clara could occasionally see the back of Ollie and Annie's buggy whenever they crossed the headlights of her and Fionn's.

Once aboard the buggy, Clara's hangover (and general feelings of nihilism) could've gone one of two ways: hellish or slightly less hellish. Luckily she liked rollercoasters and anything vaguely adrenaline-adjacent and she couldn't but laugh as they flew over the dunes.

'So,' Clara yelled, bracing on the dashboard as the buggy leapt over another hill. 'What's this I'm hearing about no calls or texts while you're away filming? Seems a bit precious, babes. A bit,' Clara adopted what she called her RADA voice, *'I am an actorrrrrr!'*

'Alright, alright.' Fionn grinned ruefully. 'I'm trying not to be all "I am an *actorrrr*" about it! You don't understand, there's a lot of pressure ... a lot of eyes on me when I'm on set. I have to deliver. It's like ... I think they'll all suddenly notice that I'm just some random guy from Dublin who was basically a failed actor until forty when he stumbled into a good thing.'

'Ah, Fionn.' Clara was surprised. Of the group, she and Fionn had always been the most confident. Him in a nice laid-back way and her in a borderline obnoxious but hopefully still lovable way. It was why they'd always gelled so well. 'You know you're good, right? We all think you're incredible. Obvi we fast-forward your sex scenes cuz *vom*, but you're a world-class actor.'

Fionn smiled, but then just as quickly his grin evaporated. 'Did Maggie say something to you about the no-phone-on-set thing?'

'Yeah. Not in a super-angry way but … obviously it affects her if you're not in touch at all and then Brody's telling her not to worry about affair allegations in the press.'

'That wasn't an affair allegation.' He gripped the steering wheel. 'It was a blind item about someone *else*.'

Clara stared at his profile; his expression had suddenly darkened. She sighed. 'Whatever it is, she's dealing with it on her own and that's the problem.'

The abrupt vibe shifts on this trip were starting to give her whiplash. If it wasn't her own shitty relationship bringing her down, it was someone else's. The thoughts of Ollie cheating clutched at her afresh. God, how was this where they'd got to? After all these years?

On the brow of the approaching hill, against the darkening blue of the sky, she could now see the silhouette of Edwin Ensel's ramshackle shack. It looked more like the carcass of an ancient sea creature than a house. The sagging veranda with its splintered and worn railings resembled the ribcage of a whale, while, on the other side of the structure, what looked to be an outhouse kicked up from the undulations of navy sand like a tail.

A few minutes later, they pulled up in the lee of the shack, where Ollie and Annie had left their buggy parked. Wind spiked with salt whistled through the sand grass in the dark around them and low murmuring could be heard coming from inside the shack above.

'It's creepy,' Clara whispered, deciding to move on from the sullenness of their last exchange. She slid down from her seat. 'Imagine being out here on your own. No lights or anything.'

'Yeah …' Fionn had thawed too and sounded wistful. 'It'd be creepy but incredible. So meditative.'

They followed the little trench in the sand that led around to the shack's sagging wooden steps.

'Meditative!' Clara scoffed. 'You've gone so fucking LA, Fionn!'

He came to a sudden stop and turned to her.

'What?' She looked up at his shadowy face.

'Just try and be chill in here. With Edwin, I mean. He's a total master of cinema, he's a legend. And he takes things seriously.'

'Okay! Relax, Fionn! I'm not a child, I know how to be a guest in someone's house. I won't shit in the sink, like.' She could sense rather than see his wince at her words.

'It's just that this meeting is important for me.' Just then behind them Maggie and Conor's buggy approached. As they turned to wave, Fionn leaned down slightly and muttered, 'Don't tell Maggie that I called this a "meeting".'

'Come in, come in!'

Clara peered around Fionn's broad back to see the source of the tinkly voice that was beckoning them warmly from the crooked little door at the top of the stairs. A stunning woman of about seventy stood there in bare feet wearing a yellow dress with a long orange suede waistcoat. Her white hair was cut into a blunt bob and she had a pronounced gap between her two front teeth that gave her beauty a sweetly girlish quality.

'Oh, I'm so glad to meet you all. I'm Pauline, Edwin's wife. Well done for getting here in one piece.' She stood to the side and ushered them past her into the long, candle-lit timber room that served as a kitchen, living and dining room. Pauline shut the door after them all, drew a thick woven curtain across it and turned to face them. 'You're all so young and gorgeous! Sit, sit.'

Clara and Maggie joined Annie and Ollie, who were already on the bench seat that ran down one side of the wooden table. Clara was glad to avoid sitting beside Ollie, though she knew she was going to have to scream at him sooner or later.

Conor located a stool and perched at the other end of the room in front of a large curtain that hung from the beam of a loft above and divided the space, while Fionn took a chair at the head of the table.

Pauline smiled pleasantly as each of them introduced themselves and Clara took the opportunity to take in the curious space around them. Every tiny shelf and neat little nook had a purpose. The ladder up to the loft doubled up as a bookshelf, home to dozens and dozens of faded paperbacks. In the window above the sink sat a planter of mint, basil and parsley above which was a rack for drying the dishes. From where she sat she could see that the freshly washed plates from dinner were dripping water down onto the herbs below. The whole place was like a little domestic ecosystem all of its own.

Pauline, it seemed, had noticed her looking. 'Oh, we don't waste a drop of fresh water out here! Most of the shacks have a well but ours is a bit of a walk! We share it with Cuttlers' shack – they're one of the original Provincetown families who've been out here for generations.'

'We learned all about them on our tour today,' Maggie said.

Clara hadn't heard Maggie say a word since they'd arrived and she sounded a little stiff and awkward.

As she should, Clara thought, annoyed. *As nice as this Pauline woman is, why the fuck are we all out here?*

The shack was cute but it wasn't screaming 'Craic!'

Did they even have any booze? She thought longingly of the mansion on the beach where they could've been sipping something crisp and cold. Instead they were here in small-talk hell.

'Yes, the tours are fun, aren't they?' Pauline smiled, then glanced discreetly towards the curtain behind Conor. Clara followed her gaze. *Is yer man Edwin behind the curtain?* Clara wondered, remembering what Geraldo had said about the voyeur.

'So,' Ollie spoke up from further down the bench, 'are you in movies as well?'

'No, no,' Pauline wafted towards Ollie, 'I'm a painter.' She was apparently uninterested in talking about herself as she continued along the table to Conor. 'You look like a serious one.' She crossed her eyes and stuck out her tongue at him.

'She has to be micro-dosing,' Clara whispered to Maggie. 'I want some.'

Conor looked boyish, less buttoned-up than his usual self, blushing under Pauline's gaze, and Clara could better see what Annie saw in him.

'I'm not serious.' Conor gave a neat, formal little laugh.

Of the whole group, Clara knew she and Conor probably had the least in common. He was so corporate, as she often said to Maggie privately on their own thread. You'd think the robotic sex-schedule thing would be suiting him but it was clear he and Annie were not in sync on that front.

'And you're Maggie, aren't you?' Pauline had drifted back up the table. 'We've heard about you. Aren't you very tolerant of your husband working on holidays! I don't think I'd have been that patient with Edwin doing that back when the boys were young.' Pauline turned her head to the curtain and added loudly, 'I can barely tolerate it now!'

If that toady little director is squatting behind that curtain, I will actually lose it. Every man in here is a selfish little fecker. Clara fumed, spotting Maggie's eyes shoot over to Fionn, who was wiping his mouth nervously.

'Well,' Maggie muttered, 'I guess I didn't *realise* that I was being so tolerant, Pauline. I don't think I was aware that he *was* working.'

'Pauline,' Clara, by now feeling utterly mutinous, raised her hand like in school, 'I can't *not* ask … Is your husband … hiding? Behind that curtain there?'

'He is,' Pauline said, with a vaguely withering smile in that direction.

'Right.' Clara nodded, ignoring Fionn's pleading look. 'So, follow-up question – and I guess this is more of a rhetorical one – but is there a man in here who *isn't* being somewhat of a complete dick right now?'

'Clara, stop.' Maggie's tone was placating rather than angry. But Clara's blood was up now. Plus there was, as she would later reflect, probably quite a bit of the day's alcohol still swirling around in it.

'I won't stop, Maggie. This is all bullshit. Pauline's husband is making her entertain a bunch of strangers while he plays with himself behind a curtain. Fionn hasn't seen you and the girls in ages but instead of spending time with you is taking a work meeting. A work meeting he planned this whole trip around, by the way. Conor meanwhile has literally one job to do and can't fucking finish. And Ollie is giving someone else "their best time ever" while I raise his kids and use the only alone time I ever get to scream into pillows inside the hot press. So, no, I won't stop. And Ollie,' Clara stared her husband down, 'just so you know, two people can cheat. I scored a really hot guy today and he said my breasts were, and I quote, "to die for".' Clara stopped to draw a ragged breath.

The shack was totally silent, until a disembodied voice with a German accent said, 'I am not playing with myself. This is a crucial part of my casting process.'

CHAPTER 9

Maggie sat frozen as Ollie gripped the table and pushed himself up to standing. He stared at his wife. 'You fucked some guy today? Are you being serious right now?'

'What if I am?' Clara glared.

'Clara! You didn't!' Annie interjected. Maggie could see she was frantic.

'Okay it was just kissing but anyway what do *you* care?' Clara spat at Ollie, ignoring Annie.

'What do I *care*? What are you talking about? I'm your husband.'

Maggie clenched her fists under the table. Oh God, Ollie looked like he was about to cry. *Bit rich, though*, she thought. Meanwhile, beside him Fionn looked deeply stressed and was also getting to his feet.

'Guys, this—' He held his hands up and began to speak in a placating tone.

But Clara was on one of her rolls now. She pointed at her husband. 'What did you think, Ollie? That you could go behind my back and I'd just sit around crying about it?' Clara was snarling now. Across the table, Maggie spotted Annie shaking her head emphatically.

'Clara,' Annie was trying to interject again, 'it's not what you—'

'Annie! I love you,' Clara shot across. 'But not now. I am tearing my cheating husband a new one.'

'She really is,' Pauline observed, and then scooted over to the dividing curtain. 'Edwin,' she hissed, 'get out here.'

Clara continued, not noticing the diminutive director slip out. 'You always said we were a team,' she spat. 'You always said you would never do what your dad did.'

Maggie hadn't seen her like this ever and it was equal parts terrifying and heartbreaking. Clara was so fierce, but behind the fury Maggie could see this was breaking her.

'What did his dad do?' Edwin leaned over and muttered to Fionn.

Is he taking notes? Maggie spied a tiny battered notebook in his hands. Fionn hesitated, looking uncertain about giving an answer.

Clara barrelled in instead. 'Ollie's dad cheated with the babysitter and then fecked off on the family. And now my darling husband's continuing the tradition.'

'I am absolutely not, Clara.' Ollie smacked the table in frustration. 'Where are you getting this?'

'I saw the text, Ollie. Now I know why you're never off your phone. You piece of shit. And the bank statements.'

'What text? What bank statement? Can you stop verbally abusing me for two fucking seconds and tell me what the hell you are talking about.'

Clara rolled her eyes. 'Don't you dare keep lying to me. Have the balls to just be honest. You disgusting prick.'

Ollie's face darkened. 'That's enough, Clara. You've clearly been drinking all day – while *I* minded our kids, by the way. You're acting *beyond* irrational and I really don't appreciate being humiliated like this.'

Clara shook her head and laughed bitterly. 'You think *you're* being humiliated.'

'Clara!' Annie spoke sharply and Maggie could hear there was something close to a warning in her voice. Did Annie know something more? Oh God, this was painful.

'Annie, seriously.' Clara held up a hand. 'I'm in the middle of something.'

'Yeah, and you're also in the middle of all of us,' Conor muttered sarcastically, to which Clara scowled.

'So.' Ollie's eyes had noticeably hardened and Maggie found him suddenly unrecognisable; in two decades he had rarely been anything but affable. 'Let me get this straight,' he continued. 'You think I'm cheating on you. And so you head out and score the first guy you see.'

Clara shrugged, looking utterly defiant.

Maggie could see hurt trickling through Ollie's expression, and the enormity of what they were all witnessing struck her. This was Clara and Ollie. *Clara and Ollie!* Coming apart right in front of them.

'Did you really, Clara?' Ollie stood, hands hanging. All his anger seemed to have ebbed, and everyone was silent.

Clara held his gaze though, as if knowing she was on the edge of something permanent. Maggie could see there was some modicum of hesitation in her eyes. Still she plunged ahead, regardless. 'Yeah, Ollie. I'm not a doormat. You don't get to make me the sad victim in your, frankly predictable, mid-life crisis.'

'I would never, ever cheat. But you did.' Ollie was speaking deliberately and breathing hard as Clara's bombshell sank in. 'I truly can't believe this. You kissed someone else.'

He stared around the cabin as though only just remembering the rest of them were there. 'I'm going back.' Head down, he crossed the room without looking at Clara again, opening the door and shutting it quietly behind him.

Maggie felt a knot of anxiety tighten in her chest. Clara sat back down at the table looking winded from the fight but not remotely repentant. 'Look, I'm sorry about that but—'

'Someone should go with him,' Conor interrupted, standing up as one of the dune buggies' ignitions sounded outside in the darkness. After some grappling to get past them on the bench, he hurried out the door and could be heard calling for Ollie as the door swung closed behind him.

'Would anyone like a drink?' Pauline asked with a strained smile.

'I feel like Clara's maybe had enough.' Fionn's mouth was a tight line across his face. 'Clara, this was not the time or the place for that.'

Maggie's anxious knot tightened further but she also felt defensive of her friend. 'Fionn, Ollie's been texting someone else.'

'You know what?' Pauline started to shuffle towards the door, pulling her husband by the arm. 'We're going to go for a little walk. Give you all a chance to …' She looked stumped at what exactly to suggest they do and didn't bother to finish the sentence. 'We'll be back. Help yourselves to anything.'

Edwin Ensel looked over his shoulder with a vaguely longing expression, no doubt wanting to take more notes on the action. But

Pauline was firm, and in a moment they had been swallowed by the salt-laden night.

Fionn groaned and rested his head on his hand. 'This has probably cost me the biggest opportunity of my career so far, Clara.'

At his words, Maggie felt a churn of disgust. 'That is so far from what's important here, Fionn,' she snapped.

Clara sat back, folding her arms. 'I'm sorry,' she said, with not a trace of apology in her voice. 'I thought I could play nice tonight but I won't be made a fool of. I'm not someone who can just suck it up.'

Maggie couldn't help but stiffen. *She's not talking about you*, she told herself.

'He's a cheat,' Clara continued.

'Except he's not.' Annie looked pained. 'I fucking tried to stop you.' She rounded on Clara, who looked sceptical.

'I told you what the text said, Annie.' Clara pulled out her phone, having none of it. 'I even took a photo of the phone screen.'

'It's not what you think it is,' Annie said forcefully.

'What is it, then?' Clara snapped.

Maggie massaged her temples; there was a sourness in the air between them and she could feel a headache coming on. None of their trips had ever been like this and she had no idea what the hell they were going to do about Clara and Ollie having such a serious bust-up. Nothing like this had ever happened before between any of the couples.

'Me and Ollie talked on the way here.' Annie shook her head at Clara. 'He's not having an affair, he's training for a marathon.'

A moment of complete silence followed this statement and Maggie felt like she could practically *see* Clara metabolise the magnitude of this information and then resolutely change tack.

'Well, if that's true, that's frankly worse,' Clara retorted.

'What exactly about that is worse, Clara?' At the top of the table, Fionn was incredulous.

'Why should he get to have that? I don't have time to piss by myself. I'm lucky if I even get to piss in the *actual* toilet.' Clara was clearly wrongfooted but was not backing down.

'I'm sorry, but where do you piss if not in the toilet?' Fionn asked.

'That's not what's up for discussion right now,' Clara snapped. 'Look. I don't think secret marathon-training requires clandestine texts and sex toy purchases.'

'Read the text from earlier.' Annie pointed to the phone.

Clara rolled her eyes. 'It said, "I had such a good time tonight ... yada yada yada".'

'You're paraphrasing. Read it word for word. It's from his training buddy. Stephen aka Stevie.'

Clara impatiently flicked the screen to unlock it and checked the picture she'd snapped of the text preview. Maggie craned to see it. 'Oh shit,' she cringed. 'They're talking about their PBs, not sex.'

From her years of punishing exercising routines, she knew all about the dogged pursuit of the personal best. *Shit, shit, shit.* Now Clara was the lone cheater in this situation.

With Ollie's childhood, Maggie couldn't imagine him getting over this anytime soon. *Maybe me and Fionn can give them money for couples therapy.* She silently searched for solutions, trying to ignore the voice pointing out that they could possibly do with a bit of couples therapy themselves. Though with the way things were, Fionn would probably send Brody instead of actually showing up himself.

Clara was still staring at her phone, her lips silently forming the words over and over again. When she looked up and found Maggie's eyes, Maggie could see that a tinge of worry seemed to be overtaking her indignation of the previous hours.

'But,' Clara pulled at her bottom lip, 'he's out at weird times. And the showers ...'

Maggie reached over to rub her shoulder as, across from them, Annie sighed. 'He told me he's trying to train when it's not full-on kid time. So that he's not leaving you with all the parenting.' She delivered this unhappily.

Oh God. Poor Ollie. Maggie stole a glance at Fionn to see if that had landed with him at all, but he was looking at his phone. God, even in the middle of their friends' crisis he was distracted. Her eyes narrowed just as he glanced up. Catching sight of her expression, he quickly mouthed 'sorry' and slipped it back off the table.

'Clara, you need to talk to him,' Annie was saying urgently. 'We googled the wrong website this morning. He wasn't buying stuff off HardBodies.com, he was buying stuff off HardBodies.ie – it's a protein bro site. For supplements, energy gels and stuff.'

Clara was staring down at the table now, looking uneasy. 'Right.' She drew a slow breath. 'Ballsed this up spectacularly, didn't I?'

Maggie raked her fingers through her hair and tried to ignore the headache building behind her right eye. 'He'll understand. Explain that the guy was gay. Gays don't count, surely.'

'Maggie,' Annie snapped, 'that's a fucking shit thing to say.' She looked furious as she mimicked Maggie's words, '*Uh… gays don't count.* That's fucking horrible.'

'I just meant …' Maggie's eyes began to sting in response to Annie's anger. 'Oh, I don't know what I meant, okay? You're right. I'm a shit person.'

Annie just gazed at her, making no attempt to argue on this point, and Maggie slumped back against the shack wall. These seemingly endless spikes of tension since the start of the holiday had been exhausting.

From the off, every one of them had been mired in their individual dramas. With hindsight, it now seemed inevitable that they'd ended up ringside at *someone's* cataclysmic confrontation. And jabbing tetchily at each other in the aftermath. Maggie wished they weren't in this glorified shed miles from anywhere. Slivers of icy breeze were breaching the wooden wall behind her back. She shivered, cold to the bone and utterly spent.

Clara looked no better – not so much upset as utterly shook – while Annie was grim-faced.

'I think we should get going.' Maggie began to rise. 'Me and Fionn can go in one buggy and you two in the other. Do you feel okay about driving it, Annie?'

'It'll probably take about ten hours to get back but yeah, grand.' She stood and nudged Clara. 'Come on, you.' They made their way outside.

Maggie turned to Fionn, who was still sitting. 'Do you want to look for a piece of paper and pen to leave Pauline and yer man a note?' she asked.

'Eh ... suuuure,' he said slowly, though he made no move to get up.

She noticed Fionn's phone was back on the table. Was there even signal out here? It also occurred to her that this was the first moment they'd been alone together in months. She turned and started to scout around for a pen or paper on the window sills cluttered with ancient-looking tchotchkes. Beyond the glass panes, she could see Clara and Annie's buggy crawling up the track before dropping below the dune closest to the shack.

'Maggie?'

'Hmmm?' She glanced his way as he tugged on her hand, pulling her towards him and then wrapping his arms around her. He lay his head against her stomach, which she automatically sucked in while trying not to completely tense her whole body.

'I've missed you,' he whispered.

She bent slightly to nuzzle his hair and inhale him. It was crazy that even after the last tumultuous years and the, let's face it, pretty lonely stretches without him, his arms, his smell, still meant home to her.

'I've missed you too.' She knew it was just so much easier to simply play nice. She didn't want to waste the time they had together picking apart the trickier things in their marriage, especially after the blow-up they'd just witnessed. Clara and Ollie's anger had been so potent, it'd overtaken the whole place like a storm system. Maggie couldn't face a confrontation, it just wasn't worth it. Fionn was her best friend; she couldn't forget that. It was natural that there would be adjustments as his career continued to evolve. *We will get to spend more time together. I'm happy for him. He's worked so long and hard for it. It won't always be like this—*

'Listen.' He interrupted her thoughts. 'I kinda promised Edwin that I'd stay here tonight.' He continued to hold her, nuzzling her and not meeting her eye.

Maggie's tentative optimism withered, a sudden cold front chasing out the warm feelings she'd been having towards him just seconds before.

'Of course you did.' She straightened up but remained in his embrace, mainly so that she wouldn't have to look at him either.

'Maggie ...' His wheedling tone scratched at her. He sounded like one of the twins trying to get something out of her. She glared at Ensel's curtained wall opposite. She hadn't seen the auteur speak directly to her husband the entire time they were there. This staying the night business had been planned in advance. Clara had said as much during her rant.

'Maggie,' he repeated, in the exact same pleading voice as before. He pulled back from her and looked up, trying to find her eyes.

'Can you not say my name like that?' She pulled his arms from her body and stepped back.

He blinked. 'Like what?'

'Like I'm your mother and you're trying to get permission to stay out late.' She walked around the table to pick up her phone. 'No probs, Fionn, I'll just drive back to the house in total darkness.'

'No! I didn't mean for you to do that,' he protested vehemently. 'Of course not. I'll take you back and then I'll ... you know ... come back.'

Maggie's head was now fully pounding. She wanted to tell him to fuck off and just stay but she was also terrified of the idea of making her way out of this remote landscape alone.

'Fine,' was all she said, feeling a bit like she was compromising her own self-respect but also like she really didn't have any other options. Was her whole marriage starting to feel like that? Yes, in her absolute heart of hearts, she knew it was. Her own wants and needs had been stamped down by his huge fucking career.

Sometimes she pictured a different future. She wondered what it would be like to leave. But she felt stymied by practicalities. How would she afford it, for starters? She hadn't worked at all in the last five years. How would the twins handle veering between luxury and normality? What bloody continent would they all live on?

She always stepped back from the precipice of these thoughts. She didn't want that. She still loved Fionn; they'd grown up together. But she also didn't know how to feel better about her life as it was.

'I'll wait outside.' Maggie hurriedly left the shack and took a seat in the buggy. Fionn followed a couple of minutes later.

'I was just leaving them a note explaining that I'll be back,' he said with a trace of awkwardness.

Maggie wanted to ask when the plan for this meeting and sleepover had come about but she didn't have to. The entire journey back he babbled about the preamble to this encounter. He was breathless as he described cryptic calls from Edwin in the previous weeks. The potential project they would collaborate on – the details of which he knew nothing about because famously Edwin Ensel's process was so secretive and so esoteric that there was nothing as banal as a script to look at.

'So you were taking his calls on set the last few weeks?' She clenched her fists but kept her voice devoid of emotion.

Beside her, he fell silent, hunching further over the steering wheel, as he focused on the track rushing towards them illuminated only by the small pools of light from their headlights.

She thought bitterly of Fionn billing this night as a surprise earlier, as if his agenda wouldn't become patently obvious the second they'd reached the shack and met Edwin Ensel.

'Why did you bother dragging us all out there with you?'

'I'm sorry, it was a bad call. I thought you'd all get a kick out of it. See the movie madness up close.' He glanced at her but she couldn't bring herself to look at him.

When they finally arrived back to the house they sat in silence for a few minutes. Maggie seethed and Fionn, clearly sensing as much, tried to placate her.

'It's only for a night or two, Maggie.' He took her hand and squeezed it.

Maggie stared at the house in front of them, looming in the darkness. The glowing fairy lights on the back deck were just visible beyond the clapboard siding. Someone was still up.

'I know it's terrible timing ...' he continued quietly. 'I want to spend time with you guys. I love when we're all together and we can just be normal.' He sighed. 'I know work is pulling me away a lot. It's just ... I've got this momentum right now and I have to lean into that. Nothing's guaranteed, it could all disappear tomorrow.' He cupped her face and turned it gently towards him. He had an imploring look. *He wants me to absolve him. To give him permission to do whatever it takes even if it means putting us second.*

She softened slightly. After all, she thought sadly, she didn't know – would never know – what it might feel like for all your dreams to come true and how that might lead to another place of anxiety and uncertainty, always waiting to run out of road and fall back to where you started.

'Fionn …' she began. 'It's not easy. Seeing awful stuff on socials and then *you're* not even the one telling me that it's not true, it's Brody …'

'I know these stupid blind items are horrible, dragging anyone and everyone into it. I heard it's Cormac O'Shea. He's on location right now.' He paused and took a breath. 'Though, eh, Brody thinks we should be papped together this week.' He shook his head, seemingly at the oddness of their life, but Maggie detected a slight question in his tone. *He also wants us to be papped*, she realised.

'The story … it's really not you?' She hated asking.

'Maggie!' He turned fully around to her. 'Of course! Oh my God, please don't believe for one second that I would ever look at anyone else.' He stroked her face. 'I have loved you for twenty years.'

'I've changed a lot in those years …' Maggie leaned back, out of his reach.

'We both have.' He reached for her again. 'Please, Maggie, don't pay any attention to the wankers on the internet. You're the mother of my children, you're my best friend—'

'Best friends see each other from time to time,' Maggie said dryly, trying not to sound petulant. She felt pathetic enough.

'I know. You're completely right, we need to get more time together and we will, I promise. I'll be back from Edwin's in a couple of days and we'll have an amazing time. It's only two days out of two whole weeks. It's an amazing opportunity to do some serious work with Edwin – it'd be a strong follow-up to *Fires in Vermont*. Really cement me as more than the *"Endurance guy"*. I do have to think about my career.'

He didn't say it but the unspoken words – *how else would we afford all this?* – hung between them as they gazed at the beautiful sprawling property perched at the edge of this paradise.

Maggie didn't have much of an answer to this, except maybe that they'd been happy before, when they'd had very little. Even if their careers weren't stellar. Before the big time, they had still been able to make their art and make ends meet. Kinda. Though she did get that things back then had been more frustrating for Fionn. As an actor, he was at the mercy of casting directors. As a writer and director, she had more agency in her work. She could write in their flat even if no one would ever see what she created. Fionn couldn't do monologues to no one in the box room.

'I'll see you when you get back, I guess.' She unbuckled and slid out of her seat. Making her way down the side of the house and towards the stairs to the deck, she could feel his eyes on her back.

She knew he just wanted her to smile and accept his new life. He craved her unquestioning support. He didn't get that she *was* trying but he never seemed to think about what she was sacrificing for him to get everything he'd ever wanted.

In the first year or two of the 'fame storm', as she'd come to think of it, he'd still encouraged her own work. He'd pushed her to get nannies for the girls so she could focus on projects. He didn't seem to follow the logic of that idea – if he was gone for months at a time and Maggie was immersed in her theatre work, Dodi and Essie would be alone with a pale imitation of a parent on the payroll. Despite what Clara and Annie might assume, Maggie had never got a nanny – she had a housekeeper, Betty, who ran the house, cooked and helped with babysitting the odd time, but Maggie tried to always be there for the girls, the only constant in their strange, unsettled lives.

She paused at the foot of the steps as Fionn's buggy engine growled to life. She would not look back: that was her tiny act of defiance.

She would push down these feelings like she always did. Fuck it, things would look different when the bleached light of another beautiful day in Provincetown dawned in a few hours' time. She would cope and put on a show for their friends, who would no doubt pity her, maybe even think she was a pushover for going along with Fionn.

There was a simple way to cope, a simple way to bury the humiliation of her marriage.

This whisper of a thought unfurled in her mind like a tendril of blood in water. There was a route to numbness. The problem was, she had nothing in her room that would soothe her. Eating had always been her refuge from the discomfort of living. Even before she had become 'officially' unwell during college she had never really eaten normally. Growing up, her mother had monitored the size of her own body closely and that toxic focus had eventually extended to her daughter's body when, as a teenager, Maggie had started to gain weight. Maggie knew her mother loved her and that her urging Maggie to give up chocolate and watch her portions was not a conscious effort to hurt her. But feeling endlessly observed at the dinner table eventually drove her eating underground and into the lonely, dark corners of her life. It became routine to eat little at dinner and then sneak as much food as she could late at night after her family were in bed. This pattern produced two contradictory effects: a soothing, almost tranquilising sense of peace and a feeling of drowning in a soup of shame and self-loathing which, of course, was when the purging had started to creep in.

It was just from time to time at first. It was so hard to hide until she became scarily adept at it – a dubious brag. Then in her flat in college with so much more autonomy and privacy, the grim habit started to become a rampaging force. The answer to everything, college stress, fights with Fionn, success and failure, was to eat and purge, eat and purge. Maggie closed her eyes against the memories rising – puking in Portaloos at festivals, being spattered in the face with toilet water when she flushed to try and hide the sounds she made as she hunched over retching. Now her thoughts darted to the kitchen. Would the staff lock it at night? She continued to hesitate on the threshold where the beach met the house.

She felt the urge gathering inside her, like a wave surging up. It had been years since she'd last done it but being sick in the restaurant the night before had felt undeniably good and these thoughts, once unleashed in her mind, were dogged. Insidious and insistent. Eat and blot out the uncomfortable feelings. Sure then the shame, familiar as her own hands, would soon come and smother this temporary relief. And then a simple way of dealing with all of it. The thing people had never seemed to understand was that there eventually came a time when being sick didn't feel gross but satisfying; ridding yourself of everything was a narcotic high in and of itself.

She wondered if she could slip into the house from the front and get to the kitchen that way without running into anyone.

'Maggie? Is that you?' Clara's voice came from above her and Maggie froze.

Maggie debated creeping away but the thought of slipping back into the shadow of the house and stealthily finding her way to the kitchen caused more dank humiliation to wash over her. Sometimes she wished that she was a secret drinker instead – anything seemed less shameful than bingeing on food. But for whatever reason, for her, alcohol and drugs didn't have that same seductive pull.

Footsteps on the wooden boards above sent fine sand down from the underside of the deck. 'Maggie?' Clara was now above her, leaning over the railing. 'Are you okay?'

Maggie pulled on a smile. 'Yeah, sorry, I was just admiring the view.' Maggie gestured towards the beach.

Clara's slightly bewildered gaze followed the direction of Maggie's hand. There wasn't a whole lot of 'view' visible out in the darkness, where the black sea was barely distinguishable from the black night above.

'Hmmm ... quite a view alright.' Clara was sombre, though her words were loose and a teeny bit slurred. 'Please, come up and tell me I haven't totally ruined my marriage, will you?' She turned and disappeared from view.

Maggie made her way up the steps and over to the two lounge chairs at the edge of the deck. Clara slumped onto one and Maggie took the other. 'How are you doing? Where's Annie?'

'She and Conor did some cursory comforting and then hightailed it upstairs. Obviously they had some sex business to attend to. I guess who in their forties *doesn't* get a boner from watching the fights of their married friends?' she joked bleakly.

Maggie took in the half-empty bottle of Pinot Grigio and the one empty wine glass and couldn't help feeling a flicker of judgement – *does she really think more booze is going to help?*

Maggie regrouped and tried to settle her expression into one of compassion, even though she was not feeling the most thrilled with Clara. *Why does she have to get so wasted and make her problems everyone else's problem?*

Clara's palms were pressed to her eyes but she seemed to intuit Maggie's thoughts. 'I know the last thing I need is more booze but ...' She hung her head, leaning forward. A curtain of hair obscured her face and Maggie couldn't tell if she was crying. 'When we got back here, Ollie said exactly ten words to me, Maggie. He said, "Sleep somewhere else, I can't look at you right now."'

'Clara,' Maggie breathed. 'I'm sorry.'

'He was so cold.' Clara's shoulders began to shake. 'It was only a kiss but he's acting like I had sex with someone else.'

Maggie thought about how she'd feel in Ollie's position. It didn't take much imagining. She'd had to work through the sickening discomfort of seeing Fionn kiss other actors all through their relationship. The fact that she'd worked in theatre had helped her compartmentalise somewhat. It was storytelling, she told herself.

Though his scenes with some of the most beautiful women in the world still felt fucking shit sometimes. When the urge to take refuge in food started to creep in, it was often these images that she was running from.

Kissing someone else in real life is still a betrayal, she thought. *It's intimate.*

She shifted her focus back to Clara. Maggie knew she still had to be her friend, even if she *had* fucked up. They had all done it for each other at various times. That's what made a twenty-year friendship: sitting with the other person, staying by their side even when you knew they'd been a bit of an asshole.

And also lying to them a bit when necessary. Maggie put her arm around Clara. 'I think you will feel better able to handle this in the morning, darl. He'll come around. I'm sure he will. It's Ollie.' Maggie forced herself to sound confident, though privately she wasn't sure at all. Everyone had their limit, and Ollie had always been very clear about *his*.

Plus, if Ollie felt he had to hide something as innocuous as a hobby from Clara, then God knows what state their marriage was in. Maybe all their jokey slagging wasn't as playful as it seemed. 'Give him some space. Come up and sleep in my room, Clara. Then you two can talk it out properly tomorrow.'

Clara looked up at her. She seemed lost, diminished from the turn the night had taken. 'Is Fionn not there?' she asked.

'No, Fionn went back to the dune shack, long story.' Maggie resurrected her forced smile from earlier. 'Come on, it'll be like a sleepover. A grim, grim sleepover.' Maggie stood and tugged Clara to her feet.

'Thanks, Maggie.' Clara wrapped her arms protectively around herself. 'I thought I'd have to go in with the boys and then the thoughts of looking at them while they were sleeping and just … Ugh, I have this overwhelming sense that I may have, like, destroyed their world just cuz I was gassed up on … what? I dunno … wine and self-righteousness.' Clara shook her head sadly as Maggie steered them towards the doors.

CHAPTER 10

Annie watched her friends make their way into the house from above. She'd felt guilty for not staying downstairs with Clara but she'd also felt more than a little bit pissed off with her. They were all here together. Things on the holiday hadn't been perfect so far but was it really the time to act like a bratty teenager and revenge-cheat on your husband? And revenge-cheat for something that hadn't even been confirmed?

Annie sighed and turned around to face the empty room. Conor was in the bathroom – when was he not? She went over and listened at the door. She could hear the rapid-fire audio shifts that could only be someone flicking through TikTok. Hiding in the bathroom seemed to be something of a theme in long relationships – Clara had reported similar with Ollie. She shuddered at the mental image: forty-something men, hairy knees and trousers pooling around their ankles, thumbing a phone. Massive ick. She made a mental note to never, ever touch Conor's phone again. *You'd miss dating women*, she thought wryly. It'd been a long time since Ellie, her girlfriend before Conor. Plus that came with its own issues – she vividly remembered their PMS syncing up. Chaos.

'You better not be stalling!' She tapped on the door, making a concerted effort to sound upbeat. 'We're on the clock for Fertility Window July 2025!'

The toilet flushed within and Conor slid the door open as he dried his hands. He was frowning slightly. 'Are you serious?'

'Eh, yes.' Annie caught sight of her furrowed brow in the bathroom mirror behind him and consciously tried to relax her face. She wasn't trying for alluring, exactly – after all this time, that would be too much of a reach – but she could at least look less stern for the person she was trying to have efficient sex with.

'I dunno, Annie.' Conor shuffled out past her. 'It's been a really weird night. It'd just be forced.'

'It's always forced,' Annie said, trying to cover her impatience by sounding playful. 'That's what everyone has to do, they just don't talk about it. You *have* to make the effort! Forced is practically the *point* when you're trying to have a baby.'

'I don't think that's the point, Annie,' Conor said quietly. He sounded exhausted, though whether it was exhausted from the emotional maelstrom of Clara and Ollie tearing strips off one another or exhausted with their own unproductive project, it was hard to say.

He sat down on the bed. 'I can't believe Clara did that to Ollie. It's so messed-up.'

'Yeah.' What else could Annie say? *Ugh, apparently we're going to talk about this and waste precious time. Fucking Clara.*

'I'd nearly forgotten that Clara could be like this.' Conor shook his head. 'She is such a drama queen.'

Annie didn't want to spoil the already decidedly unsexy mood by disagreeing with Conor, but, despite her own feelings towards

Clara, she also felt protective of her. 'To be fair, she did *think* he was cheating and he actually *was* lying to her.'

'Oh c'mon. Lying about *jogging*.' Conor gave a scathing laugh. 'Clara is a goddamn mess. She was the same in college, running around drunkenly fucking up and then crying on the stairs at house parties. Getting sick in people's handbags.'

'That's not fair. She got sick in one person's handbag, one time.' Annie began to undress in the hope that it would move them along in the proceedings.

'They're the worst advertisement for parenthood I've ever seen.' Conor remained seated, not so much as taking his flip-flops off.

'That's harsh. They love those boys.' Annie undid the buttons down the front of her dress. She wasn't wearing a bra, she never did with this dress. She'd worn it especially because at one stage in their relationship Conor had actually liked unbuttoning it for her and reaching inside to touch her breasts. She moved closer to the bed and started to slide her straps down. 'Can we not talk about this now, please!'

Conor looked up with an unmistakably pained expression. 'Annie.' He reached up and, to her dismay, pulled the front of her dress closed.

'What are you doing?' She took a step back, pushing his hands away and holding the material in front of her chest.

'I can't do this, Annie. I'm really sorry.' He dropped his head and let his hands hang between his knees.

This snub caught her like a kick in the gut. She blinked rapidly because the thought of crying while holding her dress closed like this was too embarrassing. Begging Conor for sex, literally getting her tits out. It was too much. The will to lock in another chance at this month's window came to a dead stop. It was just so demeaning. She stared down at him.

'Conor. I know, okay? I get it. It's awkward timing with the holiday and I know it's all getting a bit stressy at this point.' Her words were tumbling out over one another but if she stopped talking she was afraid she might start sobbing. 'I don't mean to be so … hyper-focused on it. It's just important to me.'

'I know.' Conor spoke softly, looking at the carpet between his feet. 'I know it's important to you.'

'It's important to *us*,' she corrected herself.

He made no move to echo her sentiment. *It's important to* us, *isn't it?* was a question she didn't dare ask in case he gave an answer she didn't like. The feeling in the room seemed to palpably shift, as though their sadness had the power to increase the gravity.

I have to let this month go, she thought. Though every month counted, especially at her age. *There's always next month*, she tried to reassure herself silently.

Annie buttoned up her dress again and knelt down in front of him, ducking her head to try and catch his eye. 'It's all good, Conor, there's always next month and then, ya know, there's options.' Her false brightness died in the heavy atmosphere around them.

'No, Annie, you don't understand.' He looked distressed, and Annie felt cold fear slice through her. He shook his head. 'I'm not doing any of this. I don't want to do IVF. I don't know how to say this … I don't want to have a baby with you anymore. I don't want to be …' He faltered and finally looked up at her. 'I don't want to be together anymore.'

Something cracked in Annie then. She actually felt herself break –

a fissure beginning in her heart and running down into her stomach. She couldn't seem to fill her lungs.

'I'm sorry, Annie.' Conor sounded distraught. 'But all this has changed us, you can't pretend it hasn't.'

Despite the pain in her chest and the airless choke of sudden sadness, the moment had a strange inevitability about it. This inevitability settled down around her like a shroud. It was as though she'd seen this conversation play out already somewhere deep in her subconscious during long nights awake and alone in the dark. The thoughts of this moment had even scurried beneath the surface of her busy daytime thoughts.

She moved to sit beside Conor on the bed, her limbs suddenly leaden. She couldn't summon words, perhaps because at the same time as her sadness was rising, so too was a thrumming rage.

'Annie?' Conor was tentative. 'Please say something.' He took her right hand and Annie stared down dispassionately. He continued, 'You had to know this was coming. I thought you'd maybe be the one to say it first.'

At this, Annie withdrew her hand. 'No, Conor. You don't get to act like this is mutual. You don't get to put this back on me.' She kept her voice even. She was not a scene-maker, never had been. And after all the indignity of the last year when she'd practically had to beg him to have sex with her every month, she wasn't going to stoop any lower, she wasn't going to scream and cry. If this was truly it for them, she was walking away with her back straight and some modicum of composure.

Conor was now twisting his hands awkwardly in his lap. 'I'm sorry, Annie, I really am. I didn't do this … deliberately. I swear.

When we started, a family with you was all I wanted but this thing has taken over every part of our relationship … We're different people now. I've been trying to figure out how to say it …'

Annie shook her head. 'You've wasted so much of my time. You were the one putting it off.'

Conor dropped his head to his hands. 'But it's been so bad between us, you can't deny that. What would a baby have done to us? Look at the state of our friends' marriages. Babies are renowned for making things *more* challenging, not fixing things.'

'So we needed to be fixed?'

We did. The thought prodded at her even though she didn't want to accept it. *We did, we did, we did* went the sorry refrain.

'And what?' Annie spoke as calmly as she could. 'Now it's too late to be fixed?'

'We've both changed.' He made to reach out to her again and Annie swerved, evading his touch. She stood and backed away from him.

'I am going to be forty-one this year, Conor. This … what you're doing here … this will ruin my life. You realise that. I will probably never have a baby now. You're taking that away from me.'

'Annie, listen to what you're saying. If that is your immediate thought here, then it's true. You don't want to be with me anymore. You only care about what I can give you. And that makes me feel like shit and has done for a long time now. All you think of is how hard it's been for you but you've never once thought about what it must be like for me. What it's like to know that all you are is a means to an end in someone else's grand plan.'

His words pierced Annie – there was truth in this statement, she couldn't pretend otherwise. He was right, and in a bid to turn away from this unpleasant truth she moved to the wardrobe and pulled out her suitcase, which was still half-full.

'Annie, don't pack.' Conor held up his hands. 'I should be the one to go. Look, Ollie and I talked on the ride back tonight and we're going to stay on the yacht for the rest of the trip.'

Annie wheeled around. 'You can't just call it quits on a twenty-year relationship in one fifteen-minute conversation, Conor. We have a life together. We're basically, for all intents and purposes, married. We have a home together.' She was aware her calm facade was crumbling and she consciously tried to slow her breathing.

'I know that, Annie. I'm sorry. I really am. It's just … how I feel.'

How could she argue with that? You couldn't talk someone back into loving you.

'Well, I wish you had figured out how you *felt* at literally any time before this.'

He nodded silently, causing Annie's rage to rev up. 'God, you're being so fucking *fine* about this. How long have you been planning to break up? Because your timing is frankly *baffling*. We're on a goddamn holiday.'

'I know.' He had the decency to look shame-faced. 'I had thought that we would talk it out when we got back. I didn't realise that you were going to be ovulating. And trying to … you know … *try*.'

'It's on the shared calendar,' she snapped. 'If you had ever bothered to engage with the process, you'd know this.'

He looked pained as he pinched the bridge of his nose, a gesture of his that Annie had always felt looked somewhat priggish. *Won't have to look at* that *anymore in my new barren future*, she thought bitterly.

He sighed and shook his head. 'It's 2 a.m. I think we should get some rest. Tomorrow's going to be hell, what with Ollie and Clara.'

'And us,' Annie said flatly.

'And … us,' he echoed quietly.

'Can't wait for breakfast,' she said sarcastically.

'Em, we might try to get out of here by then. Brody said he'd send a boat for us as early as possible to bring us out to the yacht.'

Annie exhaled sharply. 'You have it all figured out. No mess, no fuss. Nothing sticks to you. You're Teflon, aren't you?'

'It's not like that, Annie. I wouldn't be leaving if I didn't have to. I'm going so Ollie isn't on his own. I don't want you and I to hate each other. We've grown up together. All of us have. We've all been friends for so long.'

She laughed sourly. 'As if that'll be the case after all this. We'll be working out joint custody of our friends.'

'We could still all be friends after a while,' he ventured, sounding as unconvinced as she felt. He moved to the wardrobe and retrieved his bag.

'All packed, I see.' Annie glared.

Ignoring this, Conor inched towards the door. 'I'm going to go up to Ollie. We agreed I'd crash on the sofa in his room.'

'Nighty-night. Great fucking talk.'

Conor winced and then slipped quickly out the door, awkwardly catching the bag in the frame as he went.

Annie stared at the peculiar blankness of a door that had just closed behind a person who was walking out of your life. She lay down on the bed and inhaled and exhaled and tried to sort through the fevered churn of anger and sorrow raging inside her.

It was hard to admit it, but what Conor had said was true – their relationship *was* fucked if her overriding thought above all else at that moment was about the baby that he was robbing her of.

She closed her eyes as tears began to slide down her cheeks. *I have been robbed*, she thought. It wasn't an attempt to comfort herself but a bid to make what had just happened feel real. Robbed was exactly how she felt, like a house ransacked and cleared out – the only things remaining were still and empty rooms where the ghosts of her hopes and beautiful imagined life hovered, vaporous and now utterly and completely impossible to hold onto.

The finality of it all was crushing.

CHAPTER 11

Clara woke up in Maggie's bed facing the wall. She could sense rather than see her friend behind her, scrolling. For a brief moment, she registered nothing else but the pristine brightness of the room. And then it all flooded in – Ollie's fury, the mortifying reckoning that had played out in full view of all their friends and, worst of all, the foreign feeling of the young guy's tongue in her mouth. *Why, why, why? Clara, you dumb bitch.*

She rolled towards Maggie and prepared to put a brave face on things. God, what were the girls thinking? And Fionn and Conor? Probably that she was a monster and that it served her right that she'd been so utterly, wretchedly wrong.

The image of Ollie kissing a faceless woman came at her, accompanied by a nauseating anxiety. She *would* be devastated. She *had* been devastated when she thought that *was* the case. Underneath all her aggrieved bravado, she'd felt so small, as though she'd been discarded. *Ollie feels like that right now*, she thought. *I have to talk to him.*

'Morning.' She massaged her head, where a headache hammered mercilessly. 'Thanks for subletting Fionn's side of the bed.'

'Ah, yes, well, I'd love to tell you that you're a better bedmate than he is but you've been snoring and you reek of booze.' She didn't sound mad, thank God.

Clara pushed herself up to lean against the headboard. 'I'm sorry about the snoring. It drives Ollie insane at home ...' She trailed off. With the mention of their home, the scale of what she'd done overwhelmed her all over again. What was going to happen when they got back?

Maggie was silent, perhaps thinking the same thing.

'Guess my snoring isn't the worst thing about me anymore ...' Clara said quietly.

'Ah, Clara,' Maggie murmured gently.

Clara chewed on the inside of her cheek. 'I know I don't really have much of a leg to stand on but there was a lot going on in my head yesterday. It was ... kind of a misunderstanding, like?'

'I know. You weren't in a good place,' Maggie agreed, though Clara felt certain there was more Maggie had to say on the matter that she was withholding.

'I only got the guy to kiss me as payback. It's not like I fancied him.' Even though Clara knew, with the spectre of the blind item hovering, that Maggie was probably not the audience for a speech on why kissing someone else could be in some way justified, she couldn't help but continue. 'I know Annie said it was homophobic or whatever to say a gay guy didn't count but I swear I actually don't think I'd take it seriously if Ollie scored a lesbian ...' She paused, doubtful. 'Well ... maybe ...?'

Maggie sighed. 'My advice would be to skip that argument when you have your conversation with Ollie. I don't know if you should be trying to get out of this based on a technicality. A homophobic one or otherwise, you're in morally dubious territory.'

Maggie stood and pulled on a beautiful kimono that looked like hand-painted silk, and Clara struggled to her feet as well. 'I suppose you're right ... you don't want to be a cheater *and* a homophobe ...' She tried to laugh but trailed off. 'Best abandon the gay-guy argument.' She began straightening the duvet.

'You don't have to make the bed, Clara, someone will be in.'

'Oh yeah ...' Clara straightened up and fixed the dress she was still wearing from the night before. She hadn't dared go back to her room on the way to Maggie's in the wee hours of the morning. She found her phone and checked the time. Only 7.30 a.m. She needed to go to Ollie but she also needed to not be dressed like someone just off a bender and a one-night stand. 'Can I borrow something to wear, Maggie?'

'Yeah, anything.' Maggie indicated the clothes rail. 'Though they'll probably be too big.'

'Oh.' Clara faltered. What was she talking about? They were pretty close in size. 'I doubt it, Mags. If anything, they'll be too small.' She joined Maggie at the rail and started flicking through the hangers.

Maggie pulled out a dark green sleeveless jersey maxi dress with a high neck. 'This is nice? I dunno why ... but I feel like you should go demure. The last mention of your boobs was some guy admiring them ...'

They both laughed in spite of everything.

A knock on the door interrupted them then and Annie appeared.

'I cannot believe anyone has found a reason to laugh this morning.' She shut the door behind her, peering around the living room and into the bedroom. 'Fionn's not here?'

'No,' Maggie replied. 'He stayed over in the shack. He'll be back at some stage.'

Clara watched Maggie, trying to discern how she was really feeling about this. Maggie could be very hard to read.

'Oh-kay.' Annie frowned. 'Was that the plan?'

'It became the plan,' Maggie replied firmly.

'Ah.' Annie crawled onto the rattan sofa nearest the window. 'So? What's so funny? Did you speak to Ollie, Clara?'

'Not yet.' Clara concentrated on getting Maggie's dress on. 'Nothing is funny. We were laughing in an "oh everything's apocalyptically fucked" kinda way, not a "ha-ha" way.'

'Gotcha. I relate,' Annie said flatly. She was staring at the ceiling above, where the sunlight seemed to dance as the curtains behind her stirred in the breeze. 'Does everything being fucked actually feel worse in a really idyllic setting or is that just me?'

'What's happened to *you*?' Clara tucked her bra straps under the shoulders of the dress, noticing that Annie was so drawn even her lips seemed pale and bloodless.

'I didn't sleep. It's …' She trailed off. She closed her eyes but Clara could see pearls of tears gathering on her lashes.

Clara looked at Maggie for answers but it was clear from her face she had no idea what Annie was talking about.

'Did something happen with Conor?' Maggie asked.

A brisk knock startled them all and they instantly froze.

'Oh God,' Maggie whispered. 'Please let it be one of the staff.' She hurried to the door.

Even amid the taut atmosphere in the room, Clara snagged on Maggie's phrase. *The staff.* Truly, what had happened to her friend?

Maggie opened the bedroom door a crack and peered through. 'Ollie!' Maggie said brightly. 'Hi! Hi!' She could not have sounded more bizarre, but Clara knew Maggie was speaking loudly to alert her and give her a minute to gather herself.

'Hi, Maggie,' Ollie replied stiffly. 'Can you tell Clara that if she wants to have an actual conversation like an *adult*, I'll be in our room packing for the next half an hour. We're leaving at half eight.'

'Right, okay ...' Maggie started to reply but from the way her words trailed into silence, Clara deduced that Ollie had already walked off.

Clara looked at Annie. 'Who's "we"? Him and Conor? They're *both* leaving?'

Annie swept her fingers under her eyes, catching her tears. She nodded.

'What the fuck.' Clara couldn't believe it. 'I know Ollie's pissed off, but like ... leaving?' She couldn't find words. Mainly because she didn't quite know *how* she was feeling. Stupid, yes. Ashamed. But also now ... slightly indignant? 'He's not *completely* blameless here,' Clara said, ignoring the look Maggie threw to Annie. 'I know I kissed some guy but I had reason ...'

Maggie scrunched up her face. 'Oh God. Good luck justifying it, Clara.'

'Don't be a bitch, Maggie,' Clara volleyed back, and immediately regretted it.

'Guys, stop.' Annie pulled herself up. 'We're all supporting each other here,' she said firmly.

Clara nodded vigorously. 'I'm sorry.' She moved to stand in front of Maggie. 'You're not a bitch, *I'm* a bitch. I know I am. I was a train wreck yesterday.'

Maggie sighed. 'You better go talk him down, Clara.' She sat down beside Annie. 'This is salvageable. It has to be. It'd be insane of him to ... you know ... do something permanent.'

Clara grimaced. 'He wouldn't, he's just going to lecture me, I'd say. I bloody hope.' She glanced at Annie. 'Why is Conor going? What's happened?'

'We broke up,' Annie replied heavily. 'He doesn't want to do the baby thing anymore. Doesn't want *me* anymore.'

'*What?*' Clara was stunned as Annie nodded silently. Clara couldn't believe it. She tried to imagine the shape of the group if Annie and Conor were breaking up. Even Fionn becoming a household name and star of fifty-foot billboards hadn't fractured them. But Annie and Conor separating? Things would change, of that there was no doubt. The group would probably split off into two camps, Camp Annie and Camp Conor.

The same could happen with me and Ollie, she thought, with renewed panic.

'Annie,' Maggie turned to her, 'are you sure? This can't be true. You guys are such a good couple. It's probably just the stress of trying for the baby. That happens to couples. Please let me and Fionn pay for the IVF. We *want* to.'

Annie shrugged her off. 'Maggie,' there was an edge to her voice, 'money doesn't fix everything for everyone, you know.'

'Gals, we can't turn on each other, remember?' Clara interrupted. 'The guys are the shits here. Conor's a youth-stealer, Ollie's making a big to-do about nothing and Fionn has already disappeared two seconds into the supposed family holiday.'

'Clara!' Maggie sounded furious. 'Fionn is *working*.'

Clara rolled her eyes, which she could immediately see from her friend's face was not the thing to do.

Annie stood up. 'Clara, your peace-making skills need work.' She shook her head, trying to turn her towards the door. 'Go talk to Ollie.'

'So you two can bitch about me when I'm gone?'

'Yes, probably,' Maggie said mildly.

'Okay, I deserve it, I know.' Clara obediently gathered up her shoes, her headache intensifying as she bent over. 'The guys won't leave.' Clara made an effort to sound convincing. 'They won't.'

Annie gave a morose shrug. 'I can't imagine coming back from the conversation we had last night.'

Clara watched Maggie pull Annie into a hug as she shut the door.

She made her way along the corridor. *They won't leave. They won't. It'd be stupid. This is all fixable. They won't leave.*

Outside her bedroom she paused, debating whether to knock or just walk in, when the door swung open right in front of her. Ollie stood motionless, his expression hard to read.

'Hi,' said Clara.

'Hi.' Ollie was terse as he turned and walked back into the room.

This, Clara knew, could go either way. Ollie was a patient man and everyone who knew him would say he was extremely laid-back. Affable to a fault. But Clara's pet theory was that often the super chill people were the real psychopaths – they were the very people who could go postal if the right provocation came along.

Ollie had a bad mood about once a year and, my God, could the man pull a strop.

'So ...' Clara shut the door behind her. Logically she knew she should go the abject apologising route but she was starting to find his histrionics a bit dumb. 'Annie says you and Conor are leaving. Are you really storming off over this?'

Ollie remained with his back to her but she detected tension rippling across his shoulders. 'As if you wouldn't throw a complete and utter tantrum if I went and cheated on you.' His voice was icy.

'Come on, Ollie. It was nothing.' This was not the way to de-escalate, but also it was impossible to not defend herself. 'It was a misunderstanding. A misunderstanding that wouldn't have happened if you hadn't been *lying* to me.'

Ollie said nothing, shaking his head slowly from side to side. Clara put her hands on her hips, a feeling of mutiny starting to completely overtake the anxiety of earlier. The silence between them stretched. *I am not speaking first*, she told herself, already knowing that she probably would.

'C'mon, Ollie,' she blurted.

Goddamn it. He was so much better at rowing than her. Which was weird, seeing as how he so rarely did it. Maybe all those months of being the 'cool', 'sound' guy he was actually honing his fighting skills.

'Do not "c'mon Ollie" me. You fucking cheated on me *yesterday*.' He turned, scowling. Clara stilled at the sight of him. This was not an Ollie that she remotely recognised. He looked furious and she found herself paralysed with a sudden cold fear that this was no regular fight.

He began to pace as she continued to stand stock still, her limbs locked.

'Did you really not expect me to have a feeling about my wife cheating on me?'

'It was a kiss, Ollie.'

He ignored her. 'Scoring someone a few miles away from where I was playing with our *children*.'

Unmistakable disgust stirred through the fury on his face, and Clara's indignation flared once more.

'How dare you bring the boys—'

'How dare I?' Ollie barked bitterly. 'You are something else, Clara, do you know that? You couldn't just come and talk to me. You have to be the main character of every situation. It's always a drama. You go off and get absolutely plastered with the work crowd—'

'Jesus, this again? That happened once! Let it go. I have to blow off steam. Being a mother is relentless.'

'So is being a father. That's having a family, Clara. And it's especially hard when your co-parent acts like her family is some big imposition.'

'I do not. That is so fucking unfair.' She crossed her arms. 'You know, you're pretty checked out at times. Always bet into your phone—'

Ollie rolled his eyes. 'I work for myself. I have to be responsive. It's hard work.'

'I work hard too. I work so fucking hard for our family. At least you get to do a job you actually like.'

'I've never stopped you from changing jobs.'

'Money stops me from changing jobs, Ollie. Money you're spending on HardBodies.ie.'

'You spend money too, Clara. The packages are always arriving. Do you actually need more clothes?'

'I buy a few bits off Depop here and there, for fuck sake. What about all your sneaking around? Am I really such a bitch that you couldn't tell me that you'd taken up running? "Oh my horrible wife".' She put on a particularly cruel version of Ollie's voice. '"She's such a weapon, she won't let me do my marathon." Making me out to your friend to be some control-freak-wife stereotype.'

'You *told* Annie and Maggie that I was a doormat. A *doormat*,' he spat.

'I did not.'

She totally did, she remembered the conversation. It was about six months before and she had specifically *told* Annie to not mention it to Conor.

Ollie was shaking his head. 'I know you did. Annie told Conor, who told me.'

I will kill Annie, she thought. Although being honest, Clara had told Ollie plenty of things Annie'd said to *her* about Conor. What else did people in long-term relationships talk about other than the dreariness of their friends' long-term relationships?

'It was a *compliment*, Ollie. You're missing key context.' Clara glared at him. 'I was saying you're really good at sex which is surprising cuz you have such a doormat demeanour. That was all.'

'Fuck. You.' He pointed at her. 'I am not up for being treated like a joke by you anymore.'

'Ugh, you are being such a little bitch about this.' Clara stalked to the bedroom door. 'Can you just cop on so we can get back to the holiday?'

'No, Clara.' His voice was steely.

She ignored this and pulled open the door. 'I'm going to get the boys up.'

'The kids are already up and down at breakfast. If you'd cared to check, you'd know this.'

Clara felt the dam that had barely been shoring up her anger break. Her drive to make peace evaporated in an instant and she screamed the next words, not giving a shit who heard.

'Stop acting like I'm some neglectful, part-time mother. I do everything for this family.'

'So do I,' Ollie screamed back.

'What about when you're sneaking off to do four-hour runs?'

'You mean my training runs that I've been doing in the *dead of night* so as not to disappear from doing my bit of the parenting? And sometimes your bit of the parenting too when you go off to Annie's for "a couple of wines" and then end up sleeping on their couch.'

'Don't be so *sanctimonious*.' Clara threw the word like a punch. 'After women have kids, all their hobbies are housebound hobbies like *knitting* and *online yoga challenges*. Shit that they can do with kids stepping on their faces. After men have kids, you know what they do? They take up golf and running and cycling. Every sport that requires a minimum of six hours out of the house.'

'You're such an exaggerator,' Ollie scoffed. 'I'm trying to have one thing to keep my mental health from disintegrating. You know what I hate about you, Clara? You're so self-obsessed. You can only see how this is affecting you. As always,' he finished, exhaling roughly through flared nostrils.

You know what I hate about you ...

That truly stung. She had never considered that Ollie might hate something about her. Even when she thought that he might be cheating, she'd been so angry and felt so rejected, but she hadn't thought that it was because he *hated* something about her.

'Well, you know what I hate about you?' She looked across at him with as much contempt as she could summon. 'You act like the cool guy. You love everyone thinking you're so chill but you're actually so self-righteous. Watching packages arriving. Judging me any time I even slightly cut loose and get a teensy bit messy. Fuck you. How dare you judge me.'

Clara shook her head, fending off a wave of exhaustion that was suddenly bearing down on her, no doubt from the speeding adrenaline that had just fuelled the worst fight she and Ollie'd ever had.

Ollie said nothing and she said nothing. She was unsure how you wrapped up a conversation where each person had hurled the most hurtful things they could think of at the other. She hadn't realised how much resentment was buried in their marriage.

Finally, Ollie spoke: 'Well, thanks for fucking up the entire holiday. I'll be sorting out seeing the kids while we're staying on the yacht. Brody said he could arrange handovers.'

'What are you trying to do, Ollie, skip straight to joint custody? Because that's not how this works.'

'Only *you* would cheat and then make it a me-problem,' Ollie roared.

'I fucking thought *you* were *cheating.*' Clara's voice rose to match his. 'And it is a *you* problem because I was semi-right. You *were* sneaking around and lying to me. And about something so *stupid*, and that's nearly worse. And the way you're acting right now about this dumb drunken kiss is not even about me at all. This is all your unresolved shit about what your father did. You should really think about dealing with that.'

Ollie snatched up his suitcase and stormed past her to the door, banging it shut behind him.

Clara dragged herself to the sofa by the window. Did he really have unresolved issues about his father? Or was she deliberately deflecting from the issues she obviously hadn't been taking seriously between them? Feeling irritated with your other half when it came to parenting was normal. But she had kind of assumed it was just *her* irritated with *him*. She hadn't considered that he was getting so pissed with her.

CHAPTER 12

Maggie sat at the table at the edge of the deck tapping into her family group chat, which had been kept abreast of all the drama as the holiday spectacularly unravelled over the last two days.

> *Maggie: Morale is so crap, they've all decided to go home early.*

Of course, she hadn't mentioned to her family that Fionn was also M.I.A. It was bad enough that the girls had witnessed their shaky reunion, she didn't want her family worrying about them. She continued to type.

> *Maggie: It's 9 a.m. and is it bad that I am literally counting the hours till they all leave tomorrow? To say things have SOURED. I am literally looking out at the boat moored 30 feet from the beach where Ollie and Conor have stayed for the last two days.*

She glanced back at the house, where she could hear Clara and one of the nannies grappling with the boys. Annie, she knew, was down in the gym. She ran a finger through the leftover maple syrup on her plate and licked it, watching 'Donal typing' at the top of the screen.

Donal: No sympathy for the Rich Lady on her private deck.

She smiled to herself and wiped her fingers to type back.

Maggie: You're such a little bitch.

Dad: Language.

Emer: Being rich is very hard on Maggie, Donal ... She has to spend time with her povvo friends. Well, until she ships them off early from the 'vacay'.

Maggie: Shut up both of you. I know you're joking but it's not funny. I begged the girls to stay but they're insisting they go home. Relationships imploding are a bad vibe on a holiday.

Mum: This is all very sad, Maggie. The poor girls. I keep meaning to say I've put the order in for Donal's birthday cake. Aubergine emoji-shaped as requested. They just need a confirmation of the delivery date. They can do day of the party or day before?

Maggie: Yup, sorry, meant to text. So Friday 25th July is the party. I'll be arriving in Dublin the day before so if they could drop it to the house then, on the 24th?

'Morning!' Brody had just appeared at the bottom of the stairs at the other side of the deck. He started up and Maggie swiftly nudged the syrup-streaked plates over to the other side of the table.

She turned her phone face down and looked up at him. 'I haven't been able to reach Fionn.' She sat back watching Brody's smooth, bland smile that revealed exactly nothing.

'Oh?' He took a seat at the table and within seconds one of the waitstaff materialised. Brody ordered a coffee and sat back, crossing his legs.

'Have you spoken to him?' Maggie made a concerted effort to not sound furious.

'Well, we've had the occasional check-in, just keeping him up to speed on the inbox.'

Brody's coffee arrived and Maggie took this moment, as the server cleared a few plates, to try to calm down. If Brody ever rolled on them and became a 'source close to the family' in *People* magazine, she didn't want him making her out to be the crabby, pathetic wife always on the outside of Fionn's life.

'Have you updated him on the fact that our friends are having a cold war? And are leaving early? Is he coming back for the party tonight? The party he's throwing?'

Brody raised a hand in what he apparently considered to be a calming gesture. 'Maggie, I am here right now to collect the twins at his request. He wants them to come out to see the dune shacks and then he's coming straight back for the party!'

'I suppose his need for "total isolation" was just total isolation from me,' Maggie sniffed, and then rose, to communicate to Brody that she was keen for him to go. She wanted to go to her room.

She'd been trying so hard to resist the old urges but once the thought had wormed into her head when Fionn left her in the shadow of the house the other night, it'd become like a parasite. It felt almost inevitable that she would eventually succumb. She just wanted to feel some relief from the seething churn of emotions the holiday had stirred up.

It was okay. She'd had little stretches of returning to the old habits over the years and had always been fine again. It wouldn't become compulsive; she knew better than to let it.

She moved towards the doors. After eating so much she was eager to be rid of it.

Brody threw up his hands, exasperated. 'Maggie! It's a beautiful day. We are having a star-studded party tonight! This is all supposed to be *fun*.'

'Uh-huh. He didn't tell me he wanted to bring the twins to the shack. What if I had a plan for the girls? I haven't even gotten them up yet.'

Brody shook his head. 'I updated the itinerary last night, so the childcare staff know I'm picking them up. You should have received an alert that the schedule had been altered.'

'Brody, I'm not checking my emails.'

'Now, Maggie, we've talked about this. You do have to keep up with it all – it's a moveable feast!' Brody grinned broadly as though this was all part of the fun of being an A-list family, instead of it feeling vaguely dystopian. 'I also spoke to Ollie and Conor and they're going to collect Ollie's kids for a last trip out in the boat.'

'Sure, *he* texted last night,' Maggie said pointedly. 'Clara's getting them ready.'

'Great!' Brody ignored her obvious sullenness and pulled out his phone. 'I'll let them know.'

Maggie left him sitting there and pulled open the doors. The volume of Clara's boys leapt up as she entered. She couldn't quite make out the words but somewhere beneath her feet she could hear Clara speaking in a placating tone and the shrieks of hyper kids with no intention of doing what they were told.

I should go down, Maggie thought. *Help Clara. Get Dodi and Essie.* But the feeling of her shorts digging into her stomach and the sense of rising pressure in her chest drove her upstairs instead. *I'll be quick. The nanny will give the girls to Brody and they'll be so excited to see Fionn, they won't notice that they haven't even seen me.* She shoved the guilt down and hurried upstairs, relieved to make it to her room without encountering anyone.

On the floor of the bathroom, her knees complained as she knelt on the hard tiles. She leaned forward over the bowl. In the silence, her breathing echoed.

She paused.

Don't do this. The thought was just a feeble whisper compared with the roaring urge to rid herself of her mistakes at breakfast.

It's just once. I just shouldn't have had quite so much. If I do this, then it's a clean slate and no more from now on. It'll be easier back in LA.

In LA, Betty cooked for them and she found it easier to keep on track. In LA, she hardly ever went out, so there was nothing to interfere with her strict food regimen. At the beginning, Fionn tried to bring her to all the industry parties but she'd come to loathe them. Around the stars, it was like the no-eating Olympics. Canapés and dessert tables went entirely untouched.

Now on the cold floor, she breathed deeply and started the routine that was old but instantly familiar. After a few seconds, her stomach complied. Her body spasmed painfully but then the discomfort was swiftly replaced with a reassuring emptiness. She got to her feet a little shakily and cleaned up. She applied some tinted moisturiser. She examined her eyes, which were a bit bloodshot from her exertions. She thought back to the eye drops she used to use.

I could order some online. The thought rose as if independent of her.

No, this is not becoming a regular thing, she reminded herself. *This is a one-off, just to combat the holiday eating. A few more days and then it's back to good habits. Egg-white omelettes and almonds in my handbag.*

She gave the bathroom one last once-over and sprayed some perfume. The ornate glass bottle clattered a little as she returned it to the marble counter. She was unsteady. A bit out of practice. How long had it been? Definitely a few years at this stage. She'd had a bit of a bad phase when the twins were toddlers and her body had still felt like a stranger's from pregnancy and childbirth.

She walked through the bedroom, avoiding the full-length mirror, and headed back down the stairs. At the bottom, she hesitated and peered cautiously around to the right through the lounge area and out the doors to the deck. Brody was gone and with him, presumably, her daughters. Maggie could see Clara waving the kids off at the edge of the deck while Annie sat eating at the table. Maggie checked her phone; it was coming up to 10 a.m.

I could order more waffles. They don't know I already ate.

She straightened and shook the thought away. But it prodded at her.

This could be my last chance of the day to eat much. For the rest of the day she'd be with Annie and Clara. She didn't want to be stuffing her face with them. When she was in one of her phases, eating with other people was almost a nuisance. It was irritating trying to act normal around food – she just wanted to go at it in private.

If it's a different server from earlier, I'll order more, she decided. She glanced back up the stairs behind her. *I can always …*

Right at that moment, a young girl in pressed shorts and a collared T-shirt appeared carrying plates of fruit and yogurt. It was a different server than earlier.

'Hi!' Maggie held up a hand to stop her.

'Hi, ma'am.' The girl beamed. 'Are you having a nice day so far?'

'Yes, eh, thank you.' Maggie threw a glance back to the deck, then turned back to the young girl. 'Could I order waffles and bacon, please.'

'Of course, no problem. I'll get that for you right away.'

'Also …' Maggie paused.

She tried to pull back from the new idea that had just struck her but found that the words kept coming: 'I think my girls are getting hungry between meals. Do you think one of the staff could go to the market and pick up a big bag of snacks for them? Just chips and cookies. A few different candy bars. That kind of thing. And put them in my room?'

Maggie knew Fionn would be back later but she'd have time to intercept the stuff and put it away before then.

'Absolutely.'

'Thanks,' Maggie murmured, while at the same time thinking, *What am I doing?*

I just want it for tonight. It'll help with the party. Back to normal then, she silently resolved.

She imagined herself escaping upstairs later while the party carried on below. She could almost feel the monumental release that would come with the binge. She felt a swell of anxiety but also delicious anticipation. The satisfaction of churning through all that food, the comforting numbness that would follow. She deliberately steered her mind away from any thoughts of the self-loathing that would also inevitably follow.

The other thing will take care of that, she reminded herself. That was the beauty of the system. It was all like it never even happened.

The server continued out to the deck and Maggie followed behind, feeling buoyed by her plan.

Clara had joined Annie at the table. They both had a slightly haunted look to them.

'Did I miss Ollie and Conor?' Maggie asked, airily sitting down and tugging at the waistband of her shorts. They still felt tight. *I am going to seriously take myself in hand when we get back.* She poured a cup of coffee from the steel carafe and helped the server make space for the food she was carrying.

'You missed the handover,' Clara replied. 'And what must've been record-breaking levels of awkwardness.'

'Conor looked at me like I might attack him and syphon off some of his sperm any minute,' Annie remarked.

'Ollie didn't look at me at all.' Clara poked at her smoked salmon with her fork.

'I can't believe we all have to get on a plane together tomorrow.' She sighed.

'Why don't you two at least swap seats and that way you're each sitting with the other's ex?' Maggie suggested.

'Ollie's not my ex,' Clara yelped. 'Not yet, at least.' She dropped her head into her hands. 'God, I actually don't know what's going to happen, though. He's so angry.'

Maggie's waffles and bacon arrived and she paused, wondering if tucking in was a bit insensitive at that moment.

Annie caught Maggie's hesitation and instructed her to eat. 'If you wait to eat until our relationships are unfucked, you'll be waiting for a very long time.'

Clara popped a forkful of eggs into her mouth and chewed morosely.

After a subdued breakfast, they decamped to the beach and debated what time it would be acceptable to start drinking.

'Maybe never for me,' Clara said sadly. 'I should probably be making more of an effort to be contrite. Even though I swear if he doesn't stop being so holier-than-thou, one of us is going to have to move into the car when we get home.'

'I've decided I'll be drinking heavily today,' Annie announced from under the shade of the large canvas umbrella. 'It is literally the only upside of not trying for a baby anymore. Instead of a baby, I'll be welcoming a beautiful, bouncing eight-pound bottle of vodka.'

Maggie and Clara laughed tentatively.

'Too soon for us to be laughing at this?' Clara asked Annie, who shrugged.

Maggie felt the buzz of her phone on the towel beside her. She picked it up and rolled onto her stomach. She shaded her eyes to see the screen. It was a Google notification. She would never be telling the girls that she'd set up notifications for the keywords 'Finn + Strong + Wife'. She tapped the link that had come up.

SPOTTED: Finn Strong's Wife Bravely Bares All On Vacation While Husband Cosies Up To Reclusive Director.

Maggie swallowed with some effort. Her throat had immediately clenched. How did the paps get her without her noticing? She continued to scroll down, despite the swelling dread in her chest. She did *not* want to see these pictures, but she also had to see them. She had to know how bad it was.

And there she was 'bravely baring all' as she bent to apply sun block to Essie. The rolls, the billowing flab of her upper arms, her cellulite. Maggie sucked in a breath and scrolled further. A few pictures down were shots of Fionn and Edwin Ensel walking together in the dunes, deep in conversation.

Why in the fuck did they put her front and centre in this article? *I'm a nobody here.*

She knew the answer, though. There was one thing that was more clickable than movie stars, and that was women's bodies on display, particularly ones considered anything less than perfect. Shaming women even when it was packaged up as some warped feminist body positivity was just irresistible. She could see the comments section was teeming with the thoughts and input of the people who avidly consumed these things. She would not be reading those comments. It took everything but, thankfully, a modicum of sense prevailed. She clicked out of the article.

She rolled over and sat up to pull on her sleeveless linen dress. She scanned the beach in both directions and swivelled to check the dunes behind. Scattered all around them, other holidaymakers were grouped around colourful parasols, but she couldn't see anyone who looked like they were wielding a zoom-lens camera. Of course other tourists could've supplied the pictures. This had happened before with that crowd-sourced blind item Instagram account. Pictures of Fionn bringing Dodi to the ER for a broken finger had once surfaced and the internet people had lost their minds about what an 'amazing' dad Finn Strong was. Sheesh, the bar was on the floor for men. Maggie reached for the top that matched her dress, to cover her arms.

'Are you getting dressed?' Annie asked her.

'No, just putting this on, just chilly.'

'Chilly?' Clara's eyes remained closed. 'Are you joking? It's boiling!'

'Ha. Yes, I know. Sorry, I meant covering up for the sun. I don't want to look like a bloated boiled ham at this party tonight.'

'You could never,' Clara said firmly. 'Okay, distract us with some of the celebs who are coming tonight so I can mentally prepare myself for not fawning too hard.'

'Well, there's the Coen brothers, obviously. Maybe Penélope and Javier ...'

'Oh it's just "Penélope and Javier", is it?' Annie frisbeed her hat over, teasing.

The sun had dropped to just above the horizon when Maggie got back to her room to change. It was just gone 7 p.m. According to

Brody, Fionn would be there at 8 p.m. He'd probably arrive at about the same time as the other guests. The snacks Maggie asked for had been laid out neatly on the coffee table and she swiftly gathered them into her suitcase which she transferred to the floor of her closet. She surveyed the haul. Pretty good. Doritos, Cheetos, Butterfingers, Snickers. She picked up the share-size bag of peanut M&Ms and pinched a corner to tear it open. Crouching by the wardrobe doors, she ate a big handful, and then another and another. The crunching down over and over again was so immensely satisfying, and a deep sense of calm took over her mind.

I'll just have one bag and that way I won't be eating at the party. The thoughts of eating in front of all the tiny, doll-like starlets did not appeal. However, in what felt like seconds, the bag was empty and she'd started in on the second one. As she shoved the food into her mouth, a force seemed to take over, pushing her to eat more and more.

She remembered this feeling well. There came a point in every binge when something else would assume control and she didn't even feel like it was her doing it anymore. It wouldn't even matter if she liked what she was eating, it was just out of her hands somehow.

She opened more packets. Reese's Peanut Butter Cups and then Doritos. She wiped her hands on the floor to get rid of the orange dust from the chips. She worked at a Snickers, her jaws feeling oddly fatigued, though when she surveyed the amount of wrappers when she finally stopped, it made sense. She felt a straining from inside and the sensation that the last of the food was piled right up to the back of her throat. She gathered all the rubbish and stuffed it in a zip compartment of her bag. She'd go for a walk tomorrow and find a public bin.

She checked the time and realised with a dull shock that she'd been eating for twenty minutes straight. Fionn would be here soon. She needed to get on with the routine before he came barrelling in on her. She headed to the bathroom. She only had half an hour but she was going to have a shower right after she was finished and was confident the smell of the soap and shampoo would mask any lingering odour.

CHAPTER 13

Annie, tugging at the dress she was now convinced was too short, made her way to Maggie's room twenty minutes before the first party guests were due to arrive. Her phone was pressed to her ear to listen to a voicy from Rachel. Annie had only now had the energy to give her the update. For the first two days, Annie was just grateful to be with Clara and Maggie who didn't need any explanation – they already knew every scrap of Annie and Conor's life to date. But she needed to tell Rachel because she knew when she got home, it'd be Rachel helping her pick up the pieces more than anyone.

Jesus, darl. Even just Rachel's voice soothed Annie a little. *I am so sorry this has happened. I really don't know what to say. I can think of some things that'd probably be really bad to say. Like ... Conor's an idiot. And a shit. And, I dunno, is there some comfort in not having gotten pregnant with him after all? If he's changed so much? Is any of this remotely comforting to hear? I'm sorry if I am making you feel worse. Listen, anything you need at all, please tell me.*

Annie stopped outside Maggie's room to dash off a quick reply, reassuring Rachel that she wasn't making anything worse and promising to get back properly after the party.

Inside, Maggie was pulling out a garment bag that bore the day's date and time.

'You're so lucky.' Annie made her way through the lounge area to perch on the little sofa where a couple of days ago she'd felt so hopeless. Her mood had not improved. 'You don't even need to decide on what to wear, it's all done for you.'

Maggie threw an exasperated look at her. 'It's not all it's cracked up to be. For a start, the stylist can't seem to get it through her head that I'm not some size zero waif. Like, who the fuck can wear this?' Maggie rooted in the bag and extracted a floor-length chiffon dress in the most gorgeous crimson with delicate straps.

'*You* can wear it, Maggie!' Annie was unnerved. This distorted view of her body was definitely not a good sign, given Maggie's past.

'Please don't, Annie,' Maggie said, shaking her head grimly. 'I know what I look like, thanks.'

'Maggie, I am serious, you know. Hollywood is messing with your head if you don't realise that you are not far off waif-like.' Annie flashed back on the restaurant toilet from a few nights ago and felt the pull of anxiety.

Meanwhile, Maggie grimaced and pulled the delicate straps off the hanger. 'Of course Hollywood is messing with my head. These actresses ... they're on juice diets or coke and, a lot of the time, both. Just standing in their vicinity is excruciating. You'll see what I mean.'

Maggie swept into the bathroom with the dress and shut the door. It was perturbing – Annie'd seen Maggie's boobs countless times in the last two decades, so why was she hiding?

'Maggie?' Annie called through the door. 'Is everything alright?'

'Yeah.' Maggie sounded distracted. She pulled the door open a crack to peer at Annie while she pulled on the dress. 'Why?'

Annie hesitated. *She sounds totally normal.* She didn't want to confront Maggie and risk her getting defensive. Though given Maggie's history, saying nothing could be riskier.

'I just …' Annie tucked her hair behind her ears to have something to do with her hands. 'It's just that … the other night in the Canteen place. You were okay … yeah?'

'Oh!' Maggie blinked. 'Oh God. *That.* I wasn't feeling too good after the rich food. My stomach was a bit upset. I was sick in the jacks, bit mortifying.' She paused, holding Annie's gaze. 'You thought … I was … ? Oh my God. Seriously?'

Annie pressed her lips together. At least Maggie sounded more surprised than annoyed or defensive.

'I was just a bit concerned. I know things are stressy with you right now. Your life …' Annie gestured vaguely, slightly stumped at how to sum up in words the confluence of mind-fuckery Maggie had to navigate while just being fame *adjacent.*

Maggie stepped forward to hug Annie and Annie felt reassured that her friend wasn't having a big reaction to the conversation. Maggie pulled back to look at Annie, her eyes soft.

'Annie, you're so good to be worrying about me, but I'm good. I seriously am. I mean, obviously, I'm not "good" about everything. Stuff's hard, the A-list world is still not the easiest place to be in, even though it's been years at this stage. But I would never go back to the old ways. I swear. I couldn't do that to the girls. I don't want to go all "as a mother" as if mothers have more at stake or more empathy or something. You know I hate that crap. But having the twins … I feel like it did cement my recovery. I'm lucky too, having Betty cook three meals a day for me – it's perfect for keeping me nourished.'

Annie nodded. She hadn't considered that Betty's presence added stability; that was reassuring. 'And you're still seeing a therapist?'

'Of course.' Maggie grinned. 'I'd say I'm a lifer on that front. Britney will be able to retire off of my mad head.' Maggie stepped out of their embrace and adjusted her neckline.

'I thought your *PT* was Britney?'

'Oh, they're *all* Britney in LA.' Maggie laughed.

'Hello, slags.' Clara's voice rang out from the door. 'I found the Booze Boy!'

Annie turned around to find Clara leading a nervy-looking young guy in a white shirt and black trousers. He was carrying a tray heaving with receptacles of various types from high balls to martini glasses. To Annie, the colourful drinks gleamed like jewels and, while another drunken night on the awkward holiday from hell seemed like a disaster waiting to happen, getting pissed was far too tempting. At least Maggie was one thing she could stop ruminating on. Annie surveyed the Booze Boy's portable bar and picked up what looked to be a G&T.

'I'll do a martini.' Clara plucked one from the tray and twirled away into the bedroom. 'Maggie! You are such a ride. Love the dress.'

Maggie rolled her eyes at Clara. 'Yeah, right.' To the Booze Boy she added, 'Prosecco for me, please.'

'Of course.' He hurried forward and Maggie took her drink, immediately downing half before recoiling slightly from too much fizz.

She's nervous about the party, Annie observed, sipping her own drink.

'Has anyone arrived yet?' Maggie asked him.

'No ma'am, not yet.'

'Cool.' Maggie finished the rest of her glass, catching some rogue bubbles with her cupped hand, then swapped it out for another full one. 'You head down. We'll be right there.'

'Take it easy, Maggie.' Clara giggled as the door shut behind the boy. 'Or maybe one of us is always destined to be a messy bitch on this holiday? Though given that you're the only one still speaking to your partner ...' She trailed off suddenly, looking awkward, and Annie cringed inwardly. From what they'd seen, Fionn and Maggie had really only exchanged a smattering of words since his arrival.

Clara, swiftly switching tack, made her way over to Maggie. 'This dress is insane. You look amazing.' She ducked behind Maggie and peeked at the label. 'Oh, it's The Row, of *course*. It's divine. This dress is probably more than my mortgage this month.'

This seemed to make Maggie self-conscious. She turned briskly and tucked the label back in. 'You don't have to make everything about my money, Clara,' she said.

Clara narrowed her eyes and Annie felt a surge of panic. *Don't say anything,* she silently tried to plead with Clara.

Clara took another sip of her martini and evidently decided to choose violence. 'To be fair, Maggie, it's kind of Fionn's money.'

'Why are you being so fucking mean to *me*, Clara?' Maggie shot back. 'Money doesn't mean my life is perfect. You're taking your shitty mood out on me. It's not *my* fault that *you've* messed up with your husband.'

'At least my husband has made an appearance on this holiday.'

Fury swept over Maggie's face and Annie jumped up. 'Gals, we're all on edge. Let's go down and eat something.'

Annie turned to gather her phone and silk blazer and tipped back some of her own drink. Things had really nose-dived, she thought regretfully. It was a bad sign that even when it was just the three of them, things were so strained. It had never been like this before. They'd always been so easy with each other. She thought back over the countless nights that they'd performed this exact ritual, getting ready in one or other of their bedrooms: drinking, swapping clothes, mildly bitching about the lads or re-enacting disastrous moments from that day at work. Never bitching at each other. In twenty years, the most serious row they'd ever had had been the great Centaur Porn Debate of 2015. It was the kind of batshit debate she could only imagine having with the girls. Clara had become passionately enthusiastic about a new erotic fiction novel called *Centaur in My Valley*. To Clara's chagrin, Maggie had insisted that this fell under the umbrella of bestiality, while Annie opted to remain impartial, which inevitably infuriated the other two so much they joined forces against her. To this day, whenever they all got drunk and nostalgic, the idea of getting matching centaur tattoos would come up.

Annie realised with sadness that she was really looking forward to getting home and out of this atmosphere of perpetual tension. Even if going home meant dealing with the logistics of her relationship falling to pieces, at least she'd get to see Rachel.

'I'm sorry, Maggie.' Clara shifted in her heeled peep-toe leather boots.

Maggie's expression remained stony.

Annie stepped forward. 'Gals, we can't turn on each other. Not before we get the centaurs on our arses.'

At this, Maggie seemed to thaw slightly and Clara moved to put her arms around her. Maggie grudgingly tolerated the hug. 'That was a stupid thing to say. And not true …'

'Well,' Maggie sighed, 'it's not *not* true.' She looked gloomy but then shrugged. 'Annie's right, we can't be sniping at each other. You both need all your energy to resist losing it with Ollie and Conor.'

A chilly dread blew through Annie at the thought of Conor. Ugh, to have to see him and act nice, not to mention sit on the same plane for six hours. And then what? Share a taxi once they got back to Dublin? Back to their sad, airless flat. She thought of the pristine guestroom they never used. That was going be the only way to get away from each other until they sorted something more permanent. And the way things were in Dublin, would that even be possible? She knew plenty of couples who had to stay living together even after they'd split because they couldn't afford to move out.

A profound weariness washed over her. What does it take to dismantle a twenty-year relationship? Forget the logistics. Who was she now? She'd never even been an adult without Conor at her side, each helping the other through this project that was life. Her sense of loss held a real weight; it was a leaden sadness that dragged at her. Conor had been her partner in the real sense of the word – they'd been a team for so long. Though thinking about how close they'd been during the last two decades was forcing her to examine how that closeness had deserted them when they should have been more together than ever. Still, even though she could see why he was calling time, it was like some crucial part of herself had vanished overnight, the part that was stable and knew what the fuck was going on. She felt rickety and anxious every time she thought about the formless future ahead of her.

'Annie?'

She looked up at the sound of her name. 'Sorry … yeah?'

'It'll all be okay,' Maggie said, apparently having read Annie's thoughts. 'Try not to project too far into the future. I know it's easy for me to say but … anything you need, we're all here. Well, not all of us,' she corrected herself.

'I guess the friend group is kinda no more,' Clara mused, staring into her now empty glass.

Annie nodded slowly. 'It's actually mad. No more dinners or holidays or anything. I'd always thought we would end up forming either a commune or a cult in our old age.'

'Look, did the boys really bring that much to it?' Maggie tried for a smile that immediately wilted.

'We still have Fionn,' Clara piped up, but Annie knew she was only saying this for Maggie's sake. If this holiday had shown anything, even *Maggie* barely had Fionn, never mind his friends from college.

'Let's go down, it's quarter past.' Maggie stuffed her hand into a stack of delicate gold bangles and picked up a gold chainmail purse containing her phone. 'You guys won't believe how boring this party is going to be. Everyone imagines celebrity parties are gonna be fascinating but, really, they are just full of the most dull, needy people in the world.'

An hour later and Annie was now in full agreement with Maggie. The party was one of the most uptight, stilted events she'd ever attended. It was worse than that British funeral she'd once gone to.

Everyone was clearly so obsessed with how they were appearing to others that they seemed unable to even take in what was actually happening right in front of them. Annie was fairly certain that she could have literally stripped off and started a one-woman nude food fight and not one of the famouses would notice.

Contributing to the general stiffness of the crowd were the clothes. Most of the women were wearing tiny swatches of material tied to their bodies by dental floss; it wasn't a comfortable look. The men, Annie noted, were allowed to be fully dressed.

When she, Maggie and Clara had first come down to the deck, which was hung with strings of vintage light bulbs, Annie had experienced a couple of jolts at seeing faces she'd only ever experienced on a screen. She spotted Cameron Diaz, who she'd always liked. Nearby George (Fucking!) Clooney was making his way down the side of the house to the open-sided marquee that had been erected on the beach. Off to the side of this, a string quartet was set up on the sand playing instrumental versions of some of the biggest songs of the summer. Dozens of waitstaff whipped efficiently through the guests dispensing champagne, which everyone accepted, and canapés, which most people declined.

When Annie, Maggie and Clara had descended the steps, they immediately spotted Conor and Ollie standing awkwardly together and, without a word, the girls took themselves over to the opposite side of the tent.

'In a funny way this is kind of nostalgic,' Clara announced. 'Remember in college, we were always icing out the guys for whatever bullshit fight one of the couples would be having.'

'Yeah,' Annie smiled.

'God, yeah.' Maggie nodded, though Annie could see she had a faraway look as she intently watched the people arriving. Searching for Fionn, no doubt, Annie thought. It was coming up to 9 p.m. and he had still not appeared. He'd even sent the twins back with Brody earlier.

'Remember the Great Whose-Genitals-Are-More-Ugly Row of 2008?' Annie tried to catch Maggie's eye to distract her from the misery of waiting. 'Conor said vaginas were just as visually off-putting as dicks and we all lost our stupid little twenty-one-year-old minds and fell out with the lot of them.'

'Oh God, yes.' Clara clapped her hands. 'I mean, really! They couldn't have possibly thought vaginas were uglier than cocks. They were just trying to piss us off. That was pure trolling.'

A few minutes later Annie had, most unfortunately, been captured by a creepy director and was immediately in a conversational hostage situation. His slippery lips flapped at speed as he delivered a detailed dissection of the previous eight decades of film that she had in no way asked for and had already tried to escape from several times.

After a couple of attempts to participate in the conversation, she realised that he required absolutely zero responses from her and so she settled back and allowed his words to wash over her as she took in the rest of the crowd.

There were essentially two types of people in the tent. The first were the rising stars who were clearly making a concerted effort to be in the eyeline of the more established A-listers at all times, as though, should they stumble across the gaze of any of these giants (mainly men, of course), all doors would magically open for them.

The up-and-comers were so focused on being noticed that their faces, unbeknownst to them, had frozen into pained expressions of equal parts hope and anguish.

The other cohort were the mega-famous, and they had a different countenance altogether. They peacocked from the centre of clusters of people who laughed uproariously at everything they said. What a weird life. No wonder they all ended up in rehab and cults and endless marriages or, worst of all, sycophantic documentaries about their careers that were produced and funded by themselves. Annie shuddered.

She wanted to find Maggie. Despite their reassuring chat earlier, Annie still felt a whisper of concern, especially as she knew this party was not easy on her friend.

She found Maggie pinned in a corner of the tent by a young actress she vaguely recognised. Looking at the actress's body, Annie had a jolt of shock, quickly followed by sadness. The skin on the girl's back was ridged with the fine bones of her skeleton. Her shoulder blades were so pronounced that Annie felt certain the girl must feel them in bed at night, the delicate skin stretched and no doubt rubbing against her sheets when she changed position.

An image of Maggie back in college stole across Annie's mind. This was before they'd realised that Maggie was in a bad place. Annie had gone to wake her up one morning and had noticed that her friend slept with a pillow between her knees. Annie didn't understand why until much later.

Annie made sure she was smiling pleasantly as she slid around the actress to stand beside Maggie.

'I just think you are so brave,' the actress was gushing. 'So body positive.'

Maggie was nodding wearily. 'Uh-huh.' She offered up a stiff smile. 'This is my friend Annie.'

'Hey.' The girl lifted a frail arm towards Annie. Her hand looked oddly huge dangling from the painfully narrow wrist. 'I'm Erica! We're just waiting on Finn!' she said brightly, each sentence a nervously delighted exclamation. 'I was in the second *Endurance*! So I'm super stoked to catch up with him!'

Annie genuinely struggled to know where to rest her eyes. It was hard to look at this poor girl. Her mouth was so big in her pinched face. Annie glanced at Maggie, hyper-conscious that this could be very triggering for her.

But Maggie was only gazing blandly at the girl. 'Hmmm, I'm sure he'll be *super stoked* too,' she murmured.

I guess maybe she's used to it, Annie thought. The Hollywood love affair with thinness had been in full swing for years now and Maggie did live at the epicentre.

At that moment, a fever of excitement ignited among the crowd to their left. It was the arrival of Fionn aka Finn Strong aka What The Fuck Has He Done To His Teeth – as she, Conor, Ollie and Clara sometimes called him in their side chat, a side chat that was now, most likely, dead, of course.

Fionn was barefoot in weathered khakis and wearing a positively ragged shirt that was barely even *attempting* to cover his defined torso. He raised one arm in greeting to his star friends; on the other arm was Alabama Gere. She too was barefoot and wearing a barely there long dress of faded grey jersey.

They both looked unwashed but also somehow magnificent. Annie spotted Maggie's face collapse into confusion and hurt at seeing Alabama. She recovered fast, however, as though it was muscle memory at this stage to rapidly rearrange her features from disappointment to calm.

Annie knew Alabama was definitely not the girl from the blind item. She and Fionn had never worked together before. And anyway, Maggie had told them that Fionn insisted the blind item was about another actor.

Still, Annie did *not* like Fionn showing up with another woman. What was he at? He'd supposedly been out at the shacks, so where had he found *her*? On the way back?

'Sorry, folks.' Fionn's ratio of Irish accent to American twang was gradually tipping in the wrong direction, Annie thought, as he continued. Maybe it was because he was with his celeb friends. 'We're so late because we were out in the dune shacks working on something I'm so …' He glanced down at Alabama, who looked back up at him and gave a slight smile and a shake of her head. 'Well,' he pulled Alabama closer to give her a squeeze around her shoulders, 'we can't say too much but I'm so moved by the work we're getting to make.'

'We lost our shoes,' she giggled, covering her mouth like a little girl. The guests laughed appreciatively at this non sequitur.

Beside her, Annie could practically *feel* Maggie's mask hardening into place. Annie glanced around to find Clara to gauge her reaction to Fionn making his grand entrance with a woman who was decidedly *not* Maggie. Over by the musicians, Clara was shaking her head in outraged disbelief. *The woman does not bother with a poker face,* Annie thought, mildly amused in spite of her own rage.

At least Fionn seemed to have sense enough to release Alabama and head straight to Maggie, though Alabama did trail him over.

'Hey, it's my beautiful wife!' He pulled Maggie into a deep and, Annie felt, slightly showy kiss. He'd obviously caught Maggie's expression when he'd walked in.

Maggie extracted herself and leaned around him to look at Alabama. 'Hi, I'm Maggie.'

'Of course. I know who you are.'

'Sure.' Maggie nodded with an expression that was part smile, part wince.

'Hi, Finn!' Erica piped up. 'Can't believe it's been, like, six months since we were … *enduring* … *Endurance 2*!' She said this in a way that suggested this was a private joke between them, but Fionn only looked back at her with the benign vagueness that Annie'd seen him deploy with people who claimed to know him and who he had completely forgotten.

'Ah yeah, crazy.' Then he flashed one of his dimples at her and she looked like she might lose consciousness with delight.

She draped her hand limply on his arm. 'I was just saying to Maggie that she is, like, my idol! Her body positivity is so inspiring to young girls like me! She's a role model! And it's so cool that you're still together.'

Maggie, apparently having reached the end of her tolerance for bullshit, turned to Fionn and said, 'I think that's code for "your wife's surprisingly fat and old".'

Yikes, thought Annie.

'Oh my God! No!' Erica staggered a bit as she tried to form a reply but Maggie had already swept through the gap between Fionn and Alabama and beelined for Clara.

'I didn't mean that *at all*.' Erica was babbling, while Fionn stared after Maggie, looking shocked. He immediately started to follow her but just then an A-list actor Annie couldn't remember the name of stepped into his path. 'Finn, buddy! My agent tells me you got the script. I know we're not talking business tonight but I just really wanted to tell you in person that I wrote the role for you.'

Annie stepped around them and went after Maggie and Clara who she had spotted ducking out of the other end of the tent and into the darkness beyond, where the waves were crashing on the sand.

As Annie left the clamour of the tent behind, her eyes adjusted to the darkness of the huge ocean and sky before her. She moved towards the silhouettes of Maggie and Clara, who were sitting watching the silver-edged waves breaking a few feet in front of them.

Clara's ranting tone was unmistakable over the roar of the surf, while Maggie's replies were quiet, only perceptible by the small silences that punctuated Clara's tirade.

'Gals,' Annie called. They were cross-legged, their shoes dumped beside them.

Maggie and Clara looked up and immediately shuffled over to open up a little Annie-sized gap between them. Annie settled herself in and Clara dropped her head to Annie's shoulder. 'All of the guys …' she fumed. 'I don't know who to hate the most.'

'Don't hate Fionn on my behalf.' Maggie was drawing patterns in the sand.

'But what was he doing showing up with Alabama Gere?' Clara clearly wasn't seeing the warning grimace Annie was shooting her way.

'It's his work.' Maggie shrugged. 'I'm gonna head to bed.' She pulled herself up. 'Sorry, I'm just pretty beat.' Annie couldn't make out her expression in the dim light before she turned and left.

Annie and Clara watched her head back, giving the tent a wide berth, slipping down the side passage of the house and presumably entering through the front.

'Have you spoken to Conor at all tonight?' Clara asked.

'No.' Annie rubbed her arms briskly; this late in the night, the sand was chilly and unpleasantly clammy. Annie could feel her dress absorbing the damp. 'I'm putting it off for as long as possible. What about you and Ollie?'

'Oh, same.' Clara slouched defeatedly. 'You and Conor are so lucky. At least you can make a pretty clean break.'

'Did you just say I'm so lucky? About my relationship of twenty years ending?'

Clara straightened up again. 'Oh my God. Am I just saying and doing all the wrong things on this cursed holiday?'

'Yes,' Annie answered without hesitation.

Clara gave a depressed little laugh. 'What are we going to do about everything?'

'Who knows?' Annie gazed forward at the glittering horizon. 'Who fucking knows?'

CHAPTER 14

It was 8 a.m. and Clara was already sweating, despite having done nothing more than wake up, brush her teeth and dress and feed her boys. Nobody warned you that parenting was cardio; there was a lot left out of the beatific posts on Insta. It had been three weeks since they'd arrived back from Provincetown and to say things had been tense was such an understatement it verged on comical. This morning, she had yet to lay eyes on Ollie. When she'd come downstairs at seven, he'd already stashed away the duvet and pillow from the couch in the TV room and disappeared out of the house.

Now that they were barely on speaking terms and Clara was apparently the Worst In The World™, he was done with trying to be considerate about his marathon training. He was gone for hours at a time with no notice or explanation whatsoever.

She glanced over at the chaotic family calendar on the fridge. At 11 a.m. that day was 'CC' – code for couples counselling. Maybe today would bring some clarity to the situation. She definitely wasn't up for being the Cheating Bitch Wife From Hell™ for the rest of her life.

It was their first session with a man called Dr Evans. She'd tried to push for a woman but since it was Ollie who'd actually made the effort to arrange everything, she'd had to accept her fate: being trapped having to tolerate not one but two men talking about feelings. She rolled her eyes and started speed-tidying the kitchen. Weetabix seemed to be encrusted to every bowl in the house. *Why does he refuse to steep anything?* After some aggressive chiselling, she frisbeed the bowls and the rest of the dishes into the dishwasher. Then shoved it closed, employing the special knack required. She doubted Ollie even knew there was a knack. Maybe she could bring *that* up at the appointment. *Sure I kissed someone else and there may have been some light hand-to-boob contact, but Ollie does nothing around the house. Just keeping the boys alive, while I'm out at work, seems to take every ounce of his focus.*

Although, she knew this wasn't entirely fair ... if pressed, she wouldn't be able to name who their home insurance provider was. Or whether or not the car was taxed. She didn't even know for definite that cars needed to be taxed. But what good is having the admin sorted when you live in a literal sea of shite?

'Muma!' A shriek interrupted her thoughts. She grabbed the cloth and ducked out to the dining room to see who'd called her.

It was Reggie. 'Muma, I-I-I. Dodo, Muma. Muma?' At three, his demands could be a bit mystifying.

'That's lovely, sweetheart.' She kissed his soft little head and began wiping the crumbs and abandoned crusts on the table into her hand.

The front door slammed and the boys all bolted out to the hall.

'Dad!' They jostled to be the first to greet Ollie.

'Bro, you are so sweaty,' Josh told him, sounding unnervingly teenage for a ten-year-old.

'Can we watch TV?' came Tom's adorably high-pitched voice.

'For fifteen minutes,' Ollie answered. 'Then you're leaving to go to summer camp.'

Clara heard the boys thunder next door to the TV room as Ollie came in.

'Hi,' she said tersely. 'Good run?' She didn't look at him.

Ollie didn't even acknowledge her question. 'You've to bring them to camp this morning. I need to do a pretty thorough warm-down after that distance.'

Ollie filled a glass at the sink and began chugging it.

Anger ripped through her. 'I've to get to work, Ollie. Coming in late and then taking early lunch to go to this ridiculous, not to mention *expensive*, therapy would not look good.'

He continued to drink and gave a maddening shrug.

'Fine.' Clara marched out, stepping on a Lego as she went.

'Fuck off.' She shouted, kicking the piece away.

In the living room, she heard Tom squeak, 'Muma said "fuck"!'

'Ugh, fuck,' she said again quietly to herself and carried on up the stairs to get dressed.

In Dr Evans' spartan waiting room, she sat in her most 'I'm not a bitch' outfit – tapered khaki joggers with leather sliders and a long loose tunic-style top. There was no sign of Ollie yet and she was glad – being alone together was something they were, by silent mutual agreement, avoiding since returning home. She opened up Slags For Life to see what they were planning to wear to the party Maggie was hosting for her brother Donal's birthday.

Clara: So what are we wearing tomorrow?

Annie: Nothing new. Borrowing a dress from Rachel, she's my plus one. Or as she puts it: my 'conjoined twin in spinsterhood'.

Maggie: Oh God, with all the organising/getting the Dublin house ready, I haven't had a minute to find anything.

Clara x'd out of the group and over to her side-chat with Annie.

Clara: I'm sure the stylist will be curating something fab that costs more than my car loan ...

Annie: Don't be bitchy. If we learned NOTHING in Provincetown, it's that her life is pretty ... well ... crap.

Clara felt bad and hastily typed back.

Clara: You're right. I'm being catty cuz my own life is a literal shitemare.

Back in Slags For Life, Clara could see Maggie typing.

Maggie: Have ye figured out what to do about the guys? Fionn will be there, but obviously he gets that Conor and Ollie might not be ...?

Annie: Conor is coming. We already discussed and agreed to do everything in our power not to so much as stray into each other's eyeline.

Clara: Me and Ollie flipped a coin to see who could go and I won. He's working late anyway so my mum's covering the hour with the boys. I can't believe you and Conor are having 'discussions', Annie. How does it feel to be so disgustingly emotionally healthy?

Annie: Lol. Well, discussions are kind of unavoidable when you're trying to divide up your stuff ... as long as I don't let myself think about how he has fucked up any chance I have to have a family, I can tolerate it.

Clara frowned. Jesus, poor Annie. If she could donate one of her kids, she would, but, as annoying as they could occasionally be, she was pretty attached.

Maggie: Maybe it's not the end of that though, Annie.

Annie: Thanks so much for having Rachel btw.

Maggie: Of course. Dying to meet her.

The door to Clara's right opened and in came Ollie.
'Hey.' She put the phone away.
'Hey,' he answered, and took a seat opposite.

They both spent the next two minutes in complete silence, each pretending to be interested in the few plants that were the only adornments in the room. The awkwardness seemed to be building steadily with each second that passed. She was nearly tempted to try and say something, maybe along the lines of 'This is crazy, do we really need to be here?'

Then the second door opened and Dr Evans greeted them warmly.

'Ollie, Clara, great to meet you both.' He stepped aside and directed them through to the office beyond, which was even more sparsely decorated than the waiting room. *Probably to deter clients from throwing things in anger*, Clara thought, slipping into a grey suede seat with prominent armrests. Ollie settled himself in the identical one beside her. Dr Evans' seat opposite was larger and more imposing, Clara noted.

'So.' He clasped his hands together and sat forward earnestly. He had the kind of face you could forget even while you were still looking at it, and his shirt and trousers were a perfect colour match to the blank office around him.

'Clara, Ollie has,' he indicated her husband, 'updated me on the situation that has prompted this visit, but I wondered, Clara, if you wanted to tell your side of the matter.'

Clara mentally gathered herself. 'Honestly, no,' she said simply. 'Whatever Ollie's said ... it's probably fairly accurate. I made a mistake when I was drunk. But it wasn't a malicious mistake. I was hurt at the time. I thought he was having an affair. And the fact is he *was* keeping things from me.'

Beside her, Ollie was already shaking his head, which caught Dr Evans' attention. 'Do you disagree, Ollie?'

'Yeah, I do,' he said, which took Clara by surprise.

'On what bit?' She knew how indignant she sounded, but she couldn't help it. What part of what she had said was incorrect?

Ollie didn't look at her, directing his answer to Dr Evans. 'She's not talking about our deeper problems. It's not all about the incident in America. I mean, of course it is, to some extent. I'm hurt and it's even more hurtful that she would think I would ever cheat on her but in the last few weeks since we've been home ... just thinking about it all and about us and our marriage – I think it's made me realise there's this disconnect between us. And there's inequities in our marriage about parenting and the day-to-day life stuff.'

'Oh, is there?' Her words were spiked with sarcasm, but before she could get going, Dr Evans cut across her.

'Let's avoid definitive statements, Ollie,' he said. 'In relationships, there's not necessarily an unimpeachable reality; there's the experiences of two people.' He held up two fingers helpfully. 'These experiences can align or they can diverge. So maybe, Ollie, you could say ... I *feel* there's inequity.'

Clara twisted towards Ollie, folding her arms. 'Is the inequity that you get to do a job you love and I have to work the steady paycheque job that I hate to make sure we have enough every month?'

'Will you stop throwing that in my face? You never told me that you resented your job so much.'

Dr Evans cleared his throat and Ollie quickly re-arranged his words.

'I *feel* that you've never told me any of this.'

'What would be the point?' Clara sighed. 'Nothing's going to change. We've got a mortgage, we've got three kids. This is just the reality I'm living in.'

Ollie shook his head and stared off to the other side of the room.

'Ollie?' Dr Evans sat forward. 'How does hearing Clara say that make you feel?'

'It makes me feel like I'm right in suspecting that she doesn't like our life.'

'That's such bullshit, Ollie,' Clara fumed. 'How can you say that? I love the boys more than anything.'

Ollie turned to her. 'When you're with us it's like you resent parenting. When we go to the park, you listen to your murder podcasts.'

'Oh my gawd. I have *one* earphone in. I can still interact with the boys while half listening. It's not a crime to find the park boring. Sometimes I just want a bit of distraction. Some adult voices. Motherhood is fucking lonely.'

'*I'm* there too, you could talk to *me*.' He turned back to Dr Evans. 'We practically lead separate lives already.'

Dr Evans nodded. 'I'm hearing you. You say "already", which sounds – and correct me if I'm way off base here – but it sounds, to *me*, like leading separate lives is something you would like to trial, Ollie?'

At exactly the same time that Clara laughed, she realised that Ollie was nodding.

'What?' She swivelled to fully face him. 'Ollie. Lol. We couldn't even *afford* that – don't be stupid.'

Suddenly Ollie stood and, with his back ramrod straight, walked to the door. Clara struggled to compute what she was seeing. Where the hell was he off to?

With his back to the room, Ollie spoke quietly but firmly: 'Listen to how you talk to me.' Then he left the room.

Shocked, Clara gripped the arms of her chair, her thoughts rushing between two courses of action: go after him, or burst into tears.

In the end, she did neither. She just remained in her seat feeling winded. *He left??*

'That came as a shock, Clara?' Dr Evans asked gently.

She could only nod.

'We still have time. We can finish out the session with some of your—'

'No.' Clara didn't let him finish. 'Thank you,' she added, 'but no. I just want to … I should get back to work.'

'No problem.' He nodded. 'My secretary will forward the bill on Monday, no need to worry about payment today,' he said as if this was some incredibly compassionate gesture.

Clara checked her pockets to see that she had everything, and made her way out.

On the street, she tried to steady herself – what was happening? How was he the one who got to storm out?

She took out her phone and typed a message to Ollie: *Announcing that you want to separate just to punish me is pretty fuckin immature.*

Her head thrummed with irritation as she watched Ollie typing.

Ollie: I didn't say that to punish you, that's something YOU would do, frankly. I said it because I feel it.

Clara stared at the words, fear rising over her annoyance. *He's serious?* She debated replying but the shred of pride she was clinging to stopped her. *He is being so ridiculous, so childish.*

She could see he was still typing. Another message dropped in.

Ollie: Enjoy the party tonight. Tell your mum that I'll be finished at the O'Malleys' place by 9 so prob get home about quarter past.

Clara gaped at her phone. It was a warm day in the city and hurried people streamed around her like she was in the middle of racing rapids. Eventually, with no idea what else to do, she turned in the direction of her bus stop and joined them.

That night Clara did her make-up in the corner of the attic to the thumping soundtrack of Tom and Reggie taking turns jumping from the bed to the chest of drawers and back again.

Beside her, Josh was watching her intently. 'Are the lines on your eyes supposed to be straight?'

'Ha.' She leaned closer to the tiny, grubby mirror she'd propped up under the skylight. 'In theory, yes.' She closed one eye and tried to tidy up her admittedly abysmal efforts. Maggie was so lucky, she was being glammed to within an inch of her life by professionals at that very moment. She'd asked Clara and Annie if they wanted to join her and her mum and sister for it but Clara couldn't get out of the house any earlier. Her own mother liked to keep her grandmotherly duties like helping with the boys to the bare minimum.

Josh picked up a cotton bud and suggested she start over.

'Thanks, but I truly cannot be bothered.'

A particularly loud thump from Reggie bouncing off the bed

startled them and Josh got up with hands on hips and went over. 'This house was built nearly 150 years ago and it is holding on *by a thread*, you two.'

Clara laughed. It was verbatim what she was constantly telling them as they dangled from banisters and sat on the top of doors, swinging back and forth like miniature lemurs. Psychotic ones.

Josh intercepted Reggie as he scrambled to get back up on the drawers. 'No more jumping, boys.' He sounded more authoritative than Clara ever did. *He'll be a good co-parent if I end up on my own*, she thought sadly, watching them in the mirror.

At the sound of the knocker downstairs, all three boys immediately snapped to attention and then fled the room at speed. The noise of them flying down three flights of stairs made her smile and also made her grateful that she didn't have a visual on it – having three extremely rowdy kids was round-the-clock, heart-stopping anxiety. She could hear them dragging her mum into the hall with exuberant shouts.

Clara stood, and stooped to see what she could of herself in the mirror they had nailed to the back of the attic door. She looked grand. The dress was an oldy but a goody – a dark red strappy number with a plunging neckline. She added some big gold hoops and pulled her thick dark hair into a ponytail – casual to offset the pretty revealing outfit.

In her gold strappy heels, she took the stairs carefully. Downstairs, her mother Jean was distributing bags of Haribo to the boys.

'Hello, darling, you look gorgeous.' Her mother blew Clara a kiss as the boys swarmed her, riffling through her pockets to make sure they'd extracted all the sweets she had on her person. She fended them off, laughing over at Clara. 'Making the most of your breasts' final years, I see … well done.' She winked.

Clara laughed, and hurriedly gathered her jacket and clutch bag. The taxi app said the driver would be at the top of the lane in less than one minute and Clara was relieved that there was no time to catch up with Jean properly. If things in her marriage were actually as bad as the day's counselling session was suggesting, she had a long conversation with her mother in her future.

She kissed everyone goodbye, reassuring her mum that Ollie would be back soon, and hurried to the waiting taxi.

On the way out to Dalkey, the ridiculously gorgeous seaside town where Maggie and Fionn's Dubin home overlooked the sea, Clara scrolled her Insta, trying to rid herself of the day's emotional upheaval. She didn't want to think about Ollie's accusations from therapy. She thumbed her feed for distraction:

Look, Paul Mescal being interviewed by puppies!
Look, a woman doing a tutorial for homemade cereal!
Look, a girl journalling in a treehouse!
Look, take this quiz! Is my marriage over?

Oooof. Clara blinked. Nowhere was safe. The algorithm was probably listening in Dr Evans' office.

'We're here. It's one of these, I think?' The taxi driver had slowed and was peering up at the terrace of five houses, currently backlit by the streaks of pink and orange from the sun setting behind.

'Yes, this is it,' Clara replied. 'You can leave me here, you won't be able to drive down.'

The guy obeyed and Clara hopped out at the sign that read *Vehicle access for residents only.*

Even before Maggie and Fionn owned one, Clara had known these houses – everyone in Dublin did. Miavita Terrace. Lots of wealthy streets in Dublin had these kinds of names. The rich Victorians who had built them were full of notions after their European travels and had convinced themselves that Dublin Bay was basically the Bay of Naples. These houses had always held a fascination for Clara. What were the lives of the people inside like? Clara had imagined a lot of gliding: gliding down wide staircases, gliding out to the back terrace, gliding over the road to the sea for a swim, gliding back for a shite in the gold-plated toilet.

Four years ago, after they'd bought number four, Maggie texted the news to Slags For Life and Clara had immediately burst into stunned, envious tears.

She and Ollie only had two kids back then but already their house felt like it was shrinking around them. It was hard not to believe that life would be exponentially easier if they just had enough space. And a shit ton of money.

Now, Clara made her way to the house, which was lit up and giving off that vague hum that houses always did when a party was in full swing inside.

A man in a blazer and tie opened the door to her, then a woman with an iPad checked her name off a list. Another member of staff took her jacket and yet another person on the payroll handed her a glass of champagne.

The hall of number four was about as wide as Clara's entire house and every room that led off it was high-ceilinged and quite simply massive – could-fit-a-swimming-pool-in-there levels of huge.

Polished original wood floorboards gleamed underfoot and fresh flowers cascaded out over the gargantuan vases which stood on the many delicate-footed walnut tables dotted around the rooms. The borders of the ceilings were edged in ornate cornicing, and what appeared to be intricate wallpapers on many of the walls were actually hand-painted murals by an artist Maggie had commissioned.

The crowd was densely packed. The full alphabet of Ireland's celebrities – from Z-list reality stars to D-list panto stars to A-list *star*-stars – were draped on sofas and leaning against the many high-top tables that had been brought in for the occasion. As always with a Maggie and Fionn bash, the normies were easily picked out. The normie women's blow-dries were becoming battered, their foundation could've been better blended and their eyeliner was in the process of migrating up to their brow line. The normie guys were obvious by the Marks & Spencer blue jeans and the shiny white shirts that screamed 'I came in a pack of three'.

Clara checked her own reflection as she passed the giant gold-framed mirror on her right, to confirm that her own make-up was similarly wayward already. She swiped a finger under each eye to try to tidy it up a bit and then spotted Maggie's mum and sister in the mirror behind her, looking dazzling. They each had the same raven hair as Maggie and blow-dried to perfection, no doubt by the parade of stylists and make-up artists. She waved and headed over.

'Hi, gals!'

'Clara!' Emer, Maggie's sister, embraced her. 'So sorry to hear about the holiday and everything.'

Oh God, how much did they know? Judging by their faces ... a lot. Maggie might not see her family much but they were very close, constantly WhatsApping. Clara decided to feign nonchalance as she did not feel like raking over things again.

'Ah yeah, it was annoying having to leave early.'

'Yeah, Maggie was deffo disappointed.' Emer sipped her bubbles.

'It's good timing that she had this to come back for,' Maggie's mum added brightly.

'I think she is more homesick than she lets on,' said Emer. 'She hasn't actually said anything but she's flat out on the group chat sending TikToks from Irish comedians about Ireland. "Top 10 ways Irish people say goodbye without saying goodbye" or "You know you're from Ireland when ..." That kind of stuff.'

'Oh yeah.' Clara laughed. 'We get a fair bit of that in ours too!'

'I didn't think anything of it but then me and Donal did the numbers on the timestamps and realised she's carpet-bombing us with this nostalgic bullshit at 2 a.m. LA time ...' She arched a withering eyebrow in that way only siblings can.

Suddenly Donal ambushed them and crushed Clara in a hug. 'It's the chief slag!'

'Happy birthday!' Clara kissed his cheek.

After a few minutes of Donal's impassioned monologue about how forty was the new twenty-five, Clara extricated herself to go and locate Maggie and Annie.

Ploughing through the giddy crowd, she finally found them in the garden, lounging on wooden Adirondack chairs, passing a bottle of Buckfast back and forth and observing the great and the good of south Dublin. Beside them was Rachel, Annie's friend who Clara had met the odd time in the pub for after-work drinks. She liked Rachel and was glad she and Annie had become so close. Clara felt bad that she wasn't always free to see Annie as much as she'd like. Thank God for WhatsApp – it was probably the only thing keeping millennial friendships alive.

'Hey, gals.' She dispensed kisses and the usual compliments and knelt to lug a hefty stone bench closer to them to perch on top. 'I very much support the Bucky, by the way – who brought that?'

'Rachel did the honours,' Maggie slurred merrily. 'We have more hidden inside! The staff are under strict instructions to protect the stash. Let's get you some.'

'Nah.' Clara sighed. 'I'll probably have to refrain. Me coming home pissed would no doubt give Ollie more points on the Great Leaderboard of Marriage.'

'Oh … if you prefer …' Maggie lowered her voice. 'There's cocaine in the third-floor bathroom.'

'Maggie Strong!' Annie pretended to be shocked.

'What!' Maggie laughed. 'We have to have it for the models. It's like their version of crudités, we couldn't deprive them. And Donal's marketing buddies are frantic for the stuff.'

'Being coked up would also put me behind on the whole trying-to-prove-I'm-not-a-mess thing,' Clara said darkly. 'More fodder for the stupid counsellor.'

'So, how did the first session go?' asked Annie.

'Let's talk about literally anything else.' Clara forced a grin. 'Wanna talk about Conor?'

Rachel rolled her eyes, while Annie shook her head vehemently. 'He's here somewhere,' she hissed.

'Oh of course, sorry,' Clara whispered back. 'Any plans for moving yet?'

'Actually, yes.' Annie smiled at Rachel. 'She's taking me in.'

Rachel gave Annie a squeeze and said, 'She's literally our little lost orphan Annie.'

'That's nice.' Clara picked up her glass. A small bit of champagne wouldn't hurt. 'Where do you live, Rachel?'

Three hours later and Clara was buried in a plush white sofa listening to Fionn and three of his very nearest and dearest, wildly famous Hollywood friends: Saint Fire, rapper and entrepreneur; Hugo Thomas, actor-director; and Seb Wade, actor-director-rapper-entrepreneur. Clara's 'bit of champagne' had turned into 'a bit of champagne' and a 'fuck it, give me the Buckfast'. The bottle of which she had just handed to Saint Fire, who was now grimacing violently.

'This tastes like something you should be putting in an engine, not drinking!'

Clara giggled. 'It's one of the few English things Irish people will admit is amazing. It's made in Devon by Benedictine Monks – they know what they're at.'

'So, you are … Clara?' Hugo Thomas peered at her and then glanced at Fionn. 'Is she your new …?'

'My new what?' he asked.

'Your new mistress, my friend,' Hugo said knowingly, as Clara and Fionn looked at each other and then shook their heads, laughing. Hugo arched an eyebrow. 'C'mon, Fionn – no mistress yet? Aka wife number two! You're coming up on "The Time". The old Hollywood Trade-In. If you don't start collecting wives now, how do you hope to have as many ex-wives as me by the time you're my age?'

'Yeah,' Seb Wade chimed in. 'How else you gonna lose all your money if it's not getting sucked away on alimony?'

'Ewww.' Clara glanced at Fionn. Were they really his friends?

'It's tradition!' Hugo grinned.

'Not for me, thanks.' Fionn's bright expression dimmed and Clara was relieved. At least he's not participating.

Hugo just laughed. 'How many ex-wives you got, Saint?'

'Three – four if you count the Vegas marriage to my divorce lawyer's legal secretary.'

'Seb?' Hugo swivelled his head in a move reminiscent of a lizard. His whole vibe was a bit lizardy, now that Clara thought about it.

'Ah, only two.' Seb flashed that grin that used to beam down at Clara from the posters on her teenage bedroom wall. He carried on: 'But what I save in alimony I more than make up for in shelling out child support.' He laughed wryly, shaking his head. 'Seven kids total, plus one son still with pat test pending.'

'Paternity test?' Fionn asked, not very successfully hiding his disbelief.

'Ah, yeah.' Seb Wade waved a hand vaguely, then took the bottle of Buckfast from Saint and proceeded to examine the label with far greater interest than he'd just displayed when talking about his potential eighth child.

'You're all so lucky,' Clara chirped. 'I can't even afford one divorce, never mind multiple.'

'You tryna get a divorce, honey?' Saint took out a small weed pen and took a pensive pull.

'It's looking that way.' Clara glanced over at Fionn, who seemed uncomfortable. She wondered what Ollie was saying in their group chat. She relieved Seb of the Buckfast and took a swig, before continuing, 'Today we did counselling and it was not good.' She looked at the other men. 'Any of you ever do the try-to-make-it-work thing?'

'No,' said Hugo promptly. 'Very boring, I'd imagine.'

'Hmmmmm.' Clara nodded. 'Yeah, it's not really my scene either. But we're pretty stuck on all fronts – money-wise, house-wise, kids-wise.'

'But it's you and Ollie, you guys love each other.' Fionn looked pained and, while it was *her* bleak life causing this look, it did make her appreciate that he was still his old self in many ways. Conor had always been the smart one and Ollie was the goof of the group but Fionn had a gentleness to him. He had a lot of empathy. She supposed all artists did – you needed it to make art. It was why he was good at creating characters and portraying their stories. Obviously, like all men, he had his lapses – like ditching them on their holiday. But at least success hadn't made him a dead-eyed cynic like these reptilian men.

'You know who you should talk to ...' Seb straightened up suddenly. 'What was that guy's name again?' He started clicking his fingers.

'Oh yeah!' Saint piped up from his nearly prone position. 'The producer guy. Reality TV guy.'

'Simon,' Fionn said quietly, to cheers from the others.

'Yeah, man. That's the one.'

Fionn turned to Clara. 'Ignore them, don't talk to Simon. He's doing this thing but it's really seedy and it's ... just ... a big bowl of wrong.' He leaned closer to her. 'I know Ollie is really upset right now. To be honest, I think maybe he *is* overreacting a bit, which I've said to him. That didn't go down well ...' Fionn shrugged helplessly. 'And, like, I know he's talking about walking away and that's—'

'Wait, he's said that to you?' Clara gripped the neck of the bottle tighter.

'He's just very—'

'Look!' Seb interrupted them. 'There he is, that producer dude!' Seb waved over towards a small, muscular, bald man with an all-over bronze tan showcased by the shimmering gold tank top he wore over matching loose shimmering harem pants. 'Simon,' Seb yelled. This caught the guy's attention and he sloped towards them, entirely unhurried as he crossed the room accepting slightly sycophantic greetings from some of the Irish reality stars in the vicinity.

'Hello again, fellas.' Simon leaned on the back of Seb Wade's sofa. 'What can I do for you?'

'It's for her.' Saint exhaled a plume of smoke in Clara's direction.

'She's in the market for a divoooo-rrrr-ce,' Hugo Thomas sang cheerily and, through her booze haze, Clara felt a wriggle of disgust. The way these men talked ... clearly no one had been anything less than entirely deferential to them in years and it showed. How did Maggie tolerate these people on the regular?

The producer, Simon, looked down at her and leaned forward to extend a hand. 'I'm so sorry to hear you're going through a tough time. I'm Simon Hayes.'

'Clara … eh … Delaney. For now, at least.'

'Clara,' Fionn interjected, 'it will all settle down, I know it will.'

'You weren't in our session today,' Clara shot back.

'Session? You're in couples counselling?' Simon gazed down with sympathy.

'First appointment today. And probably the last. Fucker charges a fortune and Ollie – that's my husband – stormed out early anyway. And it was *his* idea.'

'It's a very challenging time.' Simon nodded.

'Yeah.' Clara brought the Buckfast up for a swig. 'So. Why were these guys saying I should talk to you? You're a producer?'

'I'm doing a reality show for couples who are finding themselves in difficulty in their relationships. We're casting in the next few weeks to start shooting in just over a month. It's a short shoot – just three weeks – but the location is stunning. The Greek islands. Still gorgeous in September at that time. Think *Love Island* meets *Wife Swap*.'

'Wow.' Clara nodded politely, a bit unclear as to how this guy was supposedly going to solve her mess.

'Tell her what it's called!' Seb yelled. *Ugh*, Clara thought, *it's a shame he's so insufferable.* All her teenage fantasies were now ruined.

Simon grinned. 'It's called *Divorce Island* because the prize for the winning couple is an all-expenses-paid divorce!'

'Seriously?' Clara laughed in disbelief. *How desperate would you have to be?* Then she flashed back to Ollie leaving the appointment earlier and swallowed down a sickly surge of anxiety. She wasn't exactly the most un-desperate person herself right now. God. But Ollie couldn't really have meant what he said. He was just punishing her. They were in a very bad place. If they could just get their heads above water for more than five minutes, they could be good again.

'Simon, it's completely deranged,' said Fionn flatly.

'Thanks!' Simon laughed. 'We like to think we're pushing the reality TV envelope and we are *helping* people. Believe me, there are way crazier reality shows out there.'

'What if the winning couple change their mind about wanting the divorce?' Fionn asked.

'No problem!' Simon clapped his hands together. 'In that case, it's a financial prize equal to the value of a divorce – a divorce in the UK, that is. So about 30K. Not sure how much it is here.'

That made Clara sit up. 'What do the couples have to do on the island?' she asked curiously.

'Fun stuff,' Simon said airily. 'Team-building challenges and trust exercises – that kind of thing.'

'So how does a couple win?'

'Oh, it's entirely based on popularity with the viewers. They vote on the couple they like best.'

At that moment, Maggie came into view behind Simon. 'Birthday cake time in two minutes, everyone. Spread the word!'

Clara spent the last hour of the party trying to sober up a bit. She'd even been tempted to pop upstairs for a little bump to sharpen her up, but coke had never really been her thing. Plus, she was afraid she wouldn't sleep till Tuesday – the joys of nearing middle age.

She was also, if she was being honest, half hoping to run into Simon Hayes again. Maybe he'd have no interest in a couple as old as them for his show, maybe it was all hot young ones they were looking for, but she still wanted to see. If only to say it to Ollie and call his bluff. *He thinks he wants a divorce so bad, see what he thinks of this …*

The crowd had thinned significantly – most of the famouses had left before 10 p.m., no doubt to get up early for green juices and stem cell enemas. The next wave to leave were the people dashing back to relieve stroppy teen babysitters. Clara was in the third wave, the people who were having fun but still needed to function the following day. By midnight, she'd kissed the girls goodbye, avoided a rogue grope from Hugo Thomas and was getting her coat when Simon Hayes appeared beside her and gallantly held the jacket for her to slip her arms into.

'Hi.' She smiled. 'I was actually looking for you … while pretending I wasn't.'

'Oh yeah?' He raised a tweezed brow. 'The show, right?'

'Well, look, we – my husband and I – might not be what you had in mind. We're not glamorous … we're old, we're broke, we have three boys …'

'No, no.' Simon shook his head. 'You two sound *perfect*. There's real *stakes* there, tug-of-love kids, financial woes. That's what we're after. We need meaty storylines.'

Clara frowned slightly. *God, when you put it like that … it really seemed so bleak. Making a storyline of her family, her boys.*

Obviously catching her look, Simon started rummaging in his pocket and came up with a business card. 'Listen, it's a lot to take in and obviously lots to discuss with your husband. Think about it.' He handed her the card and they said goodbye. Clara let him go out ahead of her and she hung back so she wouldn't have to walk down the street with him. She needed time to clear her thoughts.

CHAPTER 15

The Sunday after the party, Maggie sat on the back terrace of the Miavita house with a coffee and a bowl of fruit salad, waiting for the cleaners to finish in the kitchen so she could get something more to eat before Fionn came back from his run with Ollie and Conor.

Donal's party had raged on into Saturday morning, culminating with a mass drunken skinny dip across the road, scandalising the early-morning walkers. Naturally a couple of pictures, snapped by passersby, had surfaced on a few of the Irish celeb websites and Maggie had been enormously relieved that she had kept her clothes on and just watched.

She'd felt a bit embarrassed that the party had been *so* celeby. Brody had taken over the guest list and sent out what he had called 'strategic invites' to most of Ireland's big names. 'This business is all about making the connections,' he'd insisted. 'It looks good for Finn to be partying with these people.'

Thankfully, Donal seemed only delighted to have his birthday slightly hijacked by actors and models and musicians, and at least Maggie had been able to hide with the girls for most of the night, though *they* had escaped home before the swimming in the nip had begun.

After the dip, the party's final holdouts had come back for a big 'full Irish' served amid the detritus of the night before, and then they all finally drifted home. The cleaners had started in earnest on the Saturday afternoon but they'd had to come back this morning, still battling to right the place.

Maggie texted Annie to let her know that Fionn, Conor and Ollie had still not returned. She and Annie were going for a swim together before Maggie and Fionn flew back to LA later that night, but timings were tricky as Annie and Conor were pretty committed to not crossing paths. Maggie was supposed to give her the signal to come once Conor had cleared off.

Maggie flicked idly through the summer programme for Dublin's Regent Theatre that she'd found among the post when they'd arrived on Thursday night. There were interesting shows on and it made her think about what it'd be like to actually spend some time in Dublin as opposed to always flitting back to LA. What could a life in Dublin look like for her now? She'd be in this beautiful house more; she'd see her friends and her family more. The twins could have a more grounded life.

Dublin would be so lovely but she knew the price of that would be Fionn making fewer and fewer appearances in their lives. Coming back to Ireland would widen the distance in their marriage. He needed to be based in LA. He would also have a *lot* to say about this idea. He already missed so much time with the twins due to work; if she made it even harder for him to see them on his down time … things could get very tense. Despite his occasional forays into slightly self-centred bullshit like disappearing with Edwin Ensel in Provincetown, he adored the girls.

She skimmed a review of the new Marina Carr show but her

mind was still elsewhere. She'd never really made a social circle in LA. It was so hard to make new friends as an adult. But she also hadn't made much of an effort to explore the different sides to the city. She knew next to nothing about the theatre scene there. It seemed like theatre in LA was entirely dwarfed by Hollywood. Though perhaps it was more that her *life* in LA was dwarfed by Hollywood. She could probably be going to incredible shows but when she did go out it was usually to industry parties or premieres with Fionn.

She turned a page, only to find a familiar face, Selena Crossan, being heralded as 'the most bold and exciting voice in theatre right now'. Maggie swiftly closed the booklet. Selena had been in the same year as Maggie in college. She did not need *that* in her head. Her mood had been good in the last couple of weeks despite all the recent press. She was on the upswing of a new weight-loss plan, always the most optimistic time in such endeavours. She was practically high off the sense of control that had been restored to her since she'd begun to quietly catalogue her meals on the app.

After Provincetown, she'd gotten back on her training schedule. She let Britney go – too soft on her, and also privy to Maggie's history and therefore not willing to enable any pursuit of weight loss. She'd secured Caroline instead – the hard-bodied, domineering woman who'd worked on *Endurance* with Fionn and was now ordering Maggie from machine to machine in their stifling subterranean gym in the LA house.

Of course, she wouldn't be broadcasting that, as it wasn't fashionable anymore. Every woman just had to privately restrict and strive for weight loss while publicly shrugging off their gorgeous bodies as an accidental byproduct of their 'lifestyle'. Plus,

Maggie couldn't so much as say she was trying to eat *healthier*, without everyone around her worrying that she was going to take it too far. They didn't understand the sense of safety sticking to a strict plan gave her. She liked logging her foods in the little app. She liked the feeling of order. Lots of people seemed to find dieting annoying but she'd always found it oddly comforting, in contrast to how completely out of control she felt without rules around food. And when she sometimes went a bit off-piste with the food when she was on her own, she could remedy it with a quick trip to the loo. No harm, no foul – it wasn't like it was every day or anything.

Through the kitchen windows she could see Fionn's commanding figure entering, and the resulting effect this invariably had on any woman in the vicinity. A flurry of nerves clearly caught the two girls who'd been idly chatting and stacking dishes. They immediately stopped and gaped, before recovering a couple of seconds later. Maggie smiled. On bad days, watching these encounters could depress her. She didn't like to be reminded that all the time they were apart Fionn was having these moments with men and women literally across the world. Today, eight pounds lighter than she'd been only two weeks ago and she was feeling better. Not better enough to actually have sex with her husband, let's not go mad. She was still about twenty pounds off that, but luckily with all the travel and social engagements, not to mention the twins occasionally climbing into their bed during the night, she was pretty sure Fionn was putting the lack of sex down to circumstances rather than any avoidance on her part.

Or maybe he doesn't even care? Maybe he's in no rush to have sex with you either.

The mean little thought stabbed at her but was quickly dispatched as Fionn came out the doors towards her, grinning.

'You are looking very lady-of-the-manor, Mrs Strong.'

'Ewww,' she teased, but gave a little spin in her long, delicate lace dressing gown. The pale lilac was good with her dark hair and she'd made a note to tell Sylvia to source more things in this colour.

'Hey, Maggie.' Ollie came out after Fionn, followed by Conor, who raised a hand in greeting. They were each dressed in different takes on the sporty-middle-aged-man look. Lycra for Conor, grey sweats and a ratty T-shirt for Ollie, while Fionn was in a Stella McCartney-Adidas one-piece that was way too high-concept for most Irish men. The shoulders had some kind of aerodynamic fins.

'How was the run?' Maggie leaned back on the low stone wall supported by small columns that bordered the terrace. 'Did anyone hurl abuse about this outfit?' She gestured at Fionn.

'There were a lot of attempts that were swiftly aborted when they realised who he was,' Conor said wryly.

'How far did you go?'

''Bout 12K.' Ollie nodded at her amiably, but was definitely more muted than usual.

'Nothing for this guy.' Fionn clapped Ollie on the back.

'Oh yeah ...' Maggie fussed with her hair. 'How's the ... eh ... training going?'

'Good.' Ollie pressed his lips together. 'Especially now that I'm not tryna fit it all in in the middle of the night. No need to be killing myself being considerate to Clara; she wouldn't be to me.'

'Right.' Maggie had no idea what to say and desperately wished they would leave so the awkwardness could end.

Unfortunately, from the look of concern on Fionn's face they were going to be getting into it. 'Ah man, you guys'll work it out, right? You and Clara were always such a good couple. Chaos but good.'

Ollie's face hardened further and he shrugged dispassionately. 'Things change. Kids change things, money – or lack thereof – changes things. No offence, but you two don't have that stress. I'm not trying to make you feel bad but, fact is, you don't have the first idea of what that can do to a couple.'

Maggie bit back words that she would regret voicing. *Not seeing each other because you're rarely in the same continent puts pressure on a relationship too. One person achieving their dreams while the other is left floundering in the wake of that, pretending they're fine with their lot, puts stress on a relationship.*

After five years of having more money than she'd ever dreamed of, Maggie felt like she finally knew the answer to 'what is being rich really like?' It's like your surroundings, your clothes and all the furniture in your life undergo an insane upgrade but you yourself barely change. All the fears and insecurities you've always grappled with are still there, oftentimes even worse than before because being rich affords you a lot of time and empty hours in which to ruminate and berate yourself for having everything and somehow still being miserable. And now spoilt as well to top it all off.

Sympathy for rich white ladies was in short supply and she could recognise that that was fair enough. Though it didn't take away the regrets that seemed to be scratching away at her as the years were passing. *Any normal person could just revel in the money and the glitz,* Maggie sometimes admonished herself. She should just get on board and enjoy the ride, as Eva advised.

'Yeah, man. I know. Or ... I can imagine.' Fionn nodded, visibly agonising over what to say next. 'You know ...' he threw a quick glance at Maggie, 'you – or Clara – you could come stay here for a bit. Get a bit of a break ...'

'Yeah,' Maggie chimed in. 'Get a bit of space from each other. It could be exactly what you need to get back on track. To see that you love each other.'

'We'd even throw in the private chef.' Fionn grinned, obviously warming to his idea.

It wasn't the right thing to say. Ollie shook his head. 'Guys, I know you're trying to be nice. But I am a forty-two-year-old man. I don't need to be saved by my rich friends.'

Maggie felt Fionn palpably sag beside her and Maggie sincerely wished they'd all just leave – she missed the days when they'd all been so easy with each other. The days when they'd all been in similar places in their lives. In their twenties, they'd hung out for entire weekends, hungover, watching shite telly. Good-naturedly slagging whoever had been the most shitfaced the night before from under their blankets in the ratty house shares the six of them had lived in – the smell of damp just present under the haze of weed and fires made with briquettes.

But maybe all groups of friends were destined to disintegrate eventually?

Finally Conor spoke up. 'Guys,' he looked at Maggie and Fionn, 'relationships in the real world are more complicated. It's not as simple as Ollie taking a luxury mini-break in south County Dublin.

Why should *he* have to leave his kids? Why does Clara get to stay in her home?'

'Okay, thanks for schooling us on the *real world*,' Maggie snapped. She'd had enough. 'I'm sure you learned a lot about the *real world* growing up on the mean streets of Foxrock, Conor.'

'Maggie …' Fionn held his hands out palms down in a placating gesture, the international sign for 'calm down' which had never in the history of the international-sign-for-calm-down successfully calmed anyone down.

'He's acting like we were born to all this.' She gestured at Conor. 'We come from more normal backgrounds than you do, Conor. Fionn was raised by a single mum, for God's sake. My parents worked their asses off and still they couldn't afford to give us any money for college.' She grabbed her phone. 'I'm heading out.' She'd text Annie to meet her down at the swimming place instead – she was truly over the guys at this point. 'Enjoy the rest of the day,' she finished sarcastically, and charged into the house to get dressed, aware that storming into her eight-million-euro home on the richest terrace in Dublin was probably undermining her point slightly.

As Maggie made her way down the ramp to the swimming spot, she was surprised to see Annie there already, holding her runners and dipping a toe in to test the temperature of the water. The swimming spot wasn't a beach; it was, like many bathing areas in the city, a concrete platform surrounding an old Martello tower with steps down into the sea. There were whitewashed stone structures for changing under, and in recent years outdoor showers had been added.

'Hey,' Maggie called, waving.

Annie held up a hand in greeting and started towards the end of the ramp.

'How're you here already?' Maggie squinted as the weak sun tried to assert itself in spite of a stubborn cloud cover that had come down over the day.

'Well, Rachel's place is only over in Blackrock, remember? And we were out for coffee in the village already, so I figured I'd just head on over. Start psyching myself up for getting in.' She nodded at the steely Irish Sea that looked inhospitable even in late July.

'Ah.' Maggie nodded, laying her towel down and slipping off her long, striped Adriana Degreas kaftan, automatically pulling her stomach in. 'Listen, not sure if you can sense it on the wind but Conor is still up in our house. So is Ollie.'

Annie gave a shrug. 'They're like pubic lice, they get everywhere.' She pulled off her oversized T-shirt. 'Well, not Fionn. Sorry.'

'Since when have you had pubic lice?' Maggie grinned. 'In fact, stop, I don't need the visual!' Maggie kicked off her flip-flops. 'Anyway, Ollie is in the worst form I've ever seen him in. Like a different person.'

'Yeah,' Annie echoed. 'Clara is even more unhinged than usual.'

'Oh?' Maggie sensed Annie was referencing something specific, and from the slightly abashed expression now spreading across Annie's features, she had not been supposed to say anything.

Annie shuffled her shorts off and snapped the edges of her swimsuit to adjust it. 'I love your togs.' She tried to deflect.

'Na-ah. What's she saying to you that she's not saying to me?' Maggie raised an eyebrow, ignoring the slight prick of hurt that sometimes came when the girls seemed to be leaving her out. *Not important, Maggie. You're a grown woman!*

'Okay.' Annie rubbed her upper arms where goosebumps had appeared. 'Do not say anything. She'll tell you herself anyway. Look, she was chatting to some TV guy on Friday night and he was telling her about some mad show he's doing about divorcing couples. Basically she said it's like *Love Island* but for couples who hate each other. The prize is an all-expenses-paid divorce.'

'Oh God.'

'I know,' Annie agreed. 'It's called *Divorce Island*. The couples do tasks to help them decide whether to stay together or split up.'

'She doesn't actually think this is a real option, does she?' Maggie felt, somewhat to her surprise, a rising irritation with her friend. After the tetchy exchange with Ollie, she'd been firmly on Clara's side, but God, she made supporting her difficult sometimes.

Annie looked uncertain. 'I really don't know how serious she is.'

Maggie shook her head. 'This is the stupidest thing I've ever heard. *I'd* pay for her divorce. I'd pay for them to rent another house for Ollie to move into. Ollie was just giving me shit for offering them *our* house to stay in but, like, if the choice is go on a reality TV show or take some money …' She threw her hands up in exasperation.

'Maggie!' Annie looked to be trying to modulate her voice. 'Can you just … not. I think Clara and I have said it enough times at this stage. Money between friends is weird. Don't you think you constantly trying to pay away our problems is … well … patronising. I know you mean well, but it doesn't feel good and I would suggest you stop.'

Shame swam through Maggie and she felt a little panicky. *Well. They've clearly talked about this one between themselves.* It was not a nice thought.

'Okay,' Maggie said quietly, looking at the large stone slabs underfoot.

Annie slid an arm around her. 'Don't get upset, Maggie. I won't see you for ages. Let's swim. It's alright. Clara will cop on and they'll get sorted.'

Maggie put an arm around Annie as well. 'What about you?' she asked as they made their way over to the lapping water.

'I'll be fine too.' Annie reached for the handrail of the steps and Maggie followed behind her, each of them starting to squeal as they lowered themselves in. At the height of summer, the sea was barely warmer than on the coldest day of winter. A lot of Irish people swam all year round – knitted beanie hats bobbing around in the water was not an uncommon sight in the chillier months.

When they were fully submerged, gently treading water and their breathing had calmed, Annie spoke again. 'I feel a lot better, you know.'

Maggie looked at her but Annie's gaze was trained on the horizon – in the grey of the day the edge of the ocean made a defined navy line across the bay. Maggie said nothing, giving Annie the space to share.

'I feel better than I thought I would,' Annie continued. 'I had a real low the week before last when I got my period. At least it was a pretty light one, the universe giving me a break for once. I didn't put it in Slags For Life. I just needed to be quiet with the feeling or something. Like I'm grieving the thing I thought I'd have – a family and whatever. But I also have this feeling of ... a kind of release. There's this space opening up in my mind of "okay, if not this, then what do I want the rest of my life to look like?"'

'That's really good, Annie.' Maggie spoke softly so as not to disrupt her friend's train of thought.

'I was reading this thing that said that the most intolerable state for humans is uncertainty. That we would literally prefer a bad outcome over having to live in a state of not knowing. I really get that. I feel like the bad thing has happened now and, as shitty as it is, now I know and I don't have to be in this constant state of waiting anymore. Living my life on tenterhooks.'

'I get that, sweetie.'

Annie's eyes seemed to come back into focus then. She turned and smiled at Maggie. 'I know it's only been a couple of weeks but I'm loving living with Rachel. It reminds me of our twenties, hanging out on the couch for hours on end just talking shite.'

Maggie nodded. 'Sounds nice.'

'Though obviously there's still so much to get my head around. I've been with Conor my entire adult life. Like even on a good day, I've about twenty "what the hell has happened?" moments ... Anyway, all we've talked about is me and Clara's fuckery. How's everything been since Provincetown? Did Fionn stick around after the party or did he have to go back to yer man's shack?'

'Eh, he was sort of back and forth.' Maggie kept her tone breezy, though the reality was that it'd been a lot more back than forth. 'Things seem to be getting going on that project and Fionn's excited.' Maggie could think of nothing else to say about the trip that wouldn't sound super depressing: *I watched my daughters play on the beach from under a large hat and towel so no more pictures of my body would appear online; I snuck into town one night in a baseball cap and sunglasses to buy donuts and Doritos because, by that point, I couldn't ask the staff to get me any more 'snacks for the kids'.*

'Did you know that Selena Crossan has a play on in the Regent?' Maggie asked.

Annie shivered. 'Will we get out? My hands are numb.'

'Yeah.' Maggie nodded and began swimming back to the steps.

When they reached the top of the steps and were squeezing the water from their hair, Maggie decided to probe again. 'So? Selena?'

'Oh, yeah.' Annie straightened up. 'Yup. She's definitely doing good.'

'She was always good at networking,' Maggie sniffed, heading for the towels.

'She was,' Annie agreed.

'Is the play any good?' Maggie swiped her towel over her body.

'I haven't gone.' Annie shrugged.

'If I wasn't flying out later, I'd actually go,' Maggie said. 'See what the "most bold and exciting voice in theatre right now" has to say.'

'Maggie …' Annie seemed to be searching for the right way to articulate her next words.

'Yeah?' Maggie pulled on the kaftan and felt relieved that she could relax her stomach finally.

'Why don't *you* make something? Like Selena?'

'Selena doesn't have kids.' Maggie pushed her hair back roughly. 'Kids just suck away all your time. And your brain is just mush—' She stopped abruptly, seeing Annie's gentle concern drop from her face. 'Sorry. I'm being really insensitive. It's not just the brain mush,' Maggie hurried on. 'If I do something, it's just going to be so *nothing* compared to Fionn. And either people will feel sorry for me and think I have this little vanity project paid for by my husband, or if I make something actually good, no one will think I succeeded in my own right.'

Annie was dressed now and stepping into her runners. 'Maggie, I'm saying this with love – even though I deserve a Nobel Prize for life-coaching my millionaire friend …' Annie was smiling, and Maggie could see she wasn't being snippy.

'Go on.' Maggie nodded faintly.

'You have something no artist has.'

'Talent?' Maggie ventured hopefully.

'A full staff,' Annie deadpanned, and Maggie laughed.

'Okay, okay.' Maggie threw her hands up in submission. 'I know I can make time. A lot of time. But maybe that's what's so intimidating? I've no excuse if it's just shit. Also, I wouldn't know where to start. I'm out of practice. I've wasted years. While Selena Fucking Crossan was getting established, I was trying to deal with having twin babies in a tiny flat in London and then I was looking after our daughters while trailing around after my A-list husband. It probably doesn't sound like a good excuse on paper but after Fionn's career took off, our whole life seemed to accelerate to this crazy pace.'

'Just start,' Annie insisted. 'Get yourself an office when you get back to LA. Start seeing theatre again. Look for a story you want to tell. You were amazing at this, Maggie.'

Even after the optimistic chats with Annie, by late afternoon, Maggie was stressed. The house was back in order but the packing was getting on top of her. She had also spent a few ill-advised minutes googling Selena and learned that not only was she 'the most bold and exciting voice in theatre right now', she had also been awarded the Rooney Prize the previous summer. This was one of the most prestigious honours in the arts in Ireland. To top it all off, Fionn had 'nipped out' exactly three hours ago to show Saint, Hugo and Seb 'a few spots'.

'They came over to the party especially to see me, I gotta hang with them,' he'd said in that cajoling tone that Maggie was growing to despise.

The thing that was annoying her most was that she wanted to nip out *herself*. Instead, she tore around Dodi and Essie's pale pink bedroom on the third floor. The room's vibe was like an extravagant cake, frosted in frills and lace with two large four-poster beds with white sparkling canopies.

She threw favourite teddies, blankies and charged tablets into the two little wheely cases her daughters always brought on board for long flights. As fast as she was packing, the girls were undoing her work.

'Mam.' Dodi fell upon her bag. 'I want my iPad for the taxi.'

'No, no. Please just leave it in there,' Maggie begged. 'I just need to keep everything in its place right now so I don't forget anything.'

'Stop annoying Mam,' Essie shouted at Dodi from her position, jumping up and down on her bed, completely fucking it up in the process.

'That's antique.' Maggie grabbed Essie's hand to halt the jumping. 'Do you like the princess bed? You don't want to break it.'

'But we can just get another one?' Essie sounded genuinely perplexed that Maggie would be worried about a broken bed when there was an unending line of possessions streaming into their lives at all times.

Oh God. Maggie didn't even have time to start spiralling about the girls' growing sense of entitlement.

She zipped up the bags and pulled them into the landing and checked her phone: 4.30 p.m. Fionn had still not blue-ticked her message from an hour ago. They were leaving for the airport at six. She chewed at the inside of her lower lip. Fuck it, she would just bring the girls with her.

The three of them were in the car five minutes later, her daughters bombarding her with questions about their destination. 'I just have to get petrol,' Maggie said, steering them away from the house.

'What's petrol?' one of them asked.

'Gas, honey,' Maggie corrected herself.

'Why do we need gas? We're leaving.' The other joined the interrogation.

'We're getting it because we don't want to leave the Dublin car empty.' *Well, that didn't make a whole lot of sense*, she thought. And if the girls mentioned the outing to Fionn, he would definitely think it was an odd thing to prioritise.

She glanced at the matching blonde heads in the rearview mirror. 'Also, I've to get special Irish tea bags to bring home to LA.'

'Can we have Olivia Rodrigo?' Dodi asked.

'Sure.' Maggie handed the phone into the back seat so her daughter could cue up the music. At the next lights, she made a right towards the petrol station that was further up the coast road. She hadn't actually planned on it, but her petrol excuse was actually kind of good because she could safely leave the girls in the car while she got everything she needed and could go into the station's toilets.

Inside the shop, she kept an eye on her car through the long window in front as she picked up a fat stack of Cadbury's chocolate bars – they were more compact than any of the bags of crisps. She felt she'd get the bars into her pockets and so look fairly normal going into the loos.

All it took was five frenzied but satisfying minutes to dispatch the chocolate and then less than a minute on the floor of the toilet to rid herself of it. After three days of being constantly in the company of others and unable to do her routine whenever she overate, it was a huge release. Back in the car with her daughters, she chewed gum to hide the smell. She felt dizzy but pleasantly sedated. She took a couple of breaths to savour the lightness in her mind and body, before pressing the ignition button.

'Mam. Mam.' Essie tapped at her. 'Where is the special tea?'

Shite. Fair point, Maggie thought.

'Oh my God, I'm such a silly.' She smiled at Essie. 'I'll be right back.'

CHAPTER 16

Annie circled the dining table, tidying away the Sunday roast she'd made for herself and Rachel. Through the timber-framed, slanted windows under which the table was tucked, she could see the low, flat-roofed structure at the other side of the tiny garden where Rachel painted when she wasn't in her studio in the gallery in town. The garden was completely overgrown which, coupled with all the delicate glass panels at this end of the house, reminded Annie of the Victorian glasshouses in the Botanic Gardens.

The house itself was also Victorian. From the front, it looked like a storybook house. Two sash windows flanked a jaunty yellow door that was tucked under the sharply pitched roof of the porch. Inside, the attractively wonky floorboards seemed to gently curve and swerve through the hallways and rooms. Every inch of the walls was covered in beautiful things to look at, from ornately framed paintings and prints to Rachel's huge collection of eccentric ephemera. There were tax bills covered in scenes rendered in watercolours. Endless postcards arranged into a vast mosaic in the kitchen. The fabric limbs of slack puppets trailed on the mantelpiece in the living room, while hooked on a nail in the toilet there was the skull of what Annie later found out was a dog with the words 'get well soon' written above one of the empty sockets.

On the tiny second storey were two dreamy little bedrooms under the eaves, each with a small dormer window looking over the back garden and Rachel's studio, with the foothills of the Dublin mountains in the distance. Annie was positive that she would be way more traumatised by everything that'd happened in the last five weeks if she hadn't had this incredibly soft landing in Rachel's home.

She stacked the dishes and brought them into the little galley kitchen. She loaded the dishwasher and then checked on the two little individual trifles in the fridge that she'd made that morning. The custard was setting very nicely. Since she'd moved in, she'd been flat out behaving like the dream housemate. Well, apart from the few nights at the start when she'd gone too heavy on the white wine and had insisted they listen to the ten-minute version of 'All Too Well' on repeat. Rachel had been very patient about this and, miraculously, now, more than a month since the split from Conor, Annie seemed to have moved through the furious 'fuck that guy' stage of break-up grief and into the vaguely more optimistic 'what the hell do I do with my life now?' stage.

She and Rachel had even done some light vision-boarding which Rachel said wasn't quite cliché enough so they threw in a spell-casting they'd seen on TikTok. This went great until the ceremonial burning of old 'negative-energy-holding knickers' got a bit too smoky and they couldn't get the fire alarm to shut up. Eventually Annie had smashed it down from the ceiling with the broom handle and Rachel pronounced her the best housemate ever.

Annie returned to the table to give it a wipe. From the clock on the oven, it was coming up to 8.30 p.m. and the sky above their garden was pinking up nicely. Annie picked up her phone and texted Rachel:

Annie: *Trifle and Sopranos?*

Rachel: *Amazing, just tidying up in here.*

A minute later, Annie spotted the lights go out in the studio and Rachel, red hair tumbling as always, stepping carefully through the tall grass to the back door.

They settled themselves in the living room just off the dining room. On the TV, Tony and Carmela were having a row while Rachel offered a running commentary between spoons of trifle.

'Truly, how does she tolerate the breathing thing? I swear, 85 per cent of his dialogue is just rhythmic nasal congestion.'

'She likes being the queen of New Jersey,' Annie suggested.

'This is so good, by the way.' Rachel raised her bowl of trifle.

Annie shifted around, trying to get more comfortable.

'You okay?' Rachel looked over.

'Yeah.' Annie picked her trifle up again. 'I'm just crampy. I feel like PMS used to be the support act and now it's becoming more of a ball-ache than the actual menstruating part. Period's not even due till the end of the week.'

'Poor Annie.' Rachel found Annie's ankle amid the jewel-coloured velvet pillows on the couch and gave it a rub. 'Will I get you paracetamol? Or a hot-water bottle?'

'Thanks, but I think I'm okay. I'm too clammy for a hot-water bottle.' She grinned. 'But, yeah, if you would grab the paracetamol for me, that'd be amazing, I am absolutely wrecked. Who would be a woman?'

They paused Tony and Carm while Rachel went to hunt out the meds and Annie took out her phone for a quick scroll. She tapped the Insta icon and then got a mild jolt as a red-carpet picture of Fionn, Maggie, Dodi and Essie was at the top of her feed.

It'll never be normal, she thought ruefully, looking at them posing for photographers.

She tapped to expand the caption and see where her friends were. A premiere for the new Pixar movie. Annie examined the picture more closely and zoomed in. Maggie was wearing a scoop-necked dress. Annie looked at her clavicles, wondering if they had been this pronounced at Donal's party. Worry crept through her and she took a screenshot.

She opened WhatsApp and took special care to make sure she put the screenshot in her thread with Clara and *not* in Slags For Life. This was the minefield that was life in the modern era.

'What's the face for?' Rachel had returned.

'Oh, I'm kind of worried about Maggie.' Annie paused, wondering if it would be wrong to tell Rachel the full story, though at the same time, Annie wasn't sure there was anyone she trusted more. She pulled Rachel down to sit beside her.

'Listen, Maggie had an eating disorder when we were young. In college. It got seriously out of hand.' Annie unlocked her phone again and brought up the image of Maggie to show Rachel. 'Does she look smaller to you? Since we saw her two weeks ago.'

'Okay.' Rachel pinched the screen to zoom in on Maggie a bit.

'She looks … slim,' Rachel murmured. 'But,' she looked up, 'you'd know better what Maggie usually looks like. And I guess eating disorders don't always look how we think they're going to look.' She handed the phone back. 'Sorry, I feel like that is no help. Have you talked to Clara about it? Or Fionn even?'

'Clara … a bit. Not really. It was hard to get a moment alone together in Provincetown. At all times things seemed to be going to shit. I just sent her that pic, though.' Annie grimaced at the cramps, then continued. 'I had a few moments in Provincetown when I felt like something was off with Maggie and I did talk to her but she seemed grand. She's still seeing a counsellor, so that's good. But we didn't chat for long and then I suppose everything got completely overshadowed by all the drama. I feel like if I went to Fionn, Maggie would see that as a complete betrayal. Also, I just don't know how much he is actually around her anymore. Which is obviously a worry in itself.'

'It's so grim.' Rachel popped two paracetamol out of the packet and handed them across to Annie along with a glass of water. 'They're really not selling the old "lifestyle of the rich and famous", are they? The house is insane, though.'

'It is. Did I tell you she offered it to Clara and Ollie to stay in while they're copping on to themselves and getting over this stupid divorce idea?'

'You did. A true testament to how deranged Clara is that she is picking a reality TV show over a well-meaning handout from a friend.'

'I dunno.' Annie paused to swallow back the pills, then cleared her throat. 'Maybe you'd have to experience having two friends become insanely, mind-bogglingly rich to understand. It does something to the relationship. I think if I were in Clara's position, I'd be the same. No charity from friends. It's infantilising or something. Plus, in a weird way, this reality show is totally Clara's kind of thing. She is feckin' delighted to escape her real life for three weeks. Pretend she lives in a bikini on a Greek island and has no responsibilities. She can take the time off work because they're renting the house out while they're gone so that'll cover the bills.'

'I'm still shocked that she got Ollie on board.' Rachel pressed her lips together, shaking her head.

'Oh, he is still iffy. She's working on him, been leaning into what an amazing experience it'd be for the boys.'

Rachel snorted. 'I am sorry but *what?* Surely there's nothing in the world more toxic than your parents competing for a divorce on national television?'

'She's focusing on how travelling to Kos for three weeks will broaden their horizons, yada yada yada. Cuz it's a divorce show, most of the couples have kids, so the producers have a whole educational programme organised to run alongside the filming.'

'That is smart.' Rachel pointed a playful finger gun at Annie. 'So, what is the thing on Saturday about? We're still minding the boys?'

'Yeah. Saturday's the auditions.'

Rachel frowned. 'I thought this was all organised.'

'It is,' Annie explained. 'The producer told Clara they were cast but didn't want anyone accusing him of preferential treatment so they have to go to the casting like anyone else. Also, the show will be recording lots of stuff at it to use in the first episode.'

'Right.' Rachel grinned. 'So, what'll we do with the boys? Should we just bring them straight to a therapist?'

'Ooof, yeah.' Annie winced slightly. She didn't want to be

judgy, especially as she really didn't have the first clue what Clara's life was like, but going on a reality show seemed beyond drastic.

An hour later, lying in bed, Annie finally got a reply from Clara about the picture.

Clara: Are we looking at the dress? The kids? Fionn? Jack Black in the background?!

Annie rolled her eyes but then caught herself. Wait, it's a good sign that Clara's not seeing it. Annie started typing.

Annie: You don't think she looks smaller?

Annie waited. She could see Clara was still online, no doubt taking a closer look at the shot.

Clara: She looks slim but not bony or anything like that. I'm not seeing anything dramatic.

Clara: Then again, we completely fucking missed the warning signs last time.

Annie: I know. And there were a couple of 'off moments' on the holiday …

Annie watched 'Clara typing' for several minutes before her reply dropped in below.

> *Clara: That whole holiday was one big long 'off moment'. The one good sign is that she seems to be in a great mood in the group chat. She's buzzing about this new play idea – the Medea one. It's so exciting to hear her talking about creating again. Just checking ... Medea is the one where the woman finds out her husband's leaving her for a hotter, younger woman and she freaks out and kills the kids?!*
>
> *Annie: Yeah. The Greeks were so extra. But you're right, it's amazing to hear her so excited about her work after so long.*

Annie put the phone down for a minute. Outside the little window opposite, darkness had descended, but it was only after lunch for Maggie. She might even be in the office she'd set up in the house – the picture she'd sent them showed a tan leather swivel chair and a pale wooden desk placed before double doors leading to the pool area. Annie picked her phone back up and typed.

> *Annie: I suppose as long as her mood seems good, it's probably okay, isn't it? Surely she wouldn't be working on the project if she was struggling with food again.*

Clara replied:

Clara: We can just keep an eye on it. Don't worry, Annie, I'm sure she's grand, sure she's surrounded by people at all times.

This was true, Annie reflected. She was reminded of Betty, the housekeeper. It was great that she was there every day.

The following Saturday, Annie was still knocking back painkillers. Going by her discomfort, her period was imminent. As she got into Rachel's car to head for the hotel where the *Divorce Island* auditions were being held, she was trying to avoid thoughts of how every twist and cramp was a reminder of how not pregnant she was. All she had to look forward to now was menopause. Yay.

Beside her, Rachel was looking summery in a matching gingham top and shorts, and Annie found herself looking down at Rachel's pale, thick thighs and felt a throb of desire. Unsettled, Annie quickly crossed her legs and pulled on her seatbelt.

I can't get like that about Rachel.

Annie felt a little breathless. They started up Church Street and joined a queue of cars trying to get onto the main road. She was also suddenly hyper-aware of how close they were in the car. The throb was becoming more insistent and Annie rearranged herself again to try and shut it down. Of course, she'd thought Rachel was attractive, gorgeous even, from the moment they'd met but she'd been so preoccupied with Conor and trying for a baby that she'd never gone there in her mind. And now that they were living together, it definitely wouldn't be the best plan. Plus, Rachel was straight. *Cop on*, she told herself firmly. Entertaining a crush on one of her best friends when she was quite possibly on the rebound and living in said best friend's spare room would not be smart.

At the Elmore Hotel, they parked and followed the signs for Too Real Productions that led from the reception to a long, carpeted corridor that was crowded with couples predominantly in their forties. The atmosphere was noticeably un-buzzy. From what Annie had seen on shows like *The X Factor*, reality show auditions were usually more upbeat, full of optimistic hopefuls believing that, should this one encounter go well, their whole lives might change. Instead, *these* people all bore an expression of being completely *done* with life.

'Annie!' Clara appeared in the melee, waving. 'Thank you so much for doing this.' She embraced Annie and turned to Rachel. 'Are we on hugging terms yet?'

'Well, I'm minding your kids while you try to convince some TV producers that your marriage is on the rocks … so yeah?'

Clara laughed and gave her a hug. 'We really appreciate it. Ollie is in there now, then I go in and then they interview us together. The kids are just in here.' Clara steered them into a large room off the corridor.

'I'm still unclear.' Annie followed, frowning. 'I know they're doing education stuff but how are you going to manage the actual childcare during filming?'

'They talked us through some of that earlier. Basically there's a main villa where the show is recorded. Then all the families sleep in a separate "cast villa" on another part of the compound. There's childcare there and the producers have really cool day trips planned for the kids and tutors on site. Plus, we're not shooting all day and all night – there'll be plenty of time off.'

Annie could see Rachel looking sceptical as, all around them, kids ran about while grandparents and minders tried to marshal them.

'And Ollie is actually on board now?' Annie asked as they made their way to Josh, Tom and Reggie, who were on a sofa crowded around an iPad.

Clara looked defiant. 'He's been a sanctimonious shit for over a month now, a sanctimonious shit who doesn't have money for a divorce.'

'But Clara …' Annie searched for the right words. 'What does this really achieve? Even if you get the,' she lowered her voice 'divorce out of all this … life will still be life. Where will you all live?'

'Annie,' Clara wheeled around, looking exasperated, 'I don't have all the answers. But this is *something*. I cannot go on without something changing in my life. Everything is so …' She shook her head. 'It's so *sour*. I need to get out of that house. Get my kids out of that atmosphere.'

Rachel, sensing Annie and Clara might need privacy, walked ahead of them and approached the boys. Over the din, Annie could hear her introducing herself and presenting them with three little bags of jellies.

'Clara, I know it must be awful. But don't you think the price is too great? Putting yourselves on TV like this? What does your mum say?'

'Ah, Jean thinks it's mad.' Clara waved a hand impatiently. 'Of course she does. It *is* mad. But honestly, I'm looking forward to it. It definitely beats therapy; it beats going to the call centre for the next three weeks. If Ollie thinks I'm such a shit wife and mother, he can say it on national fucking television.'

'Clara ...' Annie smiled at her friend despite the bizarreness of the situation. 'If this is you calling his bluff, don't you think it's a bit extreme?'

'I'm feeling extreme,' Clara snapped. 'We're forty! We gotta get busy living or get busy dying.'

'Okay, this worries me. You only ever quote *Shawshank* when you are truly deranged,' Annie deadpanned.

'Look, better deranged than totally beaten down like all these poor bastards.' She threw a hand back towards the corridor of misery. 'Yeah, my marriage is fucked but ... you know what? Let's make it showbiz.'

Annie sighed. 'Is there any point in suggesting you just take some money off Maggie and Fionn and spare us all?'

'Is there any point in saying the same to you for IVF?' Clara replied. Her words were harsh but Annie knew she wasn't being unkind.

'I'm not doing IVF, Clara! I can't think about baby stuff right now! I'm in mourning ... ish.' Annie flashed back to the murmur of desire she'd felt for Rachel earlier. The very inconvenient murmur of desire that could not be entertained if she didn't want her life to fall apart further.

Annie shrugged. 'Listen. You're insane, and Ollie is so stubborn he should be studied. But grand, I support this.'

Annie and Rachel took the three boys to the park just across from the hotel while their parents prepared to potentially ruin all their lives for a free trip to Kos and an all-expenses-paid divorce.

As the kids charged at the hapless hordes of pigeons ahead of them, Annie found herself trying to explain the phenomenon that was Clara to Rachel, who'd been quiet since they'd left the hotel.

'She's a bit of an unstoppable force,' Annie said. 'You'd need to know her as long as I have. She adores those boys and she is a really good mother but she's ... unusual.'

Rachel laughed. 'Listen, I've gathered that much.'

'I just don't want you to think badly of her,' Annie continued. 'Look, whatever we might think of getting up on telly and blabbing about our lives ... Clara just doesn't take things that seriously, I guess. Not in a bad way, but she doesn't care what people think about her is what I'm trying to say.'

'Don't worry.' Rachel pulled her tangled curls down over one shoulder. 'I'm not thinking anything bad about her. I get it, I don't know her life.'

'I was just worried that you might be feeling a bit ... I dunno ... you know ... about the kids thing.'

Rachel was smiling. 'Are you aware you basically didn't say any actual words there? What? You think I'm thinking that your friend doesn't deserve her kids cuz she's crazy and her relationship is a mess?'

'Well,' Annie bit her lip, 'I'd be lying if I said I didn't have thoughts along those lines about people the odd time in the last couple of years. Like, sometimes it seems the worst people in the world get to be parents while the likes of us don't. Josef Fritzl had fucking kids. Some people should be sterilised.'

'Annie Sweeney! The eugenics enthusiast!' Rachel laughed.

'Ha, shut up.' Annie pretended to swipe at her.

'Look.' Rachel sighed. 'It is hard when you know that there's kids out there who need a home, and the process is shit even though I know the Adoption Authority are doing their best. But no, I'm not generally coveting the kids of strangers. So if you're planning a kid heist, I am not your gal.'

'I don't want to steal a kid. So much leg work and people are sooooo paranoid about their kids – very hard to get one alone.' Annie mugged.

Rachel giggled and Annie felt a giddy swoop – she loved making her laugh.

'Anyway,' Annie pushed her hair behind her ears, 'I think going it alone sounds really intimidating.' Then rushed to add, 'Of course, I think you're amazing to be doing it – Reggie, stop giving that bird the finger,' Annie yelled.

'Yeah …' Rachel looked a little sad, staring down at the path they were taking that had brought them to a small pond where the more docile children of other families were gently feeding the ducks.

'What?' Annie felt a spike of alarm. 'Is everything okay? I've said the wrong thing.'

'Ah no, you haven't said the wrong thing. I was kind of putting off telling you …' Rachel sounded flat and Annie stopped walking, reaching for Rachel's arm.

But before Rachel could say any more, Tom had bounded up to them. 'How do you kill an animal without marking their body?' he asked cheerfully.

'Ah.' Annie struggled to adjust to this new conversational direction. 'I guess … asphyxiation?'

Tom skipped off back to his brothers. 'Annie said asphyxiation too. *Told* you I was right.'

'I maybe shouldn't have answered that? Though apparently he knew,' Annie mused, and then refocused. 'What's happened?'

'So the determination on my last application came through and I didn't get the Declaration of Eligibility and Suitability. The financials and lack of partner are scuppering me.'

'Oh darl.' Annie stood in front of Rachel and placed her hands on her friend's shoulders. 'That's just so fucking unfair. What're the next steps, then?'

'The next steps for me are …' Rachel paused and rubbed her face. 'To call it a day.'

'Seriously?'

'I just don't have the will anymore, to be honest. It feels a bit hopeless. I think I need to probably sit with the idea that this isn't going to be my path. In my therapy session, we talked about it and it's been useful. I can see that there is joy in both outcomes: having kids or not having kids. And there's loss in both outcomes too.'

'But what about the international options? There could be … a route that way, no?' Annie tried to remember the adoption info she'd seen during late-night googling back when she'd first started worrying that it wasn't going to happen for her and Conor.

Rachel shook her head. 'From what others on the forums are saying, you need a rake of cash for international. It's so frustrating.' She pressed her hands to her eyes.

'Would you foster?'

Rachel shook her head. 'I dunno, that's a whole other thing. And right now, it's all just taken it out of me. All the disappointments.' She looked at Annie. 'I know you understand.'

Annie nodded grimly and pulled Rachel to her, the sadness spreading through her. 'We could get a hamster,' she muttered.

Rachel pulled back. There were tears in her eyes, though she was managing a tremulous smile. 'Hamsters die at the drop of a *hat*. They can die from stress. Stress, Annie! What are they so stressed about?'

'Probably climate change.' Annie gave a solemn nod, and Rachel laughed.

Annie's phone buzzed and she took it out to see a new message from Clara.

Clara: Success. We are Kos-bound in less than two weeks, baby!

Annie showed Rachel the text.

'Now, there's a woman who doesn't stress about anything,' Rachel said, with a degree of admiration.

'She could probably do with worrying just a shade more.' Annie turned back towards the park and set off to round up the boys.

A few days later, Annie sat at the kitchen table, troubled. According to the app in her phone, her period was late.

As the darkness gathered outside, she hunched over, examining the calendar, checking that her previous period was marked in on the 18th of July. It was now Friday the 22nd of August. Just about a week late. She put the phone down and began spinning it nervously.

I'm not pregnant, I can't be. She pushed the thought away because a) it wasn't possible and b) because the tiny bubble of hope that was already insistently expanding inside her would only hurt more when it inevitably popped. She'd been down this road so many times and knew what the fallout of hope was – sickening, crushing disappointment.

Why is it so late? Could there be something wrong with me?
She put the question to Slags For Life and Maggie got back straightaway.

Maggie: Are you sure sure you couldn't be pregnant?

Annie: I wish. The last time me and Conor had sex, it was for barely a second and he didn't come. Also, I've had my period since.

Maggie: Ah okay. Sorry, luvvie.

Annie: Ugh, don't be. No more half-floppy dicks for me. Think I'm gonna go back to women full-time.

Clara: Just catching up. You're not thinking of Rachel?

This gave Annie the slightest jolt – was Clara literally inside her head?

It's not a crush, she reminded herself. *I'm not entertaining an inappropriate crush right now!*

Annie: NO. Rachel's straight. And my landlord.
Clara: It could be a sound financial arrangement: Head For A Bed!

Annie smiled, despite the free-floating anxiety that had invaded her upon seeing how late her period was. She'd already googled 'late period not pregnant cancer' and had diagnosed ovarian cancer.

Annie: Clara, I'm trying to have a crisis here!

Maggie: Look, first things first. Call the GP and make an appointment for Monday and then just do a test to double double DOUBLE check that it's not the other thing …

By the time Rachel had come home from the pub, Annie had rooted out a pregnancy test from the box where she'd chucked her old stash when she moved out of the apartment. She had also peed on it and left it up in the toilet upstairs.

'I have a favour to ask you,' Annie called, as soon as she heard the front door shut.

'Shoot.' Rachel hung up her denim jacket and Annie made a concerted effort to not notice how pretty she looked in her floral dress with the sweetheart neckline. Head For A Bed was *not* a good plan.

'My period is kind of late. So naturally, I am having the classic cancer panic. The girls suggested I do a pregnancy test before I go full funeral planning.'

'Okay …' Rachel came over. 'And you're sure it's not possible that you *are* pregnant?'

Annie shook her head. 'I've had my period last month. It was kind of light but I had it since the last time with Conor. And that last time with him was cut short anyway.'

'Right.' Rachel nodded. 'So what's the favour?'

'I just really could do without seeing yet another negative test until the day I die. So, I did a test a while ago and it's in the bathroom. Could you just check it for me?'

'But when did you do it? Do the tests not go weird after a while?'

'It's a digital one. They don't.' Annie sighed. 'Trust me, I've a PhD in pregnancy tests at this point.'

'Okay, on it.'

Annie listened to Rachel's footsteps on the stairs, then felt her moving overhead. Annie stared at the clock on her phone and watched a full minute go by.

She's trying to figure out how to break the news gently, Annie thought, swallowing and trying to diffuse the gathering pressure of tears.

Why am I getting so upset? She struggled to sort her thoughts. *If I am pregnant …* She didn't even want to dare to hope but also being pregnant now would hardly be the dream scenario. She hadn't spoken to Conor in weeks. The sad truth of their relationship had been entirely laid bare back on that night in Provincetown. Love hadn't been what kept them together in that last year but a shared, desperate hope. And once that'd been spoken aloud, Annie knew they could never go back; they'd always know they were settling for each other.

Still … a baby? She welled up again. Stop. It'd be impossible. *Don't hope, don't hope, don't hope.* She turned her focus inward, trying to intuit any kind of inner shifting that might hint at something momentous taking place inside her.

Rachel was coming back down now. Her tread on the stairs was gentle, from which Annie inferred that this was definitely going to be just another negative in a long line of negatives.

'Annie?'

Annie didn't look at her. 'It's okay, you don't have to say it.'

'I actually think I do, to be honest.'

Annie looked up, to see Rachel beaming with a mixture of utter joy and slight disbelief.

'You're pregnant.'

The world tilted then and Annie gripped the table.

'Shut up.' Her voice came out strangled as Rachel rushed forward to hug her.

'*Annie!*' Rachel squealed. 'It's happening.'

'Shut up,' Annie repeated, as Rachel's coconut-scented hair trailed over her face.

'I won't shut up! I'm so happy.' Rachel was crying, and then Annie realised she was too.

They pulled apart and looked at each other. Rachel held Annie's face and gently thumbed the tears from her cheeks, only for more to immediately fall. It was a strange sensation; she wasn't actually crying but tears were spilling out. It was like a new expression of happiness. As though the joy building inside her had to come out in some form or another. She began to laugh – a high-pitched, disbelieving laugh. She stood up and then sat down again and then stood again.

'I don't know what I'm doing.' She giggled, the tears continuing to stream. Through the blur she picked up the test to read the word 'pregnant'. She read it again and again.

'This doesn't feel real.'

'It's real, Annie.' Rachel squeezed Annie's hand. 'And it's wonderful.'

An hour later, Annie lay upstairs in her room. There was only so much time two people could spend at a kitchen table joyfully saying 'what the fuck' at each other. And so, she'd gone to bed, to be alone and to try and let the news sink in.

In other words, overthink in peace.

Her thoughts pinballed between exhilarating delight and paralysing anxiety. The anxiety was particularly baffling. *I've wanted this for so long. Why is my bitch brain now trying to scare me out of being happy?*

Of course, she'd wanted it with Conor. She'd wanted it in their old life. She'd pictured this day in *their* home and had imagined having a baby in *their* future, the one that they'd been building towards.

Being pregnant when she'd just been cast adrift, alone for the first time since she was twenty and with no clear idea of what the next years may hold, was scary.

Then another gust of incredulous joy took her. *But I am pregnant. I'm going to have a baby.*

She placed her hands on her stomach, trying to imagine having a bump in a few months' time, and she felt almost narcotically high and happy.

She took a deep breath. *I can do this. I have a good job. I'll have Clara and Rachel close by and my family will do everything they can to help. I won't be alone. This is happening.*

She squeezed her eyes shut and allowed all the hope that she'd been tamping down for nearly two years to swell and envelop her.

This is happening. It's just not how I thought it would look.

She thought of Conor.

This was happening, but it wouldn't be without its complications.

CHAPTER 17

The journey to Kos was eight hours of pure hell, what with five acrimonious couples and nine kids of varying ages and levels of annoying. Clara was extremely grateful it was over.

On the plane, Clara had tried to get a read on the competition. There was Liz and Paul – both in their early forties as well – with two kids in tow. Darina and Richie were late thirties and had no children. Rob and Sean were with their toddler, Viva, and lastly, Mary and Derek who were the youngest – both in their early thirties – with three kids.

There was a fairly clear dynamic among all the couples. One partner who was buzzing to bring their shitshow life to the masses and one partner who was here under duress, though evidently had been sold on the idea that this was a route to getting free from their head-wrecking partner once and for all.

On the disappointingly rundown compound, there were villas and two swimming pools but the place had clearly had its heyday twenty years before. *Not unlike ourselves*, she'd thought grimly.

When they'd arrived the night before, everyone had been given chicken and chips and then shown to their bedrooms in the

Family Villa. It was at this point, at 10 p.m. on the first night, that Clara and Ollie realised they'd forgotten to ask a crucial question: what were the sleeping arrangements? The answer? Bunk beds. Their room had cold tiled floors and a window looking on to a row of scenic bins. The boys, who slept in bunk beds at home, were happily leaping on the wafer-thin mattresses as Clara and Ollie had eyed up the last set

'Top or bottom?' Ollie had said, which was how Clara was now waking up with her face just inches from a grimy ceiling on the first day of filming.

She slid her phone out from under the pillow and snapped a pic of it to send to Slags For Life.

Clara: The glam life of reality TV: view from my BUNK BED, gals. Ollie's on the bottom. Fitting. He's always had bottom energy.

Maggie got back in seconds – she was clearly still up. It was still yesterday there, as LA was ten hours behind.

Maggie: You were born a top, Clara. How are you feeling about it all?

Clara considered how she was feeling.

Clara: I'm feeling like the only option is to completely commit. No regrets. Filming starts today. The first episode airs tomorrow, our filming will be a day ahead of what's being broadcast all through it.

Maggie: I'll be watching. One of the staff has set me up with a VPN.

Clara: Amazing. Any feedback on my facial expressions/ general demeanour are most welcome. Tell me how we're coming across. I'm still not sure what emotional mark we should be aiming for. Like, are people more likely to vote for us if we're non-stop fighting or should we be peddling a sob story. @Annie How are you feeling? How's the nausea? Tell us everything when you wake up!

At that moment, Clara's alarm started up. She silenced it quickly and rolled over. Annie was having a baby! It was a week since she'd sent the pic of the positive test and explained that her last 'period' must've been an implantation bleed. Clara had started crying immediately. She'd never known that you could feel this happy for another person. She'd even gone straight up to the bathroom where Ollie was in the shower to tell him, her joy overriding the strangeness of the fact that it was the most intimate moment they'd had in nearly two months. Ollie had also choked up. Annie had said she wasn't ready to tell Conor. Her first appointment with the doctor was in two weeks so she had time to figure out what this whole baby thing might look like now that they were no longer together.

Ollie was argumentative on the matter of keeping it from Conor. Knowing such life-changing information about his friend without he himself knowing seemed wrong, and she and Ollie'd had a few tetchy words about it. Clara had managed to talk him down, arguing that Annie was going through a lot and deserved space to process before the conversation with Conor.

'Muma! Get up for breakfast.' Tom appeared at the top of the ladder down by her feet.

'We've already had ours,' Josh called up to her. 'The yogurt is disgusting.'

'Coming now.' Clara, still prone, started to slither towards the ladder – apparently the only viable way to exit the bed. 'I'll put honey in your yogurt,' she told Josh.

Clara found Ollie and Reggie at one of the fold-out trestle tables that had been arranged in a large dining room next to the kitchen. All around them were more tables, where the other competitors sat. The atmosphere was awkward as people collected cereal and fruit from the sideboard in silence.

Beside Ollie's table were Paul and Liz, who were silent except to occasionally tell one of their kids to inform the other parent of something.

'Amy, tell your father that wet towels don't belong thrown on a bed and that, as a forty-three-year-old man, he should really know this by now and maybe if his relationship with Granny wasn't so smothering and co-dependent, he might have actually become a functioning adult.'

Amy, who looked to be about twelve, rolled her eyes, clearly more than accustomed to this tiresome routine. 'You catch all of that, Dad?'

'Tell your mother that flirty messages with ex-boyfriends don't belong in her DMs.'

Amy swivelled around to her mother. 'Stop sliding into DMs, Mum.'

Jeez, poor Amy, Clara thought. At least she and Ollie would never make the boys be go-betweens like that.

At that moment, Paul and Liz did actually start speaking to each other, though it sounded more like hissing. Clara did her best to catch what they were saying. Were they talking strategy? Should she and Ollie be figuring out their reality TV personas? Probably. Though the dining room was definitely not the place.

From the other side of the room, Clara heard a cold voice: 'If you lick your knife one more time, I'm gonna stab you with it.' It was Rob of 'Rob and Sean'; across from him Sean was very deliberately bringing his butter knife back up to his lips and running his tongue the full length of the blade.

In the highchair beside them, their daughter Viva began to do the same.

'Do you see what you're doing?' Rob indicated the child. 'Don't do that, sweetie, Daddy is just a gross person with no manners.'

On the other side of Rob and Sean sat Mary and Derek with their three kids. They were staring in opposite directions and Mary in particular looked very morose. From the ages of their kids, Clara guessed that Mary and Derek must've gotten started young. She suspected they were one of those couples who forgot to break up with their secondary school boyfriend or girlfriend. Then wound up married with kids before their frontal cortex had finished developing. Of course, admittedly, she wasn't that much different, having forgotten to break up with her college boyfriend.

Just then, the last couple, Darina and Richie, sauntered in. Late thirties, no kids and no frown lines. They looked irritatingly well-rested. They stood close together and perused the breakfast options.

'Hey,' Clara muttered at Ollie, who was cleaning the back of Reggie's head – somehow there was ketchup back there despite there being no condiments in sight.

Ollie glanced over with a questioning look. He seemed to be rationing the amount of words he was saying to her, so she just continued.

'They're standing right beside each other,' she whispered, flicking her eyes over at Darina and Richie.

'So?' Ollie looked bored mixed with lightly hostile.

'So,' Clara leaned towards him, 'I wouldn't stand that close to you if I had a choice in the matter. Plus, they were chatting on the plane yesterday. *Chatting*,' she added, meaningfully.

She looked back at them and spotted Richie's hand drifting towards Darina's lower back before a quick retraction took place. 'Ollie?' She moved even closer. 'He went to touch her there. I bet they're faking being over to try and get the cash prize.'

'You have coffee breath,' said Ollie, leaning back in his chair.

Clara rolled her eyes. 'That's nice, Ollie. So glad you're ready to be a team player.'

'We're not a team.'

'Look, if they have a strategy, we need to have a—'

'People! People! Good morning.' A tall woman in a white linen suit arrived, cutting Clara off. She waved her hands in an exaggerated fashion. 'I hope everyone is settled in? I'm Caroline, your cast coordinator.'

She didn't wait for anyone to answer, instead turning to usher in several young women dressed in matching khaki trousers and brightly-coloured T-shirts. 'Now, kids,' the woman lowered her gaze at the smaller contingent and smiled in a way that suggested she had never been in close proximity to a child before, 'this is the Fun Brigade! When Mum and Dad are busy doing their "work" the Fun Brigade will be in charge!'

Clara and Ollie glanced at each other – she'd used air quotes on the word 'work' as though she didn't think children were actually sentient.

Josh raised an eyebrow at Clara. 'I thought this was a holiday?'

'It is.' Clara patted his arm. 'Dada and I just have a few jobs to do at different times.' She smiled widely to reassure him/gaslight him into thinking everything was normal.

The children filed out with little resistance and Caroline smiled benignly until the last child had left. Then she turned back to the adults and looked around sternly.

'Right, as you already know, we have an extremely tight shooting schedule. *Divorce Island* is going to be appointment television, with episodes going out every night for the next three weeks. The public are hungry for drama. Let's make sure we give it to them.' She paused to glare around the room before continuing. 'For an hour after each broadcast, public voting will open, then each day a leaderboard for all the couples will be posted on our socials. *Divorce Island* is a highly interactive show for our audience: members of the public are encouraged to comment via the hashtag #DivorceIsland and in the Confession Pod we will be showing you all updates from these online conversations to film reactions and generate compelling content. You'll be handing over your phones now to Eric.' She indicated a young guy, who moved forward with his electronics case.

Ollie shot Clara a look that seemed to say something along the lines of *Hope you're happy*, while around the room other couples were murmuring to one another.

Liz raised her hand, which Caroline steadfastly ignored, continuing with her rundown. 'We have, of course, already shot introductions for each couple at the auditions, and our celebrity host Jez Fuller will also be providing context where necessary. Our trust exercises are beginning today, as you know. We will be leaving for the main villa, Casa Amore No More, in thirty minutes to film Jez detailing what's on the agenda. I suggest everyone is camera-ready, as from now until lunchtime there won't be much time for touch-ups. Attire will be Beach Booty; no one-piece bathing suits, ladies, bikinis only. Are we all clear on everything?'

Liz waved her hand in the air with more urgency and Caroline, not looking directly at her, snapped, 'Save your questions for on-camera.' She turned and marched out of the room, sparking an instant hubbub among the other couples.

Clara turned to a mutinous-looking Ollie and shrugged. 'We knew what we were getting into.'

He just shook his head and Clara continued. 'Look,' she said beseechingly, 'eye on the prize. We can win this thing. And trust exercises are grand – they'll probably have us closing our eyes and falling backwards into each other's arms or whatever.'

As all the cast took their places on high stools arranged around the swimming pool, Clara noted that Casa Amore No More was significantly nicer than the living quarters. Through the sliding glass doors into the lounge area, she could see the walls were adorned with framed torn-in-half photographs of celebrities who had divorced: Jennifer Garner and Ben Affleck (who had the distinction of appearing twice on the wall) were there, along with Brad Pitt and

Jennifer Aniston and individual photographs of Jennifer Lopez with all four of her ex-husbands.

Production crew scurried around adjusting lights and affixing mics to the straps of the women's swimsuits and the collars of the men's open shirts.

Jez Fuller was nearby, dressed in a white shorts suit. He cheerily greeted them all while two wardrobe women knelt at his feet applying fake tan to his legs.

'Hi, gang,' he called. 'Are we ready to make some landmark television?'

Darina and Richie whooped, further cementing Clara's theory that they were in no way on the rocks and definitely cos-playing a couple in trouble for the thirty grand. The other couples gave murmurs of assent with varying degrees of enthusiasm.

'Okay.' A man with a headpiece strolled into the centre of the group, clapping his hands together. 'I'm Mickey, I'm the director of *Divorce Island*. I've done stints on *Love Island*, *Big Brother*, *Bake Off* – you name it. So don't worry, gang, you're in good hands. This pool area will be our base for a lot of our filming but we also have a number of smaller production units that will follow individual couples as you complete challenges each day. Right, let's kick off.'

Mickey moved to a monitor behind one of the cameras and called to different members of the crew. 'Sound? Lights? And we are go. Action.'

Jez, facing one of the cameras, began to read the words scrolling on a teleprompter beneath.

'Welcome to *Divorce Island*, the first show of its kind in the history of reality TV. I'm your host, Jez Fuller. For the next three weeks we'll be following five couples as they compete to win an all-expenses-paid divorce. *Or,* perhaps ... decide their miserable marriages are worth salvaging. The best part? You, the public, will pick the winning couple. They've arrived in the stunning Casa Amore No More, so let's meet them ...'

'Cut,' shouted Mickey. 'Excellent. Here we'll be inserting the previous segments we shot at auditions, getting to know you all as couples and individuals. Next up we want a quick bit of B-roll. Everyone up. I want you arranged around the pool.'

Several production assistants came forward and began to lead Clara and the others to loungers and tables dotted around. 'That's right,' Mickey called. 'Mix up the couples. Everyone pretend to talk amongst yourselves but also if we could have individuals shooting worried or annoyed looks to the other members of the group that would be great. But shake it up, laugh, chat, look suspicious – whatever feels right in the moment.'

Clara found herself beside Darina and Sean, while Ollie was handed a bottle of sun block and put sharing a lounger with Mary. The three cameramen mobilised to capture each group.

Clara smiled at Darina and whispered, 'This feels way weirder than I was expecting ...'

'No talking, please. The mics are hot and we just want ambient sound and reaction shots here, thanks. Let's think "candid", everyone.'

Clara straightened up and moved her hands, pretending to be in conversation with Darina.

'Great,' Mickey said after a few minutes, nodding approvingly. 'Okay, for this shot, Ollie, I want you to apply sun cream to Mary's back and, Clara, we'll then cut to you for your reaction.'

'Eehh.' Clara froze. Where were the bloody trust exercises? She didn't expect the crew to be straight into churning up drama between the couples.

Though, would she watch a show about dreary couples doing trust exercises and talk therapy about respecting boundaries? Probably not.

Ollie's brow furrowed and he looked over to Clara before announcing, 'I'm not doing that.'

'Don't blame ya, mate!' Mary's husband Derek called over. 'After the three kids, she's not what she used to be.'

'Fuuuuuuuck,' Clara cried, as Mary's face crumpled.

'Save it for the cameras, guys.' Mickey seemed unfazed. 'Come on now, Ollie, your wife doesn't mind, do you, Clara?'

Clara hesitated. 'Well …' Poor Mary's husband was clearly such a bastard, the least she could do was sublet Ollie.

'It's what you came here to do, guys,' Jez piped up helpfully.

'I didn't want to come here,' Ollie replied sullenly.

'Half of us didn't,' Rob muttered audibly.

'Guys, guys,' Mickey said in a beseeching tone. 'You're wasting TV gold here. For the next three weeks we want all airing of grievances to be when the cameras are rolling!'

Ollie sighed and positioned himself behind Mary, and Clara looked away as he began to rub in the sun block.

An hour later, they were back on the stools being filmed as Jez revealed the day's 'trust challenge'. *Finally*, thought Clara.

'So everyone, it's day one in Casa Amore No More and we have a very important challenge ahead. Each of you is going on a romantic date with a member of another couple.'

'What?' Mary yelped.

'That's right, gang. You will all be running the gauntlet of the ultimate temptation of any long relationship – someone new, exciting and mysterious.'

Unrest rippled among the partners who were clearly Camp Didn't Want To Do This Stupid Show. These people, it was becoming clear, were Ollie, Mary, Liz and Rob. Darina and Richie's motives continued to be hard to ascertain.

Clara fiddled with her hair anxiously as a camera moved closer to her. This was not what she'd been expecting. The producers had not mentioned anything like this. There'd been promises of on-site psychologists and a lot of chat about the production company's 'duty of care' and the cast's 'well-being' during the 'extremely delicate circumstances' of the show. She looked around at the others. Sean and Rob were looking particularly sceptical, no doubt wondering who *they'd* be going on dates with.

Jez continued. 'For the next hour, our couples will be, for all intents and purposes, single and ready to mingle. Anyone can ask anyone out and whoever's left over without a date will be paired off. Sean, Rob, we've procured some local gays for you both.' He turned back to camera. 'Okay! Let's find out if our couples find greener pastures with someone else's husband or wife!'

Everyone slid off their stools and were herded into the lounge area where waitstaff were serving colourful, sparkling cocktails. Clara, now in a slightly *fuck it* mood, took two and retreated to a white leather couch. Ollie was talking to Mary on the other side of the room. No doubt complaining about being there. The cameramen roamed about, capturing the interactions. Rob and Sean were in a heated exchange, the words '*local gays?*' rising above the din in the room.

Paul came over and took a seat beside her. He was about her age and, judging by his torso, was a devotee of some kind of hardcore, no doubt boring, exercise routine.

He caught her looking and grinned: 'Hyrox,' he said proudly. 'Eight kilometres of running combined with eight functional workout stations.'

'Wow.' Clara pretended to be impressed.

'Yeah, it's pretty intense.' He nodded, then took a gulp from his glass. 'So. It's Clara, right?'

Clara nodded. 'And you're Paul.'

'I am. So, listen, I'd love it if you'd come on a date with me.'

'Right,' Clara replied, and stalled by draining one of her cocktails in one go. On the one hand, she was extremely relieved that she was being snapped up and wouldn't be one of the dud leftovers, but on the other hand, she felt sorry for Ollie – what if no one asked him out? Sure, *she* thought he was a ride but Middle-Aged Stoner Hot was a specific taste. While the other men had embraced the brightly coloured form-fitting swim shorts favoured by the *Love Island* boys, Ollie was wearing the SpongeBob SquarePants swimming trunks he'd been wearing since 2004. They may not have been the best choice.

She looked back to Paul. 'I guess that's what we're here to do.'

He grinned and nodded, then looked smugly over to his wife Liz, alone in the far corner.

'She cheated on me,' he said, not taking his eyes off Liz. 'If no one asks her out ... good enough for her.'

At the end of the hour, the cast were once more arranged in couple formation on the stools outside. Cameras were rolling and Clara's stomach was pitching around from the cocktail concoction. Beside her, Ollie was staring straight ahead.

Jez cleared his throat. 'Our cast have rubbed shoulders – and who knows, maybe even other bits? – and now they're ready to date. Let's find out who was chosen by another spouse and who was left on the shelf! Everyone who asked someone out, step forward.'

Paul, Richie, Darina and Ollie stood and moved into a row beside Jez. Clara tried not to let her apprehension show. Ollie had asked one of the women out?

'Okay, gents and lady.' Jez gave a slight bow to Darina. 'Who asked who! Ollie, kick us off.'

Ollie delivered his answer while staring straight at Clara. 'I asked Mary.'

Clara swallowed. This felt way worse than she'd anticipated.

'Excellent. Take the seat beside your lovely date! You two make an adorable couple.'

'Darina? Who's the lucky man?'

'Derek,' she smiled, and made her way to the stool beside Derek, where she gave him a giggling, flirtatious slap on the arm – a nearby camera zooming in at speed to capture it.

Richie was next and announced he'd was 'super stoked' to be taking Liz out.

Jez clapped and turned to Paul. 'And you snagged the gorgeous Clara?'

'I did, I'm a lucky guy.' Paul grinned and took the seat Ollie had vacated moments before.

'Excellent, excellent.' Jez nodded approvingly. 'And now ... Bring in the gays!'

Two young men with flashing white teeth and frighteningly chiselled abs appeared around the side of the villa. They each took a place behind Rob and Sean and draped their arms around their shoulders. Rob immediately slipped out of the guy's arms and stormed off inside.

'And cut!' Mickey shouted. He turned to the cameraman beside him. 'Did we get that exit? That was too perfect.' He beamed. 'Good man, Rob,' he shouted after him through the open doors of the villa.

Jesus, Clara thought, if the round-the-clock filming and messed-up challenges didn't finish these marriages off, the rows about even getting involved in the first place no doubt would.

She looked over at Ollie and Mary, who were chatting away. *He's putting it on to punish me*, she told herself.

Isn't he?

After lunch, where each couple had to pretend to be completely happy and normal in front of their children, the cast were allowed to change into clothes that covered marginally more of their bodies, though there were still rules. No trousers or skirts below the knee for the women, no shirts buttoned past the navel for the men. After they went on their dates, each couple would do a joint debrief in the Confession Pod.

While the children were taken horse-riding on the beach, their parents reconvened at Casa Amore No More at 2 p.m., where five cars were waiting for the paired-off couples. The cast were all instructed to hold hands as they got into the cars, which Clara and Paul duly did.

From the back seat, she noted with a sick feeling that Ollie was taking it a step further, casually slinging his arm around Mary.

'It's not fair to use her like that,' she muttered to Paul. 'Her husband's already clearly a dick and now Ollie's …' She trailed off as she noticed the camerawoman in the front seat of their car turning to get Clara in shot.

'Hey,' Paul said in a soothing tone. 'This is our time. Let's focus on us.'

Oh God. He'd obviously gone deep on *Love Is Blind* and the other American shows where cast 'fell for each other' faster than you could say 'get to fuck!'

'"Focus on us?"' Clara laughed. 'Paul. I met you six hours ago.'

He ignored this and took her hand. The clack of the camera zooming in joined the growl of the car's ignition. The driver pulled away from the villa and Clara stared at Paul's hand, feeling deeply conflicted. She knew she should put on a good show for the viewers and make them root for her and Ollie. But root for what? Them to win a divorce? That was the name of the game, after all. For the first time it occurred to her to seriously wonder: was she actually able for this?

The date with Paul was an endurance test. He was a Bio-Hacking Bro, which in Clara's book was worse than an incel. Who knew there was quite so much to say about Hyrox? Or macros? Or mouth taping? His preoccupation with protein intake bordered on mania and Clara found her mind constantly drifting to thoughts of Ollie on his date somewhere else on the island. She wondered if Mary was prettier than her but it was hard to gauge – they looked nothing alike. All the couples were objectively attractive but Mary was Clara's opposite in every way: she was tall and more athletic while Clara was small with big boobs. As Derek had so cruelly noted, Mary did look like a woman who'd had three kids, but then so did Clara. As was to be expected of two women who had had three kids!

Even the beautiful surroundings provided no distraction from her fretting – they were being served a delicious dinner of grilled fish, flatbreads and grilled peach and feta salad on a large, tiled terrace overlooking the Aegean Sea. But she had no appetite and Paul's monologuing was unceasing. The camera hovered in and around them at all times.

'Do you use the powders?' Paul's baffling question brought Clara back to the present.

'The powders?' she asked.

'Yeah, the protein powders? I find it very hard to hit my protein goals without them.'

'I eat yogurt?' Clara replied.

'That won't do it, Clara. You need to be consuming one to two grams per kilo of body weight. And that's per day.'

'Right.' Clara nodded, forking some tabbouleh into her mouth just so she wouldn't have to say any more.

Finally, mercifully, the date concluded with them doing a few shots walking hand-in-hand on the beach in the sunset and then it was back to Casa Amore No More for the on-camera debrief with Ollie.

Each of the couples were being called into the Confession Pod separately while the others sat around the lounge. Ollie was in deep conversation with Rob – probably about the gays that'd been shipped in. She made a beeline for an empty sofa, delighted to avoid Ollie. She was nervous of looking at him and potentially seeing in his face that he'd enjoyed his date.

She gazed at her hands in her lap, until a camera drifted into her field of vision and she immediately rearranged her features into what she hoped looked like a not-too-forced approximation of insouciance.

Mary appeared to her right and asked to join her. The camera continued to hover and Clara made herself smile at Mary.

'Sure, sit.' Clara patted the space beside her.

Mary curled up in a girlish pose, feet tucked up under her. 'How was your date?'

'It was grand.' Clara pressed her lips together, then added, 'Paul's ... very ... eh ... chatty. I didn't really have to say much.'

Mary nodded, then leaned toward her. 'Clara, can I just say, you are so lucky with Ollie.' Mary clapped her hands together. 'He's *so* funny! We just laughed all afternoon.'

'Great,' Clara responded weakly.

'I cannot even imagine why you would want to split up with him.'

'Well ... it's complicated.'

'I know.' Mary tilted her head sympathetically. 'He told me.'

'Right.' Clara cringed inwardly at the thought of Ollie confiding in this woman. 'Well then, maybe you can imagine why we're here.' Clara tried not to sound snippy.

'But he's just so … *fun!*' Mary was not getting the hint that Clara wasn't enjoying this conversation. Of course Clara knew how good Ollie was on a date. She had bloody first-hand experience of how fun he could be. She remembered the days when they were in their twenties and would get stoned and play mini golf – an activity that, on paper, probably sounded boring but with Ollie was hilarious. She used to have a literal pain in her face from laughing. Spending time with him back then when they first got together had her in a perpetual state of excitement. Between dates, she'd be tormented by giddy anticipation for the next day they'd spend together. When she wasn't around him, she talked about him so much that Maggie eventually had to put the foot down and instate a rule that Clara could only mention him three times in each conversation. Marriage seemed to have a way of completely stamping out all that lovely exuberance.

Maybe if we'd kept on going on dates? she thought sadly. All the websites and relationship podcasts were flat out banging on about the mythical, problem-eradicating properties of 'a regular date night'. But who had the time, money or energy?

'Clara? Ollie? You're up,' a production assistant called from the door leading to the pod. Darina and Richie sauntered out, looking vaguely victorious. Charlatans.

'Good luck!' Mary whispered, which Clara didn't bother replying to.

She and Ollie followed the production assistant into the pod, which was snug. There was a much-too-small couch for them to squish into – clearly a ploy to ensure that the couples were uncomfortably close. In front of them hung a large mirror, behind which they'd been told sat the director and a psychologist who would offer commentary to the viewers on body language and such. Cast members couldn't hear what was being said behind the mirror except when the director spoke into the microphone to ask probing questions.

'Clara, Ollie,' Mickey's disembodied voice filled the pod, 'you each went on dates with another person today. Clara, let's start with you. How did it go?'

'It was fine.' Clara shifted a little, conscious that she might be squishing Ollie. She was hyper-aware of the heat of him and his particular Ollie smell, a smell she realised she hadn't noticed in a long time. They simply hadn't been this physically close since Provincetown.

'Just "fine"? Anything else to add?' Mickey persisted.

'I learned a lot about macros,' she replied.

'Hah! Okay, it's only the first day, you're probably trying to protect your husband's feelings. There's lots of time to get more honest, Clara. We'll make sure of it—'

'Excuse me,' she interrupted. 'I *am* being honest. I didn't have a good time. I'm not pretending anything.' She was suddenly desperate for Ollie to know this. Especially as Mary's response to her date with Ollie was bringing it home to Clara that he could easily get snapped up out here, SpongeBob SquarePants shorts and all.

Mickey ignored her little outburst – the cast not fancying members of the other couples was clearly not the narrative he was looking for. 'Over to you, Ollie. Any sparks fly?'

'Mary and I had a lot in common,' Ollie began. 'I really think we connected. We both feel that our partners don't respect us.'

'Ollie!' Clara cut across him but was immediately cut off by Mickey's voice.

'Clara, this is Ollie's truth. Let him speak. This is a safe space.'

'Ha!' Clara folded her arms. 'A safe space with thousands of viewers.'

'This is what *you* wanted,' Ollie said, not looking at her. 'Anyway, as I was saying. Mary's a really attractive, sensitive person and we had a really good time. Lots of laughs and, honestly, it felt like a holiday from my problems.'

Clara was crushed. It hadn't been the plan for him to get into the competition. Although, this moment was starkly highlighting just how lacking in any plan she really was. She'd been so focused on getting onto the show and calling Ollie's bluff about wanting to end things, that she hadn't really considered what the reality of this whole enterprise would be. She didn't know what the hell outcome she even *wanted* – divorce or money – she'd assumed by the end of the three weeks she'd know.

But now, hearing Ollie describe Mary as attractive, she was certain she definitely couldn't handle him actually liking anyone.

'That's really good to hear,' Mickey said. 'For the couples who gelled well on the dates, we're offering to extend the dates in the Intimacy Pods.'

The what? Clara reeled.

Apparently reading her mind, Mickey continued, 'The Intimacy Pods are quiet spaces for new couples to get to know each other on another level. There are no cameras, but audio is still captured.'

'I'm sorry, but what are you talking about, "new couples"? "Intimacy pods"? This is the first we've heard of this.' Clara erupted. 'Where's all the counselling and trust-building bullshit?'

'These are trust-building exercises of sorts,' Mickey replied patiently. 'The dating of other people and the Intimacy Pod assignations help each couple feel the reality of what divorcing might be like in a controlled, safe environment.'

Ollie spoke up beside her. 'If Mary's up for it, I'm happy to take our date to the Intimacy Pod.'

'Ollie! What?' Clara turned to him. Their faces were just inches apart and Clara's eyes swam with angry tears.

'You wanted to be here, Clara. I'm playing your game.' His voice was quiet, and Clara knew Ollie well enough to know that, despite what he was saying, he definitely wasn't happy.

'This is not what he wants.' Clara turned to the mirror desperately. 'This is not fair on Mary. This is … he's only doing this …' She turned back to Ollie. 'This is a Spite Crush.'

Mickey, meanwhile, was jubilant. 'Congratulations, Ollie. Mary also wanted to go to the Intimacy Pod, making you two our first couple to do so!' Clara was struggling to fully grasp what was happening.

'And cut,' Mickey said. 'Okay guys, well done, that was perfect – really fascinating. Clara, can you return to the cast villa? And Ollie – Mary will meet you in Intimacy Pod number 1 shortly.'

CHAPTER 18

In the bright morning light of Lime Orchard Road, Maggie's fingers sped over the keys of her laptop. She was propped up in bed trying to finish a scene that she felt close to cracking. The Medea project had come into sharp focus in recent weeks and that all-consuming drive to create – something she thought had abandoned her forever years ago – had returned. She wasn't finished the first draft yet but in a burst of impulsive excitement had sent a proposal off to a couple of theatre companies in New York. Incredibly, one producer had got back saying he wanted to discuss. She was meeting him over Zoom the following day.

The alarm on her phone went off, signalling the end of her writing window. She'd been pretty disciplined about working from 6 a.m. to 8 a.m. each morning. Now it was time to get the girls up. They were due to go to their Sunday horse-riding lesson in a couple of hours and it was a solid thirty-minute drive to Sunset Ranch in Beechwood.

In the gloom of her daughters' bedroom, Maggie stepped around the Lego, dolls and Plushies scattered across the carpet and peered into Essie's bed. As expected, Dodi was snuggled in beside her sister, her thumb in her mouth, while the other hand was tangled in

Essie's hair, which she liked to play with. Love swelled in Maggie's chest. They'd basically slept in the same bed since they were babies. Even now, though they started in their own beds when Maggie read them their stories before going to sleep, at some point in the night one would migrate to the other as though by some invisible twin magnetic pull.

Maggie gently lifted the blanket and slipped into the warm bed beside them, pressing her face into Dodi's unruly hair to inhale the indefinable essence of her baby – even with the tinge of slightly stale morning sweatiness, it was so delicious.

The girls started to stir and sleepily find their way to her. Dodi literally tumbled over Maggie, so that they each got a side of their mother that they could cuddle into. It was these exquisite morning moments that pulled Maggie through the more trying parts of parenting. She wished that thoughts of what her body must feel like to her daughters didn't snake in to disturb the sweetness. She found she couldn't help but try to arrange herself so that the loose pouch of her belly didn't drape so obviously to the side. From when they were little and always seeking Maggie's warmth and reassurance for hugs and cuddles, Maggie had felt amazed at how her daughters seemed so at home with her body despite its obvious imperfections. She often wondered when they would realise that she was ugly. And would they feel ashamed of her?

She refocused on the day ahead.

'Girls, we're going to see the horses in a bit! We gotta get up.'

In the kitchen, she made them pancakes in the shape of teddy faces with chocolate buttons for eyes and a nose. Fionn had been away filming once again for the past few weeks but would be back the next day.

On Sundays all the staff had the day off. Maggie didn't want the girls to look back at their childhood and only have memories of a rotation of strangers flitting around them cleaning up after them and preparing their every meal. Lately there'd been other advantages to having the house completely to themselves once a week. Sunday had become her 'cheat day'. She could order takeout and more food on DoorDash without any eyes on her. Getting food in the quantities she needed had proved surprisingly hard with so many witnesses around the house at all times. Trying to intercept the staff getting to the door before her was nigh on impossible.

Then there was the disposal of wrappers. She was afraid to put the bags in the main garbage bins, where the cleaners threw all the other household waste and might see. She couldn't bring the bags out on walks with her because Lime Orchard Road was a street of gated mansions, not a place dotted with handy public bins. So Sundays had become the best time to get rid of the week's evidence when she drove the twins to the horse ranch.

After she dropped the girls off, she turned back and headed towards the Hollywood Hills Hotel. The bin area was fairly accessible and she'd taken to disposing of her crinkling trash bags there and then going for a coffee. The hotel – despite its gorgeous views of the city and Japanese-influenced architecture and ponds of koi fish – was not a celebrity haunt, so she felt safe there. If anyone caught her at the bins, she could just pretend to be a witless tourist and scarper.

With her drop-off completed, she went around to the restaurant and ordered the blue crab Benedict that was served with asparagus, crispy rice and Béarnaise sauce. A part of her Sunday treat. Since Provincetown, she'd managed to keep herself in check for the most part. She'd established a routine that she felt was balanced, without allowing old compulsions to take over. She ate very well for five days of the week – egg-white omelettes, grilled fish and the like – and then on Wednesdays and Sundays she could engage in what she referred to in her head as her 'little routine'.

She checked the time and pulled out her tablet to tune into the episode of *Divorce Island* that was airing at that moment in Dublin. On Sundays, they would be milking the week's content for all it was worth. From 6.30 p.m. to 7.30 p.m. they were going to recap events of the week with a supercut of the biggest dramatic moments. Then, straight after, there was a new episode with all the goings-on of the previous night.

She slipped in her earpods and smiled at the waiter as he set down her plate. She carefully propped up the device and clicked the various links that eventually brought her to the stream of the show.

The opening credits scrolled through pictures of each couple being destroyed in different ways: torn apart, set on fire, being crumpled up. Clara and Ollie's picture had a red liquid poured over it, seemingly to represent bloodshed. The last picture dissolved to reveal a smirking Jez Fuller.

'It's been quite the first week at the villa, with many of our couples road-testing the Intimacy Pods while others seem to be regretting the decision to let their partners stray quite so far … Let's take a look.'

Maggie ate her food while scenes of the other couples fighting and crying played, with Jez narrating. Finally, Clara and Ollie appeared on screen and Maggie sat forward.

'While Clara got romantic with Paul on the beach at sunset, Ollie and Mary were clearly developing a strong connection and were the very first couple to escalate their budding romance to an Intimacy Pod.'

Maggie rolled her eyes at the hyperbole. Clara had looked openly bored with that guy Paul, and from the audio recorded of Mary and Ollie in the Intimacy Pod, their so-called 'budding romance' was entirely centred around how much they were hurt by their respective partners.

Maggie knew Ollie was hating every second of being on the show but, Jesus, the man had follow-through when it came to grudges.

More footage followed documenting more of the week's 'challenges', which included contestants playing spin the bottle with the option of declining to kiss other members of the group if they didn't want to hurt their spouse. On the night that had aired, Maggie and Annie, who often texted as they watched, had been enormously relieved that both Clara and Ollie refused to kiss anyone. Though, as Annie had said, they weren't displaying any increased warmth towards one another either. Slags For Life had been quiet as Clara's phone had been taken by the producers.

Jez reappeared. 'Let's leave our would-be divorcees for a moment and see what you the viewers are saying about the goings-on in Casa Amore No More.'

Graphics of social media posts began to scroll as Jez provided voiceover. 'Imelda from Swords says: "It's a toss-up between Paul and Liz and Mary and Derek for who's most on the rocks on

#DivorceIsland." Meanwhile Eadaoin in Kerry thinks Clara and Ollie have a chance to reconcile: "Ollie is clearly hurt by what Clara did but the fact that every time he's with Mary he's talking about his wife speaks VOLUMES. #DivorceIsland." A very interesting insight.' Jez clasped his hands earnestly. 'Our resident body language analysis also has high hopes for this couple.'

The screen cut to a heavily made-up woman with glasses and a serious expression. 'From my observations of Clara and Ollie, these are two people who still love each other and may have a shot, if they can overcome some of the material issues in their lives.'

Well, that's vague, Maggie thought, mopping up some of the Béarnaise with bread. Everyone's trying to overcome the material issues. She thought of Fionn flying in tomorrow. Being in the same room was one of *their* material issues. From the calendar, he actually had a pretty clear stretch of time in the next few weeks and Maggie had mixed feelings. It was so good that he would be spending time with the girls. But she knew her own routine would be affected, though she hoped to be able to work around that. She'd already identified a couple of out-of-the-way drive-thrus she could get to on Wednesday. Then there was also the problem of sex. In Provincetown, Fionn was more shacked up in Edwin Ensel's shack than shacked up with her and they hadn't even attempted to have sex on the nights he was in the house. It wasn't that unusual for them. With the age their girls were and the intensity of their schedules, they didn't get to do it as regularly as other people.

When they were home in Dublin, they'd had one 'middle of the night, don't even turn on the lights' session. Depressingly, this mode actually suited Maggie now; she found that in the dark she could relax into it more.

Of course, Fionn would be wanting the full audio-visual experience as soon as they had a private moment. She flashed on a memory of her body in the gym mirrors the night before, then hastily shook the image away.

Eva was the only person she'd confided in about feeling so inadequate on that front because, with her director husband routinely casting and directing hot young actresses in his films, Eva knew how hard it was. *Of course* Eva was rake thin and Botoxed to oblivion. Though at least she was so dyed-in-the-wool Hollywood, she hadn't pretended Maggie looked amazing, like Clara and Annie insisted.

'Why don't you just get lipo and a tummy tuck?' Eva'd asked, baffled. 'Everyone in town has, even the Hollywood dogs get work done.'

Maggie had made mutterings about being fearful of major surgery but the truth was she mainly just preferred her way. It was the sense of total control. The exquisite abandon of eating without the fear of permanent damage and then the rush of the release afterwards when she could relinquish it all in a series of long, searing but somehow satisfying spasms. The high of emptiness was something not a lot of people could understand.

She signalled the waiter and ordered a coffee, then made her way to the toilets. A few minutes kneeling on the cubicle floor and she was free of the whole $50 breakfast. Her body was lighter, a deliciously numb feeling passing through her while her head felt instantly clearer. Still looking into the bowl, she pressed the flush and watched it all disappear.

'Think of every flush as a year taken off your life, Maggie,' a particularly hardline, aggressive therapist from her college days had said to her.

In a mode of therapy that would probably get your licence revoked now, she'd made Maggie kneel in front of the toilet as she repeatedly flushed, saying, 'There goes another year. And another. And another. Is this worth it, Maggie?'

It had scared Maggie, though probably a better word was 'traumatised'. Some of the warnings issued in that barbaric woman's treatment room still crowded Maggie's head at night. Long-term effects on the cardiovascular system. Words like 'stomach rupture'. But she knew those were things that happened to the severe cases. She was not severe. Before this summer, she'd barely purged since her twenties. There'd been the bit of a stint after the twins were born, and, okay, the odd time in the lead-up to one of Fionn's premieres the urge had overtaken her, but they had been short stretches. Just like this one would be.

Back in the dining room, she resumed watching *Divorce Island*. Clara and Ollie were involved in an exercise that involved building a raft together and having an argument about how Clara had never once helped to assemble a piece of furniture in the history of their relationship. Maggie pulled out her phone and texted Annie:

Maggie: Watching the show and I am actually not even sure I know what the objective is … Like, the public votes but what are they voting for? The couple most clearly in need of a divorce or the couple they like best?

Annie: The public are notoriously stupid … I wouldn't trust them to vote in a dog show.

Maggie: Lol.

Annie: I feel really bad but I'm relying on Rachel to give me updates cuz I keep falling asleep the second I get home from work. The tiredness is insane, I can't do anything, it's cock-blocking my life!

Maggie: Ahh don't worry, that passes. The second trimester is way easier. Do you know for definite how far along you are yet?

Annie: Going off the Provincetown date, maybe 12 weeks? Still can't believe after nearly two years of trying, a bitta pre-cum did the job! Next week I'll get final confirmation, scan is booked.

Maggie: And Conor?

Maggie frowned, watching Annie typing. Surely she's bloody told him by now?

Annie: Maggie ... I can SEE what face you're making even through text. I'll tell him in the next few days. I'm just enjoying me and Rachel being in our happy bubble right now. She's taking such good care of me. We're so excited.

We? Maggie thought. Before she could reply to question the wisdom of nesting with her friend, another message dropped in from Annie.

Annie: So how's the project going?!

For a split-second Maggie had a jolt thinking Annie was referring to her 'getting healthy' project but of course she meant the work she'd tentatively started with the theatre project.

> *Maggie: Actually good, I feel like this idea has been building inside me all this time and so when I go to my office, it starts pouring out. It's really evolved so fast. I have that Zoom tomorrow! It probably won't lead to anything but you never know! At least this producer didn't ignore me. I used my maiden name. I do not want anyone calling me a Nepo-Wife if anything actually happens with the show. Have to go get the girls from their horse-riding. Tell Conor!!!*

The next morning Maggie raced through the obstacle course that was getting her two girls ready for school – they'd only just started back after the summer holidays. As she furiously plaited hair and reassured them about the new classroom they were still getting used to, her mind was elsewhere, ricocheting between her meeting with the producer Drew Schwartz that morning and Fionn's arrival in the afternoon.

Once the girls were gone, she did a thorough sweep of the bedroom to make sure she hadn't left anything incriminating in her usual hiding places. She binned a clutch of candy bars she'd forgotten were in her underwear drawer. She considered eating them but she'd started the day so well with a green juice and it was a Monday so she wasn't allowed to purge. She also knew that if she started, there simply weren't enough bars in the house to satisfy her – the floodgates would be open and she'd soon be down in the kitchen trying to sneak more food without Betty seeing. It would throw the whole day – she'd be too distracted with the thoughts of the next binge to focus on the meeting. No, no, no. Today was going to be a good day. A light lunch and a normal dinner with Fionn.

At 11 a.m., she settled herself at her desk with a peppermint tea and logged on to Zoom. It was just after lunchtime in New York, which she felt was a promising time for Drew to have scheduled the meeting. If he'd suggested later in the afternoon, she'd be feeling way less optimistic. The last meeting of the day was never a good sign.

She clicked the Zoom link of the Google invite and in seconds he appeared on her screen.

'Maggie!' Drew was New York Attractive, meaning he still had his original teeth and a pleasingly dishevelled look. He was probably around fifty. 'So good to meet!'

'You too.' Maggie smiled, trying to hide her nerves.

'Thank you so much for meeting me so quickly. I know it was too short notice for your agent to join us but also it's nice to have a more informal chat before the business side starts!'

Maggie had lied about having an agent so she just nodded, smiling. *The business side STARTS?*

She quickly quelled the elation. In America, showbiz people could be very intense – they'd claim to love you and love your idea and then, out of nowhere, ghost you. Maggie had no frame of reference for American *theatre* people but she knew she should manage her expectations. She tried to dial down the wattage of her smile.

'So,' Drew clasped his hands together, 'I thought it'd be good to start by telling you a bit about Peek Show Productions. I'm assuming, since you're west coast, you might not have caught any of our shows before.'

'I've heard amazing things,' Maggie supplied, trying to sound interested but not off-puttingly eager. 'And I saw clips from the adaptation of *The End of Alice*. That sounded like some show, congratulations on the Tony.'

'Ha! Yes, thank you.' Drew grinned. 'It just goes to show that a little controversy can sometimes help.'

'Yeah … it's some story. I read the book years ago. I'm sure it took a lot of convincing of investors to get it on a stage.'

'Well, theatre, in my opinion, is the last real arena for challenging narratives. Cinema is a sanitised marketing machine now. Art has been commodified into oblivion. I think when it comes to making theatre … everyone kind of knows we're gonna be making a loss so why not just say "fuck it" and make the work we want to make!'

'Yeah absolutely …' Maggie agreed, in what she hoped sounded like the knowing voice of an insider. She was self-conscious about how long she'd been out of this world.

'So a modern *Medea* in Hollywood? I have to say we loved the pitch and, of course, the sample scenes you sent. Where did the idea come from? It's so simple and yet feels so fresh!'

'Well,' Maggie stole a glance down at the notes she'd positioned in front of her, 'I guess I find the Hollywood wives to be intriguing. How do they cope with what their husbands are doing at work all day? The scrutiny. The rumours. Power corrupts and infidelity in Hollywood is just rife. Plus, the whole trading in for younger women is practically a Hollywood rite of passage for male stars. The parallels with *Medea* feel so obvious but when I went to see if anyone had done anything with the idea, there was nothing.'

Drew nodded. 'I loved the echoes of self-mutilation in the cosmetic procedures that your Medea undergoes to try and keep Jason. And the translation of Medea's obsessive passion in Euripides' version to the monumental self-relegation that women of hugely successful men must do to further their partners' careers. Such urgent themes. So incredible that a play from the fourth century BC is still so relevant. This is a seriously exciting prospect, Maggie.'

'Thank you so much.' She beamed, barely able to believe how well it was going.

'So ...' Drew paused, apparently selecting his next words carefully. Maggie braced for the inevitable let-down. Maggie knew how these things went from Fionn's endless meetings with execs back in the early days. They'd love-bomb him and then never call again. She smiled, trying not to betray any disappointment. It was only the first meeting, after all.

Drew clasped his hands together, looking serious. 'You are no doubt fielding a lot of interest from different companies but we would love it if you would consider entrusting us with this project. I am confident that we could have this up by next fall and we will put our blood, sweat and tears into making this a landmark production.'

'Oh my God.' A jolt of happiness caught Maggie completely off-guard. 'I can't believe you want it.' She quickly tried to right herself; desperate was *not* the look she was going for. 'Ehm, obviously I'll need to talk to my agent ...' Maggie flailed, mentally trying to decide who'd be playing her agent in this lie, before settling on the obvious choice. 'Her name's Eva.'

'Of course, naturally.' Drew nodded. 'There's a lot to discuss for you. I know you want this work to be with the best of the best.' He paused and winked. 'I do think we are the best of the best, but I might be a bit biased on that front.'

Maggie and Drew wrapped up their meeting just before lunch with plans to meet in New York in two weeks' time, with Drew meeting with Maggie's 'agent' over Zoom in the meantime.

Maggie immediately called Eva to update her that she'd been promoted from 'friend' to 'friend and agent'. Eva gamely agreed to do the call with Drew, saying that Leon had done theatre in the past so she could talk to him and brush up on the kinds of deals struck between writer and producers.

Maggie didn't care if she got the shittiest deal ever – she'd pay *them* to stage her play. Money was not the goal; she didn't need it, and lately she had resolved to stop feeling bad about that. It felt like Fionn's career had been somewhat stifling her life for years; she may as well enjoy the perks.

The elation was intoxicating and she was feeling celebratory. She updated Annie and her family WhatsApp. Then she went to the kitchen on a kind of autopilot and liberated the Butterfingers from the bin where she'd thrown them earlier. She also slipped into the pantry and gathered whatever she could find there that didn't require cooking. It wasn't the best haul, but a force that she didn't question and couldn't stop was driving her. Up in her bedroom she began to gallop through the food. There was not a lot of time before Fionn would arrive and the girls would be back from school. At some point, it felt like it almost wasn't even her peeling back packaging and forcing more and more into herself. The pacifying effects of so much food was divine. She ate and ate, as any sense of being in control deserted her. It was the exhilaration of falling, but without the fear because she knew it would be all reversed in a few minutes' time.

Gradually she neared the edge of her capacity; she felt like she was literally packing all the crackers and nougat and chocolate down like you'd push garbage into a rapidly-filling bin. When it felt like the tideline of the food was just at the top of her throat, she lurched to the bathroom and began to vomit. With every cascade, waves of peace surged over her. Even while her heart drummed in her chest and she needed to gasp for breath between each contraction of her body, the sense of lightness and of control returning was so soothing.

Then everything veered sideways and went black.

Maggie opened her eyes and realised with a stab of terror that she was lying on the bathroom floor, her cheek glued to the tiles. Her head was pounding and she had no idea what time it was. She pushed herself upright, wincing as the pain in her head intensified. Her right hand was caked in dried vomit. *Oh fuck.* If the mess had dried, how long had she been out for? *Shit, shit.* She rolled onto all fours and pulled herself up by the sink. She washed her hand and then turned to the mess in the toilet. The room reeked and she desperately started to spray perfume as she flushed the evidence away.

A year of your life, Maggie.

She silenced the thought. She needed to clean herself up. She hurried into the bedroom to check her phone: 3.15 p.m. Fionn would arrive any minute. *Shit, shit, shit.* The girls must've gotten home an hour ago. She frantically stuffed the wrappers into her underwear drawer in the walk-in. Back in the bathroom, she rinsed her mouth, washed her face, hurriedly applied make-up and lit a candle before she flew downstairs, ignoring her headache.

Betty was serving Dodi and Essie snack plates and all seemed completely, reassuringly fine. She tried to look interested as Betty detailed the evening's menu but her mind was circling one roaring thought: *I was passed out while my girls came home from school and someone else took care of them.*

Maggie hugged both her daughters, being careful to keep them slightly at arm's length in case they smelled anything off her.

All is fine, all is fine, she intoned silently. *Nothing bad happened.*

Dinner that night was so normal that, to Maggie, it almost felt like they were actors in a play. A mum and dad and two little girls digging into the Thai-inspired feast followed by frozen yogurt with at least a dozen choices of toppings that had been laid out on the kitchen island.

Dodi and Essie were buzzing at having Fionn there and Fionn was the most present he'd been in ages. Full of funny stories about the calamities on the set of *Shake It Up* – a romcom about the unlikely love story of the widower owner of a milkshake stand and the plucky manager of a nearby vegan ice-cream place. The tagline was going to be 'Lactose-crossed lovers'. It was a movie he'd gotten tied up in before all the Oscar buzz and he had to honour the contract. He wasn't worried it would hurt his career, though. He was pushing for them to use the paycheque to buy a ski property in Utah.

By contrast, Maggie felt untethered to the scene around her. Distracted and detached. She was smiling and nodding along, but all the while endless thoughts streamed through her head. Mainly about whether or not to purge after the dinner that she'd barely picked at.

It's a Monday.

But the day is already ruined. You did it earlier, may as well go again.

But look what happened.

That was a one-off. Do it and then back to good habits tomorrow.

'So, yeah.' Fionn was gesturing with his spoon of fro-yo. 'Brody was kinda leaning towards me breaking contract but Elise – you know, Elise Parks, she was on the movie with me – she's doing a Lars von Trier movie next so I think everyone's bouncing between high and low these days. Look at Nic Cage. Oh, I met Maya Rudolph on set too. She's something else. A real artist. And she has four kids!' He put his arm around Maggie and nuzzled her neck to the chorus of amused protest from the twins. 'I think we should take off this weekend. Yosemite for camping? Or Palm Springs? Less time spent driving and the girls haven't been to the desert yet!'

'That could be good …' Maggie replied. Though her mind had snagged on the Maya Rudolph thing. It seemed to her like the words 'real artist' had settled between them with a dreadful weight, though Fionn looked oblivious. She picked up her wine. It was a low-calorie variety owned by one of the Real Housewives.

'Can we play Fortnite?' Essie chirped, while Dodi noisily scraped her bowl clean beside her.

'Sure,' Maggie smiled. 'But you know what you need to do first.'

The girls hopped up, launched their bowls into the dishwasher with a clatter and sped out of the kitchen.

'Are we letting them play Fortnite now?' Fionn raised his eyebrows.

'Well … are you spending more than twenty nights a year in the same house as them?'

'Ouch.' Fionn looked blindsided.

Even Maggie was a little caught off-guard by her own cattiness. She was irritable. Probably because she hadn't eaten much at dinner and didn't feel too good after the blip that afternoon.

'I'm sorry.' She shook her head. 'That was shitty. And an exaggeration.'

She didn't want to row. Sure, sometimes his return to family life could bring up mixed feelings, provoked by his stories of all the fun he was having and the obvious pleasure he was getting from achieving everything he'd dreamed of. But she never wanted to punish him, not least because it would surely only serve to push him closer to his acting buddies.

'It's okay.' Fionn pulled her close again. 'I really do wanna get this ratio of work and family into better balance. There's no point in working so hard if we don't get to enjoy it all together. I feel like once this Oscar stuff is done with, I'll be able to take the foot off the pedal a bit. The Oscar campaign is wild. I'd never appreciated that studios basically lobby the Academy for nominations.'

'It is crazy.' Maggie started to gather up the rest of the dishwasher bits on the table. 'But I've a good feeling.'

'Leave the clean-up, Maggie. Let's have another drink. I wanna sit on the terrace with you and soak it all up. I've missed you.'

On the terrace, Maggie couldn't focus. Fionn was full of questions about *Divorce Island* as he hadn't seen any of it yet but, inside her, as the few calories from dinner were being absorbed, the unsayable urges were nagging her to the point that she could barely form answers.

'Do you think they're doing well on the show? I still can't quite believe it's for real.' He tipped back some more wine with obvious relish. He rarely drank when he was in the full swing of a movie.

'I know what you mean,' Maggie said, vaguely trying to remember his question amid the panicked cacophony of her brain. *Just go to the toilet, Maggie. Then you'll relax and you can enjoy the evening.* She couldn't argue with that. She *would* relax if she just got on with getting it done. She could focus on Fionn, maybe even have a nice fucking evening with her husband. She thought longingly of the peace that awaited her on the other side if she could just do it. *Why am I resisting? It's not like it's hurting anyone.* The feeling of the cold tiles against her cheek when she woke up earlier revisited her, along with a flash of her vomit-caked hand.

'Maggie?'

With a start Maggie noticed that Fionn had taken that same hand and was staring intently at her, his incredible chiselled face glowing as, across the city, the sun dropped behind Mount San Antonio. 'Are you okay? Is everything alright?'

'Sorry, sorry.' Maggie smiled wanly. She needed to *not* give him cause for concern. The last thing she needed was anyone wondering if she was okay. That'd be a fast track to them trying to stop her. Just enough of her brain was unpolluted by the cancerous spread of her obsession to know that what was happening was not ideal. If the others found out, they wouldn't understand that she had it under control. They wouldn't understand how much better, how much *safer*, it made her feel.

'Everything is cool.' Maggie smiled. 'I'm a bit worried about Clara and Ollie. I feel like this whole show is a big game of chicken for them – like, who's gonna back down first. But the stakes are too high … Anyway …'

Maggie paused. She hadn't fully decided whether to tell Fionn about the Medea project or not. A part of her wanted to wait for when things were definite to surprise him. An echo of his earlier words about Maya Rudolph drifted through her mind. *She's a real artist. And she has four kids.* Maggie decided to tell him.

'I actually have some pretty exciting news.' She slipped out of his concerned grasp.

'Yeah?' He perked up.

As she detailed the morning's meeting, she watched his face closely. She didn't detect anything but genuine happiness, even when she explained – she made absolutely sure that she was *not* asking his permission – that she'd be going to New York in ten days' time.

'I want to get some intensive writing done and I'll be meeting with Drew.' She looked at him steadily. 'So you'll be fielding the twins.'

'Perfect! And we can come join you! The *Endurance 2* premiere is around then! This is amazing, Maggie!' His eyes were shining.

'I cannot tell you how amazing this is to hear. This is what you should've been doing all along.'

A twinge of irritation caught her momentarily – *maybe I would've been if your career hadn't been hogging all the oxygen?* He clearly didn't notice her pulling a face because he was continuing enthusiastically. 'Feels like the old Maggie!' He clapped his hands and she decided to let this slightly insulting observation slide. He was genuinely delighted; she knew he wasn't trying to put her down.

'So a reworking of *Medea*? Amazing. I'm a bit hazy on that story ... We definitely did a Euripides in college but can't remember which—' The buzz of his phone on the table caught his attention and he frowned while examining the screen, then turned the sound off. 'Not important! We have *got* to celebrate ... I can think of a good way.' He winked. 'We could sneak off now before the girls' bedtime.'

The thought of 'celebrating' her good news, naked in their bed, gave her a jab of apprehension. He had literally just wrapped a shoot spent doing romantic scenes with one of the most gorgeous twenty-four-year-olds in Hollywood. The age disparity in the leads in movies was seriously depressing. God forbid a forty-four-year-old man should have to touch a forty-four-year-old woman. Though in this town no forty-four-year-old actress looked remotely close to a normal forty-four anyway.

'Sure.' She smiled. And the lie of her smile made her feel suddenly lonely. *We're not in sync*, she thought. *He doesn't know the full truth of my life right now.* This was the unfortunate side-effect of her routine. It could put distance between you and the rest of the world. She tugged at her waistband; she felt so full. Even as she pondered the downsides of it all, the thoughts pressed in on her. *If I do it now,*

I can come back, and he won't notice anything. Having sex would feel ten times better.

Her resolve evaporated. 'Let's finish our wine first,' she suggested. 'We've got time.'

A few minutes later, she excused herself. She picked the en suite of the furthest guest room and in mere seconds felt freer, lighter and calmer. All the good things. Her mind felt clearer; her perfect routine had instantly muted the cacophony of anxiety. She brushed her teeth with a brush from one of the many guest vanity kits that all the bathrooms were stocked with.

After they'd finished the bottle, Maggie hovered in the dressing room off the bedroom.

'You are coming out here eventually, yeah?' Fionn called playfully.

'I'm giving it some careful consideration.' She kept her voice light and jokey as she searched through the many drawers of the mirror-topped island in the centre of the wardrobe. The fancy underwear drawer was definitely one of them; the stylist tended to arrange the pieces once she'd bought them and Maggie wasn't sure that she hadn't moved the drawers – it'd been a while since Maggie had gone hunting for a lacy something or other to wear so Fionn wouldn't have to look at her whole body. She liked the one-piece kind that held in her stomach and kept her breasts roughly where they used to be. She crouched at the lowest drawer and found the various delicate confections neatly folded among layers of tissue. She picked a lacey lilac one, shimmied out of her dress and pulled it on.

In the mirror, she did a speedy assessment. *Still a middle-aged heifer?* Check. She turned and craned to check the status of her back flab. *Overhangs hanging?* Check. She snapped the elastic around her thighs and was about to embark on stuffing her back fat down under the top of the one-piece when Fionn appeared in the doorway.

'You look so hot.' He stared at her and Maggie turned, sucking in her stomach as best she could which, from the glimpse she caught of herself in the mirror, did absolutely nothing. She smiled stiffly at him.

He came closer. 'I don't know why you bother putting things on.' He touched the strap and trailed his fingers along the lace edge that was taut against the swell of her breasts. 'I like it but …' He looped a thumb under each strap and slowly began to tug them down. 'You know I only want to take it off.'

As her breasts were released from the lingerie, he lowered his head to run his tongue over each nipple and Maggie gasped quietly. Despite how good it felt, it was a struggle to stay in the moment. Right at that very second she knew somewhere the internet was scrolling on, pseudo-feminist articles were applauding Maggie's astounding ordinariness and gossip forums were picking apart her family.

Fionn's lips found hers, drawing her away from the thoughts. He squeezed her tits and pushed her back against the wall of the dressing room, his hard-on pressing against her. He knelt down and pulled the lingerie all the way down and tossed it aside. He sat back on his heels for a minute, looking her all over. 'You're so beautiful.' He reached up to take her breasts in his hands and then leaned forward and began to gently tongue her clit. Maggie squeezed her eyes shut. It felt incredible. He pinched her nipples and her breath quickened.

As she began to feel the delicious pressure build, he gripped her ass and licked harder.

'I'm gonna come,' she whispered urgently. He pulled back abruptly and stood. 'Not yet,' he breathed in her ear, one hand still gripping her ass, as he undid his pants with the other. He'd barely bothered to get his trousers down before he pushed his dick inside her. She felt pricks of pleasure burst as he held her hips and lifted her higher against the wall. In the mirror opposite, Maggie could see his perfect ass tensing and releasing as her legs trailed over his hips.

'Do you wanna change or come like this?' he asked, grinning. 'I can't last much longer, I'm sorry. You're so fuckin' sexy.'

Maggie hesitated. She liked that, up against her like this, he couldn't really *see* her. She was suddenly conscious of how well lit it was in the dressing room. Her eyes flickered to the mirror opposite; if they moved now, he'd see her from *two* angles – God, she hated her brain. Fionn seemed to catch her glance and looked to the mirror also. He pushed into her again. 'Don't get distracted,' he whispered to her. 'You're so fuckin' hot. I'm gonna lick you till you come and then I'm gonna fuck you from behind. You want that?'

'Mmmmm,' was all Maggie managed as a response. Fionn held her against him and turned around to lay her out on the top of the island. He pulled out and, running his hands all over her body, he began to flick his tongue over her again. As her hips began to buck, he pushed his fingers inside her, which was all she needed to finally peak and start to orgasm. She'd barely recovered when Fionn flipped her onto her stomach and, gripping her hips, entered her from behind. In three sharp thrusts he was coming. In the mirror she watched as he threw his head back, the muscles of his neck pulling taut like ropes as he groaned a long satisfied 'fuuuuuck'.

Later, while Fionn had gone to read the twins a story, Maggie showered and did her skincare. She was relaxed and content. *Why did I dread it so much?* she wondered, patting in her serum. *I feel so much closer to him.* She had to remember this feeling going forward. The intimacy was so important. She couldn't let her head get in the way.

CHAPTER 19

Annie picked up her phone to check the clock for what felt like the twentieth time since she'd sat down outside Bear Café: 9.45 a.m. Conor wasn't even late; she'd just shown up half an hour early because she could no longer pace the hall of the house without potentially causing actual wear to the rug. She'd been battling a growing guilt for the last three weeks since she'd found out she was pregnant and had continued, day after day, to not tell Conor. She'd just felt so all over the place about everything. Her internal monologue whirred constantly, prodding her with questions about the logistics of single motherhood and co-parenting with an ex. Adding Conor's reaction – something she was struggling to predict – to the chaos was too much. She hadn't even told her family yet. Not because she feared *their* reaction – they would be thrilled and, given her parents' own unorthodox setup, wouldn't bat an eyelid at her going it alone – she just felt bad enough for telling her friends before Conor and so had resolved to wait until he knew.

The fact was a big part of her wished she didn't have to tell him at all. He hadn't wanted a baby in the end, so why should he get to be a dad now? Why did she have to share this with him? She knew her feelings were irrational but it was hard not to feel a bit resentful.

Every day she'd resolve to get it over with, and every day she'd lapse into stasis until finally it would be 10 p.m. and too late to start the conversation

Now, sitting at the little iron table under the canopy that shaded her from the weak mid-September sun, all she could do was jiggle her leg rhythmically. She uncrossed and recrossed her legs in the other direction, tugging at the waistband of her leggings. At twelve weeks, she was already starting to show slightly, but in her clothes it wasn't obvious.

For distraction, she started scrolling the *Divorce Island* hashtag to catch up on the public's reaction to the previous night's instalment during which the couples had been sent on an elaborate scavenger hunt to 'find the magic'. Literally. They were all searching for a close-up magician called The Dazzling Bob. Cue Clara and Ollie having a fifteen-minute debate about whether they should even bother trying to find him given how annoying close-up magic was.

In just two weeks, Clara and Ollie had become the fan faves. Annie read the comments under one post:

@sineadmkell: I could literally watch Clara and Ollie hunt for change in a handbag #DivorceIsland

@cassielorraine: I just want the best for them ... which in the context of the show, I'm not even sure what that is? Win? Lose? Someone help! #DivorceIsland

@instaneasa: I get Ollie's point about Clara kissing the gay guy but as a gay guy, FORGIVE HER, OLLIE!!! #HomosForClara #DivorceIsland

Annie tapped on a clip where Clara and Ollie were standing on a beach, Ollie reading a clue: 'If it's the magic ye seek, search on the beach.'

'Are you sure that's what it says?' Clara stood in a polka-dot playsuit, her hair piled on top of her head in a matching head scarf. 'It doesn't even rhyme.' She turned to camera. 'Who's writing this stuff, Sean?'

A voice from off-camera replied stiffly, 'Please don't address the camera, Clara.'

Ollie turned to the camera as well. 'Why? C'mon, Sean, do you think the viewers don't realise we're standing here with a cameraman and a boom operator?'

Clara giggled. 'We're more married to you and Mike,' she waved a hand to the sound guy, 'than we are to each other at this stage!' She turned to Ollie. 'Can we keep them? Please!'

From behind the camera, Sean could be heard laughing.

'Come and help us raise our children, guys,' Ollie said imploringly.

The scene cut to Clara and Ollie pushing a row boat into the water while Jez Fuller narrated.

'Clara and Ollie are our first couple to guess correctly that The Dazzling Bob is waiting on this floating pontoon just twenty metres from the beach.' The camera zoomed to a small man in a suit surrounded by water. He waved his arms elaborately and a flock of doves rose into the air behind him.

'Will The Dazzling Bob help them "find the magic"?' asked Jez as the camera focused on Clara and Ollie's boat which, it immediately became clear, was travelling in the decidedly opposite direction to the magician.

On her phone, Jez regrouped: 'It appears Clara and Ollie have something else in mind ...'

Annie grinned. It was such a relief that they were actually having fun together. Somehow, on a show called *Divorce Island*, they seemed more together than they had in months.

Another boat, containing the crew, appeared, giving chase, then the scene cut to Clara in the Confession Pod. 'We just weren't arsed with the dazzling lad,' she explained.

The clip cut to Ollie's talking head: 'Once I was in the boat, I realised I hadn't been alone with Clara in days. We keep having to "date" other people.' He did rueful air quotes.

It cut back to Clara. 'Have you *met* the other people on this show? Not to be mean, but it is literally a collection of rejects, as in they're people being *rejected* by their other halves. I know I am too but ... whatever. And like ... Ollie's hot. Maybe he's not everyone's "hot". But he's my kind of hot. Not that hotness can make a marriage work but ...' She shrugged. 'It helps. Thirty grand would help too,' she added impishly.

It cut back to Ollie. 'Would I take the cash or the divorce if we won?' The camera cut to his hands twisting in his lap as tense music ratcheted up before the clip cut to black.

Annie put the phone down and tried to focus on the menu. It was impossible to know what to eat. All day, every day, she had a kind of swaying nausea in her stomach, nausea that was sometimes assuaged by eating something and, at other times, made far, far worse by eating something. She read the Bear's breakfast special and then picked up her phone again to text Rachel:

Annie: Bear would be a cute name for a baby?!

Rachel: Yes! And good for a girl or a boy.

A picture dropped into the chat underneath Rachel's reply. She'd added 'Bear' to the blackboard in the kitchen where the list of baby names was growing by the day. Other picks included Nancy, Lia, Oisín and Jamie.

Annie smiled, momentarily distracted by the unpleasant business at hand. This would be the first time she'd spoken to Conor in nearly four weeks. The four days they'd spent moving out of the apartment in mid-July had been strange; the atmosphere was oddly formal. They were polite with each other. They'd even strayed into a kind of bleak nostalgia from time to time as they unearthed the ephemera of their two decades together: tickets to gigs, pictures from college days, a set of knee and elbow pads – relics from the slightly improbable summer when they'd actually regularly gone rollerblading together.

While they had both attended Donal's birthday party, they had successfully avoided each other – a cursory nod passed between them at the beginning and that was the extent of their interaction.

Annie's fury at him had initially burned bright, but it flamed out quicker than she expected. She knew deep down that she and Conor had been crumbling in the last six months of their relationship.

Now she'd left it to the very last possible moment to let him know about her pregnancy. Her first scan, at which she would find out for sure how far along she was, was that afternoon. Conor, who meticulously planned his days from hour to hour, would not be happy with the swerve his day was about to take and Annie was secretly hoping he wouldn't be able to make it and it could be just her and Rachel.

She craned her neck to look up and down the street. No sign of him. *I could just bail out. Never tell him? Never admit it's his baby?* It was not a thought she was seriously entertaining; for starters, they had the same friends so keeping a secret of that magnitude would be impossible. She just didn't want to be dragged from her bubble of joy, which facing the reality of co-parenting a baby with her ex would definitely do.

Extreme happiness, Annie'd found, felt a bit like walking on a tightrope: at any moment it could be snatched away. She'd tried to explain this to Rachel, that the happier you were, the higher the stakes. Rachel had hugged her, inadvertently giving Annie another problem as the softness of Rachel's arms around her, coupled with her unique Rachel scent, had sparked a dizzying rush of yearning in Annie that felt beyond anything a normal friend hug would inspire.

'Hey, Annie.' Conor had at last appeared. He pulled out the wrought-iron chair opposite her.

'Hey.' She half stood, reaching to hug him before abruptly pulling back. *We don't hug anymore*, she remembered. Too late. At the sight of her embarking on a hug, Conor had gotten to his feet and was now flailing because she'd abandoned the hug. He completed the greeting awkwardly with a half-hug, half-arm-pat combo.

'That went well,' remarked Annie dryly, and he grinned weakly.

'How've you been?' he asked.

'I've been good.' She thrust the menu at him. 'I've picked.'

'Oh-kay.' He turned the menu the right way up.

'I'm getting the breakfast special,' she blurted. 'And I'm pregnant.'

Conor looked up from the laminated sheet, his mouth a perfect 'o'.

'I know what you're thinking ... immaculate conception, right?' Annie jabbered as Conor continued to stare at her, his knuckles now white from gripping the menu so tightly. 'But I googled it and it turns out you can get pregnant from pre-cum.'

Conor finally closed his mouth to swallow with what looked like effort.

'I ...' he began.

'I know?' Now that she'd started talking, Annie found she couldn't stop. 'I actually didn't realise for ages because I thought I'd gotten my period after Provincetown but it turned out it must've been an implantation bleed or something. Obvi I'd read all about those the last few years – you know, when we were trying. Back when I was tracking my cycle so closely, I was always watching out for anything at all in my knickers. Sorry if that's a gross image for pre-noon.' Annie grimaced. 'Though it's all about to get a *lot* grosser down there! Ha. Ha.' She squeaked out a nervy, high-pitched laugh.

'Yeah,' Conor breathed. His face appeared to be slowly shifting through several different emotions: disbelief, confusion, worry and back to disbelief again.

'Are you two ready to order?' A young woman with a partially shaved head and many delicate piercings adorning her ears appeared at Annie's elbow, bending to place glasses and a carafe of water on the table.

'Yes, please.' Annie smiled up at her. 'I'll have the breakfast special and a decaf Americano.' She and the server looked to Conor, who still seemed to be in a state of suspended animation.

A couple of seconds passed during which Conor's gaze had drifted from Annie to the waitress, but still no words were forthcoming.

Annie took the menu from his hands and handed it to the girl. 'He'll have the breakfast special as well and a regular Americano. Thank you.'

'Perfect.' The waitress bounced back through the café doors.

'Can you speak?' Annie dipped her head to catch Conor's eyes. 'Will I get you a pen and paper?' Annie poured out water for each of them and pushed Conor's towards him.

He gratefully accepted and downed the glass in one. 'Sorry.' He ran a hand over his face, massaging his brow. 'I'm back.' He shook his head. 'This is wild, Annie.'

'I know.' She sipped from her glass. 'I feel like I should tell you this up top: I'm really happy and I don't want any negativity about it.'

'Why would I be negative about it?' Conor looked surprised. 'We've been trying to make this happen for so long!'

The 'we' jabbed at Annie. She didn't want to be a 'we' with Conor. Not anymore.

Also, he was the one who put a stop to the trying.

'How far along are you?' He took out his phone and pulled up the calendar app. 'What were the dates of Provincetown again?'

'I think I'm about twelve weeks but it's going to be confirmed today. I have my first hospital visit.'

'Today?' Conor's eyes bulged slightly. 'But why are you only telling me now? I have to clear my schedule.'

'You don't,' Annie protested. 'My friend Rachel is coming with me.'

He stared at her. 'Rachel? But I'm the father.'

'Yes, but ...' Annie said delicately, 'Rachel and I have been doing lots of the things together.'

'What do you mean "the things"? What things? How long have you known about this?'

The waitress reappeared with a tray and set their plates and coffees down before them. Annie was grateful for the brief pause. For a moment she considered lying but she knew that it was pointless, it'd come out.

When the waitress left, Annie picked up her knife and fork just to have something to busy herself with. 'I've known for a bit. I took a test about three weeks ago.'

He absorbed this for a moment, his eyes narrowing as he digested it. 'Three weeks! Annie, what the fuck?'

'I just wanted ...' Annie trailed off. 'I dunno.' It seemed mean to say the truth, which was that she hadn't wanted to have a downer of a conversation with him during the happiest weeks of her life.

'But ...' He took a breath. 'Okay. Sorry. Let's not dwell on that. This is so huge, Annie. It's amazing, sure, but also we have so much to sort out. We need to find a new place.'

There was the 'we' again. Annie floundered a little. Find a new place? What was he expecting?

'*We* have a place.' Annie placed a hand over her stomach. 'I'm living with Rachel now. You know that.'

'But ...' He looked exasperated. 'What are you talking about?

We're having a baby, the baby we've been trying for for so long. We're getting back together.'

'No way.' The words were out of Annie's mouth before she could put any sheen of kindness on them.

'No way?' Conor's eyebrows shot up.

'No way,' Annie repeated firmly. 'Two and a half months ago you told me that you didn't want me. And now I'm pregnant and you want me again? No fucking way to *that* plan. I have Rachel and the baby, we're looking at moving into a three-bed so we'll have a room for the baby.'

'What?' Conor sat back in his chair. 'So it's all about Rachel now, is it? She's going to the scan? She's gonna see my child before I see it.'

Annie resisted the urge to eye-roll because she knew he absolutely had a point. 'No,' she said, with exaggerated patience. 'Look, come as well. If you can,' she added.

'Oh, how good of you to extend the invite.' His words were steeped in sarcasm.

'Conor, can you just not?' Annie shook her head. 'I realise I played this pretty badly. Things have been crazy. A lot happened in the summer. And even though I am happier than I ever thought possible, I'm also scared. Like …' She lowered her eyes, speaking softly now. 'I'm scared that it'll all go away.'

Conor's expression thawed. 'Yeah, I get that …' he said softly. 'But don't you think we should be … at least living together? I'm not being old-fashioned but maybe this could be what gets us back on track? *Not*,' he raised his voice slightly as Annie began to protest, 'in a "I only want to be with you cuz you're pregnant now" way but in the way that things had become so hard between us because this thing wasn't happening and now … it's happened. Maybe we need to give *us* a chance again? To be a family?' He gazed at her, his eyes hopeful.

She felt a twinge of guilt. She didn't know where to begin answering that so instead she leaned into the logistics.

'The appointment is at 3 p.m. If you can't get away from work, I'll send pictures straight away, I promise, and no more booking appointments without making sure you can come.'

'Right.' He sighed, and Annie felt even worse.

'Hey.' She reached over to touch his arm. 'We'll still be doing this together, you know. This is our baby. We've been friends for a long time. Maybe this is not the worst setup ever, right?'

She smiled gently. Sure she'd been hurt by Conor, but she'd known him for two decades. She knew he was going to be an amazing father.

And maybe friends raising kids together could be the next evolution of the family unit? Why was Friend Love always downgraded, as though it was lesser than romantic love?

She thought of Rachel then. Everyone said raising kids took a village … Rachel would be a part of that village too.

Of course, a part of Annie knew that when it came to Rachel, she was never just going to be a random villager. It wasn't Friend Love budding inside her along with little Beanie, but facing that meant facing a lot of knottier questions too, and more than anything, she didn't want to lose Rachel.

In the waiting room of the ultrasound department of the maternity hospital, Annie kept catching herself staring at the other women and their gargantuan bellies.

Apparently reading her mind, Rachel leaned close. 'I can't wait till you have a big bump!'

'Or a fuck-off gigantic one,' Annie whispered back. She took out her phone and, pulling Rachel close, took a selfie of them to send to Slags For Life. She checked the time. Ten past three. The appointments were running behind and there was no sign of Conor yet, though he had said that he'd be coming.

'Look at this one.' Rachel nudged Annie, showing her the MyHome listing. 'Three-bed in a newly built estate in Ballycourt! That'd be good, still on the tram line for us to get to work.'

Annie examined the pictures; it looked airy and minimalist with all mod cons, though it didn't have the character Rachel's cottage had.

Again, seeming to hear her thoughts, Rachel whispered, 'We'd make it our own. It'd be a really good blank canvas. There's a crèche in the estate for when you go back to work after mat leave!'

Annie drifted into an image of her and Rachel wheeling a buggy on a sunny morning next summer, dropping a baby to crèche and getting the tram to town.

'Am I too late?' Conor's voice brought her back to the cramped waiting room.

'They're a little behind,' Rachel said, as Conor budged in to sit beside Annie, giving Rachel only the most cursory nod.

As Annie handed the phone back to Rachel, he spied the screen. 'House-hunting I see.'

His words were barbed but Rachel didn't notice. 'It's hell out there,' she said ruefully. 'And I'm not exactly a big earner. I'm an artist. But we'll find something.' She gave Annie's hand a squeeze.

'Might make more sense for me and Annie to find something, don't you think?' came Conor's retort.

Rachel's eyes flicked to Annie, who tried to communicate silently and subtly: *Ignore him. I in no way want that!*

Annie was grateful when the nurse appeared in the door and called her name, though of course an issue immediately arose as all three of them stood.

'Oh, we only allow one person to accompany Mum,' the woman said.

'That'll be me, then.' Conor stepped forward.

Annie bit her lip and turned to Rachel. 'I'm sorry,' she whispered.

'Don't be,' Rachel said softly. 'It's okay. I get it. Ireland's obviously not ready for throuples to have babies.'

Annie grinned. The *thought* of throupling with Conor was a specific kind of hell. Though what shape her family would take was uncertain. Annie followed Conor and the nurse down the hall towards the examination rooms. She was already imagining her and Rachel at crèche drop-offs together. What did that mean? Annie gazed at Conor's back walking ahead of her. He's the baby's father. What were she and Rachel gonna do? Become sister-wives to him? *Lol.*

These competing thoughts vied for her attention as they were brought into a windowless room with a bed and various pieces of medical equipment. However, a few minutes later, when the delicate but determined throb of their baby's heartbeat filled her ears, all conscious thought evaporated. She lay there in quiet awe as tears trickled into the fine hair at her temples.

CHAPTER 20

'Muma! Muma! Be Sea Donkey! Be Sea Donkey!'

Her youngest's shrill demands abruptly jerked Clara out of her latest grim terror-spiral (not remotely based in reality) about Ollie hooking up with Mary. Reggie, in water wings and brandishing a pool noodle, was splashing water directly in her face. Delightful.

They were bobbing about in the small, grotty swimming pool outside the cast villa. In the deep end, Tom and Josh were ducking and diving and generally trying to drown each other. The pool at Casa Amore No More was azure blue and bordered by marble. It was also largely ornamental – the cast weren't allowed in it unless there was a scene of engineered drama involving couples treading water in tiny bathing suits and whispering together while their other halves glared from nearby sun loungers.

The pool she was currently in looked and felt like a large toilet. Still, the boys loved it. They didn't know the difference. In the three weeks of being there, they'd become incredibly attached to their lives on the sunny Greek island where there were always other kids to play with, lessons on the beach and a swimming pool in their front garden. Home would be a bit of a land when they got back there in a couple of days.

She complied with Reggie's request and stood obediently while he clambered onto her back and held the straps of her swimming togs like reins.

As she and Ollie and the other couples had become more and more embroiled in the director's messed-up 'vision' for the show, she was increasingly concerned that even if they won and opted for the cash over the divorce, all that money would be funnelled straight into therapy for their kids.

Unfortunately, she was having this attack of panic about a month too late.

At night, wedged under the grotty ceiling of the bedroom, listening to the soft snuffling snores of her boys, the guilt could choke her. Clara was afraid the boys would be plagued by her stupid idea for years to come. Would the kids at school make fun of them? The other kids' parents were no doubt already saying a thing or two. She shuddered to think of the WhatsApp side chats.

Divorce Island had been a bad fucking idea but it was Clara's bad fucking idea and she had no idea how to begin rowing back from it. Plus in another thirty-six hours it would all be done anyway. Tonight was the last challenge. Then the votes would come in and, in an elaborate ceremony on the beach at dawn, they would learn if it had been remotely worth it. One at a time, each couple would stand on an altar and each partner would be asked if, should they win, they would be taking the money or if they wanted to divorce their spouse. Then the couple chosen by the voting public would be announced. Clara and Ollie had been receiving the highest votes night on night, so it was looking likely that their answers were going to have some real-world ramifications.

Any time she thought about the unknown of Ollie's answer, she felt an icy shiver of fear down her arms. It was scary that she really had no idea where his head was at.

They'd been having a lot more easy, lighter moments in the previous couple of weeks, moments when they felt like their old selves. But could that really be enough to bring them back from the brink? For her part, it kind of had been. Whether it was simply the time together without the strain of their life in Dublin or perhaps the heat of the Greek sun, her resentment towards him had burned off. All she could see now was how childish she'd been and she was haunted by regret. Though she hadn't yet managed to voice any of this to Ollie with all the cameras around. *The cameras I brought into our lives.*

'C'mon Sea Donkey.' Reggie kicked impatiently and, struggling under the considerable weight of the three-year-old, she began the arduous swim to the other side of the pool. 'Hurry *up*!' he demanded tyrannically, and Clara laughed.

'God, where did you get such a *lazy* Sea Donkey, Reggie?' she exclaimed in mock horror. 'I wouldn't put up with it if I were you. You should have me put down and made into glue!'

'Jesus! Clara! You're going to traumatise him!' Clara turned around, to find Ollie on his hunkers at the other side of the pool.

Despite his admonishment, he was laughing, and Clara felt a trace of optimism and also a flutter of nerves. She'd been having them more and more around him. It felt like the early days of their relationship. In a strange way, being on the show had helped her see Ollie as a person again, not just as her husband of nearly twenty years – a husband who had come to feel a bit like an extension of herself, a sentient limb, rather than a person in his own right.

She had realised that he still had the ability to surprise her and make her laugh – their flight from The Dazzling Bob on the high seas had reminded her so much of the hijinks of their twenties, minus the class A's, of course. She wondered if he was experiencing anything like this with her. She hoped so.

'We're their parents, our *job* is to traumatise them,' she called back playfully.

God! Why'd I have to drag us to Greece and onto a TV show to make me realise how much I don't want to lose him?

Maybe she'd needed something dramatic to shock her out of her marriage complacency? Maybe *Divorce Island* wouldn't be the disaster she feared it'd be? They *were* getting on better – she was sure *that* wasn't wishful thinking on her part.

'We're parents of the year so.' Ollie stood and pulled his T-shirt off over his head and kicked off his flip-flops. His hair was mussed up and his smile lopsided as he took a couple of steps back.

Clara, realising what was coming, yelped, 'Ollie, noooo!', trying to swim backwards without drowning their son. Too late. Ollie cannon-balled into the pool right in front of her, sending a sheet of water over her head. He surfaced looking thrilled with himself and jauntily expelled an arc of water from his mouth.

'I was trying to keep my hair dry for tonight's shoot,' she lamented. 'Also, I wouldn't let that water near my mouth if I were you. I weed in this pool earlier.'

'*Clara!*' Ollie cried, vigorously spitting.

She shrugged. 'Grow up, Ollie, everyone pees in pools.'

'No! They don't!' He laughed.

'The rule is: any body of water is fair game,' Clara said reasonably.

'The rule is: the *sea* is fair game – it's the law of the ocean. Pools, on the other hand, are a sacred space.'

Clara laughed, then wondered if she looked like shit. *Why do I care? The man has watched me literally shit out three babies.*

But she cared. She really cared.

'How're you feeling about tonight's "trust exercise"?' Ollie casually picked up Tom, who'd paddled over, and threw him over his shoulder into the water.

'Me next!' screamed Josh, swimming down to their end of the pool. Ollie obliged, chucking him after his brother.

Clara rubbed under her eyes, trying to stop her mascara running. 'I guess I'm wondering if they'll man up and actually give us something interesting to do.'

The previous trust exercises had been largely tame. Lead each other blindfolded around the island for the day, and such. Though that particular one had really soured when Paul left Liz standing on the terrace of the local taverna after becoming distracted by Darina in a white and gold bikini across the road leading Richie. The producers had loved it but Paul abandoning his wife definitely didn't go over well with the viewers. The audience had given the majority of that night's votes to Clara and Ollie who, in an attempt to make things more interesting, had both worn blindfolds and generally stumbled around the place causing chaos and having quite a lot of fun doing it.

Ollie stretched out to float on his back, only for Reggie to leap from Clara's back onto his stomach. 'Waaah.' Ollie leapt up, winded but unperturbed. He hoisted Reggie onto his shoulders and started to bounce up and down. 'With the finale tomorrow, I'm sure they're going to have to up the ante.'

Jez Fuller stood opposite the couples on the other side of the pool. It was just after 7 p.m. and behind him the white walls of Casa Amore No More had a rose gold glow, reflecting the spectacular sunset taking place. Clara was wearing a purple sundress patterned with tigers. Ollie, as instructed by the cast coordinator, was shirtless, wearing a sarong, as were all the other men – the sarongs had been distributed just before dinner. In front of each man was a cinder block and heavy-duty scissors. In Clara's hands was the length of rope each woman had been given on arrival.

'Are they giving us the option to drown the men?' she muttered in Ollie's direction.

'Feel free to do it,' Ollie replied, staring straight ahead. 'Put me out of my misery. I'm not a sarong guy; they do nothing for my calves.'

'Your calves are looking well,' Clara replied, trying for flirty.

'Clara, Ollie. Can you guys say all that again on camera when we're rolling?' the director called.

Clara and Ollie rolled their eyes at each other and, again, Clara felt the funny little swoop of nerves.

He likes me. Doesn't he?

The slightly preposterous thought surprised and then amused her.

Of course he likes me, we've been together for two decades.

But she knew it wasn't a given anymore. It hadn't been ever since that stupid day in Provincetown and really, if she was honest, maybe before that too.

'Rolling,' shouted the first assistant director.

'Tonight,' Jez held the camera's gaze and spoke with a breathless intensity, 'on the final night of this incredible journey, we are inviting our couples to participate in our most intense test of trust yet. Now, once and for all, you the viewer can judge who deserves to win freedom from the shackles of a dreary, unhappy marriage. Or,' he paused to dial up the drama, 'who will choose each other.' At these words, cameras on all sides mobilised and began to circle Clara, Ollie and the rest of the cast. It felt a bit like being devoured.

'*Cut!*' the director yelled. 'Playback,' he demanded, and then hunched forward in his headphones to watch the monitor. Apparently satisfied with whatever he saw there, he leaned back and addressed the waiting crew. 'Reset, guys.' Then he stood and approached the contestants.

'Guys, you all look great. Mary,' he swivelled towards her pulling on her sleeve, 'lose this little shrug cardigan thing, luv. It's not 2002. You're only thirty-something – we want the viewers to believe Derek could still want you.'

'Prick,' Ollie muttered, and Clara spotted him shake his head at Mary in commiseration. Clara did not love this but also this was Ollie. This was why she liked him, wasn't it? He was a good one. She was fairly certain that Ollie didn't fancy Mary. She *did* dress like someone arriving on Ellis Island in the 1800s. *She's so dreary,* Clara thought uncharitably. *Oh God, why am I being such a mean bitch?*

Then it hit her: *I am jealous.*

The director was moving along the line, adjusting the men. 'Let's show a little more leg.' He fussed with Richie's sarong. 'Right, you two,' he pointed at Clara and Ollie, 'let's try and work in that interaction again on camera. The audience is loving your natural banter.'

'Yes, so natural,' Ollie deadpanned.

The director slid back to his seat and checked in with the lighting and sound guys, then called action.

Jez stood before them and looked at each couple in turn. 'Tonight, these men are going to place their ultimate trust in their wives. And husbands,' he hastily added to Rob and Sean. 'Ladies and Rob, you are probably wondering about the ropes you've been given. Gents, you, no doubt, are feeling growing concern about the cinder blocks in front of you.' He paused here and Clara could already imagine the ridiculous music they would use to up the tension. Jez then looked pointedly at her and Ollie and they repeated what they'd said to each other a few minutes earlier.

'*Silence!*' Jez thundered, and Clara suppressed a giggle.

'Okay, wives, you are to kneel down in front of your husbands.' He'd dispensed with acknowledging Rob, Clara noted. She tugged at her dress, then got to her knees in front of Ollie. It was a troubling sensation to be doing something that she suspected would eventually no doubt be meme'd to within an inch of its life and quite possibly haunt her to her grave.

Think of the money. Or the divorce if Ollie chose that. She winced both at the hard marble slabs under her bare knees and the thought that, after everything, maybe Ollie was leaning towards divorce.

'Clara, Liz, Darina, Rob and Mary, now tie one end of the rope around the genitals of your spouse.'

What! Clara thought at the same that several of the men yelped the same.

From her position, eye to eye with Ollie's crotch, Clara glanced to her left at Liz, who was grinning malevolently up at Paul. 'Maybe you shouldn't have gone into the Intimacy Pod with Darina yesterday,' she said with an arched eyebrow.

'That's it, ladies, go ahead,' Jez called. He turned to the camera. 'The sarongs are no fashion statement. They are to keep us broadcasting before the watershed.' He winked at the unseen viewers.

Clara looked up at Ollie, who nodded, looking tense. She reached under the material and fumbled with the rope and Ollie's poor, innocent floppy junk. When she had secured the rope she stood up, as did the rest of her counterparts.

'Now the wives must tie the other end around the cinder blocks. *But*,' he raised his hand to silence the murmured objections of Sean and Richie, 'first they must cut the rope to measure. Ladies, you will all dive to the bottom of the pool to estimate how deep it is before cutting the ropes accordingly. In a few minutes, you will be dropping the cinder blocks attached to your men to the bottom of the pool. It is up to you how much slack you decide to give.'

There was a sharp intake of breath from the men.

Then they were handed blindfolds as the women and Rob stripped down to their swimsuits and one by one slipped into the water. Clara opted for a hand-over-hand method of measurement. She tried not to think of the risks. So far none of the challenges had posed the risk of personal injury. This was serious.

Back on the edge of the pool, with the men's eyes still covered, the women and Rob set about measuring how much rope to give.

'Do we have to cut the rope?' Clara asked. 'Can we choose to just leave the full length?'

'No,' Jez snapped.

Clara concentrated. Ollie's penis had provided her with some good times; she didn't want anything terrible to befall it. She reminded herself to allow for the cinder block landing both upright and on its side and then she added another few feet to be absolutely sure.

With each man now secured to the cinder block, Jez instructed them to pick up their blocks and step to the edge.

The director cut at this point and told them that each couple would now have an interaction for the cameras. They began with Paul and Liz.

'Paul, do you trust Liz?'

'Yes. With my life! But not my penis!'

Liz smiled malevolently and Jez fixed his beady gaze on the next couple.

'Darina and Richie, there's a lot at stake here. You two haven't had kids yet.'

'Maybe don't assume everyone wants kids.' Darina glared.

Jez moved along hastily, no doubt fearing the inevitable discourse online about archaic, heteronormative expectations being peddled on arguably the most heteronormative reality show ever conceived of.

Rob and Sean were next.

'This is barbaric.' Sean folded his arms.

'So was forcing me onto this show,' Rob snapped, and gave a sharp tug on the rope. Sean winced.

'*Cut!*' the director yelled. 'Did we catch that rope action?' he asked the camerawoman closest to him. She gave the thumbs-up and resumed shooting.

It was now Derek and Mary's turn. Beside Clara, Mary looked close to tears and covered her face with her hands. 'I'm scared,' she said. 'I know there's enough rope, but,' she peered out at Derek, 'what if something goes wrong, what if I hurt him?'

Jez nodded sagely. 'That's the risk you are all taking. You've gambled your hearts by coming to Divorce Island and now you are gambling with your husband's most vital organ.'

Clara felt sick. The cameras turned to her and Ollie.

'Clara? Ollie?' Jez prompted them.

The situation was rich with opportunities for quips but, instead of taking the bait, and no doubt delighting viewers and probably securing votes at this crucial point in the competition, Clara turned to look Ollie in the eyes.

'I don't want to hurt him any more than I already have,' she said simply.

Ollie gazed back at her, and their surreal situation – cameras, lights, crew and dicks tied to concrete blocks – receded. In that moment, it was just them. For some reason, Ollie's ruffled hair and scruffy stubble were breaking her heart and suddenly she knew what she had to do.

'I don't want to do this.' She turned to the director. 'I want out. Of this whole thing.'

'Admirable, but no. You signed a contract,' the director said. 'Keep rolling, gang,' he commanded.

'Please,' Clara whimpered. 'What if I do it instead? I can tie the rope around my boobs?'

'Clara?' Ollie interrupted her. 'I trust you.' And before she could say anything else, he let go of the block. The rope that lay coiled at his feet shot into the water.

'Fuck!' one of the other guys shouted. The block hit the bottom, the muffled 'thunk' audible despite the depth of the pool.

Clara burst into tears. On the ground, all the additional rope still lay and Ollie was unharmed. She put her arms around him and breathed him in. She stood on tiptoes and kissed him where his hair curled at his neck just under his ear. She hadn't touched him like that since the cabin of the boat in Provincetown.

It took a moment to register that his arms remained resolutely at his sides. He wasn't reciprocating. She stepped back and something inside her plummeted. Hope? Any shred of optimism? Whatever it was, it dropped as fast as the cinder block had and she felt desolate.

No one spoke and then the director yelled, 'Excellent work, guys. That was gold. Full of heart. These are the moments we directors wait our whole careers for.'

Clara looked at Ollie but all the easiness of their earlier teasing had disappeared and his face was now shuttered.

She took a breath and said simply, 'I'm sorry, Ollie.' She tried to pour everything that had happened in the last three months into those three little words and then she walked away.

When she got back to the cast villa, all the children were asleep. She slipped past the night-time babysitters and into her room, where she visited each of her boys curled in their beds to place a whisper of a kiss on their cheeks. Then, in the dark, she pulled off her damp bikini – her dress still lay crumpled at the edge of the pool in the other villa. She felt around in the pitch black to find knickers and then pulled a ragged T-shirt of Ollie's from the laundry basket. She needed the comfort of his smell.

She was lying in her bunk when she heard panicked shouts pierce the night outside. Then in mere minutes sirens were approaching. Oh God. The shriek of the ambulance hit a fever pitch and the room filled with flashing blue and red lights as it charged past and sped through the compound.

Someone was hurt, and that spelled either the end of *Divorce Island* forever or the instant renewal of the series for another season. *Yikes!* Clara remained in her bed. No way was she going to investigate. She couldn't face whatever reality was unfolding over at Casa Amore No More. Ollie would be back soon, he'd tell her.

Only a couple of minutes passed before the ambulance was screeching back out to the main road, and shortly after she could hear a growing hubbub of voices as cast members returned through the hibiscus-scented night.

She heard them come into the living area of the villa. She couldn't make out words exactly but she detected an air of disbelief in the hushed conversations.

Ollie slipped into the room. 'Clara?' he whispered. 'You awake?'
'Yeah.'
She heard him scuffle around in the dark, undressing. Then the creak of the bed beneath hers as he lay down.

'You will not guess who didn't leave enough rope!' He sounded amused, maybe even a bit impressed. 'Mary! She finally stood up to that prick Derek!'

'Cool,' Clara replied quietly. She'd no appetite for the gory details. She was too preoccupied.

'Ollie?'

'Yeah?'

'I meant what I said back there. I am so sorry. I've been a complete fuck-up.'

'You have,' he agreed.

She waited for him to say more but all she could hear was the sound of his breathing.

'Are you nervous about tomorrow?' she asked.

'No.' He sounded tired. Was he tired of her? Of the day? Of the whole sorry situation? 'I know what I'm going to say on the altar.'

'Right.' Her eyes filled with tears. 'Ollie?'

'I'm going to sleep now,' he said, and the bed groaned a little as he turned onto his side.

'Okay,' she whispered, wiping her face with the sheet. It seemed best not to press him. Maybe it'd be better to try and talk to him in the morning before the stupid ceremony. She had to make him see that they were worth fighting for, see that they could get home and make changes somehow. Spend more time together. Or get space from each other, whichever they needed. Surely he had noticed their old dynamic returning.

The next morning, the couples were quiet at breakfast. It was still dark out. Clara had been woken up especially early by a crew member and hustled into recording a quick talking head as she'd missed it the night before. The kids were still asleep but would be collected for a boat trip around the island in a couple of hours. To Clara's dismay, Ollie had already disappeared, probably for one of his long runs, so her plan to plead her case was completely scuppered. There was also no sign of Mary and Derek, naturally. They'd been at the hospital all night.

One of the production assistants appeared at the door. 'Morning all.' She clapped her hands. 'Thirty minutes to show time. The vans to take us to the beach are outside. Mary and Derek – who is doing better – will be meeting us there.'

Clara raised her hand. 'Ollie's not back from his run yet.'

'He's already outside, Clara. C'mon, let's get moving, gang.'

Clara hurried back to her room to pull on the yellow and purple tie-dyed sundress she'd chosen to wear for the public execution of her marriage.

But maybe it won't be an execution. She tried to be optimistic as she grabbed her sun hat. *Maybe he's feeling the same way I am?* Though not talking to her last night and skipping out before dawn to run didn't seem to bode well.

Outside, the others were getting into the vans. Clara spotted Ollie in the one in front and pushed past Paul and Liz to get in beside him.

'Hey,' she said.

'Hey.' He looked showered and wasn't in his running gear.

'I assumed you'd gone for a run.'

'No, just a long walk.'

'Oh.' She messed with the straps of her dress. His hands were clasped in his lap and she longed to take one and feel that reassurance and comfort she'd always used to get from Ollie.

'Let's go.' The production assistant had jumped in beside the driver and now they were pulling away from the villa. 'Divorce Day, everybody!' she whooped.

On the beach, Clara felt at a remove from everything that was happening. In the distance, waves were crashing, cameras and the production team were swarming everywhere and nearby Ollie was blank-faced, but all she could focus on was the roar of anxiety inside her.

By now, the sky was streaked with soft pastels of rose and orange as the sun began its ascent from the horizon. Mary and Derek had joined them, Derek in a wheelchair with a small shawl draped over his lower half to conceal the enormous bandaging that resembled an adult nappy.

Mickey, the director, stepped onto the altar. 'This is it, folks. The moment you and an average of 650,000 viewers at home have been waiting for. Immediately after the ceremonies, we'll be heading back to the compound to record talking heads. Also at the villa, a psychologist will be at your disposal in case anyone's feeling a sense of hopeless, despair, et cetera.' He tossed this off casually and made his way back to his chair under a parasol.

The filming began with Jez Fuller reminding viewers what an incredible, envelope-pushing show *Divorce Island* had been. Then, one by one, he invited each couple up and held both their hands like he was officiating a wedding. Liz and Paul, who'd been the most acrimonious right from the very beginning, were first.

'Do you take this man to divorce or to make it work?' Jez asked Liz, who answered with defiance: 'Divorce.'

Jez turned to Paul. 'And do you take this woman to divorce or to make it work?'

'Divorce,' Paul said coldly.

'A unanimous divorce!' Jez, beaming, clapped his hands and the rest of the cast joined in awkwardly. He faced the camera to his right. 'But it's still up to you, dear viewer, to decide if this miserable couple should get the divorce of their dreams. Text voting is still open.' He winked.

Next up were Darina and Richie, who opted to make it work, which tracked – Clara felt vindicated in her belief they'd always been trying to game the show, only pretending to be having problems in order to win the money.

Rob and Sean chose divorce, as did Mary and Derek. Clara glanced at Ollie but there was still no hint at what he was thinking.

'Clara and Ollie, join me now,' Jez commanded.

They made their way past the other couples, up onto the altar. Jez took their hands and turned to Clara.

'Clara, do you take this man to divorce or to make it work?'

Clara answered without hesitation. 'I want to make it work.' She tried not to sound as desperate as she felt as she looked up at Ollie.

Ollie didn't even wait for Jez to ask him the question before answering: 'Me too, Clara.' He broke into a teary smile and grabbed her up into a hug.

'Oh my God.' Relief crashed over her. 'Thank you. Thank you. I love you, Ollie. I love you.'

Being buried in Ollie's arms after going so long without holding each other was the most wonderful feeling, and she started to cry.

'I'll be better, Ollie,' she promised.

'We both will,' he murmured into her hair, before tipping her back with panache and kissing her deeply. Even Jez was dabbing his eyes.

CHAPTER 21

On Sunday morning, in the two-storey apartment on the corner near Bowery and Delancey Street on Manhattan's Lower East Side, Maggie awoke to the sound of messages. From her phone she could see it was 10.30 a.m. A lie-in was practically unheard of in her life. Even during the girls' summer recess, they were always up early at home in LA. Everyone in LA was up early.

New York, meanwhile, was *normal*, a bit more like Dublin, which was possibly why Maggie felt more at home there. It was as though because New York was geographically closer to Dublin, it meant that New York was also *spiritually* closer. Though she could see that, ironically, this was very *LA* thinking.

Thinking of Dodi and Essie back in LA so far away caused a clench of anxiety in her chest. She felt a visceral pull at the thought of them, without her, watching cartoons with sleep-warmed cheeks and messy hair. She'd never left them for more than a night before. She'd been in New York all week working on the script.

I will be seeing them so soon! she reminded herself, rolling over to check her messages. She spotted that the first notification was from Brody.

Brody: Updated the family calendar. Please familiarise yourself with the new arrival times, etc.

She opened the app and peered at the schedule for the next few days. Fionn and the girls were flying in at lunchtime – Fionn was adamant he wouldn't be missing the start of the *Divorce Island* finale which was going out at 7.30 p.m. in Ireland and at 2.30 p.m. their time.

The family's time was loose until that evening when Maggie was heading to meet Drew Schwartz and a few more from the theatre company. According to Drew's assistant who'd sent the invite it was to be a casual get-to-know-you vibe, hence the Sunday booking, but they would also no doubt talk about the development schedule for *Medea in Hollywood*. Fionn would probably take the girls for a pizza slice and maybe up to Times Square for a wander while she did that.

The premiere of *Endurance 2* was the next day, and any time Maggie looked at the time blocked off in the schedule – seven hours for hair, make-up, red carpet, film and after-party – she felt her enthusiasm dip. It'd been a while since she'd had to be on Fionn's arm out in public and truly there was no greater torture. All the photographs and shouting and interminable small talk – at least people would stop bothering to talk to her the second they realised she was a nobody.

She pulled her mind back to the dinner that evening. The Cookhouse Restaurant in Chelsea was a favourite and she was looking forward to meeting people who were actually interested in what *she* had to say. She just needed to decide what to wear.

She dragged herself from the bed, opened the blinds and padded across the parquet floors to the bathroom across the narrow hall. She loved this apartment – a four-bed with old sash windows that looked onto a rickety fire escape – which they were renting for a staggering eight grand a month. She cringed at the decadence, but since she would be working on the play in New York on and off for the next year, it made sense.

She pulled on cropped wide-leg jeans, a slouchy grey T-shirt and ballet pumps – it was the end of the third week of September but still mild. Next she looked through Sylvia's options for dinner – a deconstructed suit by Yves Saint Laurent, a Marni dress and a knitted tunic by JW Anderson. Maggie was dubious. They all screamed 'money'. Playwrights didn't have money. She really, really didn't want them to know that she was married to a movie star yet. Or ever, if she had the choice, though unfortunately that was entirely impossible. Maybe she could just go super casual?

She checked out the clothes she was already wearing in the mirror that hung on the inside of the wardrobe – even with the massive price tag, New York apartments were so pokey when you were used to LA, though this was a fact Maggie actually liked. Her desk space was tucked under the stairs that led up to the three other bedrooms. She'd gotten so much done at this little table, she now felt almost superstitious about trying to work on the show anywhere else.

Unfortunately, in another week she'd be on the move again. They'd be back in Dublin for a few weeks and she'd have to set up another space for her project in the Miavita house. She'd manage; she was dying to see Annie and Clara and it was Ollie's marathon. Speaking of ... She picked up her phone. Greece was ahead of New York. Clara and Ollie's fate had already been sealed.

There were still no updates in Slags For Life, as Clara still hadn't got her phone back. She texted Annie instead.

Maggie: Ahhhh, I'm getting nervous. What the hell is going to happen to them?

Annie: God, I know. Rach and I are already stress-eating. I hope they're alright. Whatever's happened. Crossing everything ... for what? I don't know. 😮

Maggie threw in a gif of James McAvoy sweating nervously and fanning himself and headed out the door to grab breakfast in the deli on the corner – coffee, glazed donuts and grapefruit juice was her current order – then she'd come back and put in a few hours on the script before the others arrived.

At the desk, Maggie fidgeted. She was two hours into redrafting the outline of Act 1 but her focus was wandering. She was hungry again. And feeling shaky. That was the problem with getting back into her old routine. The ache from purging staved off hunger for only so long before she'd find herself thinking of food again.

She checked the time: 12.30 p.m. She was on the countdown to her family's arrival. She opened the DoorDash app and debated her options which, in New York City, were infinite. She could have anything from oysters to banana pudding delivered right to her. She'd been a heavy user of DoorDash for the last week. Alone in the apartment, she could order as much as she wanted at any time.

As much as she wanted at any time turned out to be ... quite a bit. On one particularly frenzied day she'd ordered four separate times, but her stomach had been in bits after each purge and, more and more, she was thinking about how she needed to nip it all in the bud. She'd put a loose deadline of quitting once she'd turned in the script. But just thinking of stopping instantly amped up her anxiety.

I can stop. I've stopped before, she'd remind herself. Then another possibility would swiftly present itself. *Why do I have to stop entirely? I could just cut back. That would be fine. Just keep it in the back pocket for certain occasions.*

Now she stood up and drifted into the kitchen.

There's got to be something here. Her thoughts skittered around. She just needed anything. She found some spaghetti in the corner press and started to boil water in a pot. She didn't have any sauce or even cheese, but it didn't matter, she just wanted the sensation of consuming. Minutes later, standing at the kitchen counter facing the blue tiles of the backsplash, she pushed the slightly undercooked, tacky lengths of pasta into her mouth. Over and over she did it. She refilled her bowl twice and then a third time until finally the dogged urge to eat abated and she made her way back to her desk with an efficient stop in the bathroom en route.

Once again, sitting before her notes and laptop, she felt a deep satisfaction with the whole situation. A perfect system. All thoughts of cutting back shelved for the moment.

A couple of hours later, Dodi and Essie were dashing around playing hide and seek while Fionn and Maggie were watching the deranged final episode of *Divorce Island* in the living room.

'*What the—? Aaaahhh!*' Fionn had screamed, grabbing his crotch, when a cocky-looking Derek had nonchalantly dropped his cinder block into the pool only to suddenly howl in pain and throw himself in after it seconds later.

'I did not think Mary had it in her,' Maggie said, stunned.

'I know!' Fionn had pulled himself into a protective foetal position on the couch beside her. 'Jesus Christ. Isn't that assault?'

'They're all release-formed to the hilt,' Maggie reminded him.

The show was cutting between the arrival of paramedics and the Confession Pods where other cast members were expressing shock after the fact.

'Mary's been worn down by his prickery,' Ollie said solemnly.

'She should be arrested.' Richie and Darina were appalled.

'She should be president!' Clara told the camera. 'Of the *world*,' she added.

The show cut back to an anxious-looking paramedic. 'The prognosis?' He ran a hand over his mouth. 'Penile trauma. A lot of bruising. A lot of pain.'

'Is there any sign that it has detached?' Jez asked seriously.

'No.' The man shook his head. 'The penis goes very ... how'd you say? Deep? Deep into the body. He is not a very happy man, though. It's a strange game you play, no?' He made the sign of the cross.

Comments on social media were exploding as Maggie watched crew members cutting the rope between the cinder block and Derek, who was lying screaming on a stretcher. Mary was standing placidly nearby.

@clang82: I did not have Mary doing a DIY peen-ectomy on my 2025 bingo card. #DivorceIsland

@jenodwyer: Not Derek getting dicked over. #Deserved #DivorceIsland

@hoorayforniamh: I'm with Clara, Mary for president. I know we love Ollie and Clara but Mary's got to win, she's earned it. #DivorceIsland

The scene cut to Mary in the Confession Pod. She shrugged and stared into the camera. 'I can't say I wouldn't do it again.'

'Oh my God.' Maggie snorted. She checked Slags For Life; still no sign of Clara but Annie'd messaged.

Annie: My preggo nausea cannot TAKE THIS. Ahhhhhhh.

She had snapped a picture of herself and Rachel pulling disgusted faces with the show on in the background.

Maggie replied with a picture of Fionn curled on the couch with an anguished look on his face with the caption: *He's taking it very hard.*

Voiceover from Jez Fuller took them through a whirlwind montage of the subsquent twelve hours in which cast members went to bed, rose for breakfast and then readied themselves for the closing ceremony. During this, footage showed Mary travelling to the hospital to help Derek into a wheelchair and bring him back to the altar on the beach.

Several of the men tried to help Mary drag Derek across the sand but the new, steely Mary was having none of it – she pulled the wheelchair backwards, tipping a screaming Derek out twice during the journey to the altar.

'Good God, this is sensational TV.' Fionn laughed. 'I should've got in as a producer when I had the chance. This show is gonna run forever – it'll be a worldwide franchise in months, I'd say.'

On the TV, Jez began to invite each couple to the altar.

'Wanna call it?' Fionn asked, still cupping his genitals.

'No, I don't want to "call it", these are our friends,' Maggie replied.

Fionn sat up. 'Don't worry. This is meaningless, Maggie. Even if they choose divorce, Ollie won't do it. He's mad about her. And she loves him. Life stuff just got on top of them.'

Maggie glanced at him. Did he have any of that insight when it came to their marriage?

A moment later, as Ollie and Clara kissed on screen, Maggie caught her own tears with her fingertips. 'I'm so relieved.'

Fionn hugged her close. 'Me too!'

The show wrapped with the unsurprising announcement that Mary and Derek had won their divorce, which Clara and Ollie, on camera together in the Confession Pod, both said was absolutely deserved.

When asked what was next for them, they seemed a bit flummoxed. Clara spoke eventually. 'I suppose we'll be doing the "work" part of "making it work", won't we?'

That night Maggie, Fionn and the girls took a town car up to Chelsea, where Maggie got out.

'I'll make my own way home,' she said, leaning back in to kiss the girls. In the end, she had stayed in her jeans and flats. She was comfortable, which was the most important thing when it came to meeting people you were decidedly not comfortable with.

'You sure?' Fionn asked. 'We could come back this way on our way home. We might do a show,' he mouthed the last bit, presumably not wanting to get the girls excited in case they couldn't get into anything.

The last thing Maggie wanted was to be collected from dinner by her A-list husband in a sleek, chauffeur-driven Lexus.

'All grand.' She smiled as she closed the door.

Inside the Cookhouse, it was hopping. The lighting was dim in the huge open space, and tables in all directions were full. The server led her to the tan leather booth where Drew Schwartz and two others, a man and a woman, were sitting beneath an elaborate pendant light that hung so low over the table their heads were nearly brushing it.

'Maggie!' Drew slid out to kiss her on the cheek. 'It's so great to meet in person!' He turned to the people at the table. 'Introducing soon-to-be Broadway's new darling Maggie Pierce. Maggie, this is Eric Averez, art director, and Jackie Kirke, my co-producer.'

Maggie shook their hands and took the place beside Drew. Eric was angular yet impish; he winked at her. Jackie was curvy and beautiful; she had the eyes of a Disney princess and a head of glossy chestnut curls.

'Maggie, the project is fantastic,' Jackie said firmly, as though Maggie had just been arguing with her on this point. 'Just fantastic.'

'It is,' Eric effused. 'I am dying to get going on an aesthetic for this. I have a few interesting names on the shortlist for costume.'

'Amazing.' Maggie smiled.

'Eva and I are still fine-tuning the contract.' Drew picked up a menu and passed one to Maggie. 'But we'll get it over the line in the next week or so. She is *cut-throat* – I love it! Where did you find her? I'd never come across her name.'

'She doesn't take on many clients.' Maggie kept her eyes trained on the menu.

'Well, she's getting you a phenomenal deal. Considering we're a poor theatre company.'

A server appeared and poured water for the table then spun away efficiently.

'Right,' Maggie said awkwardly, reaching for her glass.

'Look, Maggie,' Jackie closed her menu, 'let's just get one thing out of the way.'

Oh God. Maggie shifted in her seat. They wanted out? They wanted her to change everything? They wanted her to hand it over to another writer, someone with more experience – she'd heard of that happening …

'We know you're Maggie Strong.'

Oh. Right.

Her good mood slid a bit. 'Yeah, I guess I am …'

'To be clear, it's not the reason we adore this project. Obviously we leapt at it before we knew that.' Jackie, Maggie was quickly realising, spoke at all times like she was berating you but she was clearly passionate. 'We *adore* this project because it's unique, it's fresh and it has something to *say*.'

'Maggie,' Drew smiled, 'we were just throwing your name into Google, as you do, seeing who you are, and we saw a picture of you and your husband.'

'So cute,' Eric gushed. 'You two have been together forever!'

Maggie winced at the thought of all the pap shots of her that must've come up on that same search.

'Look,' Jackie tapped the table as though she was already bored of the subject she herself had brought up, 'will the proximity of Finn Strong to this project help with financing and marketing? Absolutely. Will casting him as Jason be something we'd like to discuss? Sure. But is he important? No. You are.' She stabbed a finger at Maggie.

'Okay.' Maggie laughed a little.

'Alright, Jackie.' Drew grinned, batting her aggressive finger away. 'We just wanted to get it said. In case you were ... feeling uncomfortable about it. And on that front, is Finn – I mean your husband, is he comfortable with the story as it is?' Drew lowered his voice. 'The A-list actor adulterer storyline, et cetera?'

God, Maggie thought, *had Drew heard about the blind item with the unnamed Irish A-lister and thought it was Fionn?*

'Of course,' Maggie lied, without hesitation. 'He fully supports my career.'

God, I hope he'll support this.

For the rest of dinner, the four of them looked at rough timelines for getting the show staged in just over a year, in time for the 2026 autumn/winter season. They also mapped deadlines for Maggie's revised drafts, and Maggie left with a rambling stream of consciousness jotted in her Notes app and more enthusiasm than she could even contain. She wanted to scream or sing or skydive out of a plane. This was how Fionn must feel every time he booked a role and she looked forward to telling him. At last something was happening for *her* that they could bond over.

She ended up walking all the way back to the Bowery, unwilling to break the spell of the evening with small talk in a cab or the bustle and heat of the subway. She walked through the glittering city and daydreamed. She was imagining insane things: chatting to Seth Meyers on *Late Night* or attending the Tony Awards. Mad shite. Fun mad shite!

Back at the apartment, shadows draped the floors and furniture. She only hesitated for a moment at the kitchen door before pushing away the temptation. Instead she crawled into the tangled sheets beside Fionn, who rolled over and encircled her waist with one thick, strong arm.

'How did it go?' he murmured.

'Amazing.' She smiled into the velvet dark of their bedroom.

'*You* are amazing.' Fionn pulled her to face him and kissed her. 'I'm glad they recognise that. It's so brilliant that you're creating again.'

Their kissing soon escalated and a little while later Maggie lay back spent but dreamily happy.

The next day, Maggie was buoyed through the tedium of Premiere Day by memories of her meeting with Drew, Jackie and Eric, as well as the satisfying ache of her body after the frantic midnight sex with Fionn.

That was twice this month. She smiled to herself as the make-up artist worked on her face. Yes, on paper it was a pitiful number, but by the last few months' standards, it was not bad at all. She was feeling less inhibited and more in control of her body for the first time in a long time and that was definitely helping her feel more confident.

While prepping for a previous premiere six months before, she had cried multiple times over how she looked in her dress (like a ham stuffed into a sequined purse, she'd texted the girls) and had convinced herself that Fionn wouldn't want her there, that he would be embarrassed by her presence. In the end, she'd pretended to be unwell to get out of it.

Today she was calm, her head clear as a cloudless sky. She had gone for a run and then donuts that morning. Then she'd gone to the bathroom as soon as she'd come home. She had become even quicker and more silent than she had been in her twenties.

'Do you want to take a look?' The young make-up artist stepped back and indicated the large mirror the stylist had brought with her.

Maggie didn't bother to stand, just craned her neck slightly. 'It looks lovely,' she told the girl. 'The great thing is, no one's going to be looking at me. Like, *at all!*'

'Oh, I'm sure they will, Mrs Strong.'

'Nah.' Maggie shrugged. 'You wait and see. Fionn will walk the carpet with one of his co-stars. There won't be a single piece of photographic evidence of me at this event – except maybe a bad shot of my upper arms from the side.'

Maggie messed with her phone. The young make-up artist paused in her work. 'You know you're, like, super skinny, right?'

Maggie just smiled. 'That's nice of you to say'. Her phone buzzed in her hand. It was Clara in Slags For Life. She and Ollie were coming back down to earth.

Clara: Well, we're home and ... it's nice. A teeny bit awkward maybe.

Annie: But why? You guys had the cutest divorce ceremony of them all!

Clara: I know. It's not that. It's more like now we know we love each other but it doesn't exactly fix anything. Also, I feel like shit. I'm having some kind of delayed panic reaction to having done the show. I can't stop thinking of the kids. They went back to school this morning and I was convinced they'd come back hysterical, the other kids saying stuff. They appear to be fine but ... how long will that last?

Maggie bit her lip. She'd thought before about her own daughters one day coming home having read or heard something about their father. But the conversation with Drew and the others last night suddenly played on her mind. It hadn't occurred to her that the twins might hear something about *her*. The show was going to be very public. A very public story she was writing about a mother killing her children. She could hide behind the fact that it was not her plot but an adaptation. Still, it was set in their world. In her mind, the scenes took place in their house in LA. Jason in the play was an actor just like Fionn. He had affairs ...

But it was a *story*. The girls would have to understand that. They would never see it on stage and it'd be years before they'd give it much thought, if they even ever did.

Still, Maggie could feel the conflicting desires revving inside her: the desire to make something, to *be* something; and the desire to protect her children.

'Well?' Fionn leaned in the door to the bedroom looking half-amused, half-worried. 'How do I look?'

'Are they shorts?' Maggie straightened up. 'Is that a leather suit?' She pressed her lips together to contain a laugh.

'Yep, it's a leather shorts suit with a skimpy cashmere vest and Chanel pearls.' He took off the jacket to show her. 'Sylvia knows what she's doing. She says all the young guys are getting more "fashion forward".'

'And you're joining them. You'd be bullied so hard at home right now.' She giggled and held up her phone and snapped a pic as he did a coquettish pose. 'This is going straight into Slags For Life.' Before this drama-filled summer she would have sent it to their old friend group chat but it'd been tumbleweeds in there since July.

On the other side of the door, Brody appeared with an earpiece and several phones clutched in one hand. 'Twenty minutes, people,' he called.

The traffic in and around Lincoln Square was the pits, not helped by the security and the fans who had all been corralled into a fenced pen that sprawled well beyond the sidewalk. Cabs were beeping incessantly and Maggie's plan to exit the car before they delivered Fionn to the red carpet was scuppered; there was nowhere to pull up discreetly without them being mobbed. Maggie's hopes to avoid the whole humiliating 'unknown wife of the star at the premiere' schtick were dashed.

The cinema's brightly lit marquee blared the words 'NYC Premiere *Endurance 2*', and beneath, the entrance was entirely revamped with eight-foot-high siding featuring Fionn's eight-foot-high face.

Opposite her, Fionn's ordinary-sized face was serious, staring intently out the window. She knew from experience that his mind was now entirely focused on the next thirty minutes in which he would have to look perfect, be nice to fans and be down to earth and funny to the journalists in the hopes of securing a few viral video moments. It was a lot to juggle. Beside her, Brody was talking on the phone.

'Okay, Finn is fifteen seconds out.'

The car inched a few more feet and drew level with the mouth of the red carpet that was flanked with barricaded photographers and fans all shouting and straining to see into the car. People in black with clipboards and earpieces stormed around looking like they were coordinating the D-Day landings. Organising these events was quantum celebrity engineering.

The car stopped and every single set of eyes were on them. It was like a rising wave of attention, the power of which never ceased to stop Maggie dead in her tracks. The sound of shrieks and screams was blunted by the windows but the force was still palpable and Maggie's nerves hit like a small tremor. She tugged at the bottom of her cropped leather shirt and wished she was wearing something else. Something plain and black and not midriff-baring. She'd felt confident that morning. Sylvia had had to have the skirt taken in two weeks ago at the first try-on but it was still loose this morning and an assistant had had to stitch it further. Now though it was occurring to her – most of the *Endurance 2* cast were men (naturally), and save for their wives, Emilene Jones was the only other woman who was going to be on this red carpet. And she was twenty-fucking-six.

Fionn gave Maggie's hand a quick squeeze and then his door was opened by security and the wave of attention broke over him. He stepped out under the lights and flashed a grin, raising his hand in greeting.

Brody slid from the car next and reached back for Maggie. She sucked in a breath, trying to quell the sense of vertigo that being this close to her husband's fame always induced.

Since Maggie had been unable to bail out of the car early, Brody had decided that Fionn would do a few minutes on his own then walk with Maggie to the front of the theatre. Then Maggie would peel off so he and the other actors could do the group shots and a lightning round of interviews with all the media outlets.

She allowed Brody to draw her out of the car and used the door for cover to adjust her outfit.

'Nice, Maggie, you look good,' he muttered to her as he put the phone to his ear again. 'Yeah we're on the carpet now.' He pressed a finger to his ear and turned slightly away from Maggie. 'No. What? That's not the—'

Maggie didn't catch the rest as Fionn took her arm and brought her into his highly charged orbit. The difference between standing there on her own and then standing at his side was dizzying. The roar of the crowd came in and out as though playing through a bad connection. The camera flashes left residual flares on her retina. The first step she took was clumsy and Fionn smiled down at her protectively and gently tightened his hold on her.

I should have eaten breakfast, she thought.

Correction, I should have kept down my breakfast.

'Finn! Finn! Finn! This way, Finn!' The chant was coming from everywhere. The photographers had the same desperate edge to their voices as the fans. But this was their income, they needed to get the right pic to appease their bosses or, if they were freelance, to sell to Getty and other vendors of celeb images.

Fionn steered Maggie forward slightly and grinned for a bank of cameras.

She smiled and tried to arch her back slightly to make her waist appear smaller. Then she tensed, wondering if this pose was causing the waistband of her dress to dig into her back flab. *This bloody cropped shirt.*

'Now one on your own, thanks,' one snapper called, flapping a hand sideways to indicate getting rid of Maggie.

Fionn's smile didn't so much as twitch but Maggie heard him say 'fuck him' under the cacophony. He turned them both around to the photographers on the other side, to audible groans behind them.

'Nice going, Alan,' Maggie heard one photographer say to the guy who'd asked for the solo shot.

As they posed and Maggie sucked in her stomach like her life depended on it, Brody muscled in front of them. He tilted his head to Fionn's ear on the other side of Maggie and she heard him whisper, 'Change of plan, Emilene is here. You walk her, I'll take Maggie.'

Fionn nodded. This hurt, even though Maggie knew that Fionn was basically in the middle of a work day and it wasn't like he didn't want her by his side. Seconds later there was another surge in the shouting as Emilene Jones stepped from her car. She was not as big a star as Fionn – online people moaned about her nepo-baby status – but she was on the rise and with her producer father was no doubt soon going to eclipse the other actresses her age.

As she made her way to Fionn, the energy from the crowd pitched upwards, hitting a zenith when Fionn released Maggie and leaned forward to kiss his co-star on the cheek.

Brody slid his very much unwanted hand around Maggie's elbow and drew her back and away from the stars.

'Let's get you a good seat and a glass of fizz,' he said, as though he was rescuing her. Which, she supposed, he was.

They made their way up through the crowd, skirting around more of Fionn's co-stars and their teams and into the theatre.

As promised, Brody furnished her with a glass of champagne, then he steered her into a corner. 'Listen, Maggie. I don't want us to be at cross-purposes.'

'Okay?' *What is he talking about?* she wondered.

'We both want the same things for Finn.' He held her gaze.

'We do,' she agreed, though she wasn't actually all that certain they did.

'What you do affects him.'

Oh fuck, she thought. *Is this about the play?* Surely he could only know what Fionn knew. Though maybe he'd given it a bit more thought than Fionn. That wouldn't be that hard. Fionn was happy she was in a better mood and doing something of her own.

It was clear he was excited for her, though he hadn't actually asked that many questions about the nuts and bolts of the show. He was understandably preoccupied. *Fires in Vermont* was coming out the following month and the whispers about the Oscar nominations were everywhere. Though it would be more than three months until they were announced.

'What is it I'm doing, Brody?' she asked.

'Ordering over $2,000 worth of food on DoorDash in the last week since you've been in New York.'

'*What!*' Maggie was stunned. It couldn't have been that much. Could it?

She panicked and made the split-second decision to go on the offensive.

'DoorDash is expensive, Brody. That's not that much food. Also, we have the fucking money.' She rolled her eyes but in her stomach fear roiled. Oh God. This was way too much reality. Did he suspect something?

'Look, Maggie, I don't care who you're holed up with eating takeout all hours of the day and night – yes, I can see the times of the transactions, honey – while your husband's on the other side of the country. But all it takes is one of these delivery guys to go to the *Post* and then all eyes are on Finn's marriage.'

Maggie felt light-headed. Brody was usually so polished, his tone shocked her. Of course, she could see why he was being so zealous – his livelihood was completely entwined with Fionn's. Every star was like a separate little economy unto themselves with so many people relying on them for work. Thank God he had the wrong idea but also, shit, she could absolutely see *why* he'd gotten a hold of it. 'Brody, absolutely nothing untoward is happening.' She cast around for a reason that wasn't *I'm bingeing multiple times a day.*

'I've been having meetings in the apartment. The producers ... working late ...' She waved her hand vaguely. 'And some friends from home came over.'

Brody didn't look overly convinced. 'Hmmmm. If you say so. But Maggie, I've been in the business a while and believe me,' he leaned right into her ear and she tensed, 'you don't wanna be a Hollywood Nobody *Ex*-Wife – it ain't pretty.'

Maggie was unsettled. She wasn't worried about Brody telling Fionn about the DoorDash thing; he clearly wanted it to go away. It was more the brush with exposure. As she made her way around the pre-show reception on Fionn's arm, her racing thoughts continued to pull her out of the moment. *I need to be more careful. Maybe I need to get a separate credit card? Or use cash.*

Fionn excitedly told everyone they chatted to about Maggie's project and it was gratifying to hear the pride in his voice and to bask in their interest. Still, she felt off-kilter even though she hadn't even finished her first drink and had been on water since. Her head was foggy and a couple of times the room seemed to shift strangely.

At the end of the film, when they all stood to applaud, Maggie's head was pounding and her legs suddenly nearly went from under her. She recovered quickly enough and managed to get herself to the bathroom without anyone noticing.

In the privacy of the stall she coaxed herself. *Deep breaths, deep breaths.* She realised it'd been hours and hours since she'd eaten that morning and she had gotten rid of it nearly as fast as she'd swallowed it. She wished she was back in the apartment. Her stomach was hurting and her heart knocked in her chest. *I'm just having a panic attack*, she told herself. *I just need air and something to eat.* She tried to stand slowly and drifted sideways but managed to keep herself upright.

Outside, she told Fionn she wasn't well and within twenty minutes was back at home kneeling on the kitchen floor eating slice after slice of Wonder Bread – a brand she hated. She just needed to shake the dizziness and she'd be fine. She resolved to keep this bread down.

CHAPTER 22

'Aaaaah! Annie! You're getting a little *bump*!' Ellie, Annie's sister, practically leapt on Annie at the door of their mother's cottage.

'I've noticed,' Annie said dryly from her youngest sister's armpit.

'Don't crush her!' Shiv, their mother, thundered as she came through from the kitchen. She then proceeded to unpeel her daughter and leap onto Annie herself.

'Are you Rachel?' Ellie was shouting down the narrow hallway from behind Shiv.

'No, she's a woman I found on the way here.' Annie laughed.

'Jesus, you're a ride,' Ellie told Rachel, pulling her on through. 'Annie, you're not bisexualing again, are you?'

'Not how it works, Ellie,' Annie said airily. 'Once a bisexual, always a bisexual.'

'Yeah but don't ye go dormant like a volcano when ye're playing straight?'

'Shut up, thank you.' Annie started trying to shunt them all towards the kitchen.

Rachel grinned. 'I'm a … friend.'

In the kitchen, the windows were steamed from the kettle boiling, and brown bread was cooling on the worn wooden table. Through the fogged window, Annie could see her dad picking his way up the slightly overgrown path.

A moment later and Annie was once again being crushed in a hug. When she was released, she introduced Rachel.

'This is Liam,' she indicated as he took Rachel's hand and made a gallant little bow. 'Garden-shed dweller and charismatic whittler,' supplied Annie.

'Are you two shattered?' Shiv was pouring out tea for everyone. 'Bloody road from Cork's still in shite since that flooding at the beginning of the month.'

'It was grand.' Rachel accepted a cup and a plate of brown bread, butter and marmalade.

'Eat up, but don't go mad,' Shiv instructed. 'We'll go down to O'Mahoney's for fish and chips later for dinner. I've put you two in the loft. Ellie's in with me for the night. Are you staying tomorrow night as well?'

Annie reached for the milk. 'We're gonna hit the road late tomorrow night. Ollie's marathon is on Sunday morning and we're all going. Fionn and Maggie are coming over and everything. She's a lot better now, she's working on a play! Has a New York producer and everything!'

'Sorry,' Ellie cut in with a mouth full of bread, 'no offence to Maggie, but *boring*! What the *hell* is happening with Clara and Ollie? Everyone I know was obsessed with *Divorce Island*.'

'To be honest, I barely know what's going on with them.' Annie shrugged. 'They're not even back a week and I think it's gonna be a while before things settle down again. Clara says people are asking for selfies when she's at the shops, and mad stuff.'

'At least they were fan faves.' Ellie swallowed thickly and jammed more bread into her gob, before continuing, 'They were the least messy couple on the show. Which is saying something. I'm really glad they'll be sticking together.'

'Let's hope so,' said Shiv.

'Aaaaand speaking of messy couples,' Ellie's eyes were dancing. 'what's the story with you and Conor?'

'Can you please sound a shade less gleeful?' Annie sniffed. 'Things are … tricky.'

'I'm not gleeful. But he did break up with you in the middle of trying for a baby.'

'We're going to work it out.' Annie sighed. 'Could I interest you in more bread to stuff your face with?' She turned to Rachel. 'It's the only way to mute her.'

That night after a big feed in O'Mahoney's, Annie and Rachel both collapsed on the loft bed.

'I love Ellie.' Rachel's arms were flopped over her head, stretching her T-shirt tight. Annie could see the outline of her breasts and quickly pulled her eyes away.

This, she was finally beginning to acknowledge, was going to be a problem.

Not if I pretend it's not happening, she told herself, knowing full well what a futile plan that was.

'She's fun,' Annie agreed, putting her hands on her burgeoning belly. 'Very cute as a baby. And with the age gap, Shiv was delighted to have the free babysitter.'

'Good you have the practice.' Rachel rolled onto her side and placed her hand on Annie's bump beside Annie's own. 'Four months today.' She smiled. 'Any moves from Beanie?

In the last week, Annie thought she'd begun to feel the tiniest of flutters.

'Nothing.' Annie tried to focus on anything other than the warm pressure of Rachel's hand. Inside her, a weird jumble of feelings spun like a washing machine. Annie was pregnant. They were talking about the baby inside her but all she wanted to do was push Rachel's hand down between her legs. She wanted to pull her close and kiss her. Being pregnant and aroused at the same time felt extremely strange.

Annie turned away and reached for the lamp on the bedside locker. 'I think I need to sleep.' It seemed to be the only solution. If she was conscious, she was thinking about Rachel. And if she was thinking about Rachel, she was then worrying because how could this work? Did Rachel think about her? Obviously yes, they lived together. But was there anything more between them? Just how straight was Rachel?

The next afternoon, she and her mother took a walk on the beach, just the two of them, while Liam and Ellie brought Rachel pier jumping. It was a nice reprieve from the endless chat.

Of course, the reprieve came with a side of motherly curiosity.

'Rachel is fantastic,' Shiv said as they padded over the dark, compacted sand where the water was receding from the beach. She glanced over. 'I sense you're falling for her?'

Annie wasn't surprised; her mother's intuition was notorious.

'Do you think that's a bad thing? Do you think I should, I dunno, pull back from her?' Annie asked sadly. Before adding, 'If I even can.'

'Annie, don't be sad. This is a beautiful time in your life and one you have waited quite some time for. Rachel clearly loves you and this baby. You of all people should know that families look all kinds of different ways.'

'I thought we could maybe team up, do this baby thing as friends. But now I feel like I'm fucked. If I could just not have feelings for her, it'd be simpler.'

'Hmmmm.' Shiv reached for Annie's hand. 'Listen, a more pragmatic person than me would probably be full of advice about disengaging. To protect your heart or whatever. But not one of us is practical in this family.' She laughed lightly. 'And we're all doing okay, yes?'

'Yes,' Annie nodded.

'My advice, if you want it, is: don't make decisions to try and keep from getting hurt. You cannot safeguard yourself against pain and, if you try, while it might keep bad things at bay, it can keep the good out too. You can cope with whatever happens. All this will be fine, Annie. It just might not look how you thought it would.'

Annie's mind circled around her mother's words all the way back to Dublin, and Rachel, who was driving, seemed to get that she wasn't in the mood to chat.

When they got back to the cottage, Rachel made tea for Annie and poured herself a glass of red wine.

'I loved seeing where you come from,' she told Annie.

'Yeah, it's quite something!' Annie said ruefully.

'Makes sense.' Rachel raised her glass. 'You're quite something too!'

What do I do with that? Annie wondered helplessly.

Was it flirty? Friendly? Tipsy?

She's only had two sips of wine, Annie reminded herself.

'I'm wrecked.' Rachel rose from the table. 'Hopefully the wine will help me sleep!'

She leaned down to hug Annie and left a fleeting kiss on her cheek, before heading out to the hall and up the stairs.

Well, that's *not head-wreckingly confusing at all!* Annie thought, exasperated.

The next morning was Ollie's big day. Town was abuzz with runners and supporters alike. Arriving at the brunch place, Annie was tired. She'd devoted at least an hour and a half to over-thinking about Rachel in bed the night before. She sat down heavily at the large table Maggie had reserved for them while Rachel got menus.

'Hey.' Conor slid into one of the seats opposite.

'Hey!' she replied wearily, and he frowned.

'Are you feeling okay?' He leaned forward with concern.

'Oh yeah, all good on that front.' Annie patted her bump. 'Beanie is starting to move a bit,' she said, trying to inject a bit of life into her voice. 'You won't be able to feel yet,' she added quickly, pulling her leather jacket closed as his hand reached over. 'Anyway, I'm grand,' she said quickly, to gloss over the awkwardness. 'I'm just tired. We got back late from my parents' last night.'

'Ah, so she's met the parents.' He sat back. 'Big moves.' He looked away, shaking his head slightly.

'Not the time, Conor,' Annie sniffed.

'When *is* the time, may I ask?'

'How about when we're not all out to brunch?' Annie hissed, glancing towards Rachel, who was leaning on the bar and chatting to the manager, a guy she seemed to know. In her twenties and early thirties, Rachel had worked in restaurants before her painting had taken off.

'She's becoming involved with my baby, Annie. I've a right to an opinion.'

Annie sighed. 'Okay. Yes. I know you do. To a point. But it's my life.'

'You know how it looks, right? It looks like you were with me to get pregnant, and now that you are, it's back to women.'

'Ha,' Annie scoffed, anger rising. Conor had never been entirely comfortable with her sexuality. 'We were together nearly twenty years, Conor. That would be some long game. What it *actually* looks like is that you left me when I wasn't getting pregnant, and now that I am, you're suddenly all over me again. Also, even though this is not the point, I am not "back" with women. I'm living with my friend.'

'I know you,' he said darkly. 'I know what you look like when you're falling for—'

A sudden jump in the volume of chatter around them stopped him from finishing, and they both looked to the door to confirm the cause. Fionn in sunglasses, jeans and a T-shirt had entered, with Maggie and Clara and the five kids behind him.

The manager abandoned Rachel and rushed over. To Annie's surprise, Fionn seemed to know him too. He pulled the smaller man into a hug and Maggie was beaming. The nine of them made their way to the table, causing a wave of interest to ripple through the restaurant just as Rachel returned and took her seat beside Annie.

'Hey, Annie!' Fionn leaned down to hug her. 'You look fabulous. Fully preggo now. Amazing.' He high-fived Conor as both Maggie and Clara kissed Annie's cheeks and patted the bump. Then the three of them moved to Rachel and kissed her too. They settled the kids at the end of the table and a waitress zipped over with colouring pencils and sheets of paper.

'Happy times.' Fionn sat down beside Conor. 'This is Danny.' He introduced the manager, standing at the head of the table. 'We used to wait tables together back in the day.'

'So did we!' Maggie added.

'And me!' Rachel laughed. 'Spot the people who never got real jobs!'

'Real jobs are overrated,' announced Clara. 'I hate mine.'

'Well, you're a reality star now.' Danny winked. 'Sorry! Not to be creepy but I know who you are. Me and my mam didn't miss a *second* of the show. Where's Ollie?' Concern flickered across his face. 'You two are still ... together? Please don't break our hearts now.'

'We are.' Clara fussed with the menu. 'We're doing okay,' she whispered, glancing at the kids. 'He's doing the marathon. We just saw him off at the starting line. I'm tracking his number on the app so we'll head to the finish line later.'

'Gorge.' Danny smiled. 'Okay, we've got divine specials ...'

'So, tell us about the play, Maggie.' Beside Annie, Rachel was shaking Tabasco on her eggs.

Maggie smiled. 'Well, I've nearly finished the very messy, shitty first draft. Adapting is easier in some ways because the structure is kind of there. And the producers are already bidding on theatre spaces for next autumn. So I guess it's real!'

'Ahhh, it is so exciting! Have you read it, Fionn?' Clara said, leaning over to squeeze ketchup onto Reggie's plate.

'Not yet.' He flashed a grin and took Maggie's hand. 'She wants me to wait for the next draft. Though I'm tempted to over-rule this! I just can't wait.'

'Annie says it's an updated *Medea*?' Rachel rested her elbow on the back of Annie's chair, a move Annie spotted Conor noting.

'Yeah.' Maggie fiddled with her pizza, cutting a thin slice. Annie could see she didn't seem overly keen to elaborate.

'It's a brilliant take,' Annie said. 'It's *Medea* but she's like a Hollywood wife!' At this, Maggie's eyes snapped up to meet Annie's. *Was there a warning there?* Annie wondered.

'A Hollywood wife?' Fionn looked at Maggie. 'Meaning … what exactly?'

'Meaning … you know,' Maggie picked up her pizza, 'it's set in Hollywood.' She took a bite and looked at Annie with something approaching irritation.

Oh shite, Annie thought, *she hasn't told him* anything *about the actual story yet.*

Annie looked over at Clara, who was evidently realising the same thing.

'I see …' Fionn said slowly.

'So!' Clara put her knife and fork together with a clatter and turned to Annie and Rachel. 'How's the house plans going, gals? Are you two still looking to rent a massive semi-d in suburbia?' she asked chirpily, clearly trying to cover for the uptick in tension at the table.

'We wish!' Rachel laughed. 'We realised that we'd have to sell the baby to afford it!'

Gah! Annie squirmed, catching Conor's frown. Maybe this conversation was not the best route to dispel the tension. They were not in 'Rachel joking about Conor's baby' territory yet – maybe one day.

'When do you think Ollie will be finished?' Annie asked, feeling suddenly desperate to be released from the table.

'Oh, hours yet,' Clara said looking a touch nervous, no doubt reading Annie's mind.

'Great.' Annie smiled weakly.

'Let's look at the desserts,' Maggie said brightly, pushing her plate away. 'I booked us in to get our nails done.' She looked at Conor and Fionn. 'You guys can handle five kids, right?'

'They can definitely handle it,' Clara remarked. 'I saw Fionn punch a tiger in the face in *Endurance 2* the other day!'

CHAPTER 23

Clara hastily pulled away from ComYOUnicate and merged with the Monday traffic. It was only 4 p.m. but, given it was late October, it was already night outside. Depressing but inevitable. The clocks had just gone back but the extra hour did little to dispel the sense that every day was spent in darkness. Working overtime meant she was already at her desk by the time it was bright out, and when she was leaving to go to her car, the inky gloom was already back. Even with leaving work early today it was *still* miserable, black and rainy. She needed to get to the Eurosaver before it closed. It was only five kilometres away but in Dublin you had to factor in that about a million people were also trying to drive somewhere using roads and general infrastructure that was, in the main, a sprawling, baffling mess. Add the drizzle and you were essentially screwed.

She inched the car forward then stopped again, which gave her the chance to pick up her phone and voicy Ollie.

I'm fucked. It's now raining so obviously people have abandoned all efforts to drive in any kind of sane fashion. And before you say it, I know I'm voicying and driving right now! *But* I don't *ever* claim to drive in any kind of sane fashion.

She hesitated as she was about to hit 'send'. Maybe this was a bit too ... much? Too chatty or glib?

She deleted it and started again:

Hiya. Can you please text me the full Halloween list? Thanks a million!

This time she pressed 'send'.

It was five weeks since they'd got back from Greece and the general vibe between them had been reasonably ... *pleasant*. But, as she'd told Maggie and Annie, not pleasant in a good way. It didn't feel normal; she and Ollie weren't fighting but this overly cordial relationship wasn't them either. The Them from before seemed to have gone AWOL.

Clara x'd out of the app and threw on her favourite murder podcast. The crime girlies were being seasonal, with a series on creepy Halloween deaths. The one advantage of the shorter days was that Ollie could do all the childcare in the afternoons with the boys. What they lost out money-wise in the gardener's slow season, they saved on crèche and afterschool-minding so they basically broke even.

The boys liked him being at home more often and Clara had noticed that he was making an effort to do more around the house.

A beep from the phone interrupted the hosts discussing dismemberment. It was the list from Ollie. That Friday, Maggie and the girls were coming over to trick or treat and drink wine. Ollie was heading out with some of his running buddies – the marathon was nearly a month ago and he was back in the saddle. Clara was making an effort to be supportive. *Just as long as he doesn't announce an Iron Man next*, she thought darkly.

Clara whipped through Eurosaver like the pro that she was. Her secret was that she wasn't above elbowing children and the elderly out of her way. She gathered the sweets and costume bits and was walking in the door of her house just after 6 p.m.

'Muma! Muma!' Reggie ran at her legs before she'd even closed the door. She swung him up into her arms.

'Hello, my beautiful little Face Sucker.' She nuzzled his warm neck as she walked into the dining room, where Tom and Josh were savaging pumpkins. 'Hey, you two, should you actually be using those knives?'

'They're only butter knives.' Josh held his one up. 'That's why they're not *working*!'

'Dad did the big cutting,' Tom informed her.

Ollie walked down the stairs, partially hidden by the enormous mound of laundry in his arms. 'Are they complaining again?'

'Yes!' said Josh loudly.

'Good day?' Ollie asked pleasantly as he walked into the kitchen and crouched to stuff the clothes in the machine.

'Yep,' Clara replied pleasantly.

'Spag bol for dinner?' Ollie asked pleasantly.

'Lovely,' Clara replied pleasantly.

'I'm going to play a bit of Xbox when the boys go to bed,' Ollie said.

'Great, I'll watch *Emily in Paris*,' Clara replied. This was their way of communicating that they would be staying out of each other's way later and no one would be trying to cuddle up on the sofa.

'Things are fine but also awful in their fineness?' Clara was pouring wine for Maggie in her kitchen four nights later.

They had brought the kids around trick or treating and now the five of them were watching *Hotel Transylvania* in a sugar-induced k-hole while Clara and Maggie whispered in the next room.

'It's so shit. I thought by the end of the show you guys were getting closer again.'

'I know.' Clara nodded vigorously. 'Me too. But now I think it was just because we were stuck with all those other people. It brought us together cuz other people are shit. It's mad how unfun the majority of people are. But anyway now … I dunno … he has forgiven me for the whole Provincetown thing, I know that. But, not to be a total cliché, the spark is gone.'

'Ah luv, it sucks.' Maggie sipped her wine thoughtfully, then spoke. 'If we're being clichés, may I suggest a date night?'

Clara laughed. 'Maybe we just need to accept that long-term monogamy is a failed experiment. The stats on it are horrible. Look at Conor and Annie.'

'If we're talking monogamy, look at Annie and *Rachel*.' Maggie's eyes widened meaningfully.

'I know.' Clara made an *eek* face. 'I think we need to let that mess play out of its own accord. I tried to suggest that bringing both Rachel and Conor to the big scan was a bad idea, and she got very ratty.'

'I know,' Maggie replied. 'Although I think they all agreed in advance that Rachel would be waiting outside.'

'Thank God everything seemed to go okay with the appointment.' Clara picked up her phone and brought up the picture of the baby Annie had sent through earlier that day.

She turned it to Maggie. 'These pics are always so generic! A fun game would be to do an anonymous lineup of all our scan photos and try to pick out our babies.'

Maggie grinned. 'Dodi and Essie would be easy – they were both rammed in there together.'

'Of course! I'm a dope.' Then Clara put her head down and spoke into the table. 'Do you think I'm a dope? Of course you do. I am a dope. Ollie and I had a really good relationship but I was too self-centred to realise. In my head it was all about who was doing more with the kids and who had it harder and the answer, according to *me*, was always – surprise! surprise! – me.'

'I get it.' Maggie smoothed Clara's hair. 'Fionn is basically on holiday from parenthood every few weeks. He's on location in Spain right now.'

Clara lifted her head. 'I'm glad you decided to stay here for a bit.'

'Me too.' Maggie nodded. 'With all the work on the script, I couldn't have managed the girls without Mam and Dad. And Donal and Emer. They've all jumped in at different points.'

'Why not get childcare, Maggie?' Clara was perplexed at her friend. It wasn't until the Provincetown trip that Clara fully grasped that while Maggie had home help she didn't, as Clara had imagined, have a full fleet of nannies – an assumption Clara now felt bad about.

'Ah, I don't need it, the girls are very easy. And the tutor has them for three hours in the morning. I feel conscious that they're growing up in a very weird situation and so I want to be there for them. And I'm lucky that I *can* be there while also getting back into work and creating.'

Maggie looked so happy every time the subject of *Medea in Hollywood* came up that Clara felt like she got a contact high from it. Clara knew the first draft was finished, Maggie's fake agent, now real agent, Eva had read and loved it, and Maggie was working on notes that the producers had sent through. The one slight blight on the project was that Maggie still hadn't told Fionn the plot in detail and he hadn't asked, which, as Clara had said in her side chat with Annie, seemed a bit self-absorbed.

Clara sipped her wine. 'When are you going to let Fionn read it?'

'Next draft,' Maggie replied firmly.

'Any worries on that front?'

'Yes. Obviously.' Maggie spun the stem of her wine glass with her fingertips. 'It's going to be a *conversation*,' she said meaningfully. 'A play by Finn Strong's wife about a Hollywood actor, his unfamous wife and two kids? There's a lot of parallels with us. And obviously in the play Jason ditches Medea for a young new co-star? People will speculate online. It's going to be tricky but I'm not going to kill the project. Fionn mightn't be super happy about it at first but I'm sure he'll get over it.'

Clara smiled. 'Yes, he will. As he should. I love Fionn and he's one of my oldest friends, blah-blah … but I would kill you with my bare hands if you gave up anything more for that man. This show is going to be amazing.'

'Thank you.' Maggie smiled, tilting her glass to her lips. 'To be honest, if he wants to argue with me about it, I don't think he's got a leg to stand on. I checked our family calendar and this year alone he's been on location more than he's been with us. He's two weeks into this project with Edwin Ensel and that won't wrap until Christmas, I'd say. Plus last week he was shooting but managed to make time to get to New York for the *Fires in Vermont* premiere.'

'Ah yeah! I read some reviews. Best actor in a leading role a cometh!'

Maggie grinned. 'We're not even allowed to *speak* about that, he's so superstitious, but yeah, fingers crossed. Anyway, what I'm saying is he's a part-time husband and father, at best.'

'Maybe that's what all parents should be?' Clara mused.

'Really?' Maggie looked dubious, 'I wasn't saying that in a positive way—'

'*Wait!*' Clara jumped up. 'That's what we should do to get the spark back!'

Standing in the kitchen with hands on hips, Ollie was looking at Clara like she'd just suggested a gangbang with the PTA.

'I'm sorry … *what?*'

'I said what if we take turns living in Maggie and Fionn's basement?'

'Are you suggesting that we separate?' He looked stricken. 'I know things are still a bit awkward but we're getting there, aren't we?'

'We are.' Clara grabbed his upper arms and took a brief moment to appreciate their definition.

My God, we need to have sex again some time in this decade.

'This might help things along. I am *not* suggesting we separate. At. All. It's a bit like a marriage restructure, rethink this whole monogamy thing. We're too used to each other. This would be like a fun shake-up. We'd take it in turns to have a little holiday from the drudgery.'

'You're calling our life together drudgery.'

'Absolutely.'

'It'd mess with the boys.'

'They'd barely notice – no one's more self absorbed than children. If I fell down the stairs, snapped my neck and was bleeding out they'd still be asking me where the Switch was. Anyway, it's probably messing with them more that we're around the place being polite freaks all the time.'

'I'd miss you.'

'Good! We need to miss each other,' Clara said emphatically. 'I'm only suggesting a weekend each, once every month. Can we just try it, please?'

'So you want to make things better between us by not spending time together?'

'Now you're getting it.' Clara held up a hand to high-five him but he didn't reciprocate. She barrelled on with her hard-sell. 'Imagine if it worked! We could write a bestselling guide: *Part-Time Marriage: Tips to Unfuck Your Relationship from the Losers of TV's Divorce Island*.'

'If I were you, I wouldn't be reminding me of your last terrible idea while trying to convince me of your new one.' He moved closer and put his hands on her waist. The move was a little robotic but she'd take it. She leaned up on her tiptoes and kissed him. His grip on her waist tightened and he trailed kisses over to her neck.

'It's been nearly four months …' He breathed in her ear.

Without pulling away, she spoke. 'See? It's working already. Just the suggestion of part-time marriage has given you a semi.'

CHAPTER 24

Maggie closed the door behind the Deliveroo driver, balancing the two hot pizza boxes on her hip. Shrieks behind her brought a smile to her lips.

'Pizza, pizza,' Dodi chanted, practically charging Maggie to grab the boxes.

'Careful,' Maggie called at her daughter's back as she headed for the stairs.

'It's Friday?' Essie bounded into the hall from the playroom. 'No Maeve tomorrow?'

'No Maeve.' Maggie grabbed her phone and nipped into the kitchen for paper napkins and cans of Coke. Returning to the hall, she climbed the stairs following in her daughters' excited footsteps, which had turned into excited thumps overhead as they entered her bedroom. This was their new Friday tradition: pizza picnic in bed with a movie.

'I thought you liked Maeve,' Maggie said, coming into the room.

'We like her.' Dodi was already kneeling on the bed arranging a mountain of pillows. 'But she's still a *teacher*.'

'We never had to do school in Dublin before.' Essie pronounced Dublin with a native flatness that contrasted with her California drawl. Given that Maggie's family loved to tease her on the subject of her American children, it gave Maggie a spark of glee to hear it. She reminded herself to make Essie repeat it to Emer and Donal at dinner the next day.

Maggie gave Essie's little bum a nudge up onto the bed beside her sister and then joined them herself to arrange the ratty old blanket she used expressly for their bed picnics. 'Ye've never been in Dublin during school time,' she explained.

'Yeeee've.' Dodi giggled. 'Yeeee sound like Granny, Mam!'

'Ye is the plural,' replied Maggie. 'So, if you're just talking to me, it's actually "you".' She grinned and pulled the two of them into a hug. '*Ye* hafta learn to speak your mother tongue.'

'What in the crap is "mother tongue"?' Essie, who mainly spoke YouTube, asked.

'Oh God. Don't say "crap".' Maggie, amused, made a further mental note to tell Fionn about their new penchant for saying 'what in the crap' on their call in the morning. He was in Spain on Edwin Ensel's movie so nearly in the same time zone for once. He was also making a concerted effort to call every second day, so he was becoming less 'part-time husband and father' and more 'FaceTime husband and father'.

They dug into the pizzas and started the movie, *Encanto* for the millionth time, which played from the projector onto the discreet drop-down screen positioned in front of the opposite wall. Maggie slipped out her phone to check Slags For Life. Clara was reporting on her and Ollie's first attempt at the monthly weekend off plan.

Clara: Part-time husband is the way forward, pals. And I like the solo parenting, feels like the boys are going easier on me cuz they know I've no backup. Good of them. I'm genuinely considering writing this book.

Annie: Maybe give it more than a couple of weeks to check that it's a solid option?!

Clara: Well, Ollie came back from his weekend in the luxury basement last Sunday in a great mood. He was actually happy to see me and we had stuff to SAY to each other. And I was actually interested in listening to him. We had dinner WITHOUT OUR PHONES.

Annie: Huge.

Clara: Plus, without him in the house taking up at least 20 per cent of the floor space, me and the lads had a great time. Very chill. I was definitely shouting less. The house was lovely and tidy. I've realised that I don't mind cleaning up after the kids, it's the cleaning up after the other adult that I swear is the downfall of modern marriages. Ollie's shoes are like fucking canoes. Though I will say the laundry piled up, credit where credit's due. He's probably doing more around the house than I realised.

Maggie grinned as she picked at the pizza – she preferred to eat properly after the girls were asleep. She opted to ignore the fact that being unwilling to eat 'properly' in front of others possibly said something about your definition of 'eating properly'. She started to type.

Maggie: I will say he was a lovely guest. Though when we went for a coffee, it was worse than going somewhere with Fionn. Ollie was star-spotted at least half a dozen times.

Clara: Ugh I knooooow. I'm getting it too. A woman in the playground told me we were 'goals'. That's Ireland, they wouldn't give an actual movie star the soot of paying them any attention but go on telly randomly for three weeks and you're famous.

Maggie: At least all the 'think pieces' about Divorce Island being the most toxic thing on telly since The Swan are going easy on you guys. Jesus, I'd hate to be Mary and Derek – people are STILL trying to ring Joe Duffy even though the man is literally retired. Every one of them probably siding with Derek if the posts on socials are anything to go by. Poor Mary.

Annie: I heard she's doing her own spin-off show, though! There's Something About Mary.

Clara: Yeah. The plan is she'll be going on Divorce Cruises through January with a crew following her new single life.

Maggie: Demented. Ireland's becoming nearly as batshit as America.

She then snapped a pic of the pizza and sent it through.

Maggie: Bed picnic and Encanto over here.

She switched over to her email to check if there'd been any updates from Drew; it was still office hours in New York.

She'd sent the latest draft on Monday and was anxious but also excited to hear his thoughts. She was quietly optimistic that it was getting close to being finished. Sure enough there was an email, the subject line of which gave her a powerful jolt of happiness.

You're a fucking genius, honey!

Drew's email confirmed she was right to have been optimistic.

A near-perfect script. I love what you've done with the ending. Medea being vilified in the press but also lionised by scorned women everywhere. It's dark but such a funny take. I can see the op-eds now. 'A merciless critique of Hollywood!' '#MeToo Returns!' 'Feminism gone too far', yada yada! And no doubt there will be some gossip in some circles about how autobiographical it might be. All excellent for selling the show. I suggest you take a break from the writing now. We're going to work on casting. We want to net a big name, which will require major forward planning to iron out scheduling conflicts. These stars always think they want to do theatre but then they realise it's a six-month commitment as opposed to six weeks on set! Obviously depending on the theatre availability Broadway shows can be open-ended. If tickets are selling, we go and go. We don't want to be swapping cast too soon. I don't want you to get your hopes up but we've been talking to Cate Blanchett's people. She did Chekhov at the Barbican at the start of the year so fingers crossed she's in the theatre zone.

Maggie stopped reading to sit with this for a moment, she wanted to savour this. Cate. Blanchett. Maggie knew how projects worked: people were attached and then unattached all the time. Fionn had only got *Fires in Vermont* because Ryan Gosling dropped out. Still, she allowed herself to picture Cate Blanchett in the opening scene spitting blind fury at Jason at the news that the press were about to expose his affair with Glauce.

She resumed reading.

Anyway, more on Cate as we have it. In the meantime, the script is with Eric now and he has started putting the feelers out for the design team. There'll be a new round of rewrites when we go to table read but that's a ways off. For now, I want you to be so proud, Maggie. This is just the beginning for you. Every single one of us at Peek Show is so pumped for this project. To be quite honest, I am amazed at what you've accomplished in two months. I'm in awe. Brava.

Maggie sat through the rest of *Encanto* in stunned joy. Every few minutes, she snuck a look at the email again to relive it. She couldn't believe she'd actually done it, she had produced a piece of work after all these years. For so long, she'd existed under a shroud of failure made all the worse by Fionn's success and the obvious satisfaction he was getting from making his art. Now she wondered if his success really had been at the expense of hers? Maybe not. She couldn't keep blaming him; it was she who had allowed herself to be paralysed by comparison.

On the screen 'All of You', Lin-Manuel Miranda's soaring ode to hope and family, started to play over the last scenes of the movie. Maggie took a screenshot of the email and sent it to the only people who would so fully understand its profound significance.

Maggie: Gals. I literally have no words.

Praise and victorious gifs streamed in from Annie and Clara, and Maggie found she had tears on her cheeks.

Maggie: Obviously, a lot of things have to line up and fall into place for this to get to opening night. And things get derailed all the time ...

Clara: Maggie. Shut UP with the caveats. Just SOAK THIS UP.

And so she did. Maggie floated through wrangling the girls into their pyjamas. She wrestled with the knots in their fine golden hair, telling them a new instalment of the Hair Fairy stories that she'd always used to trick them into tolerating having their hair brushed. When she turned off the lights and kissed them, her tears left their velvet-soft cheeks damp.

'I love you, I love you, I love you,' she told them. 'You two have made my life.'

Later, she lay in her bed. Even though she felt intoxicatingly clean and weightless after completing her routine, her abdomen was sore from throwing up. It was then that the happiness finally, inevitably started to recede as thoughts of Fionn and the play began to creep in.

She would be telling him the news no matter what. It wasn't a case of 'if'. This was happening and he knew about it already so what was the point in waiting to update him? Maybe he'd be happy for her? She resolved to do it in the morning. From the family schedule, she knew he had an early call time, so he'd be awake.

She fell into an uneasy sleep, hunger clawing her awake every hour until at last around 4 a.m. she gave up trying to fend it off any longer. It was the one problem with the system: her body needed fuel. She was only sated for so long after each session then her appetite would return. Okay, maybe not the *only* problem with the system. But it didn't matter, she'd resolved that she was going to stop it altogether after Christmas and get back to good habits in January with a fresh slate. No more binges and no more throwing-up. She'd eat clean, no sugar, no refined carbs. Betty would cook nutritious meals and she'd stick to a plan without it becoming an obsession.

On the landing, she inched open the door to the girls' bedroom and inhaled the milky, biscuity scent of their sleeping bodies that brought a rush of memories back. When they were babies, she would smell them constantly. She couldn't be near them without burying her face in the folds of their necks and running her nose over the funny little fuzzy bald patches at the back of their heads where the rub of pillows meant the hair didn't grow the same. She loved the sweaty little tendrils that curled at the nape of their necks after their naps.

The day ahead unfolded in Maggie's mind. They'd have pancakes and lie around in their pyjamas. For the first time in weeks she wouldn't be distracted by work, not needled by thoughts of scenes that weren't fitting or flowing. The three of them would bundle up and meet her family for a walk up Killiney Hill, then back to Emer's for dinner and chats.

Down in the kitchen, she began to raid the treats cupboard. She really was so hungry. She started on a packet of Jaffa Cakes. Then before she could do any more ruminating, she sent Fionn the screenshot of the email.

It was only around 5 a.m. Spanish time but call times on this shoot were very early and the message blueticked almost immediately. She pictured him in the make-up trailer reading Drew's words: 'no doubt there will be some gossip in some circles about how autobiographical it might be'. Three dots appeared to show Fionn was typing and then they disappeared again.

Maybe he'll just be supportive, like I always have been? Then she saw him go offline and a sinking feeling dragged away her optimism.

She sighed and typed:

Maggie: If we are strong in our marriage any speculation in the press will be irrelevant. It's art, not a confessional.

More dots of typing and then more nothing. It was so unfair of him to leave her on 'read'. To ignore all the amazing things the email said.

Then a FaceTime from Fionn came through. She wiped her face, in case there were signs of the biscuits she'd just been eating, then hit 'accept'.

Fionn's grinning face filled the screen; he had tissues tucked around his collar – she'd been right, he was in make-up.

'Hey!' he said, speaking quietly. 'Sorry for the delay there, I was just waiting for the make-up artist to step out. I read the email! What a reaction! I'm so glad he's aware of how insanely talented you are!'

Relief swept through Maggie.

'Yeah.' She smiled. 'I guess I was a little nervous that you'd be worried about … eh … parallels to our actual life …'

Fionn laughed. 'Don't worry, only dopes will be thinking that! And sure look, unfortunately we both know that people will say shit no matter what. All that matters is that the people in our lives know us and know that anything said in the press or on gossip sites is utter shite. The main thing is that you are going to be staging your first work in *years*! And in *New York*! I cannot wait to see it! And Cate Blanchett! That would be insane. It's just so exciting. I'll be working less next year, you'll be working more. It'll balance out. And we can all be based together in New York. We've always wanted to do a year in New York! There's so much to look forward to. I love you, Maggie.'

A few minutes later, Maggie said goodbye and hung up. She felt close to tears. She knew this was a turning point: they were getting back on the same page. It felt like the old them, like back when they were in their twenties and thirties, when they had been on parallel paths. She thought of how he'd read drafts for her and she gave him notes before auditions. They'd had a shared world. They'd both loved theatre and storytelling so much that most nights, with rollies and glasses of red wine in hand, they'd stay up at the kitchen table discussing and dissecting the art they were making. This year ahead would be just like that again.

She was so delighted at how the thing she'd been angsting about had been a complete non-issue that she barely even registered as she went to the press and pulled out more bars and jellies. She was feeling so good, she deserved to celebrate. The girls would be up soon; she needed to eat and get rid of it before they appeared.

CHAPTER 25

In the early light of the crisp Saturday morning, Annie eased the front door closed behind her. Just beyond the garden gate, smoke billowed; Clara's engine was running. Annie stuck the bottle of non-alcoholic prosecco she'd grabbed from the house under her arm and pulled her wool coat around her, even though it didn't come close to closing around her bump. Little Beanie, who they'd learned at the big scan was a girl, was asserting herself more with every passing day, it seemed. At twenty-three weeks, she now gave Annie indignant little kicks if Annie had the temerity to sit in a way that the baby didn't like, and each night when Rachel came in from her studio she'd murmur to the bump, holding it with both hands trying to coax a poke or prod from beneath the taut skin. Meanwhile Annie would silently fret about what the hell she was going to do. Have a platonic three-way co-parenting relationship with her ex and the woman she was secretly in love with? It seemed hopelessly farfetched.

Annie hurried to the car and hoisted herself into the passenger seat. Clara blew some hurried kisses in Annie's direction and pulled away from the path.

'Easy now.' Annie held the handle above her head as the car jolted over a couple of speed ramps. The balloons that Clara had already blown up floated around in the back seat.

'I know, I know. We have precious cargo but I really wanna get in before Maggie and the girls wake up to get the kitchen all set and decorated.'

Annie held up the Nosecco, beaming. 'I'm so excited to surprise her. So handy that you've a set of keys now.'

'I know!' Clara agreed, turning left and taking the coast road that would bring them all the way to Maggie's house. They had concocted their plan late the night before after Maggie had sent them the producer's email. Maggie'd been waiting so long to explore her own career, it deserved to be celebrated.

By the time they pulled into a space, the sky had lightened.

Annie got out and gathered the lengths of ribbon, pulling the balloons from the back of the car while Clara grabbed the haphazard cake she'd thrown together.

Clara opened the front door of the Miavita house as quietly as she could and Annie waited while her friend poked her head in the gap to listen out for any signs of life inside.

Clara turned back to Annie with a gleeful smile. 'Fab! They seem to be still asleep!'

Annie followed Clara down to the kitchen, trying not to knock things over with the bobbing balloons. They set to work arranging plates, decorations and glasses for the toast. When everything was ready, they debated going up to wake Maggie.

'I think it's more fun to let her come down thinking nothing's going on!' Clara replied

'Yeah,' Annie agreed. She stood still, trying to listen out for any movement overhead. The house seemed preternaturally quiet and Annie started to feel a slither of apprehension. Clara was snapping pics of their celebratory breakfast and Annie busied herself, tweaking the position of the place settings to try and stamp out her disquiet.

The pregnancy was definitely affecting her mood – she was finding she could get quite heightened about the slightest thing. She moved to the kitchen island and started transferring the used cups and glasses in the sink to the dishwasher. She also fished out a few screwed-up wet sweet wrappers from around the drain and pulled out the bin drawer, only to find an unnerving sight: lots and lots of wrappers. Crisps and chocolate bars and empty cereal boxes and packets of crackers.

'Clara,' she whispered, indicating the detritus.

Clara took a look. 'It's just a bin, Annie.' She shrugged.

'It's so much stuff, though.'

'She's probably not taking the bins out that much,' Clara said. 'It's only her and the girls.'

As if summoned by her words, a clatter above told them the others were up. Clara grinned and Annie's tension eased. Clara was probably right; kids snacked practically continuously, after all.

Annie slipped over to quietly close the kitchen door and she and Clara stepped back. Annie looked up, noticing that the footsteps above had stopped and low voices were buzzing. Annie flicked her eyes to Clara, who leaned towards her. 'If the girls come down first we have to not startle them. But if they're anything like my kids, they'll go in to Maggie before they come down. Even Josh won't go downstairs without me in the morning and he's ten. Dodi and Essie are only eight.'

A voice overhead pulled their attention back to the ceiling.

'Mam ...?' Either Dodi or Essie was obviously waking Maggie, and Annie readied herself for the surprise.

'Mammy?' The reedy voice pitched up. Annie cocked her head to listen. 'Mammy ...' they heard again. Then a strange prolonged sound.

Footsteps suddenly pounded down the stairs and landed hard in the hall. Annie rushed to the kitchen door and pulled it open. At the front door, Dodi was frantically straining to reach the latch and then kicking the door in frustration.

'Let me *out*,' she screamed. 'Let me out.'

Annie rushed forward. She could hear the little girl's laboured breathing and somewhere upstairs a faint mewling sound.

'Dodi!' Annie shouted, grabbing her small shoulders with a vague awareness that Clara was dashing up the stairs behind her.

'Mam's not saying anything.' Dodi started shaking.

Annie, trying to sound as calm as she could, asked, 'Where is she?'

Dodi trembled as some kind of shock set in. Clara shouted from upstairs, 'Get up here, Annie. Call someone.' Annie could hear sobs clutching at Clara's words. 'Call the guards, Annie. Now!'

Annie pulled out her phone as she took the stairs two at a time. 'The guards?' she said, her thoughts reeling. 'You mean an ambulance, no?' She stopped dead at the top upon seeing Clara crouched outside the open door of the bathroom holding her head.

'It's ...' Clara gasped. 'I think it's too late for an ambulance, Annie.'

In that instant, scalding terror shot up through Annie's body and her vision grew dim as she staggered forward.

'What ...' She heard her own voice as though it was a stranger's.

Everything seemed to accelerate and slow down at once; in her head was a blizzard of confusion. She had somehow moved forward and could now see into the bathroom but her mind, perhaps trying to protect her, at first only allowed snapshots of the terrible scene to come into focus. Maggie's toes gleamed with the pedicure they'd gotten only two and a half weeks ago. Her knees had bruises on them. Her paper-white face was turned to the side, blind eyes staring. Her lips had a bluish taint. Curled in her left hand was a much smaller, delicate hand and that's when, with horror, Annie finally understood the source of the quiet, strangled mewling.

Beside Maggie, Essie, impossibly little, crouched, whimpering and petting her mother's hand.

'Mammy …? Please …' She tugged at her mother's slack arm. 'Please. Mammy.'

For Annie, other sounds were now dialling back up. Down at her feet, she could hear Clara.

'Oh God, oh God, oh God,' she was intoning, like a prayer.

At her back, Annie heard Dodi. 'We have to bring Mammy to the doctor.'

The child's pleading voice finally cut through Annie's shock. 'Clara,' she said sharply. Clara's eyes snapped up and Annie instructed her to bring Dodi downstairs.

Next Annie lowered herself to the floor carefully. Incredibly, she actually remembered her bump and, feeling the heft of her baby in her womb, a new dam of pain gave out as she reached for Essie. This little girl had once been curled inside her mother, neither of them knowing how little time they would have.

'Essie,' Annie spoke softly, 'you must go downstairs. We need to …' She struggled to come up with something to say because what the fuck were they about to do?

Essie was shaking her head vehemently. 'If I leave, I won't see her again, will I?'

'You will, luvvie.' Annie didn't know what Fionn might make of this promise but right then it didn't matter. 'Please,' she coaxed, 'come out. We're going to …' Again she floundered but then, of course, she knew what they had to do and the knowledge filled her like a whole ocean of sadness. 'We've to ring your daddy.'

Essie allowed Annie to guide her out of the bathroom and Clara returned and brought her down the stairs. Annie crawled in and, holding her breath, placed her fingers on Maggie's neck. Not that she really had a clue how to find a pulse. She'd have to do a first aid course before Beanie was born. The thought shocked her. It was so self-centred. They would live while Maggie wouldn't. Her tears began to fall and her teeth chattered.

She unlocked her phone and dialled 112 as she dug further in under Maggie's jaw and was overwhelmed all over again by the terrible strangeness. Maggie was lying on the floor. Maggie would never see her babies again. Annie's tears began leaving a trail of tiny dark marks on Maggie's blue cotton pyjamas, as Annie leaned over to put a hand in front of Maggie's mouth.

'Emergency services.' A voice spoke into Annie's ear.

'I need an ambulance.'

'Okay. I'm putting you through to the ambulance control room. Try to stay calm.'

Another voice came on the line. 'What address are you at? What is your emergency?'

Annie gave the Eircode of the Miavita house and then somehow managed to assemble the words to describe the horror laid out before her.

'Okay, the call has been put through,' the responder said. 'I have also contacted the local community first responders. They might be with you before the ambulance. They're civilian volunteers but they have training and some equipment.'

'Yes.'

'Gardaí are also en route. I can stay on the line until someone arrives. Do you know how to do CPR? I'll talk you through it.'

CPR. Of course. I should have been doing CPR the second I saw her. Annie had a terrible sense that she was doing everything wrong.

She put the phone on speaker beside her and pulled Maggie onto her back. She listened to the woman's instruction, trying to ignore the mottled skin on the side of Maggie's face that had been pressed to the tiles. Annie started to feel sick but got up on her knees to push down on Maggie's chest.

'I don't know what I'm doing, Maggie,' she gasped between sobs and compressions. 'Please stay, please stay.' Next she sealed her lips to her friend's and blew as hard as she could.

In her heart, she knew that Clara had been right, they were too late. Maggie was dead. She had been dead since before they'd pulled those balloons out of the car.

Still Annie kept going until, eventually, unseen hands gently but firmly moved her out of the bathroom. She lay rag-dolled against the wall a few feet from the door and watched these strangers, a man and a woman, take over. They continued the CPR but Annie detected a sense of going through the motions as they exchanged glances and whispered quietly to each other. They were all too late. Annie shook with sobs as images of Maggie visited her. Maggie young, Maggie pregnant, Maggie laughing, tipsy with red-wine teeth, Maggie smelling her babies' heads and tickling them as toddlers in the garden. The sweetness of these glimpses was unbearably cruel.

Regrets flooded Annie so fast they were hard to parse.

We should have gone straight upstairs. We should have come last night. I should have gotten Essie downstairs faster. I should have …

More medics arrived and she shifted further away. The scene seemed to hurtle around her and she closed her eyes and tried to breathe but her lungs seemed only capable of contracting weakly.

Time passed and in Annie's disturbed state it could have been seconds or hours. A woman in a white shirt with a walkie-talkie clipped to her waist knelt in front of her.

'Can I help you downstairs?'

Annie nodded faintly and slowly got to her feet. She felt like she'd been in a state of suspended animation, though for how long she wasn't sure. Through the door of the bathroom, Annie could see the place where Maggie had lain. Maggie was nowhere; they had already taken her. Now the tiles were too pristine. The room looked impossibly perfect as though nothing had taken place at all. Annie shuffled forward across the landing, struck by the strange ordinariness of having to put one foot in front of the other when it felt like everything had just ended.

Down in the hall, Annie could see Dodi sitting in an antique chair, knuckles white as she gripped the seat, her legs dangling a foot above the floor. The guards had arrived, as had Ollie, who held Essie in his arms as he stood beside Clara's still and silent form.

Conor appeared from the kitchen carrying cups of tea, followed by Rachel who held the milk jug and biscuits.

Every one of them turned to watch Annie and she understood then that she was descending into an irrevocably changed world, a new and awful nightmare without end.

Maggie. You're gone. And it's my fault, I didn't save you.

CHAPTER 26

The night before Maggie's funeral, Clara opened Slags For Life. By an unspoken agreement, she and Annie had continued to communicate in the group chat. The thought of going over to their thread just felt too awful, like they were leaving Maggie, abandoning her. There was also comfort, however heartbreaking, in scrolling up in the chat and seeing Maggie's last happy messages.

Clara tapped out a pathetic plea.

Clara: Can you come over? I'm not okay.

Annie's reply was mercifully quick.

Annie: On my way.

Clara lay back down on her bed where she had spent most of the last four days since the worst day of her life. The rain beat relentlessly on the black square of the attic skylight above and she felt a twinge of guilt. Dragging her pregnant friend over felt selfish, but the awful truth was that since that devastating Saturday morning, she'd been having near-continuous panic attacks and she was scared to drive.

Just thinking about the panic attacks felt dangerous because she suspected just thinking about it could summon them.

'Calm, calm, calm,' she chanted quietly, pressing the heel of her hands into her eyes.

When she told Ollie about the choking shame that had settled like a vaporous entity in her body, he hadn't understood. He'd scrolled Slags For Life himself pointing at Maggie's messages.

'She was in good form, Clara, you couldn't have known.'

'She was carrying so much,' Clara had replied. 'And she felt she couldn't tell us.'

Now on the bed, she sucked in air and tried to ignore the pressure building in her chest. She tried to escape her head by looking around the room. The internet said that to stave off panic, you should pick three things you can see, but nothing around her looked right and nothing felt right. It hadn't since she'd seen the paramedics grimly performing chest compressions on Maggie that, to Clara, looked much too rough. 'They're hurting her,' she had blurted. Ollie had led her away and the next thing she remembered she was at home in bed. The car journey had melted from her mind and she had come to, frantic that they had left Dodi and Essie behind.

'Emer came to collect them,' Ollie had explained.

Later that day, Ollie had reluctantly left her on her own with the boys while he went with Conor to get Fionn from the airport.

'He's out of his mind,' Ollie had told her. It was now Wednesday and Ollie and Conor had been taking it in shifts to stay with Fionn out at the house. Dodi and Essie were with the Pierces. Everyone was falling apart in different locations, Clara's being her bed. It felt so horrible and unforgivably self-indulgent. Annie'd been doing so much while Clara completely collapsed.

Annie had, with Rachel's help, been running interference between the hospital where Maggie's body had first been taken and the funeral home that was handling all the arrangements for the next day. It was Annie who'd arranged to hold back the funeral for a couple of days to allow the American contingent time to fly in. Annie was the one who'd been savaging the reporters who dared to come near Miavita Terrace to catch 'Finn Strong in mourning'.

That was hands down the most excruciating bit; within hours, Maggie's death had become public property. Maggie's picture was everywhere. TikTokers were making videos insinuating it had been everything from drugs to foul play. Brody actually had to put together a statement on the cause of death to quash the rumours. Even though he'd kept the wording vague, there was a leak somewhere because soon everyone seemed to know and then of course every single person had something to say about Maggie's bulimia. And about her and Fionn's marriage. And about what kind of mother relapses and leaves behind two children – as if that was a choice.

Clara was grateful when a tap on the bedroom door interrupted the rampaging thoughts.

Annie came in and shut the door behind her. 'Ollie let me in. He said to tell you he's going to Fionn after he puts the boys to bed.'

'Thank you for coming over.' Clara remained lying down and Annie joined her, their heads resting on the same pillow.

'Thank you for giving me something to do,' replied Annie.

'You're doing so much.' Clara tried not to start crying. 'I feel so bad.'

'Don't, it's for selfish reasons. I'm only doing stuff because if I stop for a minute I go to pieces. I wish I could have a fucking drink.'

'I can't think of anything worse,' Clara replied. 'I'm too anxious. If I had a drink, I'd probably have a full-scale nervous breakdown.'

'At least you'd get a little trip to the psych ward out of it. Lovely diazepam, get lots of colouring done.'

Annie was trying to make her smile, but Clara knew she didn't deserve her friend's kindness. Annie should be screaming at her for not taking her concerns seriously back in the summer when Annie had wondered if something was up with Maggie.

'Why didn't Maggie get help?' Clara swiped at the tears running down her cheeks. 'Why didn't she tell us?'

'Maybe she was going to,' Annie said quietly.

'You said something was up and I fobbed you off.' Clara's shoulders shook as she tried to keep her sobs in check.

'Please stop, Clara. I didn't act either. I just—' Annie fell silent.

'Just what?' Clara turned onto her side to face Annie.

'It's the stupidest thing. I can hardly bear to say it but I thought she didn't look that thin, so she mustn't be sick.' Annie was looking at the ceiling and shaking her head. 'Like, people with eating disorders look every kind of way, we all know this now. But she didn't look the way she had back when we were younger and she was sick. So I just told myself she was fine. And then she seemed so good, so happy with the play and all.'

'Do you think it's been going on all these years?' Clara shuddered to think of her friend, so utterly alone and locked in the savage cycle of that disease.

'No.' Annie was firm. 'When me and Fionn spoke to the doctor, he was certain that this relapse hadn't been going on longer than six months. He said he could tell from her teeth.'

'Oh God.' Clara hadn't been eager to hear what the doctor had said. It killed her to think of all that Maggie's poor body had endured. But maybe it was time she faced it. Clara had let it happen, after all. She didn't deserve to be protected. 'What did he say about her heart?'

Annie shifted her bump awkwardly so that she too was on her side facing Clara. 'He said the arrhythmia could've been caused by extreme electrolyte imbalances during the first bout when Maggie was in her twenties and then when she was well for a long stretch it remained undetected. He said that Maggie's insight would be so compromised by the illness, she probably didn't realise just how dangerous every purge was. She didn't realise that she was literally rolling the dice on her life every time she made herself throw up.'

'Fucking hell.' Clara rubbed at her eyes. 'How are we ever going to explain it to Dodi and Essie? They will hate us.'

'Let's take one thing at a time. Funeral first – you can catastrophise about everything else after tomorrow,' Annie said, and Clara pulled her into a hug.

'You are being so grown-up right now. Maggie would be so impressed,' she whispered. Then added, 'Don't make me do the eulogy.'

'Clara!' Annie sat up. 'You've been in this room for four days, have you seriously not planned the eulogy?'

'Well, *you* were understanding for all of twenty minutes.' Clara laughed, and for the tiniest sliver of a second things seemed almost normal. Then she flashed back to Maggie prone on the bathroom floor and felt sick.

Annie, evidently seeing this play out on Clara's face, said gently, 'We're allowed to laugh, Clara.'

'Yeah.' Clara nodded reluctantly. 'I know.'

'So, I know you're joking about the eulogy. You've got something for tomorrow, right?'

Clara sighed and pulled herself off the bed to grab her laptop. 'Yeah, yeah. Between panic attacks I put together some pictures to play on the projector. Brody was actually kind of helpful. He digitised a bunch of old college snaps. I gave him a list of songs for this string quartet he's got and the twins are saying they want to sing 'All of You' from *Encanto*. Emer and Donal will get up with them to help them with the words.'

'Jesus.' Annie closed her eyes. 'God love them.'

The next morning, the rain had cleared but a low granite slab of cloud remained parked above the city.

They all met at Miavita first to divide into three large black cars and go, in convoy, to the beautiful old chapel in the foothills of the Dublin mountains. It had been deconsecrated years before and was the site of many of Dublin's secular funerals. A fourth black car held Maggie's coffin. Upon seeing it, the thought suddenly hit Clara that everyone would one day own a coffin – this idea rocked her. You could be going about your life and meanwhile your coffin could be already waiting for you, sitting in a warehouse somewhere.

Just as she was recovering from this strange new knowledge, she was confronted with a deeply unnerving sight. Fionn. The last four days had demolished him. He leaned listlessly against the back of the last car. His devastation was writ into his very being. His suit hung from his frame; his eyes looked too big in his sunken sockets. He looked up but didn't seem to see her.

Clara stepped over carefully in her low black court shoes on the still-wet ground and embraced him. He dropped his head to her shoulder and shook silently. 'It's gonna be okay,' she lied. 'We'll be okay.'

Nearby, Maggie's parents and Donal and Emer all looked ashen-faced and haunted. Dodi and Essie stayed huddled together and Clara's boys kept their distance. No one knew how to behave. Annie and Brody directed everyone to their respective cars and they pulled out onto the main road.

In the church, among the attendees, the sorrow and shock at what they were gathered to do was palpable. Fionn had remained drawn and vacant even as he carried his wife's coffin into her funeral, but the second the photographs and videos started playing above the altar, his reserve abandoned him. He doubled over in the pew and started to sob.

Maggie glowed in every picture. There she was, no more than twenty, screaming at a gig, her mouth wide and her teeth bared in completely unselfconscious delight. There she was sticking her tongue out, dressed as a puppy for a Halloween party. There she was in the centre of the six of them, Ollie, Conor and Fionn on the girls' backs. Clara remembered they'd all fallen over seconds after the click of the camera. The stills changed to a video of a young Maggie storming around a stage, directing one of the college productions. Then Maggie appeared with a bump so big it looked fake, with

Fionn grinning and pretending to hold it up from underneath like Sisyphus. In the next slide Maggie and Annie were dancing with a bouncing baby twin each in the tiny London flat; at one point they leaned close and each kissed the other's twin.

The images kept rolling. There were so many; how to show a whole life and friendship as big as theirs in such a dismally flat format as a projected slideshow?

Clara rose and went to the podium to the left of Maggie's coffin.

'Maggie was a girl who sparkled. And then she was a woman with astounding talent. And then she was a wife who would go to the end of the world and back for her love. And then she was a mother who gave her babies everything. And through all of this, she was my and Annie's best friend. We have a group chat called Slags For Life – who can remember where these names come from! And I guess it might sound shallow but I don't know what to do with that group chat. I've never been in a group chat that someone has died in before. It's a very 2025 problem. I just can't leave it, I can't archive it. But can I bear living with it sitting in my phone forever? I don't know. I don't know if I can bear all her messages and jokes and pictures just existing there in my pocket like a butterfly under glass at a museum. I can't believe we only got her for such a short time. When we called it Slags For Life, we were assuming that life would be long.

'Anyway, I don't even know how to begin to tell you all the ways that Maggie was magical. She was so talented and fun and hilarious and brave and smart. So instead I'm going to borrow a song from one of the best gigs we ever went to. It was 2003 and we were drinking in the Pav planning to head to see Jerry Fish and the Mudbug Club later that night. For reasons that are lost to time, Maggie was wearing just a bin liner and a pair of runners. We didn't know each other that long but I knew I wanted to know her forever. Ollie and Fionn were there and Maggie and I were on the hunt together. We both were mad about these guys but had failed to capture them and beguile them with our wares. By wares I mean boobs, obviously. Anyway, then we heard that – *disaster!* – Ollie and Fionn were going to two different house parties and that we would either have to split up or one of us was going to have to sacrifice her night for the other to net a dick. Soooooo. Then Maggie was like, "What about the secret third option? Feck the guys and we go to Jerry Fish and dance our arses off?" So we did that because I knew I could wait another week or so to shift my future husband but I couldn't miss out on Maggie for a minute. So we danced and we sang this beautiful song that has been going around my head non-stop for the last four days. Please join in if you know it cuz I am a shite singer.'

Clara cleared her throat and started, trying to ignore how much her voice was wobbling.

Day will break, stars will fall
There's always something you'll forget to say
Don't dismay
True friends never part

The congregation stood and began to sway and Clara began to cry.

SUCH A GOOD COUPLE

We'll meet again
Trust me my friend
There's no harm in goodbye
Give me your glass
Follow your heart
Wipe that tear from your eye

Ollie and Annie and Conor and Fionn all came to join her at the podium and they turned to Maggie's coffin and sang out the last lines while, on the screen above, Maggie herself spun and danced with her baby girls.

Time makes amends
Don't be afraid
You'll not let love pass you by
Remember this
True friends never part

CHAPTER 27

'Are you sure you're okay to go to work?' Rachel was filling the kettle as Annie picked through her leather backpack looking for her vitamins and making sure she had everything for her first day back since the funeral ten days before.

'I'm all out of leave.' Annie clipped the pack shut, satisfied that she was all set.

'But you're pregnant and you're grieving,' Rachel persisted.

'It hasn't escaped me that I'm pregnant and grieving,' Annie snapped.

The darkness of the late November morning beyond the kitchen windows was oppressing. A similar darkness had settled over Annie's heart in the previous week. Even Beanie's acrobatics in her belly couldn't awaken any sense of hope. Nothing would be right ever again.

Rachel didn't respond. She put tea bags in the mugs and waited for the water to boil. Her patience had become grating to Annie.

She's waiting for some day that I'm better, and it's not coming.

Rachel had come to Maggie's house that day. Conor had rung her to let her know what had happened, whatever that meant.

Annie stood. 'I don't want tea. I'm going to get an earlier train.'

'Sure.' Rachel didn't look at her. She was messing with two teaspoons and the tinkling felt oddly pointed. Annie wanted to slap them away.

'Why are you pissed off?' Annie could hear the snarl in her own voice and didn't care.

Rachel pushed her auburn curls behind her ears and pulled the sleeves of her pale pink embroidered dressing gown back up to her elbows to pour the tea.

'I'm really not.' Her voice was even, which just made Annie want to swipe at her even more.

'You're not even looking at me.'

'When I look at you, you tell me to stop staring at you.'

Annie changed tack. 'You're acting like this is all happening to you and it's not, you barely knew Maggie.'

She could see this line of attack was having a better effect. Rachel's back had stiffened but still she didn't rise to it. 'This is happening to you. I'm your friend, I love you. So, in that way, what happens to you happens to me,' she said simply, turning around and leaning back on the counter. She looked pained.

'You're my friend. You love me like a friend,' Annie mimicked. 'That's not ... it's not ... the way I need ...' Annie could feel herself running out of steam and was furious at herself. *I sound like a petulant child.*

'I don't think it's the best time for that conversation.' Rachel turned back to the counter and fussed with the spoons again.

'Leave the fucking spoons alone.' Annie tried out a shout and that felt better.

'I'm putting them in the fucking sink.' Rachel swept the cutlery off the counter and they landed with a clang.

'I'm leaving.'

'So you said.' Rachel took her cup to the table and Annie swept into the hall, dragging her coat from the hall stand and heading out into the black morning.

At work, everyone was careful around her. Maddeningly so. She messed around in her inbox until she felt it was a reasonable time to escape to the park for a bit. In Merrion Square, she walked as though she was actually trying to get somewhere. The fallen leaves underfoot were ice-stiffened and she flashed back to the chill of Maggie's cheek as Annie kissed her goodbye in her satin coffin bed. She took out her phone and opened the picture she hadn't shown anyone. She'd taken it in the funeral home for reasons she wasn't inclined to interrogate. Maggie looked serene, at peace, all the fucking clichés.

She also looked like someone else. Annie's anger spiked. Annie didn't recognise Maggie because she'd only ever seen her in motion, smiling, laughing, crying, *living*. You weren't supposed to see your friends dead.

Annie remembered the bruises she'd seen on Maggie's knees. Maggie had been doing it so much that, over time, the pressure of kneeling on hard, uncaring tiles had left a mark. But *Annie* hadn't seen a thing.

Or she had and she hadn't *done* a fucking thing. She'd been so caught up in Conor and trying for a baby. And then she'd been so caught up in Rachel. Fucking Rachel.

In her hand, the phone rang. It was Conor. Fucking Conor. She flicked the display to answer. She was running out of people she didn't hate right now. She could tolerate Clara. Just. Though her swings from hysteria to sadness were also starting to scratch at her patience.

'Hey,' Annie said.

'Hey,' he replied. 'Are you okay?'

'Is that a serious question?' Annie snarked.

'I guess not.' He sighed, then continued. 'Where are you?'

'In Merrion Square. Back at work but, you know, escaping. Everyone's annoying the fuck out of me. If one more person makes me a cup of tea, I'm going to set them on fire.'

'It's very icy to be out – be careful on the paths.'

'Yup,' Annie snapped. 'Listen, are you calling for a reason? Because if this is just a check-in, I will happily update you: Maggie's still dead; I let her suffer alone and die. And everyone's a fucking asshole.'

'Fionn's missing,' Conor interjected.

'See? Another fucking asshole.' Annie glared at the path in front of her. 'He's probably drunk somewhere. He'll stumble in when it suits him, not giving a shit that you were worried. He's got two kids – he can't pull this crap.'

Conor carried on, completely ignoring her little speech. 'No, he's *missing* missing. We were not telling you because, well, because of the baby and, also, we did keep thinking he would walk in the door. But now it's been two days, the police are involved and Brody's releasing a statement. It's going to be all over social media in the next few hours.'

'This is so fucking … self-obsessed,' Annie snapped, even as a veil of fear came down around her. *He's been missing for two days?*

'Annie, c'mon. His wife is gone.'

'If he had spent a single *second* with her when she was alive maybe he'd have known what was happening to her?' she spat, though she knew the person she was really angry at was herself.

'Annie, we need to find him. I'm scared he's going to do something bad. Rachel is on her way to collect you. I called her. There's no way you're going back to work.'

'Great. Rachel, my amazing *friend*.'

'Yeah, she mentioned you were doing the "push people who love you away" thing.'

'I'm not,' Annie railed. The baby kicked as if to say, *You are*. 'Anyway, she doesn't love me.' Annie felt herself sag and slumped onto a bench, her fury finally dying away.

'She definitely does. Not sure if it's the way you want her to but …' He trailed away.

Annie's phone buzzed against her ear, announcing Rachel's incoming call.

'She's calling, I better go. Are we meeting at Miavita?'

'Yeah, see you soon. And Annie?' He hesitated for a moment. 'I love you too.'

'Yeah, yeah.'

The journey to the house was subdued. Annie didn't apologise for that morning but she sensed it wasn't necessary. Instead she sat in the passenger seat reading Brody's statement. It was sparse in detail.

Following the death in recent days of his wife, Fionn/Finn Strong's family and friends are concerned about his well-being. Police are seeking any information regarding his whereabouts.

There followed a list of numbers to contact.

At the house, Brody distributed flyers that felt comically unnecessary.

'We should just give out *Endurance* posters,' Ollie quipped bleakly.

They paired off to start the search. Ollie and Conor had made a list of possible places Fionn would go. Annie and Rachel said they'd take Rathmines where Fionn had lived in a bedsit during college and where, occasionally, when he was in the country, he still returned to drink in some of the pubs. Ollie and Conor went further south to the beaches in Bray and Greystones. Donal and Brody were headed to the city centre. Emer and Maggie's parents were taking care of the girls, who Annie realised, with a pang, she had not seen since the funeral. Clara had had to stay home with the boys but she was calling every person who had ever so much as had a pint with Fionn.

In Rathmines, the pubs were only just opening. The staff were sympathetic, though obviously grappling with the oddness of the scenario. A city-wide search for a movie star was undeniably weird.

'We should stop for lunch,' said Annie after a couple of hours going door to door. 'I'm hungry. Beanie doesn't give a shit about a crisis.'

They settled themselves by the steamed-up window of a café called Edward's. Edward himself served them and before they'd even ordered asked them if they'd heard about 'yer man the actor'.

'The whole of Dublin is on the hunt. It's mad. The poor wife, they're trying to cover it up but apparently she killed herself. It's tragic.'

Annie was too exhausted and hungry to bother getting angry but she could see Rachel fuming. After they ordered, she followed the guy, and Annie watched dispassionately as Rachel engaged in a terse exchange up by the till.

She came back to her seat. 'We can leave,' she told Annie.

'Honestly, I can't even be bothered caring right now.'

Rachel reached out and stroked Annie's forearm. 'I'm so sorry, Annie. I promise you better days are coming.'

Rachel's hand was slightly rough, an artist's hand, callused from her work. It felt so good, so comforting – Rachel's thumb grazed Annie's inner wrist but Annie forced herself to pull away.

'Annie,' Rachel started, but then said no more.

Even though Annie had never confessed any of her feelings, somehow the truth of her love had been gradually revealing itself anyway. Annie's love made itself known when they sat on the couch at night and in the morning when they brushed their teeth at the sink. It filled the home they shared and hovered in the space between them. For her part, Annie realised she had been trying to breathe hope into this space between her and Rachel but she wasn't sure what Rachel had been trying to do.

Annie put her hands in her lap, tucking them under her bump. 'Rachel, I don't want to lose another person that I love but I'm not sure I can take this ... this friendship right now. I can't just be your friend.'

Rachel stood up looking immeasurably sad and Annie's throat was suddenly choked with unspilled tears.

Rachel came around to Annie's side of the table and laid her hand against Annie's cheek. 'I can't be your friend either.'

A vice was tightening around Annie's chest as tears gathered in her lashes.

Rachel gently thumbed the tears from Annie's eyes only for more to gather. She spoke quietly. 'It's taken me time to understand how I felt because obviously I've never been in love with a woman before …'

Inside Annie, amid the gloom of grief, a faint glimmer began to flicker. It wasn't quite enough to penetrate all the sadness and guilt and anger but it was there.

'I'm in love with you, Rachel,' Annie whispered.

'I know, Annie. I'm in love with you too.' Rachel smiled sadly. 'But,' she murmured as she leaned down and kissed the tears from Annie's eyes, 'I don't want our beginning to be forever knit into this awful time. You need to process and grieve. I'm here. I'll always be here.' And then Rachel kissed her deeply. Annie closed her eyes and lost herself and her pain and her fury for a few beautiful moments.

Then on the table the phone rang.

It was Conor. Fionn had been found alive and shit-faced. A photographer from one of the tabloids had been trailing him but got an attack of conscience when he saw the appeal to the public and had brought him home.

'Thank God for that.' Annie managed a smile. 'Now I can berate him in person for doing that to us.' She laughed a little and it felt wrong.

Then Rachel took her hand and it felt a little less wrong.

'I'm gonna go call him.' Annie rose from her chair. 'I feel bad for saying shitty things earlier. He's hurting so much.'

'You all are,' Rachel replied.

Outside, Annie paced as the phone rang on Fionn's end.

'Annie.' His voice cracked.

'Hey.' She didn't know where to begin; he was already crying.

'I'm so sorry, Annie.' He choked out the words. 'I've been in a complete blur. I didn't even realise that literal days had passed. I'm such a fuck-up.'

'You're not,' she said, though he didn't seem to take this in.

'How did I not see what was happening to her? It'd been so long since … everything that happened when we were young. I never even thought about it anymore. I've just been going around obsessed with my career. Oh God. The girls, Maggie. I've failed them.'

'Please don't say that, Fionn. We all failed. Not just you.' She leaned back against the wall as the first few drops of rain began to fall.

CHAPTER 28

On Thursday morning, Clara pushed the key into the lock of the Miavita house, trying to steady her breath. Every time she'd opened this door over the last two weeks, she'd been dragged back to that morning and all the ways things could have been different.

She stepped over the threshold and the same thought that always came rose up once more.

Go straight upstairs, Clara. Now. Run.

It was too late, of course. Would these words visit her every time she came here for evermore? Probably.

'Clara!' Dodi appeared in the door of the playroom and Clara gathered her up in her arms. Through the child's tangle of hair she could see Essie sitting on the carpet in front of the fireplace messing with some Magna-Tiles. When Maggie was alive, Clara had never really noticed how like their mother the twins were. The hair threw you off – they were fair like Fionn while Maggie had beautiful black hair – but Dodi and Essie had Maggie's big, expressive eyes. Maggie's eyes were so pretty – wide-set and round with a slight upward tilt at the edges. They'd made her look both innocent and mischievous all at once and now the girls each had an echo of this quintessentially Maggie expression.

'No tutor today?' Clara asked, trying to act somewhat normal.

'Dad says we don't have to do school yet.'

'Right.' Clara paused to listen for Fionn. She could hear the water running in the kitchen. She moved into the playroom. 'Maybe you guys might like having schoolwork again? It could pass the time.'

Dodi shrugged and Essie stayed quiet. Clara looked around the room that was stuffed practically to the ceiling with everything a child could dream of. They had a climbing wall installed up one of the alcoves and a miniature wooden tree house in the corner with a swing hanging beneath it. Boxes of Lego and dolls and even a small electric kid-sized convertible that actually drove around. The room had been exactly the same when she'd visited two days before, nothing had been touched.

'I'm going to talk to your dad.' Clara planted a kiss on each of their heads and went out to the kitchen.

'Hey.' Fionn was washing the breakfast dishes.

'Heya,' Clara replied, noticing the twin blades of his shoulders protruding through his greying T-shirt. Was it possible he looked even worse than he did forty-eight hours ago? 'Have you eaten?' she asked. 'I bought pastries.' She pulled two brown paper bags from her bag.

'Thanks, Clara.' He grabbed a tea towel and dried his hands. He sat down heavily at the table. 'I know I look like shit.' He gave a weak smile.

Clara passed him a pear and pecan plait and sat down as well. 'You have to eat.'

'I know.' He leaned back and plucked a carton from the counter behind him. 'My nutrition guy has me drinking these high-calorie, high-protein shakes three times a day. Edwin is worried about continuity so I have to get back to normal or I won't look like the guy who started the movie.'

'Edwin? As in weirdo director Edwin?'

'Yeah.' Fionn sounded unfathomably tired. 'He's been really supportive …'

'Has he? Worrying about his movie's continuity when your wife's been gone barely a month doesn't sound supportive. He should be looking out for you properly.'

'Ah, I know how it sounds.' He sighed. 'But the whole production's ground to a halt. The budget's getting hammered. Guys on the crew who work by the day are losing money. I have to go back.' He started to massage his jaw and Clara saw that even his knuckles looked oversized compared to his withered wrists and fingers.

'Fionn, you don't,' she said emphatically. 'You don't have to do anything. Maybe you need to just settle here for a while, get the girls into actual school. Rest. Have a normal life for a bit.'

'I want to. But I can't just jump into a normal life, Clara. That's the thing I finally understand about fame: you can't turn it off. Look at how it's been the last four weeks. Every day some magazine or website or dick on social media is giving their take on my life. Finn Strong does grieving. Finn Strong went missing. Finn Strong's neglecting his children. Finn Strong made his wife miserable. Finn Strong is *dating* again – where the fuck did they get *that*? Sources close to Finn Strong say he's going off the rails. Finn Strong's going to get the Oscar nomination out of pity. One website wrote an article about how much hotter I am now that I'm a widower. I can't put the girls in school where anyone could say anything to them.' His eyes flared with rage for a moment and then his face collapsed in on itself. 'How is she gone, Clara?' His head dropped and his shoulders shook with the contractions of silent grief. 'I can't stop feeling like I did this to her.'

'Fionn, it's so soon.' Clara couldn't think of a single other thing to say. It seemed pointless to tell him not to read the internet. Even more pointless to try and tell him things would get easier. She didn't particularly believe it herself.

'I want to finish this movie. That probably sounds really fucked-up. It probably *is* fucked-up, but I want to be someone else for a while. I want to just escape my life. I want to escape from being myself even if it's just for a few hours a day.'

'But the girls need you.'

'I know,' he said forcefully. 'And I need them. I can't leave them right now. I can't imagine ever leaving them again.'

'So that's the decision made then. You don't go.'

'Clara,' he looked at her and she sensed he was gearing up to something, 'will you come with me and Dodi and Essie to Spain? It'd be for a few weeks max.'

'Fionn—' she started, but he cut across her.

'I know it's a lot to ask but there's no one else. Annie's pregnant. Conor doesn't know a thing about taking care of kids. You're one of my oldest friends. We'd rent a house there; I'd be home in the evenings. The girls love you.'

Clara couldn't bear to tell him 'no' outright. 'Fionn, I can't leave Ollie and the boys. I need them so much right now and they need me.'

He didn't seem to be listening. 'After the shoot wraps, then I can disappear. We all could, you and Ollie, the boys, and Conor and Annie and Rachel. We could all go somewhere and just be together.'

'Fionn,' she spoke gently, 'we all have lives here. I have a job. I have to go start my shift right after this.'

'I'd pay you.' He lurched forward, clear desperation in his eyes. 'I'd pay you more than the call centre.'

'I don't want you to *pay* me to help you.' Clara sighed.

'But I would,' he insisted. 'You don't even like your job, Clara.'

She had no reasonable response to this. Of course she didn't like her job. Most people didn't like their jobs. It was normal.

'Please think about it.' His face was a mask of anguish. 'I know it's a lot to ask but please? Talk to Ollie. Take some time.'

Clara pushed the bag of pastries further across the table. 'If you eat something, I promise I'll think about it. Okay?'

Clara had no idea what the right course of action was. Pull the boys out of school again? Could Ollie come? What about her job? There was no more leave to take, not after Greece. But looking at Fionn's bald desperation and thinking of the twins rattling around the playroom full of everything little girls could want but the one thing that mattered most – her heart seized with the pain of it all and she felt utterly torn.

When Clara got home that night, the boys were already in bed. Ollie was playing Xbox but got up to make her tea.

'How did it go with Fionn this morning?' He handed her the mug and deposited a packet of chocolate digestives on the couch between them.

'Bleak.' Clara blew on her tea and stared at the game Ollie had paused. A small glowing creature stood in an enchanted landscape. This was Ollie's way to decompress. *We're all escaping,* she thought.

Her main escape was sleeping but it came with a terrible side-effect – every morning she woke up and for a split second she remembered nothing, until the full weight of Maggie's absence came back down on her like an avalanche.

Ollie spoke quietly. 'He texted me. About the Spain plan.'

'God … I'm not sure, Ollie.' Clara shook her head.

'I told him you'd come around. It's the ultimate part-time marriage after all.' He gave her a wry smile.

Clara put her mug on the floor and pulled Ollie's arm around her. 'I am so done with that. I want a full-time, round-the-clock, twenty-four/seven marriage. I want the drudgery and the fighting and the mess.'

'Beautiful, Clara.' He kissed the top of her head. 'I still think we should do it.'

'We?'

'Fionn won't mind us all coming. We could rent out the house again to cover the bills. Fionn wants to pay you, so what the fuck, let him. Half of the time out there will be during the Christmas holidays so the boys won't miss much school. The kids will all have a tutor, Fionn says. We'll get to dodge the worst weeks of the year here; you hate January. Having the boys there will be good for Dodi and Essie.'

'Let's think about it.' Clara sipped her tea.

Later, Clara lay in bed. It wouldn't be that long. A month out of her life. On her phone she opened up Slags For Life and tapped on their icon photo. It was the three of them at about thirty at a festival – how had it been more than a decade ago? She stared at Maggie with freckles on her nose, grinning in a pair of heart-shaped sunglasses. In this picture, three-quarters of Maggie's life was already behind her. What if she'd known she only had ten years left? What would she have done differently? Nothing? Everything?

Clara started to type:

Clara: Are you awake?

Annie: Of course, night-time is Beanie's favourite time to kick the shit out of me. I'm starting to slightly dread meeting this child. She's so ... abrasive.

Clara smiled.

Annie: So are you guys going to go with Fionn?

Clara: How did you know?

Annie: Ollie told Conor who told me at today's check-up.

Clara: I love us. We can keep quiet about nothing.

Annie: So? Thoughts?

Clara: I was looking at our group chat pic. That was over ten years ago. Imagine Maggie'd known she was on the clock? She would've kept making theatre, I think.
Annie: We're all on a clock.

Clara: I know. I was already years into customer service when we took that picture. Haven't done anything since.

Annie: Well, everyone has to work.

Clara: I know, but I could've been braver. I've always been such a martyr about Ollie doing what he loves and me taking the hit with the steady gig. But the truth is I think I was too afraid. I never wanted to try anything because I didn't want to fail at it.

Annie: Clara! You did a reality show this year!

Clara: That's not brave, it's psychotic. Though at least I put the 'hot' in psychotic, I guess.

Annie: You do. So, plan?

Clara: I guess we're going to Spain so that Edwin Ensel can finish his precious movie.

Annie: It's a good call. I think Maggie would appreciate it. Also mad but on the theatre thing, Brody emailed me really randomly. The Medea producer wants our contact details. Apparently he wants to still stage the show and, I suspect, he wants us to sweet-talk Fionn into letting it go ahead.
Clara: God, what is WITH showbiz people? It's been like a second since the funeral.

Annie: I'm up for trying. Maggie's work should be seen and if the producer thinks he can still make it happen then we should be a part of that.

Clara: Okay, deal. How was the check-up, by the way?

Annie: Actually, so special. Obviously Conor and Rachel came and, for the first time, Conor let Rachel be the one to come into the examination room with me, so she got to see Beanie moving around finally!

Clara: Ah that's gorgeous.

Annie: We've also decided on a name. It's a pretty obvious move but we're going for Margaret. We'll call her Marni instead of Maggie so that it's not confusing.

Clara placed her phone face down on her chest for a minute and allowed the tears to come. At this stage, she'd all but given up trying to stop them. She resumed typing.

Clara: That's beautiful.

Ollie came in and started to undress, discarding his boxers on top of Clara's make-up, while the socks landed on her pile of books. Then he noticed her crying and came over to give her a hug.
'Did Annie tell you about the baby's name?' he asked.
Clara giggled into his shoulder. 'Lol, yes. I was only just saying

to Annie ... What are we like? Nobody can do a thing without everyone immediately knowing.' At the same time, they both stiffened slightly and then Ollie held her even tighter. Clara knew that they were thinking the exact same thought.

Nobody can do a thing without everyone immediately knowing.
Except Maggie.

CHAPTER 29

Annie and Rachel drove out the coast road towards Miavita on a still, grey afternoon. It was New Year's Eve.

The last day of the last year of Maggie's life, thought Annie, feeling her mood sink.

This was one of the side-effects of grief that she had noticed in the six weeks that her friend had been gone. Grief came with endless calculations of the person's goneness. Three days after they found Maggie on the floor of the bathroom it wasn't just a Tuesday, it was the first Tuesday Maggie didn't live to see. The first Friday night, Annie had a similar thought. When she put on the black Docs she wore to the funeral, she realised it was the first time she'd worn them in a world that no longer contained Maggie. As Annie'd gradually gotten her appetite back – urged by Conor and Rachel to eat as much for her sake as the sake of the baby – she was mostly surviving on buttered toast and chocolate when one day she thought, with a jolt, of how at some point Maggie'd eaten her last bite of chocolate not knowing it was her last forever. Just thinking of Maggie eating and how her illness had weaponised this simple act had twisted the knife of grief in Annie's chest.

Now Annie watched the trees and houses sweep past outside, eventually giving way to a stone-like slab of unmoving ocean. It felt like the world was holding its breath as the hours tipped closer to the new year. They were all gathering to play charades and eat pizza and drink champagne as mandated by Conor, who had texted everyone the week before as they'd each been dragging themselves through separate lifeless Christmases – Annie in west Cork, Conor in Foxrock and Fionn, Ollie, Clara and the kids in northern Spain.

Conor was prescribing togetherness and Annie appreciated the effort. He'd even included Rachel. Since the morning of Maggie's death when he had texted her to come to the house, Conor and Rachel had been communicating. Annie knew that they were passing updates back and forth on her state of mind and working out logistics for the hospital appointments, which had ramped up now that she was twenty-eight weeks along. She appreciated this cooperation they'd developed; it felt like she had a wind at her back without them being overbearing and asking her twenty times a day if she was okay, which exhausted her – lying, she'd come to realise, was far more effort than telling the truth.

Rachel's hand in hers brought Annie back into the present moment.

'Are you ready to absolutely spit roast everyone in charades?' she asked.

'What an image!' Annie smiled weakly.

'Conor's really taking New Year's Eve Games Night seriously – he made a group chat for our team to discuss strategy. It's called Death To The Plebs.'

Conor had allocated teams by alphabetical order so Annie, Clara and Conor made up one team and Fionn, Ollie and Rachel were on the other. Annie surmised that he had done it to avoid a boy/girl divide as this would have meant Rachel occupying the place Maggie'd held between Clara and Annie for the last two decades of game nights. It was thoughtful. He'd stepped up so much in the past month and a half and she'd been reminded of what a good guy Conor was. She was glad the two of them were finding their way back to friendship. And not just for the baby's sake – though of course that too – but also because he'd been there for her for twenty years and she now realised she would always want him in her life.

At the house, Ollie opened the door looking flushed, no doubt from the fire that burned merrily in the large fireplace in the hall.

'Hey.' He kissed them both and led them through the playroom – where all five kids were leaping around screaming, playing a game, the parameters of which were unclear – and into the front reception room.

Dodi and Essie looked so much better than the last time they'd all stood in this room three weeks ago saying goodbye before they'd left for Spain. On that day they'd been largely silent, reacting slowly to anything that was said to them and looking more weary than any eight-year-olds ever should.

Fionn and Ollie had packed up the kids and flown to Girona only days after Clara and Ollie had made their minds up to go. It was good that Ollie had so little work on as it had seemed like a good idea to get Fionn and the girls out of Dublin and away from scrutiny as soon as possible. Clara, meanwhile, handed in her resignation and worked out her notice period before flying out after them just before Christmas.

'How's Spain been?' Rachel asked Ollie as she arranged pillows for Annie to park herself on for the next few hours.

Annie eased onto the couch. The third trimester was taxing. She worried endlessly that the boulder of loss that was crushing her was surely affecting her baby. Though it seemed Beanie was a determined little thing, if the kicking and prodding was anything to go by. The bump had expanded and expanded until finally Annie's feet were completely eclipsed. Things were becoming real. The buggy was ready, folded in the boot of the car. Impossible quantities of impossibly tiny baby clothes had been bought. She and Rachel and Conor had read the internet back-to-front and top-to-bottom on the subject of birth, breastfeeding, bottle-feeding, baby sleep schedules, baby shite schedules and winding. The only thing left to figure out was how to three-way parent a baby with your ex and your sort-of-still-somewhat-unconfirmed-and-until-recently-a-bit-straight girlfriend.

'So, nothing big or anything,' as Clara'd remarked in Slags For Life.

'Spain is good, only six more weeks to go so we'll be back before the baby.' Ollie nodded at Annie's belly. He poured a champagne for Rachel and a Nosecco for Annie and glanced through to the playroom where the volume was still turned up to ninety. 'Five kids solo is a lot.' He looked mildly haunted. 'When Clara showed up last week, it definitely felt easier. Though she's as rowdy as them, as ye know. But also,' he lowered his voice, 'she's been especially good for Fionn. She sits up with him a lot. They're out there late at night talking. Which … like … thank God because the kids have me shattered by then. And … I feel like … she's better at knowing what to say to him.'

'Heya!' Ollie straightened up as Fionn, Conor and Clara waded through kids and toys to join them. They all carried bubbles and tentative smiles.

'How's the incubator?' Fionn leaned down to kiss Annie's cheek.

'Good, thanks. Gestating away, obviously.' Annie gave him a squeeze before he moved on to hug Rachel hello.

'So.' Conor stood in front of the mantelpiece, which was nearly as tall as him. 'We're all here!'

A sort of communal flinch took place and Conor, instantly distraught, hastily added, 'Jesus Christ, not "all" of us. Fuck,' he muttered.

'Conor said "fuck",' Tom called placidly from the next room.

'Shite,' Conor said.

'Conor said—'

'Okay, thanks luvvie,' Clara interrupted, pulling out her phone and tossing it to Josh. 'Why don't you all do the pizza order?' She slid the doors that connected the rooms together closed. 'I'm taking my life in my hands letting them do it, but sure look …'

'Go on, Conor,' Annie called, trying to sound encouraging. He was making an effort to paper over the cracks in the group. He seemed to have realised that he was best positioned to do it. Fionn was mired in grief and work. Clara and Ollie were crazily busy having now practically doubled the number of kids they were trying to parent, and she was growing a baby. Plus, Conor had the best organisational skills of the lot of them, as evidenced by the bullet-pointed Games Night Agenda he'd shared ahead of the get-together. One of the points read, 'Have fun?'

Conor dragged a hand nervously over his face. 'Look, I'm ill-equipped to speak but I'm going to give this a shot.'

'Good man, Conor,' Ollie called encouragingly.

'This … none of this … is how we thought it was going to be …' He stopped and swigged his glass. Annie felt a pang for him; she'd never seen him look so uncertain, so lost. It made him look younger, which caused a further pang at the memory of young Conor holding a glass at a distant New Year's Eve in the past. The scene in her mind was dim as though degraded by time, but she knew they had all been there together, brimming with anticipation of another year unfolding before them.

Now they were together but on the precipice of a future they were dreading. A future that only seemed to promise an eternal ache and the fathomless guilt she knew they were all feeling. The baby kicked and she instinctively put her hand to the spot. Of course it wasn't all dread but it was all unknown.

'I guess,' Conor continued, 'I'm trying to say that none of us ever thought something like this could happen but we have to stay together. I don't want us to lose any more than we just have. I don't want to become those college friends who just see each other for drinks at Christmas or whatever.'

'We won't,' Clara said vehemently. 'We just can't, frankly. I would lose my mind.'

Beside her, Ollie nodded vigorously, putting his arm around Fionn, who gave a slightly tortured smile.

Annie was uncomfortably aware of Rachel's stillness beside her. This must be awkward for her. She could participate in neither their grief nor their reimagining of the future. Annie didn't want to look at her and risk drawing attention to these facts. Instead she brushed the back of Rachel's hand with her fingers and Rachel gently nudged her head closer to Annie's in acknowledgement. Though acknowledgement of what? Since the day they had searched for Fionn and tentatively kissed, they hadn't kissed again but Annie knew Rachel was trying to give her space. Annie's fury had burned itself out and been replaced by a sort of numb sadness. The thoughts of life without Maggie seemed flat and colourless. Even feeling excited for the baby was confusing, the happiness faltering when it encountered her sadness.

Rachel had more or less said that this wasn't the time for their story to begin, and while Annie understood and even agreed in principle, in the weeks since their conversation doubt had crept in. Was Rachel holding off because she had changed her mind? Or, as Annie desperately hoped, because life was just too upended and confusing right then?

Fionn crossed the room to hug Conor and turned back to the rest of them. 'I … guys … thank you for being here.' He pushed his hands through his hair. 'And … thank you for not … blaming me for … you know.' Tears dampened his eyes.

'Fionn,' Annie struggled to her feet and Conor darted forward to make sure she didn't need help, 'don't say that! Look,' she took a breath, 'in a way we're all to blame and none of us is to blame. Maggie had a disease and we thought she was better and it came back and we all missed it, not just you …'

'I just don't want any of us to ever be as alone as she was in those last months.' Fionn's voice started to catch and Conor gathered him into his arms, then picked up where Fionn had left off.

'Look, we have to tell each other everything from now on,' he said forcefully. 'Good things, bad things. Everything. We know now that there is such a thing as "too late". We have to tell each other that we love each other every chance we get. Friends don't say it enough.'

'Okay, but we're not saying it to a *sickly* extent, right?' Clara, Annie could see, was blinking away tears and trying to smile.

'Not to a sickly extent.' Annie nodded solemnly and then grinned. She turned to Fionn. 'It wasn't all terrible at the end, you know. She was so happy creating again. That's something, isn't it?'

'Yeah,' Fionn said faintly.

'It *is* something.' Clara was vehement. 'And yer man, Drew, the producer, wants to still make the play happen so other people will see her work and find out how talented she was.'

Annie felt hope glimmer among them all in the room. There would be a certain magic in seeing Maggie's art. 'That would be amazing,' she breathed.

'Yes.' Fionn nodded. 'He said the script needs only minimal tweaks and the director is game to do those. I'll get a final look to make sure Maggie's original vision is protected. I have the notes she was keeping and everything. They're still planning to open in New York in October.'

'So we're all going to New York then,' Annie said firmly, cradling her bump. For a moment she allowed herself to picture cradling her baby in a sling, walking through the chilly blue-sky days of autumn in Manhattan. Some day in the future when life might feel right again. Hopefully.

She and Rachel got home just after 1 a.m. and Annie found she could barely drag herself up the stairs.

'I think they're getting too steep for you,' Rachel said, hanging up their coats.

'I can manage!' Annie reached to grip the banister and accidentally bumped her belly in the process. 'Oh God, I'm getting too big for this house, that's the real problem.'

'You're like a zeppelin in a condom!' Rachel mugged, and Annie laughed. And then realised it was the first time in six weeks that she'd laughed without simultaneously thinking, *How can I laugh right now?*

Rachel must've seen something in her face. 'Are you okay?' she asked.

'Yeah,' Annie whispered. 'I just … I think …' She struggled to explain. 'I think I just felt kind of normal for a second there. Maybe being with the others helped …'

'Oh, Annie.' Rachel moved up the stairs to take her hand. 'I understand, you know. When you lose someone, it's like the world doesn't fit you anymore. You're out of step with everyone else. In a weird way, it makes a funny kind of sense. The person's missing, so the world has changed shape. But the moments of feeling normal will start to come more and more and then they knit together. That's how the world eventually starts to fit right again.'

Annie listened, but she was distracted by the loveliness of Rachel's grey-green eyes in the half-light of the hall.

'Rachel? You haven't changed your mind, have you? Obviously it's okay if you have. It's okay if you're straight … or whatever …'

Rachel didn't so much as blink at the sudden switch in conversation; she held Annie's gaze serenely. 'I dunno if I'm straight or bi or what. But I know I'm yours, Annie. All yours.'

Annie leaned down and started to kiss her, bringing her hand up to stroke Rachel's neck just under her copper curls. Rachel closed her eyes and gave a little sigh as Annie gently nipped her bottom lip.

Then Rachel pulled back and ran her hand over the curve of Annie's belly. 'We have to get you off the stairs – my nerves can't take it!' She smiled up and Annie felt another brief glimpse of normality. It felt right to stand here in the early hours of a new year and kiss Rachel.

CHAPTER 30

Six weeks after New Year's, Clara sat on a plane looking down at the grey sprawl of the city and the jaunty red and white of Dublin's Poolbeg chimneys, which seemed to be rising up to meet her. Reggie and Tom sat in the row beside her with Dodi, Essie, Ollie, Josh and Fionn occupying the two rows in front. They were a three-row family now. Fionn had received some double takes on board but, mercifully, no one approached him at any point on the way back to Dublin. Filming had finished, and they'd all spent a week exploring the quiet whitewashed towns that clung to the red-dirt coast of northern Spain. It was February, so the tourists had yet to arrive and they could go hours without encountering anyone on their many walks. Then they had packed up the villa and prepared to cart five kids back across the water.

On the last night at dinner, Fionn had raised a glass: 'To ditching the fame game.'

'Ah, stop that!' Clara had laughed. 'You take one holiday and you think you're cured!'

'Maybe I am.' Fionn had cocked an eyebrow. 'It's been nice not being Finn Strong here.'

'Hmmmm.' Clara had nodded, humouring him. 'You won't be able to afford me anymore so.'

In the previous two months since leaving ComYOUnicate, Clara's role on Fionn's staff had evolved to something resembling an assistant. She hadn't set out for this to happen, though she was enjoying it far more than any work she'd ever done before. She did worry that working for her friend could become tricky, but she knew with 'Finn Strong's executive assistant' on her CV she'd get another job if she had to. With Brody in LA, Fionn had come to rely on her to organise his schedule and his life in general. She'd taken care of getting Dodi and Essie enrolled in the same school as Josh, Tom and Reggie, which they would be starting in just a few days' time. She'd organised the deep clean and preparation of the Miavita house. When they touched down, her first appointment was with the caterer for Dodi and Essie's birthday party. They would be nine the following week and everyone was on edge. They would forever remember this, their first birthday without their mother, and Clara wanted it to be perfect. Or at the very least not be a site of trauma that they'd be recovering from for years to come – to this point, she was still undecided about booking the exotic animals guy.

After they'd landed in Dublin airport, the mandatory celebrity van with blacked-out windows had arrived and brought them out to Dalkey and the house that was now going to be home to all eight of them.

Ollie and Fionn began unpacking while she met with the caterer and talked her down from trying to serve a quail egg canapé to a bunch of nine-year-olds. Afterwards, Clara took the train into town and went to meet Annie near the hospital where she'd just been for her thirty-five-week check-up.

They hugged hello and Clara squealed at how far over the bump she had to reach. 'You are gloriously big! Whoohoooo! Not long now to the magical miracle that is birth and all the defecating in front of loved ones and strangers that that entails.'

'I can't wait.' Annie mimed puking.

'Oh, your gag reflex is going to need to be a *lot* stronger for parenthood, babes.'

They walked up to sit at the canal, picking up coffee and pastries on the way.

'So, the kids are starting at the new school?' Annie took the lid from her cup to blow on her decaf Americano.

'Oh no fucking *way* are we talking about my boring shite, you are tits deep in new love!' Clara took a satisfying bite of her cinnamon bun and sat back. 'I want to hear everything!'

Annie smiled. 'I wish there was something to tell. But we are doing *a lot* of kissing and not much else.'

'Oh no.' Clara swiped at the crumbs dropping on her hoodie. 'Is she a bit allerg to the clunge?'

'*Gah*, never say clunge again!'

'Sorry! What do bisexuals call it then? Dr Quirkey's Good Time Emporium?'

'Shut *up*!' Annie gave her a faux-serious reprimanding look before continuing. 'She's allerg to the pregnancy thing. To be honest, so am I. I think we're both kind of in agreement that we won't be properly …' She trailed off.

'Down to fuck.' Clara nodded sagely.

'Yep, down to fuck! Until after I'm no longer a human vending machine.' Annie rolled her eyes and then placed her almond croissant atop her bump in order to sip her coffee.

Clara hastily stashed her own pastry and grabbed her phone. 'This is the loveliest piccie ever,' she said, snapping Annie in the dappled light. 'Expectant Goth Mother With Croissant, circa 2026. We have to send it to …' She stopped. She couldn't believe she'd been about to say it. Across from her, evidently realising, Annie swallowed.

'God, I'm sorry …' Clara set her phone down. 'Shite. And we were doing sexy sex chats and everything.'

'Well, fucking a human vending machine isn't exactly the sexiest sex chat …' Annie said quietly.

'Lol.' Clara tried not to sound so morose. 'I just meant things almost felt … not terrible for like ten straight minutes there. That's got to be a record. I think the best me, Fionn and Ollie have managed so far is maybe seven and a half.'

'Send the pic to The Greatest Horseplay Of All Time,' Annie suggested, and Clara obediently opened their recently formed new group chat with the guys and Rachel. They had finally archived Slags For Life. A new beginning needed a new group chat. Ollie replied straight away.

Ollie: Bun in the oven, bun on the oven.

Clara started typing.

Clara: Ollie, if you're texting, you're not unpacking.

'So … unpacking?' Annie retrieved her croissant. 'You guys are fully doing the commune thing? Or is it a cult?'

'It's only a cult if Fionn starts shaking us down for money,' Clara said. 'And currently … it's the total opposite. What with him paying *me* and all.'

'And is that weird?'

'Surprisingly, no. Not after I started and realised how much bloody work is involved.' She laughed. 'Celebrities are like toddlers. Helpless and demanding.' She grinned.

It was true that when Fionn had first proposed it, Clara'd had the same reaction she'd had every other time her friends had tried to give her money – a knee-jerk 'no' with a side of icky humiliation at being a charity case. But she could clearly see that Fionn and the girls' need was much more important than her pride. She wanted to know that they were being cared for and she knew that she and Ollie and her boys were the right ones to do it. Family helps family and that's what they all were.

'I think,' she looked at Annie, 'with the way things are now, living all together and making a communal friend-family makes the most sense. He's talking about not wanting to be famous anymore, though I think the Oscar nomination has scuppered that, at least for the foreseeable. But I think he's very committed to overhauling his life and his career, cutting way back on work, only doing the important projects. And anyway in a few more years, when the kids are bigger, maybe even gone off to college, we'll do a re-shuffle. Or maybe Fionn will …' She hesitated; it felt weird to say. 'Maybe Fionn will meet someone else before then and he'll want to change the setup.'

'Yeah, I guess that's a real possibility.'

'Obviously,' Clara rushed to add, 'I'd like that for him. When the time is right and the girls are settled. Me and Ollie are keeping our house. The current renters are keen to stay on. The mortgage is covered. It's been an insane relief to not be feeling chased by repayments and bills every month. Anyway, that's *our* weird plan. What's *your* weird plan?'

Annie shot her a look and sighed. 'I dunno. Screw this poor child up with my messy love life before it's even born?'

'Solid.' Clara nodded firmly.

'The kid's dicking *me* over too. The midwife at my appointment said she's breech, so unless something happens over the next few weeks, I'll be getting sliced and diced.'

'Ah, the sunroof isn't so bad. When you know it's coming, that is.' Clara tried to sound reassuring. 'It'll be grand.'

'Clara! You are a terrible liar!'

'I am,' she agreed. 'Sorry. All my births were like faithful remakes of *The Texas Chain Saw Massacre*.'

Annie barked a laugh, then added solemnly, 'There's just no easy way to get people out of people. Anyway, with a situation as bonkers as ours, the birth is the least of my problems. Thank God Conor and Rachel are getting on, at least. Rachel made a suggestion but it feels a bit *Three Men and a Baby*.'

'Is her suggestion to get Tom Selleck to raise the child? Because I love that.'

'It's to semi-live-together for the beginning bit. She says Conor could stay in her studio, you know the little mews out the back of the house, and then he's on hand and won't feel like he's missing stuff.'

Clara nodded. 'Sounds very ... your parents, actually!'

'Yup,' Annie agreed. 'Obviously my mum is very pro.'

'And Conor?' Clara tried to imagine the scenario. It worked so well for Shiv and Liam because they were arty types who lived in west Cork. Could Conor cope with such an unorthodox arrangement?

'He says he wants to do it.' Annie sipped her coffee. 'He's really softened since … everything. He's making an effort with Rachel. He even agreed not to be weird about her coming with us to the antenatal class. Obviously, everyone *else* in the class was pretty weird about it, lol.' Annie grinned. 'He's also very pro me and Rachel not trying to move right now with all the stress that'd bring. Plus, we weren't finding anywhere I could imagine us living. I just hope it's going to be okay …'

'It's not. Believe me.' Clara reached over and petted the bump. 'You're gonna screw this baby up no matter what. That's not up for debate.'

'Jesus, Clara!'

Clara ignored this. 'Listen, I know what I'm talking about. I am *years* into screwing my kids up. I will be your Wrecking Innocent Lives Sherpa! The kid will hate you at different times, they'll say you've traumatised them, blah blah blah.' She made a yakking motion with her hands, rolling her eyes. 'Look, if Conor is up for this and Rachel is too then you need to stop worrying about what could go wrong and start getting *excited* by what could go wrong!'

Annie laughed. 'You're such a comfort.'

'Thank you.' Clara smiled at her friend. 'I love you.'

CHAPTER 31

The morning of Dodi and Essie's birthday party was chilly but bright. Annie stood in front of her mirror draping black dress after black dress over her gargantuan belly, trying to gauge which one had sufficient material to clothe her.

'Morning.' Rachel came up behind her and put her arms around her. 'How'd you sleep?' They had yet to sleep in the same bed, as Annie was having such a hard time getting comfortable.

'Ugh, sleep seems to have left the building.' Annie sighed. 'I'm just so full of baby. I can't get comfortable. I feel like I've swallowed a set of bagpipes. Plus, I kept getting the Braxton Hicks things, the fake contractions. All night, I was like, "Is this labour? Or is it wind? Or is it Braxton Hicks?" It's so annoying.'

Rachel patted the belly and nuzzled the nape of Annie's neck. Annie felt her breath catch as desire bloomed deep inside her.

Annie sighed as Rachel then pulled away. 'This is the longest blue ball of all time …'

Rachel smiled. 'I know. It'll be worth the wait, though. There is a *lot* going on with your body right now.'

As if her body was in agreement, Annie felt another twist and grind of Braxton Hicks starting up. 'Yeah.' She nodded. 'Plus, it'll be your first time with a woman and I don't want you to develop a pregnancy fetish.'

'Aaaand,' Rachel placed a gentle kiss on Annie's neck, 'you're in enough discomfort right now. You don't want a fumbly girl-virgin who has no idea what she's doing at you.'

'I'm sure you'd know what to do ...' Annie turned and kissed Rachel deeply. Then she pulled away reluctantly. 'I guess we've to get going. It's nearly ten. Clara is freaking out about everything being perfect.'

'Yeah ...' Rachel agreed. 'I'll go get dressed.'

Annie chose a dress covered with tiny stars that gave Beanie plenty of room and tried not to think about how Clara's mission to deliver a perfect birthday party for the girls was surely doomed. Like so many days over the last three months since Maggie's death, it was about going through the motions and pretending, as though their lives depended on it, that everything was okay.

When Annie walked into the kitchen of the Miavita house, Clara, clad in a leopard-print tracksuit with platform runners, was ranting into her phone, while Fionn fussed with an explosion of pink and gold balloons.

Clara waved to her and mouthed 'fucking cake' and then slipped out the back door.

Annie gave Fionn a hug. 'How's preparations?'

'Good.' He smiled gently. 'It's a hard day ... obviously.'

Annie nodded. Maggie used to go all-out for the girls' birthday.

'Anyway,' he made a visible effort to brighten up, 'we're not getting maudlin today! Today's about new memories ... according to my therapist, at least.' He shrugged in a bemused fashion.

'It *is*.' Annie gave him a squeeze. 'Where are the girls? Are they okay? Excited?'

'They're ... good. I think. I hope. They're out with Maggie's parents until kick-off. Where's Rach?'

'In the playroom. Conor roped her into wrapping presents the minute he opened the door.'

'Cool.' Fionn started to gather up some balloons. 'I'm gonna start putting these around. You should sit – we've got everything under control.'

'Nah, I'll help.' Annie started to disentangle the strings.

'So? Any movement from the baby yet or is she determined to come out arse first?'

'No, still as stubborn as ever. The C-section is scheduled for Tuesday three weeks so I'll be like thirty-nine weeks then and they're happy with that as she seems to be measuring big.'

'That's cool. I know a C-section's not easy but at least you can mentally prepare.' Fionn managed to free a few balloons and began to arrange them on one side of the back door. Clara was visible just beyond, gesturing and still ranting. 'Not really sure what kind of drama cakes can have,' Fionn remarked.

'So ... ?' Annie changed the subject. 'Beanie's not the only exciting thing this month ...'

As predicted, Fionn had been nominated for Best Actor in a Leading Role and Annie and Clara had had a lot of text back and forth about what Fionn was going to do about the Oscars ceremony. So far he was resolute about not going.

'Ah, don't you start. Clara's already booked a flight that I am not going to be taking.'

'But, Fionn … it's the fecking *definition* of a once-in-a-lifetime thing. You're nominated in one of the most prestigious categories of the most prestigious awards in the world.'

'I'm not interested.' Fionn shrugged. 'I don't want to leave the girls. And I don't know how to explain it but it's meaningless now, you know? Like … in the old days, I never even *bothered* to fantasise about getting nominated for an Oscar! A fucking Oscar! Wouldn't have even *occurred* to me to hope for something like that. That's how far-fetched it was. And last year when the buzz was building, I was getting so caught up in it. But now it all just … doesn't matter.' He sounded impossibly exhausted.

'It doesn't matter *now* maybe but you might regret not going and having your moment.'

'I've been getting my moment for five years now and there was a cost to that that I couldn't see at the time. Or maybe I didn't want to see …'

'Ah, Fionn.' Annie had to steer him away from this painful territory. She didn't want him going down the blame-game road; they were all trying to work on more self-compassion. 'Listen, we can do a party all together here to mark it. The kids would love it – we could dress up fancy and everything.'

Clara arrived back in. She came and briskly hugged Annie. 'Right. Fionn, stay on balloons. Annie, come with me. I want you doing quality control on the gift-wrapping.'

Clara steered Annie out of the kitchen and back towards the main hall.

'You've gone full Karen,' Annie remarked. 'I've never seen you so belligerent and organised.'

'I'm not organised, I'm panicking, Annie!' Clara hissed. 'The girls were so quiet this morning. It's really come home to me how much this day matters. This is one of the first chances to reassure them that things won't be utterly shite forever. Show them that we can have a nice party and, while their mum won't be there, it will not be terrible.' Clara whirled around, eyes wide. 'Oh God, you don't think it'll be terrible, do you?'

Annie pulled Clara into her arms even though it was awkward as hell with Beanie wedged between them. 'Of course it won't be terrible.'

'The cake is fucked,' Clara said unhappily, pulling out her phone. 'I said Minecraft and yer one heard "mine shaft" and has done this really technical cross section of a working mine. Labelled and everything.'

Clara jabbed at the phone miserably to bring up a photograph and Annie leaned in to examine what had to be one of the most visually unappealing cakes she'd ever seen. A mound of brown cake with scraps of green cut out to reveal a vertical tunnel. 'God. Right. It's brown, that's quite a choice. Did she think she was making a cake for mining enthusiasts?'

'There she was on the phone banging on about how the edible "sump pump" – whatever *that* is – is operational.'

Conor popped his head out of the playroom. 'A sump pump is a pump that can be submerged in water, crucial for dewatering mines.'

'Conor!' Clara looked exasperated, then paused. 'Okay. Wow. That *is* kind of impressive. *Anyway,* we have to find some Minecraft crap to shove on top of the mine shaft cake so it looks more fun and less like an underprivileged mining town in Durham in the 1800s.'

An hour later, the party was in full swing and everyone was doing a committed pretence at normality. The kids seemed to be reasonably happy but Clara was buzzing around with a frantic energy and Annie was already looking forward to getting home and watching something stupid on Netflix for the rest of the day. She was tired on her feet but even more uncomfortable sitting down. She really just wanted to assume a bovine position, prone on a couch, and stare vacantly for a few hours. That was when she suddenly felt the twist of a nauseating pain far sharper than any of the Braxton Hicks from the previous few days. She clenched her teeth and staggered a little. *Shit.*

'Kids! C'mon! Cake time!' Clara was rounding everyone up and doing complicated air traffic control motions to the two waiters wheeling in the baffling cake that no amount of random Minecraft merch stuck on top could make look normal.

Annie, still rattled from the shocking pain she'd just experienced, tried to steady her breathing. The clatter of the room around her dialled up in her ears and then receded just as fast. Her thoughts surged this way and that. *Is this it? Should I be sitting? Lying down?*

She looked around to find Rachel or Conor. A great pressure

was building in her pelvis and she needed to subtly communicate, perhaps by telepathy, that standing on a six-grand rug might not be the ideal place for her right now. Unfortunately it was Clara's eye she caught instead. Clara was mid 'Happy Birthday' when her gaze snagged on Annie's and she went from placid to suspicious in less than a second. She swiftly made her way to Annie.

'You better not be doing what I think you're doing,' she muttered, still pretending to smile around at everyone else.

'I'm not "doing" anything, my body's doing something. It's out of my hands.' Annie was trying not to laugh while also trying to ride a fresh wave of pain. 'Oh God, Clara,' she whispered. 'It hurts so fucking much. Is this it?'

'Happy birthday to Dodi and Essie,' sang the rest of the crowd. Fionn had his arms around the girls while Ollie filmed. Rachel and Conor were swaying and laughing and all three little boys were reaching simultaneously to jab at the cake.

Annie hunched slightly and had to remind herself to breathe through the cracking, grinding pain.

'We've got to move you.' Clara started trying to hustle Annie towards the door but Annie only laughed at the futility of this plan.

'I can't move right now,' Annie growled quietly, her fists balled to help her withstand the pain.

The 'Happy Birthday' song was nearly over and Clara tried to take Annie by the elbow. 'These poor girls have lost their mother and their cake is a failed Geography project. They don't need your vadge being ripped to shreds to be their lasting memory of turning nine!'

'Hip-hip hooray! Hip-hip hooray!'

'Okay, okay! I'm going.' Annie started to inch forward so she could make her way around the little knot of people gathered protectively around the twins. She wanted to catch Rachel's eye but ultimately she had to focus on keeping quiet and not drawing attention to herself. She made it past everyone, when she had to stop to bite back a moan of pain. A new roiling contraction had her by the guts. *Oh God.*

'Make a wish, girls,' Fionn told his daughters, and there was a collective pause in the room as the girls each took a deep breath.

Splat! Everyone looked up.

A sudden warmth down her legs, coupled with the loud slap of liquid on a wooden floor, confirmed to Annie that her baby was indeed coming early.

Annie smiled around at them. 'Sorry, gang.'

From the time she and Conor arrived at the hospital, Annie felt like she'd entered an altered state. She shouldn't feel this serene; after all, she'd gone into labour five weeks early with a baby who was still breech. But somehow she felt protected. If she wanted to get woo-woo about it, a part of her was convinced Maggie was by her side.

She was told she needed medication to try and stop her body contracting so that the C-section could be performed. Conor did all the talking with the doctors. She didn't trouble herself to listen to what he was saying. She didn't need to, she trusted him. Annie was moved from one room to another. Beneath the strip-lighting, she felt on the precipice, as though different possible lives were unfurling around her. Nothing felt real. Until she had the reassuring weight of her baby in her arms, nothing would feel real.

And then, after a few minutes of curiously painless rummaging inside her abdomen by a surgeon, a baby emerged.

A perfect curled rosebud of a baby girl called Marni.

A few hours into Marni Sweeney's life, Conor and Annie sat in the hospital ward in the state of shock and awe that visits all brand new parents on day one.

'She's stunningly beautiful, obviously,' Conor said emphatically.

'That's my side of the family.' Annie nodded eagerly, looking down at the baby slumped on her chest.

Together they watched the baby's minute movements: the twitching fingers, the subtle pulses in her almost translucent eyelids. Annie couldn't take her eyes off her daughter.

'She's mesmerising. She's better than TikTok!' She grinned at Conor, who was flitting around the bed, feverishly snapping pictures and sending them to the group chat. They had the best spot in the room they were sharing with five other new families, over by the windows. At that time of day in the late February afternoon, the shadows of the city were long and darkness would soon win out.

'The guys have sent a video.' Conor turned the phone so they could both watch a chaotic few minutes of Clara, Ollie, Fionn and the kids shrieking and jumping around and singing 'Happy Birthday' to Marni.

'Lucky the twins are already used to sharing a birthday!' Conor laughed.

Annie lay back, smiling. She was exhausted but she didn't want to fall asleep and miss Rachel. She'd said she was on her way. Annie was to stay in hospital for five days to recover from her surgery and Rachel was to be the first visitor, though they'd all agreed she would be the only one of their friends who would come to the hospital. Neither Annie nor Conor nor Rachel had articulated it but Annie felt that they all wanted to have a bit of time, just themselves together, to see how their funny little family might feel before they left the sanctuary of the hospital and, no doubt, began to butt up against the prejudices and preconceptions of other people.

'Annie.' Rachel appeared at the edge of the blue curtain at the end of Annie's bed. Annie could see tears sparkling in Rachel's eyes as she hurried forward to hug her, stopping just short upon realising that Marni was tucked into the crook of Annie's arm.

'She's perfect!' Rachel exhaled. 'My God, so tiny! I nearly didn't spot her in your arms.'

Annie smiled and rubbed her cheek over her daughter's velvety head for at least the fiftieth time since she'd been born. Annie couldn't stop touching her and smelling her and petting her; it was already entirely unconscious, as though Annie's body had suddenly become fluent in a whole other language overnight – the language of motherhood.

Conor stood to give Rachel a hug that was only slightly hesitant, and Annie appreciated the effort. 'Obviously she was on the early side,' he explained. 'But luckily she's a good weight and the doctors were very happy with how everything's looking.' He clapped his hands together. 'So …'

'So ...' Rachel dabbed at her eyes.

'So ...' Annie joined in smiling.

'Soooo ...' Conor started laughing. 'I guess we should ask ChatGPT how three people raise a baby together?'

EPILOGUE

Eight months later ...

Annie sat in the depths of the huge van that had collected them all from New York's JFK airport. They were crossing the water to Manhattan and beside Annie, in her car seat, Marni was pumping her legs impatiently.

Annie leaned in to tickle her. 'Who's the best baby in the world?' she asked seriously. On the other side of the car seat, Rachel whipped around, indignant. 'I thought you said *I* was the best baby in the world!'

In front of them, Conor turned and said solemnly, 'It's me. I'm the best baby in the world.'

Annie grinned at them both. It was funny how moments like these, moments of normality, could feel so precious. It felt like all three of them had come through something momentous. The last eight months had been both a blur and the longest of her life.

It had been disorientating, suddenly losing all grip on any sense of certainty as she scrambled to intuit her daughter's needs. The fact that she'd had Conor and Rachel flailing around with her, just as clueless but also just as committed, had made everything more doable and more fun. With three of them, they were able to get more rest and divvy up jobs like cooking and cleaning. Annie had been nursing Marni for the early months and so either Conor or Rachel would get up to help her change and settle the baby after feeds, which meant Annie got more sleep than the average new mother.

Of course, she didn't entirely dodge the sleep-deprived derangement. One night after Marni had been unconsolable, crying on and off for hours, Annie's dressing gown sleeve had caught on the door handle for the third time and she had utterly lost it. Rachel was pacing with Marni at the time and watched in utter astonishment as Annie wrenched the dressing gown off her body and started trying to rip the sleeve off.

'It keeps *catching on things*,' she'd snarled, before abandoning the attempt to tear it and simply storming downstairs, shoving it in the kitchen sink and trying to set it on fire.

'A totally normal-sized reaction,' Rachel said cautiously from the doorway. She'd followed her down with the baby in her arms. They'd both collapsed into peals of laughter, which had somehow – finally, mercifully – lulled Marni to sleep.

When Annie had related Dressing Gown Gate to Clara she'd just nodded. 'The shit you do when you're in the newborn phase and that final little thing tips you over the edge. One day, after I'd dropped a tray of lasagne, I just walked out. Abandoned Ollie and the kids. Left the house. I got in the car and started driving. I was eight months pregnant with Reggie. I was just in a T-shirt and knickers. I had no shoes on. About two minutes down the road, I realised I needed petrol and had to pull into a garage. I was *fuming*, storming around the petrol pump, muttering to myself. I could see I was making people nervous but I didn't care. Since then, I never let the tank go empty.' She'd shaken her head with a slightly haunted expression. 'Gotta be ready,' she'd muttered, then blinked and smiled again and leapt into praising the concept of the parenting triad. 'This is why you're so lucky to have three of you!'

Their new system had impressed Clara so much that she was trying to convince Annie to do a book or a podcast with her.

'Annie! You don't even realise how revolutionary all this is!' Clara had gestured wildly over wine just the week before. '*We. Are. Revolutionaries.* We could call it "Parent In Numbers: Don't Let Your Baby Beat You Down!"'

'This is in no way *our* original idea, Clara!' Annie had laughed. 'Hello? The "village"? People have been doing it like this for millennia; it's just patriarchal, capitalistic systems that messed that up.'

Conor staying in Rachel's studio had worked out well, though on nights that he was on Baby Shift, he often dozed on the chair in the corner of Annie's room. But after this trip, it would all change again. The baby had started solid food and bottles. Annie was going back to work and the next phase would begin. Conor was moving back to his apartment and their joint custody arrangement was about to kick in. It felt like this would be crunch time in terms of whether their setup could actually work, but Annie was quietly confident. They'd been through so much together in the last year that they were very different people. They had a lot of compassion for one another, a compassion that'd been forged in grief.

Annie was relieved that Marni was now a robust roly-poly baby. The newborn time had been lovely but not relaxing – punctuated, as it was, by endless sudden panics: inexplicable high fevers, mysterious rashes and impressive arching milky vomits and explosive nappies. Oh God the fluids, the endless, endless fluids.

Tonight would be a real test of concept as Conor would be taking Marni for his first night of completely solo parenting. It was opening night of *Medea in Hollywood* in the Rivet Theater a few blocks from Times Square. Clara had arranged a babysitting service to take care of Dodi and Essie and the boys but Annie, Conor and Rachel all felt Marni was still too little to be left with anyone but family. At first Rachel had insisted that *she* miss opening night; she'd only known Maggie for a few months, after all. But Conor had been adamant: he wanted to, and he still wasn't sure he definitely wanted to see the play. Maggie's parents and siblings were also grappling with this question but maybe in time they'd be ready. The show would be on for several months and may be extended further depending on how sales went, so there was time for them to decide and come over.

Annie understood their indecision. Tonight was going to be strange for each of them in different ways. For her and Clara, it felt like they were about to hear Maggie's voice from the other side. For Fionn, it'd be his first appearance in public all year. He had skipped the Oscars, as he'd said he would. He hadn't won for Best Actor though *Fires in Vermont* did scoop Best Picture. They'd had their Oscars party in the Miavita house, staying up late watching the ceremony all together. Fionn cuddled the girls on the couch, and if he was upset at not having gone then he truly deserved the Best Actor award as he'd laughed and tickled the girls and generally joked around all night.

'Okay, gang.' Up front, Clara leaned around the passenger seat to get eyes on all five adults, five kids and one baby. 'Shut up, all of you! Game plan time.' She tapped on her tablet.

Annie caught Rachel's eye and grinned. Clara even had an earpiece for her phone now: she was a born executive assistant. As she said herself, years of fielding the boys around had honed her skill for herding people with little to no sense.

'So we're about to arrive at our block. We have two apartments in the same building. Building codes and door codes are in your itineraries that I emailed you two weeks ago, so no one start on about how you can't find it, okay?' She glared around.

'Yes, Clara!' Conor replied.

'Good. Directions to the dinner place are on the doc. Dinner is beside the Rivet Theater. Drew Schwartz and the other producers and some cast are joining us for a drink at the end, then we're heading to the theatre together. Kids?'

'Yes, Clara,' the kids chimed.

'You will be located in the apartment, being force-fed pizza and sweets. Check?'

'Check!'

'And not acting the maggots for the poor babysitters?'

'And not acting the maggots for the poor babysitters,' they repeated back gleefully.

There were a lot of eyes on the opening night of *Medea in Hollywood*, for several reasons, most notably that Carrie Coon was playing Medea. When a big star was doing a theatre show it dialled up the scrutiny ten-fold. When that star was doing a show written by the wife of an A-lister who had died before it was staged, the intensity was off the charts.

Annie had expected a certain amount of interest in Maggie but had assumed people would be much more focused on the cast. Not so. If there's a dead woman to speculate about, God knows people will speculate, and Annie and Clara had to consciously shut out the noise of social media as the press had ramped up and the story of how *Medea in Hollywood* came to be became widely discussed.

Now at last they were sitting in the densely packed stalls of the Rivet Theater and about to see Maggie's work. It was a very strange sensation. They were about to hear from Maggie. It was hard not to imbue the experience with something of the supernatural. Would there be a message trailed like breadcrumbs through this ancient tale? Some hint at how it had all gone so wrong? Something to tell them?

The lights dimmed and a hush fell down around them. Annie leaned forward slightly to watch Fionn, Clara, Ollie and Rachel as the curtain rose.

Light filled her friends' faces, as Maggie's last words started to ring out from the stage.

ACKNOWLEDGEMENTS

I would like to thank the following people who are the hands down, all time best people I could ever ask for to be in my life and in my corner.

Joanna Smyth, Ciara Doorley, Elaine Egan, Aonghus Meaney and all at Hachette who worked on this.

My agents, Tanera Simons and Sheila David, who have always championed me and without whom I would be permanently lost in a bureaucratic hellscape of contracts.

The early readers of the book who provided excellent feedback and encouragement: Louise O'Neill, Liadan Hynes and Marian Keyes.

I owe a huge debt of gratitude to Dr John Legge of St Vincent's Hospital who guided me through some of the particulars of the medical system. Any errors are of course my own.

I'd like to shout out Sinéad Crowe at @intuitiveeatingireland and Jo Moscalu at @binge.eating.dietician for all the vital work they do in the anti-diet space. You're helping so many people and I am one of them.

The lyrics to 'True Friends' by Jerry Fish appear in this book with kind permission from the man himself. A wonderful artist, provider of the soundtrack of my life and an all round dote. And a special thanks to another absolute gent, Philip King, for connecting us.

All the incredible teachers and staff of St Matthew's NS who give my children such support and care along with a great education. I'm sorry I'm so bad at the homework!

I would also like to thank Barbara Tonge who is the most gentle, warm and kind person you'll ever meet and has minded my boys so well in the last few years.

To the fabulous women I am so lucky to work with: Leslie-Ann Horgan, Anna Coogan, Ailish McElmeel and Eleanor White. Thank you for always being so sound when I miss a deadline (wincey-face emoji!).

The group chats without whom my already patchy sanity would fall to shit altogether. Mother of Creep, Gut Gals, Corpso, Conjoined Twin, Mini Balding Man Club, Death Is Coming, The Book Club With No Books and the Empowered Movement Chat.

I would also like to thank everyone on Irish Bookstagram, as well as all the brilliant booksellers. You help and encourage authors probably even more than you realise (not to mention keep my TBR overflowing with recommendations). I love the Irish books community so bloody much – you're all mensches.

Thank you to all the Creeps and the Mother Of Pod gang. Making these shows is the funnest job I've ever had or will ever have and you make it possible.

Of everyone, my family put up with the most shite. Thank you from the bottom of my heart to my first husband, Seb White, who, whenever I start on about jacking in the writing, patiently rolls his eyes and reminds me that I have said this at least three times a year for the past eight years. My favourite mother, Mary O'Sullivan, who inspires me and helps me so so much, whether it's wrangling my boys so I can work or reminding me to wear lipstick. To Anne Harris for also stepping in to wrangle my kids and encouraging me to get out of my leggings and put on a decent outfit from time to time. These things matter!!! Also, thank you to all my family in the extended Harris-O'Sullivan-White multiverse.

Lastly, to my sons Rufus, Arlo and Sonny, I love you so much, you have made my life. You were, of course, the inspiration for the trio of brothers in this book though you are obviously far madder.

RESOURCES

Bodywhys (Eating Disorders Association of Ireland)
Free helpline and email support for sufferers, family, and friends
Phone 01 210 7906
Website www.bodywhys.ie

Text About It (50808)
Free 24/7 text support service for mental health and emotional distress
Text HELLO to 50808
Website www.textaboutit.ie

Samaritans Ireland
Emotional support for acute distress, 24/7
Phone 116 123
Website www.samaritans.org/samaritans-ireland

National Infertility Support & Information Group (NISIG)
Helpline (10 a.m.–10 p.m., daily) and support meetings (online + Cork/Dublin)
Phone 087 797 5058
Website www.nisig.com

Spun Out
Resources for mental health and emotional distress including eating disorders
Website www.spunout.ie